GODEATER'S
SON

Other great stories from Warhammer Age of Sigmar

GODEATER'S
SON

NOAH VAN NGUYEN

BLACK LIBRARY

A BLACK LIBRARY PUBLICATION

First published in 2023.
This edition published in Great Britain in 2023 by
Black Library, Games Workshop Ltd., Willow Road,
Nottingham, NG7 2WS, UK.

Represented by: Games Workshop Limited – Irish branch,
Unit 3, Lower Liffey Street, Dublin 1,
D01 K199, Ireland.

10 9 8 7 6 5 4 3 2 1

Produced by Games Workshop in Nottingham.
Cover illustration by Manuel Castañón.

See Black Library on the internet at

blacklibrary.com

Find out more about Games Workshop
and the worlds of Warhammer at

games-workshop.com

Printed and bound in the UK.

To my beautiful wife, Thinh. I'm lucky I found you.

The Mortal Realms have been despoiled. Ravaged by the followers of the Chaos Gods, they stand on the brink of utter destruction.

The fortress-cities of Sigmar are islands of light in a sea of darkness. Constantly besieged, their walls are assailed by maniacal hordes and monstrous beasts. The bones of good men are littered thick outside the gates. These bulwarks of Order are embattled within as well as without, for the lure of Chaos beguiles the citizens with promises of power.

Still the champions of Order fight on. At the break of dawn, the Crusader's Bell rings and a new expedition departs. Storm-forged knights march shoulder to shoulder with resolute militia, stoic duardin and slender aelves. Bedecked in the splendour of war, the Dawnbringer Crusades venture out to found civilisations anew. These grim pioneers take with them the fires of hope. Yet they go forth into a hellish wasteland.

Out in the wilds, hardy colonists restore order to a crumbling world. Haunted eyes scan the horizon for tyrannical reavers as they build upon the bones of ancient empires, eking out a meagre existence from cursed soil and ice-cold seas. By their valour, the fate of the Mortal Realms will be decided.

The ravening terrors that prey upon these settlers take a thousand forms. Cannibal barbarians and deranged murderers crawl from hidden lairs. Martial hosts clad in black steel march from skull-strewn castles. The savage hordes of Destruction batter the frontier towns until no stone stands atop another. In the dead of night come howling throngs of the undead, hungry to feast upon the living.

Against such foes, courage is the truest defence and the most effective weapon. It is something that Sigmar's chosen do not lack. But they are not always strong enough to prevail, and even in victory, each new battle saps their souls a little more.

This is the time of turmoil. This is the era of war.

This is the Age of Sigmar.

A vellum letter, fifteen years old. Despite its age, the glistening ink is still luxurious and thick. Two tasteful trifold creases run the letter's width. Filigrees in the page's borders gleam.

TO THE RIGHT HONOURABLE LADY LELLEN SE ROYE
of the Se Roye Company:

In accordance with your first decree as viceroy-regent
of Candip, the Company has undertaken a census and
survey to ascertain the wealth of your new soke, the Pale
of Bodshe. To assist in understanding our assessments,
a summary of key definitions has been provided below.

Places of Import

The Pale of Bodshe. The great territory located within
Aspiria in the Great Parch of Aqshy. Natives refer to
themselves as Palers.

The Burning Valley, Cardand. This vast valley, named
for the Yrdun kingdom that once occupied it, is the centre
of the Pale. The entire valley is filled with the kingdom's
ruins, including many ziggurats.

Candip. This subterranean city is the beating heart of
Cardand. Before its absorption into Sigmar's demesnes,
Candip was known by its Yrdun rulers as *Carnd-Ep.*

Bharat. A second Yrdun kingdom that once abutted
Cardand. (Note: Company surveyors found no record of
Bharat's continued existence. Presumed lost during the
Age of Chaos.)

The Outlands. The territories on the rim of the Burning
Valley, occasionally referred to as 'the hinterlands'.

The Ashwilds. The territories surrounding the Burning
Valley, mostly ash-desert.

The Wastes. The inhospitable territories beyond the

Ashwilds. (Note: Given the difficulty of traverse and the hostility of native tribes, the Company recommends no attempt be made to cross these wastes on foot.)

The River Losh. The ancient river system that gives the Burning Valley its shape. All of Cardand's vegetation grows in the Losh floodplain.

The Paleward Winds. The favourable winds that airships use to enter the Pale from the Great Parch.

The Parchward Winds: The favourable winds that airships use to leave the Pale for the rest of the Parch.

Peoples of Import

The Yrdun. The Palers who once ruled Cardand and Bharat. Yrdun live by a code called the *Yrdoval.* The wealthiest scions of the ancient Yrdun great houses have been Reclaimed. (Note: Yrdun commoners are open to Reclamation but offer little possible tax revenue. Their welfare is not a priority.)

The Beltollers. The Paler tribes that once submitted to the Yrdun, now scattered across the Pale. Major tribes are listed below.

The Holmon. The duardin of the Pale, often called 'delvers'. Notorious for drafting fraudulent contracts.

The Hullet. A martial tribe inhabiting the wastes surrounding Cardand. Known to mix the ash of the dead in their war-paint.

The Mukwuk. An offshoot branch of the Yrdun. Considered loyal and simple.

The Rockwrists. A tribe of diminutive folk with indigo blood. Reliable as a source of labour. (Note: The Company recommends immediate Reclamation of this tribe.)

The *Sleeps-First Clans*. An insular confederation of tribes that believe the Age of Sigmar to be a dream.

The *Sur-Sur-Seri*. An exclusively female tribe.

The *Telantr*. A cave-dwelling people rarely seen on Cardand's surface. Telantr warriors ('arrow-tongues') are known to spit poison.

The *Ushara*. Deadly nomad raiders whose warriors are called 'warborn'. (Note: The Company recommends extreme caution in dealings with the Ushara. They have been known to track and kill missionaries sent to convert them.)

Appendices complete with the Company's full appraisals of potential territorial revenues are included in the attached scrolls.

Congratulations on your accession to the viceroyalty-regency, my lady.

Yours respectfully,
Councillor T. von Deernt
Keeper of the Purse

A second letter, little more than scrawl on waxed paper with notes in the margins. Nicks, scorch marks and questionable stains mar the page. This letter was drafted piecemeal in the field.

THE PILLARS OF YRDOVAL

(commander's survey human terrain bodshe pale)
done by ~~Captain~~ Qual Micaw Boskin

YRDUN smallfolk resist SIGMAR'S LAWS,
claiming to follow an older code.

Task: Investigate Existence of YRDOVAL,
Unwritten Code of the YRDUN.

(begin survey results)

1: SANCTUARY

YRDUN tradition demands they must have
sanctuary for their people. They claim they will fight
to the death to protect those within their sanctuary.

*sceptical about this /
believe when see*

2: HOSPITALITY

YRDUN pride themselves on taking care of guests.
Show up hungry, naked and cold and YRDUN are
guaranteed to feed, clothe and warm you.

*recommend billeting forces
near YRDUN to reduce unit
upkeep*

3: VENGEANCE

YRDUN will go to any length to avenge perceived
wrongs.

Up to them to decide if and how they were
wronged.

*also sceptical / regard with
caution*

4: -??

Unable to verify rumours about fourth pillar of
YRDOVAL. THE YRDUN in CARDAND seem unaware
of it.

(end survey results)

*next survey is yours, J.
This is the last time we
bet assignments in a
card game.*

-M.B.

CHAPTER ONE

Sometimes, when I look out over my world, I want it to end.

This time, the shadow of a sailing mountain drew my cold eyes to the burning flats. In its shade a woman staggered, her patent screams drifting up the way mirages do.

My spite warred with my pity. My soul groaned from the weight of my false indifference. Because I couldn't not care. This was a priestess of Sigmar. Her Azyrite shrieks betrayed her, as did her ragged raiment and the worthless relics she carried.

The human in me wanted to help. Everything else screamed not to. Whatever the Azyrites claimed, they'd made beggars of us all. And I had not come here to save anybody. My conscience commanded me only to my sister's word.

My eyes traced the priestess' discarded baggage. Along that dotted thread, three figures gave chase. They were microscopic in the distance, yet lean and strong, accustomed to Aqshy's heat. I saw it in their lanky swagger. I felt it in the glimmer of their sand-iron.

They were warborn of the Ushara, one of the Beltoll tribes. Centuries ago the Beltollers had submitted to Cardand and Bharat: the empires of my mothers and fathers, ruled by the great Yrdun houses and clans. That was a time of balance. Of restraint.

But this was the Age of Sigmar, and the old balance was gone. The Azyrites had destroyed the old order for the sake of their own. We were their prey, now. We were each other's.

So I didn't move. Let the priestess revel in the fires her people had kindled. Her tiny figure, swathed in bright clothes, stumbled. If her pursuers didn't claim her, exhaustion would. If not that, then thirst.

If I didn't help her, she would die.

And Varry would be disappointed.

My jaw hardened. I gulped a lungful of hot air. All I'd ever wanted was to make Varry happy. I'd seen her joy in guarded moments, in the dead of night. Twinkling in her smile, fading like cinderflies. But her joy was so rare. She took care of me, and I knew the toll those efforts extracted.

Always tired, Varry. Always bleak and forlorn. If I helped the priestess, I might see Varry smile. Something in that pleased me. Something covetous, something earnest. Most of all, something true.

Were this priestess sitting in my place, on the lee of this ridge – and were I in her place, in the shadow of leering mountains – she would not have helped me. Azyrites took everything and gave nothing in return. They'd never helped us. Not when we were rag-thin and roaming, nor when we built our home on the broken hill, digging our well into the rock until our hands bled.

But the Azyrites had never had what I had. Varry was all I lived for, the only mortal in blazing creation I would have died for.

Killing a handful of warborn for her would be nothing, nothing at all.

* * *

Dust billowed in the Ushara's tracks. The nomads' coal-black flesh gleamed beneath their Idoneth-dyed shawls, which whipped in the wind. The Ushara resembled serpent-dancers in Cardand's night markets. Those dancers would gyrate like spinning tops, then plunge and roll to their feet. The warborn's movements were similar, economic but showy. But when they fought they would be savage and merciless.

The priestess scrambled through the brimstone sands. She huffed prayers for protection to her god who didn't care, who didn't listen. She clutched a handful of precious jewel boxes in quill-thin fingers and ebony hands.

'Please,' she rasped. Her plea went unheeded, gobbled by the sounds of her scrabbling.

As I watched, I sneered. The priestess was a mewling child in the manicured flesh of a woman whose life had known only privilege. I loathed her – but it was not for her I had come.

Rising, I drew my javelin. Yolk-yellow sands dusted from my arms in sheets as I quit my concealment.

The warborn halted. *'Yrdunko!'* one barked.

I whipped my arm forward. The javelin flew. My throwing thong slapped my wrist as the lead-weighted shaft speared the closest nomad's eye. He snapped down headlong, blood misting the space where he had stood, then blossoming into a pool around him.

I drew my long dirks, both Hammerhal-forged. They were gifts from Jujjar, an old friend. Before this I had only appreciated their utility in cutting cord or slitting the throats of rustled cattle. Never in battle.

Immediately the nomads were upon me. The two remaining warborn expended as little energy as possible, exposing themselves not at all, cautious the way predators are. I fended off probing strikes. The Ushara's serpentine fighting style was lethal, not a display I'd ever hoped to witness at blade's length. At least, not without a rank of Yrdun Ashstalkers beside me.

Those days were gone. But before our Freeguild Ashstalkers had been disbanded, we had trained against warborn mercenaries. I knew this foe. The Ushara fought high and far, lofty in body and spirit, so I stayed low and tight.

They circled, thrusting their sand-iron, their falchions clanging off my dirks. If they attacked from both sides, they'd finish this. I had to stay calm, maintain control.

Then tremors ran beneath my feet. My eyes flickered down. A lavamander tunnelled through earthfire beneath the sands, sacred and massive and precious. Just what I hunted for – just when I wanted it least.

The second nomad barked and struck. Impulse had mastered her sense. She spent herself in a wild flurry, and when the time was right, I lashed out and swept my feet. She toppled; I finished her with a perfunctory thrust.

Sweat ran down my tarred brow. I had to focus on the third warborn, but fighting as a lavamander migrated only made this harder. Its moving mass shivered up my bones. The beasts were as quickly lost as they were found. To have followed this one's movement now would mean losing sight of my foe. Even for a moment, distraction meant death.

Control. All I needed was control.

He thrashed forward. I parried a frenzy of blows from his sand-iron falchion, until a dirk slipped my grip. Survival in the Ashwilds required endurance, agility, tenacity. This foe possessed all three, in greater abundance than I. But rage ran in his veins like a curse. Fury had robbed him of reason. His breathing warbled as he panted hoarse oaths for the lives I had stolen. He had not mastered Aqshy's heat; it had mastered him.

He was off balance, out of control. I could best him like that.

I feinted, then disarmed him. He gritted his teeth and shoved through my guard, tackling me.

Our blades thumped to the sand. His lithe fingers locked around my throat. With iron strength, his eyes cobalt fire, he squeezed the life from me.

I couldn't breathe, couldn't prise his stone hands from my neck. The world went red, then silver at the edges. I groped through hot sand until my fingers grazed a dirk's edge. I seized the blade. Pain sang in my hand as its edge sliced through my palm and fingers. I jolted the dirk into the warborn's arm, then twisted until sinews crunched.

He screamed, spraying me with spittle, drenching us both in blood. He crumbled and nursed his mangled arm.

I shuddered at the sight of his suffering. I would have closed my eyes if I dared. I finished him kindly, quickly. Not with pride, nor vim – just a breed of patience and remorse.

I sputtered, clearing the beetle in my throat, the throbbing in my head. Sand moistened by blood had infiltrated my wraps. This gory clay abraded my flesh and painted me rust. The stench of death hung in the air.

The mountains passing overhead reminded me where I was, and I scanned for more opponents. No Beltollers remained – only I and the mewling priestess, her eyes willow-green. Her thirst-gnarled lips hung awry, like the fixed rictus of my father's death mask, a grimace that could frighten the dead.

The priestess hissed, half-mad. 'Boy! Where did you come from?'

I raised a bleeding finger to my lips, then tucked my dirks into my sash. I padded after the tremors I had sensed. Here and there I paused to listen, holding my breath. Aqshy's heat ebbed into my heels, running up my bones. My blood was hot; I fought to make it cool.

Then, beneath a shifting blur of heat, fissures split the earth. An animal's coal-rough muzzle pushed up from beneath the ash-stricken sand. The lavamander.

I went prone as the black behemoth emerged. Ranks of thick legs carried its char-scabbed trunk from the ground, shedding crumbs of earthfire like slag. The blind creature sniffed the air, and I dared not breathe. The cracks in its tough hide glowed orange with the heat of its blood, which boiled mine.

A male, a juvenile. He bleated, then groaned. His call was all bass and glottalisation, like a knotted cord pulled through my head. He dragged his outsize mass onwards, seeking out a fresh vein of magma. The lavamander nosed into the hard earth and burrowed the way dogs play in sand.

I hugged the ground, still not breathing. When the earthen crush had ceased, I lifted my head. He was gone.

Varry had once told me our father uttered special words for lavamanders. Invocations to Sigmar, the god he worshipped, in Yrdo, the tongue of our people. In the past I thought that seemed right and well. But all things seem right to children.

I tugged a scrap of fire-resistant hide from my carrying sash and clambered into the cooling crater the lavamander had left behind. Magnure resembled crackling embers, smouldering and snapping with forever heat. Even through the enchanted hide it seared my hands and roused my heart. I kept the ice in me cold, counting my breaths, fighting the scalding heat with everything I had.

I wrapped the magnure, sashed it, then emerged from the crater.

'What was that?' the priestess croaked.

I regarded her. A priestess of Sigmar, yes, but not one of *those* priests. No shaven scalp, no scar-stitched face. No platemail or hammer or storm-swell voice, holy books chained to her war-heart breast. I glanced along the trail of treasures she had dropped during her flight. The warborn must have thought her a gift from the gods; perhaps she thought as much herself. To have carried so much so far, she must have been strong. But I couldn't understand why she'd bothered.

'You come from Capilaria,' I said, in the Azyrite tongue. 'From that damn city, Hammerhal.'

She furrowed her brow. 'Yes, yes. That damn city. My damn city, damn you!'

I stared.

'Are you alone?' she asked. 'I don't care if you are, but please say you aren't. You're from Candip? You must be. Where are your spears? Your vassals? Or… your liege?'

My eyes wrinkled. 'What's a liege?'

She huffed. 'What's a liege… Well, yes. At least I'm alive. There's always that.'

I followed her gaze into the wastes, where ash danced over blistered sands.

'We brought something,' she murmured absently. '*Izmenili* of Chamon. Precious gems. Gems… shiny rocks.' She made shapes with her hands, as if to qualify the shininess of rocks. 'You'll need to go back for them with whomever's accompanied you. It's too dangerous to go alone. Beastkin overtook us at dusk. They killed my party, tore them apart.' She shuddered. 'They'll be back. Won't they? Or… perhaps you *can* go alone?'

I planted my foot on an Ushara's skull. Brains squelched as I yanked my javelin free. 'They'll be back. Eventide. Just wait.' I wiped the javelin clean, checked its shaft for cracks. 'How'd you survive?'

She exhaled. 'I don't know. Hiding beneath the wagons. I ran when I could, but they chased. Damned things they are, but they're vicious. I ran and ran through the night. Somewhy, they gave me up at dawn. Then, those…' She glanced at the corpses around us. 'Them. They came.'

'Ushara. Warborn.'

'Yes. Them.' She peered at the jewel boxes in her arms, as if all her suffering were nothing compared to their value. She held at least a dozen. More were tied into her clothes.

Then she sighed. 'I shall wait here, beneath the metaliths' shade. The flying mountain, metaliths are flying mountains. Bring water when you can. You know these lands? Look at you, of course you do. You'll have no problem, you and whomever you've brought. Yes? So. What're you waiting for? Go on.'

I peered at the ridgeline. Part of me had hoped Varry would see all this. I had saved this woman for my sister, not for charity. The priestess was not some motherless infant I would elevate to adulthood and teach my ways. She was a grown woman, strong enough to carry many things, then drop them. Thanks to me, she was still alive. She required nothing else.

The priestess grimaced. I thought she saw me for the first time, then. The flesh of my face like a nightmare's, painted in sun-daub tar mixed from stolen scrivener's ink and crushed charcoal. My matted, unbound hair. The heat shawl and wrappings I had drenched in blood to save her life, already crusty and scabbed.

Or...

Did she see a man? A mortal like her, with mortal wants and mortal needs? I had dreams, once. As she must have had – as all children had. Once my eyes were delinquent with wishes. As a child, I had possessed hope and faith.

But I don't think she saw any of that.

'You're not going to help,' she said.

I pointed to the wasteland horizon. 'The beasts are Smoulder-hooves. They move when Hysh sinks below the hills and the sky's fires dim.' Then I pointed to the ridge. More drifting mountains – more metaliths – peppered the sky beyond. 'Smoulderhooves are scarce beyond these bluffs. That way lies the Burning Valley, Cardand. And within it, Candip.' I hawked, spat. 'Your city.'

She grew flustered. 'I need help, not waypoints. I need *your* help. I need the other Izmenili.'

I palmed sand over my hand until my cuts clotted, then brushed the dried filth off. 'I did help.'

'The warborn? That was *duty*, not help. We're both children of Sigmar. *Kindred.*'

I chuckled. 'You're no kin of mine.'

She narrowed her eyes. 'What's wrong with you? Why this indecency?'

Enough was enough. My head pounded, my blood blazed, and the magnure's heat burned in my veins like a hillfire. I sipped from my waterskin and departed.

Her feet crunched into the sand behind me. 'You ingrate. You animal! You're an ashfoot, aren't you? A Paler, an Yrdun native. I've heard of you Yrdun. Miscreants and reprobates, charging extra for those who speak Sigmar's tongue! After all we did for you! After everything we *gave* you!'

Ashfoot. My shoulders tensed, but I walked on. Perhaps I need not share the events of this day with Varry.

'We raised aqueducts in Candip!' the priestess said. 'We walled your city, our armies patrol its reaches! We contain foes who would ravage your lands, you know that? *Ra-vage!* You'd be gheists but for us. You'd be thralls to the Dark Gods! This is how you repay us?'

I stopped and turned. 'Repay who?'

'Us! The God-King!'

My finger jolted out at her. 'You did nothing when the beasts came for my family. Nothing when me and my sister were alone, except hire us to fight your wars. I'm not thankful for *nothing*. I don't repay *nothing.*'

'Civilising the Reclaimed is not nothing!'

I marched onwards. 'Hail Sigmar.'

Blissful quiet followed, broken only by the rustle of wind. Then, a sizzling reached my ears. The air suddenly stank of brimstone and baking pottery.

I glowered and turned. The priestess made the old signs with her fragile fingers, trying to cast some spell. Cuneiform runes perforated the air, disturbing to behold for long.

'Put your hands down.' When she didn't, I drew a dirk and lurched out. 'I said, *put them down.*'

The priestess blanched, her skin going the shade of dusk. Her fingers danced faster. But she tugged the wrong threads of magic, and her sleeves ignited. The rune's cinders caught aflame. Her eyes widened.

I ducked just as the spell exploded. Heat washed across me. Then I straightened and stormed over, swatting away the embers of magic. I seized the coughing priestess by her ragged raiment collar – she stank of sickly perfume. I hurled her down, then pushed my blade to her neck to silence her puling.

Breathless with terror and forceless indignation, she spoke. 'What are you doing?'

I twitched, my knuckles digging into her soft neck. Soft, from a soft life of creams and silk and touching soft things. To a creature so soft, I must be jagged and ungiving.

Then the thought struck me. She thought *I* was the bad one.

For a moment, I wondered what she might have thought if we had met in Candip and not here. In the crevasse-city her people had stolen from mine, sitting on one of her priesthood's heavy palanquins as it was borne upon the stooped shoulders of my impoverished kindred. Men like Jujjar, or women like Varry. Varry believed the Azyrites deserved reverence for the salvation they brought to Bodshe. *Salvation.*

I would not kill this priestess. Not even for summoning spells against me – not even in these Ashwilds where nobody would learn of her death. True, Varry would never have forgiven such a crime. Even in her absence, I craved to please her. I yearned to be the brother she loved.

But that wasn't the heart of it. The Azyrites had already taken so much. I would give them nothing more. Not another moment – not another breath.

My eyes dropped to the hammer-faced medallion hanging from the woman's neck. I cut its cord, tucking it away. Then I released her. 'Seek the Burning Valley and Candip. There many will tumble for the chance to help you. Send them to kill me if you wish.' I rose. 'They'll get lost.'

Tears formed in the corners of the priestess' eyes. 'Please. I can't go alone. I just need help.'

But I was already gone. Her whispers became screams, then threats, then promises of reward. Perhaps her words would have swayed Varry, but Varry was blind to the truth of the realm. The gods did not love us. And just as well, for I loved nothing but Varry.

As the creaking hulks of passing mountains joined the priestess' distant noise, I clambered up shingly slopes, each step careless. Errant thoughts washed through my mind.

Then someone emerged from behind the nearest tor.

I tensed as I recognised Varry. She wore a shawl like mine, and the same tar on my brow painted hers. Tufts of sand-caked hair protruded from beneath her cowl. She had come to find me, right where I'd promised to be.

The corners of my lips rose into a smile. Varry always looked tired. Beneath her spring-water smile and starlight eyes lay a forlorn strength, the prerequisite for our existence. She was the only person who had ever loved me. But she had come much sooner than I expected.

I froze, as if stillness could conceal the distant priestess or mute her petulance, but Varry was observant. She glimpsed the blood on my clothes and frowned.

'Held, what have you done?'

CHAPTER TWO

Where Azyrites rule, freedom dies. This almost happened to the lavamanders. The sacred beasts once roamed the Pale of Bodshe, honoured and revered by my people, the Yrdun. My sister and I made our living off the magnificent beasts.

Precious few lavamanders still wandered the Ashwilds. They bled the burning magic from Aqshy's native earthfire, feeding until the lava flows annealed to smooth stone. The earthfire was their living; their waste was ours. The magnure we collected – lavamander dung – we sold to the merchants of Candip. We lived on the pittance they paid for it. From Candip, dealers exported the lavamanders' crackling feculence to the God-King's distant demesnes, to heat the stoves of laughing foreigners, to warm the steamed baths of effete lords.

This was hearsay. Varry and I couldn't know. Neither of us had ever left the Pale. Neither of us used stoves, either – not when Aqshy's scorching shale would do. And rarely had we felt the steam of anything but our own sweat and tears.

Varrianala Fall was third daughter to our dead parents. Where I had refused the struggling priestess, Varry would have helped her do anything. But Varry was a woman of scruples, and her life might have been measured in the salvation of broken things like me. Years ago, after the beastkin killed our parents and our family was scattered to the eight winds, Varry turned to the God-King for the same reason I turned away from him.

She had sought Sanctuary, that first pillar of *Yrdoval*. No safety in the realm exists other than the safety we make for ourselves.

For all the things I admired about Varry, she was a believer. She worshipped the pitiless God-King. She believed in him with all her heart. When his thunder called, she danced. When the Cursed Skies rippled in the veil of night, she cowered.

And she prayed. How she prayed.

In the days of the Yrdun's supremacy, each lavamander was bestowed a name. Names were reflections of our inner flames, unique and undying. This was as true for the lavamanders as it was for the Yrdun and the Beltoller tribes. The Ushara warborn, the Holmon delvers. The Telantr arrow-tongues and the Mukwuk and Hullet. The Sur-Sur-Seri, and the Rockwrists, and the Sleeps-First Clans.

Beneath the veil of creation, all of us were united by this inner fire. Our names were indomitable – even by the gods.

It was a decent lie. But unlike the myth of those flames, the days of the Yrdun's supremacy had ended. So had our stories and our people and our names. Time and ill fortune had toppled the Yrdun from their thrones and ziggurats. Beltollers had become savages, Cardand had become bones, and Bharat had been lost.

Only the gods remained. Only me, and only you.

You wish to know who I am. You think you already do. But you don't, just as I don't. Not any more.

Once I was Heldanarr Fall, seventh son to a dead father and dead mother, heir to a dead nation, child of her dead kingdom,

Cardand. Sometimes, I look over the lands which were ours and remember the life they inflicted upon me. I witness this dead place with its dead people and its dead name and my palms tingle and my heels itch and my stomach boils.

These times most of all, I wish to take the realm into my hands and set it ablaze. I look out over my world, and I want it to burn.

But it already has.

Once I was Heldanarr Fall. Who I am now, I no longer know. Never have I worshipped the gods. But never have I obtained the objects of my desires, either. So let this be my first and final prayer, for all the things I have not attained. Hear me, that you may know me. Do not forget me.

For soon, I'm coming for you.

Varry knew I meant to leave the priestess to fate's bitter tithe. She descended to help the woman. I feared speaking the wrong words, making a bad situation worse. Varry was already upset.

As she dried the priestess' desert tears and gathered her flimsy boxes, I watched. She offered a precious draught from her water-skin. The priestess drained it, then asked for more. Without question, I offered my flask. The priestess drained that, too.

My generosity assuaged Varry's anger, her disappointment. Still, she said nothing and pushed past me, helping the priestess up the ridge.

'Let's go,' Varry said in Yrdo, without looking.

I flinched. 'Where?'

'Home.'

The knives in her tone told me to say nothing more, and I followed.

The Pale of Bodshe was massive. A charred wilderness, a broiling kiln, yawning across forever horizons. Shrubs with branches like insects' legs speckled the Ashwilds' hard ridges and blurry sand flats, uprooting and scampering where the heat drove them. Split-nosed, bat-faced creatures basked on the cliffs, panting, their veined wings spread like tarps to gather moisture. The Parchward Winds would take them to better places, like the flying metaliths.

All creation learned to resist Aqshy's fire. The plants, the beasts, the mountains – mere existence had made them immune to the bright realm's heat, immune to their own. They were everything I wished to be.

Before the blood rains ever came – before long-necked daemons prowled the unterways and overwastes – the journey from the Ashwilds to the Burning Valley of Cardand was perilous. At day, Varry, the priestess and I passed the swelters by resting beneath the shade of stone overhangs. Then, from the aching coolness of dusk until the painful promise of dawn, we hiked below ridges' crests, through whispering brushlands, towards a place called home.

My sister had offered Sister Elene, the Sigmarite priestess, Sanctuary and Hospitality. These were guaranteed by Yrdoval, the code of our people, of which the third pillar was Vengeance. Whenever we rested, Elene made her abundant needs known. We gave her Hospitality. Sanctuary awaited her. Of Vengeance I only dreamed, for Elene had not wronged me yet.

During our journey Sister Elene explained to Varry why she had come to the Pale. In the Burning Valley lay the sun-bleached bones of the old Yrdun kingdom, Cardand. Our people still haunted its broken fastness, its crumbling ziggurats and canyon roads, its dusty markets and collapsed unterways. The ages had laid the Pale of Bodshe bare. Cardand was no exception.

In the heart of Cardand's shattered edifices lay Candip like a deep wound, an underground crevasse, a city of dreams. When the Azyrites first came to plant their banners in Cardand, they took the fortress-city *Carnd-Ep* and rechristened it Candip. They had stolen it from us.

In the time since, Candip had flourished under the careful administration of its viceroy-regent and her puppet conclave. The city had burgeoned from a remote outpost into a bustling bulwark of Sigmar's power. Now, Candip was overdue for ordination as a City of Sigmar. The simple inanities of Sigmarite politics had inflicted some delay upon the ordination, but Elene was due to play a role in it when it finally occurred.

As Elene regaled us with her people's glories, I got the impression tension marked the relations between Candip and her sovereign, Hammerhal Aqsha. In the century following its theft from the Yrdun, Sigmarised Candip had become an insurgent among her sister demesnes. Elene claimed her appointment for the ordination was a settlement meant to please rival factions – another inanity I could not grasp. But that she was nobody's first choice, I understood well.

Hammerhal Aqsha lay in the heart of the Great Parch, east of the gore-drenched Flamescar Plateau, in distant Capilaria. Save the rumours carried on Paleward Winds by Hewer Durandsson and his duardin arkanauts, I knew little of the Parch, less of Capilaria, and almost nothing of Hammerhal.

One evening I warmed trail bread over a fire. Elene dressed my ignorance with the hubris I had come to expect from Azyrites. Her people had come to teach us all things.

'The honourable Se Roye Company administers Candip,' she explained to Varry through a mouthful of bread. She never spoke to me directly, though I suspected she wanted me to hear. 'Lady Lellen is viceroy-regent.'

Varry fed the flames with brush. 'We know of the Se Royes, sister.'

'The *honourable* Se Royes. The venerable Lady Lellen was awarded a charter of nobility, decades back. For grand services rendered to the God-King, blessed be his name.' She simpered. 'What I'm saying is, don't be confused when we arrive, should you hear of House Se Roye and the Company Se Roye. They are the same, so you need not even ask. Perhaps you shouldn't speak at all. Actually, let me do the talking. I'm rather eloquent.'

I scowled. *Eloquent* was not the word I would have called Elene.

'We're not taking you to Candip,' Varry said. 'We're taking you to our home. Kharadron ply the Parchward Winds. Captain Durandsson's airship is due with us. We'll smoke him down. He'll take you to the crevasse-city, for reimbursement. But we must make good time or we'll miss him.'

Elene spread her hands, a missionary pose. 'All things happen or not by the will of Sigmar.'

'All things happen or not by the sloth of *you*,' I mumbled. 'Each night you slow us down, and we're only returning early for you. This foraging trip's been a waste of provisions and water. All for you.'

Silence passed, punctuated only by snapping flames and the sounds of Elene's chewing. 'I'm sorry,' she said, smacking her gums. 'I couldn't understand you. The Azyrite tongue requires *e-nun-ci-a-tion*. Not like your speech, I'm sure.'

I bit my tongue.

'Heldan and I,' Varry rushed to say, 'we used to live in Cardand. Just off the outworks. Beside the palisades, before they cleared tenements from the cogfort tracts. We were Freeguilders.'

Elene raised her brow. 'Oh?'

Pride flashed in Varry's eyes. 'Yes.'

I smiled. Nothing pleased Varry more than our prior service to the God-King. I'd only done it for victuals and our monthly phial of *akwag*. I had never measured the cut of those Aqua Ghyranis wages with a proofing plate, but the magic waters had kept us strong. That had been enough.

'But your home's no longer in Cardand?' Elene said. 'Why leave?'

I raised my eyes. I wondered what Varry would say.

She shrugged. 'We thought we'd do better out here.' Varry's humble glance begged me to remain quiet, so I did.

Elene's beetling brow furrowed. 'That is noble. Hard work's a thing of virtue. Sigmar demands sacrifice and toil. The honest always get back what they give.'

That evening I bit my tongue until it bled, and not only for Elene's mistaken impression her people were fair to ours. I felt Varry's embarrassment as my own. She wanted so terribly to impress the priestess, but we had nothing which might impress anyone. We had truer virtues, but Elene didn't care for those. She wanted more. She wanted us to take her to Candip.

For most of our journey home I bore Varry's sullen disappointment with a martyr's forbearance. She had rarely spoken to me since hearing Elene's screams beneath the shadow of those metaliths. I felt locked in one of Candip's market pillories, for petty offenders and the wrongfully accused. Which was I? I wondered, as we trudged in darkness and the night's mythic silence. I hadn't hurt the priestess. I had *saved* her.

The more Elene told us, the more intriguing her tidings. She spoke of the stars' lay like they were Aqshy's own geography. She spoke of our place in the cosmos as if she really knew. She described in detail the other Mortal Realms, places I had long assumed were myth.

I thought her a charlatan, until one night I spied her admiring her Izmenili, her jewels of Chamon. They twisted in her hands, changing colour and shape like desert beetles hiding from stonehawks.

I was certain nothing like that existed in all Aqshy. The Azyrites must have been powerful indeed, to have transported such treasures across creation on nothing more than their whims.

Elene explained how this was possible, too. The Great Parch was vast beyond measure, but Paleward Winds shortened the months-long sea voyages into days-long air journeys, straight to Candip. Since no realmgates had been secured in Bodshe's Pale, these voyages were necessary. Without the winds, travel between our lands would have been arduous.

'A realmgate,' I said. The word's simple beauty inspired me. Alone in all things Azyrite, the elegance of their speech has always pleased me. 'This leads to other realms?'

Elene had not forgiven my apathy to her previous predicament. She clucked her tongue, shook her head. 'Oh, child. The nature of a realmgate is not something you shall ever need to know.'

That day, drifting asleep in the shade, my chagrin was a lurking ache. Elene's words should have stirred my anger. I ought to have lashed out – and control was not what stopped me. Elene was right. As warm sand and the mellow shade lulled me to sleep, I realised I had never believed in anything before her stories. It felt trivial and obvious I need not believe in myself.

CHAPTER THREE

Varry never told Elene the truth. The Ashstalkers, our Yrdun battalion, had been disbanded on Lellen Se Roye's command – the very Lady Lellen whom Elene held in such high regard. Our pay had been miserable enough, and when our akwag stipends dried up completely, we were forced from Cardand into the Ashwilds, where we could at least earn a living.

Service as an Ashstalker had never been prestigious. All Candip had sneered at us. In Candip, Azyrites had become the locals. The Yrdun and Beltollers were displaced, strangers within their own lands. We could not afford the city's rents nor purchase simple provisions. Even drinks at certain establishments were beyond our reach.

I still remembered the day Jujjar and I completed parade training. We had hated those marches. In the history of our people, no Yrdun warrior had ever hunted nor fought in straight lines, standing stiff and still and bleeding sweat beneath the sun. Yrdun fought as skirmishers, and I saw no better way. I still couldn't understand the Azyrites' moral and tactical rigidity. But I could not understand many things.

We had thought to do as the other old soldiers did – to have a drink. But walking to an Ulcarver tavern popular among Hammerhal's Sun Seeker Freeguilders and Se Roye's Company mercenaries, strange looks came upon us. Ulcarver was an Azyrite ward populated by Azyrite bloodlines. In Ulcarver, even Capilarian veterans whose chests were laden with service medallions from Parch wars strode with held breath and tense shoulders. Pureblooded Azyrites knew who was one of their own, and who was not.

So when Jujjar and I entered the tavern, silence assailed us. Silence wouldn't pour a drink, so we approached the keeper.

Chewleaf spittle ran down her poxy chin. Her eyes were sullied from jaundice. I removed my phial and a cheap dropper to purchase drinks, just as other veterans did. Three drops of Aqua Ghyranis, for two rounds. A fair rate for anything but firewine swill.

The keeper wiped her chin. Then she placed a loaded pistol on the proofing plate and stared with loaded eyes.

Jujjar bade me look around. Every mortal in the dim room was Azyrite. Duardin, aelf, human – but Azyrite, with lightning in their eyes and aether in their blood. I saw it, in their upturned noses: contempt. We might as well have been cannibal Smoulderhooves from the wastes to them.

This had been my experience in Candip; I knew Varry's to have been worse. I could not fathom why she still believed they would ever be good to us.

Soon I recognised the hills. Their shape and cut, the give of gravel underfoot. Dawn's fleeting warmth was desolate and close, the last grasp of a dying lover.

We lived in the rugged marches between Candip and the Ashwilds, two days from the Burning Valley and the ruins of

Cardand's broken kingdom. Mount the distant hills and one would see Candip's gleaming towers nestled in the old kingdom like gems in a geode. I hoped to never see them again.

I loosened my shawl and enjoyed the familiar scorch in my lungs. Breathing Bodshe's air was like inhaling the draught of a closed stove-house. Often hot rains blew in on the Paleward Winds with rumours of distant wars. The rains soaked the lands. Strange plants blossomed, and animals emerged to revel. The Ashwilds became a place of burning vitality – not this sulphur-stricken hell.

Then the skies cleared, and Azyrite priests shepherded their maddened flocks of fanatics across the outlands. They always came, sooner or later, whipping the flesh from their backs. They crowed to the God-King for salvation, purging the wonder from the lands. Faith returned, and the Pale went dry. And when time had passed, the rains came once more to instigate their quiet rebellion, and the circle began anew.

Elene, treasure-laden, lagged far behind us. Varry stopped to glare at me from over her shoulder.

'Why'd you kill the Ushara?'

My ears perked. She was speaking to me. When I answered, I kept my voice steady. 'They would have killed her.'

'*You* would have killed her. You left her to die.'

My eyes wrinkled. 'No. I saved her life.'

'And then left her to die. I know you well, Heldan. You needn't have killed those warborn. The Ushara respect our ways. You are more *our ways* than any Yrdun-son I know. Even more than bitter Jujjar.'

I tossed my hands, exasperated. 'I couldn't have stopped them with words. So I did what I could. And I did it for you.'

Varry's eyes flickered. She was not indifferent to that.

Then she sighed. 'I deal with Ushara in Lurth. What shall I say when our paths cross again?'

'Nothing,' I said. 'Why say anything? Let them wonder what happened to their kin. It's not for us.'

'It is if we killed them. We pay our dues, brother. We get back what we give. I'm not a liar. And mother and father did not raise us to be bandits.'

'No. They didn't raise us at all. Father had his neck ripped out and mother rode lightning into the sky.'

Varry lurched forward. '*I* raised you! And I did not raise a heartless heathen!'

I recoiled. 'This isn't about the warborn.'

Varry's eyes flitted back to Elene, who still negotiated the crags below. For two days, I had gravely misunderstood Varry's silence. She wasn't angry. She was afraid.

'Censors must be paid for the dead,' she said. 'You know what those are?'

I shrugged. 'Sigmar rubbish?'

'No. Well – yes. But not rubbish.'

I shrugged again. 'Why would I know Sigmar rubbish?'

'You prefer some other sort of rubbish? Are you learning pyromancy rubbish or scrivener rubbish or some trade rubbish which'll help us return to Candip?'

I waved. 'Candip is hell. I know much better rubbish. The old ballads, by heart. *House of Sorrows*, and *The Loss of Bharat*. I know the Pale paths, in and out.' I raised my javelin, then tugged my dirks' hilts and winked. 'I know how to kill three warborn by myself.'

'Yes. Very impressive, your atrocity. But three dead Ushara means three censors, little brother.' Worry-lines marked Varry's eyes. Her frown could have been cast in bronze. She was more serious than I had seen in a long time.

'What is a censor?' I asked.

Varry's eyes returned to Elene. 'A tax. A very onerous tax.'

Tax and tribute were nothing new. I need ask no more.

Then I smirked, and Varry scowled. 'What?' she said.

'We always pay Varry onerous taxes,' I said. 'When'll we pay a Heldan onerous tax?'

Varry's lips cracked into a smile. 'I hate you. Don't do that again.'

I thrust my javelin into the sand, then removed the scrim of magnure I had carried.

Varry glimpsed the smouldering embers and gasped. 'You carried this alone? How long? I found none. I would've helped.'

'It was chance,' I said. 'The 'mander came as I killed the Ushara. Like an omen.'

Varry brightened. She loved omens, loved the idea of them.

Our eyes returned to the magnure. Its heat tugged at the strings of our hearts, simmering in our blood. That heat was a force. More than that, it was a promise. The Aqua Ghyranis we could earn for this from Hewer's Kharadron could feed us for a month or longer.

But if Varry was thinking the same thing, the notion brought her no joy. The sight of her growing dismay settled in me.

Then I remembered Elene's hammer-faced medallion. I removed it and offered it to Varry. For one singing moment, she grinned. Joy gleamed in her eyes, and her hands shook.

But she must have understood who I got it from. She grimaced and snatched it away. Her eyes flashed to Elene. 'Sister, is this yours?'

'Oh, who knows?' Elene's bright eyes lifted. 'Wait – yes! Your heathen brother stole it from me. All the God-King's grace, how could I forget?'

'Because you only think about your jewels,' I said.

Rebuke flashed across Varry's face. She returned the medallion. I glowered, folding the magnure back into my sash. I shouldered my javelin and trudged on, glancing over my shoulder.

Elene brandished the coin. 'You know what this signifies? Grace. Sigmar does so much for us, does he not?'

Varry nodded. 'That he does, sister.'

Elene tied the cord off, looped the medallion around her neck. 'Our duty is to spread that grace. So we do, here, for you.'

I tossed my hands at the hills. 'This is not grace.'

Elene scoffed. 'Grace for your souls, fool, not your feet and your bellies! We saved your *souls*.'

'Save our feet and our bellies,' I said.

Again, Varry glared.

'No,' I said. 'You cannot be angry with me. Not for this. Not for killing the warborn. If I hadn't killed them, this woman would be dead. And if I meant to save the woman, I had to kill them.'

Elene sat on a stone. 'This woman has a name.'

'Not one worth speaking.' I returned my eyes to Varry. 'So what is it? Are you angry I let her live? Or angry I didn't let her die?'

I was incandescent, ready to argue my point. Then I glimpsed the weight of the world on Varry's sagging shoulders.

'Forget it,' she said. 'It's no matter.'

I clenched my teeth, tired of guilt, tired of feeling as if I'd wronged Varry. Everything I had done was for her. 'Beastkin killed the priestess' folk,' I said, in Yrdo. 'You understand?'

Varry blanched. The Smoulderhooves did not often venture into Cardand's outlands, but they did, and only for prey. Beasts could track a spoor for leagues. I had tried to raise this point before, but Varry had not wanted to listen.

'They will follow us. That's what I wanted to avoid.'

Varry's head sank. 'We'll get her to Hewer's ship. Then she'll be safe.'

I pounded my chest. 'But not us!'

Elene crossed her legs. 'It would be quite nice to participate in this exchange. Really, just lovely.'

I ignored her, looking to the horizon. 'Let's move.'

Varry nodded. 'Come, sister. Time's short.'

Elene baulked, glancing between us. 'Could I have water and a rest?'

Why did Varry worship Sigmar? Sigmar had not protected our family, nor us. Faith was no shield. It was a false sense of security.

But Varry was neither coward nor fool. She did not seek to curry divine favour. She sought solace. All the miseries we had endured, and no succour but what we had made for ourselves. I had my own medicines for the past. The glacier in my heart, and the fighting. My hatred for the divine, deeper than oceans.

I could not blame Varry for the path she had chosen. All people found their own way. Blind she may have been, but she had done more for me than anyone in all the world. She could have left me for dead in our family's desolate croft. She could have forged a life in Candip for herself.

Instead, she had lived for me.

Perhaps there would be some unseen wisdom in helping Elene. Varry and I had gone far together. We could go farther still.

CHAPTER FOUR

Hewer and the Kharadron had come and gone.

Varry still bothered with our smoke signal, piling green brush from saddles around the ridge into our fire pit. She muttered curses and dripped sweat, seething in chagrin.

Shame burned in me, too, a sympathetic flame. I folded my arms, watching smoke plume over our home and disperse. Beholding Varry's vain effort and distress caused me hurt. Hewer never came when the sun, Hysh, was this low in the sky. His journey always brought him at midday's swelter. He couldn't have seen our signal now. He'd have been too far.

I forced my gaze away. A minor metalith loomed over our home, casting a long shadow upon the bluffs. Cordage anchored it, spell-treated and flameproof, a gift from Hewer. Our little moon had long provided cover and concealment for our home and our cracked hill. Littering the hill's uneven slopes, dilapidated shelters and tumbledown fences leaned like drunkards in Candip. This place had been a village in some near past, a settlement with weather-worn outworks and proud guardian statues which hummed when the Cursed Skies went black.

But whoever had built this place was gone. The village had been abandoned, its statues toppled, its fields left barren and unploughed. All that proved anyone lived here at all was our dwelling on the hilltop, beneath our little moon. Piled stones, a thatch roof. An ash-garden plot. The accumulated trappings of half a lifetime spent in poverty.

A broken home for broken things – yet home nonetheless. I was proud of the life we had built.

I sighed, turning. Varry's heat-chapped hands shook. She knew what I knew.

'They're gone,' I said.

'Quiet!' she snapped. 'I'm concentrating.'

Behind us, Elene dawdled. 'I suppose this means I'll stay the night?'

'Not at all,' I said.

Varry stopped, tossed her hands. 'I'm sorry, sister. Ignore him. Of course you're welcome. It's not much, but it's safe.'

'For now,' I said, in Yrdo.

Varry lowered her cowl. 'We'll make the trip to Candip on the morrow, come dusk. Tonight we should rest. And prepare.'

I said nothing. Varry would have crusaded to the ends of the realm, if only Elene asked it of her.

Sister Elene glanced around our hilltop, down its rugged slopes. Disdain twisted her ebony features. Her face became a bunched fist. 'What a horrifying little hovel.'

Varry averted her eyes; anger churned within me. Elene was an unwelcome ingrate. She had drunk our water and enjoyed our hospitality. Now she shamed Varry.

Elene ambled to the bluffs, peering across the abandoned settlement. 'An old Dawnbringer colony. Picked dry, though.'

Varry brushed sweat from her brow. 'Held, get a mat together for her, please. I'll get water from the aquifer.'

I grunted, gathering what I needed. Varry retrieved a yoke and pails by the plot.

'A mat?' Elene said. 'For who?'

'Maybe you'd prefer the ground,' I said. 'Very comfortable, here.'

'No, it's not,' Varry said, 'because the heat would kill you at day. We stuff our mats with river reeds from the Losh. They soak up the heat.' Varry glared at me. 'Be good. Make the mat. I'll be back before you know it.'

Elene froze. 'You're leaving me with this unreclaimed pagan?'

My ears perked. 'Oh I like this word. *Pagan*.'

Varry hefted the yoke onto her shoulder, pails clattering at either end. 'He's not bad when he doesn't want to be. And he doesn't want to be. Right?'

I heard that for what it was. A peace. I nodded.

Varry shot me a dead look. Then she left.

As I stuffed fistfuls of reed into a burlap sack, Elene watched. Her attention felt like unwashed grime. 'What do you two say about me in your tongue?' she asked.

'Evil, evil things,' I said.

After a pause, Sister Elene chuckled. She was so noxious. 'You must have many friends, Heldanarr Fall.'

I grunted. I crammed more reeds into the sack, imagining it was Elene's mouth.

'Who named you?' she asked.

I debated not answering, but this was something I enjoyed talking about. 'Fall, from our father,' I said. 'In our tongue *fall* means the changing of all things. The way flame becomes smoke, the way embers become ash. He wanted our family to change like that. He wanted our lives to be better.'

'Flame, smoke, ash. Aren't those the seasons of Bodshe?'

'Not ash. Flame and smoke. But two seasons, yes.'

'What of your first name?'

'From our mother. I don't know its meaning.'

Elene's eyes twinkled. 'But I do.'

I looked up.

'Heldanarr's an Azyrite name cast in your people's tongue.' She smiled, her teeth polished ivory. 'You and your sister both have them. Missionary names.'

I returned to my labours. 'That is disheartening to learn.'

'Your sister worships Sigmar, praised be his name. Your parents too, it seems. Yet you're a heathen. How is that?'

'We are not all fools.' I stuffed another handful of reeds. 'Sigmar has never helped us. I don't worship gods who give nothing and ask all.'

Elene grew flinty. 'Sigmar gave you everything.'

'This does not feel like everything,' I said. 'We don't all have fine clothing and blessed gems.'

'The Izmenili are dedicated to Candip's ordination. That is simply beyond you.'

I nodded. 'I'm grateful.'

Elene flattened her lips. Silence reigned between us, silence I had longed for. But she would not go so quietly.

'So where are your kindred?'

'My father is dead. Mother and the others are just gone.'

'Where?'

'My brothers and sisters, to Candip. Gone to the guilds. Or wherever else.'

'Your mother allowed this?'

'Not all our mothers are Azyrite princesses.'

'No. I reckon some are ashfoot drunks.'

I froze. 'Don't say that word again.'

'Then don't call me Azyrite. I'm not, no more than you are. My family's been in Aqshy for generations. It doesn't matter where our blood first flowed. I'm Parcher – blood, soul and bone. Your doltish barbs lack sting.'

I shrugged. 'Parchers, Azyrites. You're all the same.'

'Careful. You speak with a Parcher's fire on your tongue. I hear the snap, the spark. I wouldn't have missed it.'

I stared. Then my eyes thawed. 'Mother was a Parcher, yes. Took up a pan and knife when the Smoulderhooves came. Then lightning struck, Varry says, and the beasts were gone.' I returned to the half-finished mat. 'So was mother. They found my father, in pieces. But not her.'

Sister Elene's back straightened. 'That's an omen if I've ever heard one, child. Drake's teeth, I always wondered if the tales were true.'

'I don't think that one is.'

She narrowed her eyes. 'Then what do you think?'

'I think a mother left her children. I think her daughter didn't understand. And I think her son doesn't care one way or the other. Not any more.'

Elene contemplated my words. For my part, I did not care to understand the past. All that mattered were its lessons. My parents had yearned to be free. In that yearning, they had failed. Freedom required control, and control required will. But where faith reigned, there could be no will. Faith in gods made mortals into slaves.

I stitched the mat closed with a cactus-thorn and woven thread. I tossed it down, then leaned against the piled stone of our horrifying little hovel. I would not have traded kingdoms for these walls. I would not have traded anything.

A question had been brewing in my head ever since Varry and I spoke in the hills.

'What are censors?' I asked.

Elene stirred from her reflections. 'Censors? Petty indulgences, ordained by the Sect of Candip. They're unique to Bodshe's Pale.'

I blinked. Esoteric theology came so easily to her. 'How much does one cost?'

Elene stared. 'Much more than you possess, or your sister. Censors paid to the Church Unberogen protect fallen souls from the dark powers.'

She was not toying with me. I straightened and glanced at our hovel. I had stowed the magnure I found in the wastes in our hand-carved cellar. Would it be enough?

Elene's eyes sparkled with insight. 'You and your sister must pay censors for those dead nomads.'

I counted my fingers, calculating. 'We make a pint of akwag for each stone of magnure we sell.'

'What? What is akwag?'

'Aqua Ghyranis,' I said. 'We have two stones. So two pints, plus our stores. Is that enough?'

Our wealth clearly surprised Elene. I wondered if she believed her own rubbish, about people getting back what they gave.

'Yes,' she said. 'But barely. You'll have dregs left. Droplets.'

I could not believe my ears. Droplets, after months of labour. To us, even a flask of akwag was a mighty sum. Now I learned it was merely petty change before the covetousness of Elene's church. Varry's exhaustion these past days, her brooding silence – it all made sense. After we paid the warborn's censors, we'd have nothing.

'You have the power to cancel it,' I said. 'Tell me you do.'

Elene's face darkened. 'Your sister is a believer. I cannot dictate matters of conscience to her.'

'That is what all priests do. Absolve us. We saved you.'

She looked askance at me. 'You understand what the Cursed Skies are?'

'I know they rustle when the red moon passes.' I rose and paced, unable to calm my rising panic. 'I know those days and nights grow cooler. Please, you'd be a bloodstain if not for us. Release us from this debt.'

'That is not how this works.'

'Then how does it?' I snapped. 'No censor was paid for my father's death. Why do the warborn get censors?'

Elene's expression softened. If I had thought her contempt aggravating, her pity was unnerving. I had not expected compassion from her. I wanted anything else.

'Once,' she said, 'we knew what happened when our mortal coils unspooled. But those days are over. Not all souls find repose in Shyish. The realms are changing. And much more than the skies, beyond even my knowing or reckoning.' She moistened her lips. 'Sometimes, cursed realms take the dead. Realms of many hells and Dark Gods, worse than sinners' nightmares. More often, the Great Necromancer seizes their souls as his tithe, a fate no better than the first. Protecting the spirits of the faithful from these forces takes effort. Effort requires currency.'

'They were pagans,' I said. 'Like me.'

'But *mortals*. And mortals deserve rest. I daren't utter the Five's names, but those nomads were free of their taint. To leave their censors unpaid would curse them with fates worse than death, or damn them to the Great Necromancer's servitude.' She shook her head. 'Heldanarr Fall, I would not force this upon anyone. Not even ashfeet nomads who meant to kill me. Not even you.'

I didn't know what she spoke of. But I could not do this to Varry. 'They would not have paid your censor,' I said, hoping to reason with her.

'I require no censor. Faith protects my soul. Whatever wicked woman you think I am, I have given my life to Sigmar.'

My face twisted into a grimace. 'Sister Elene,' I begged.

'Now I have a name? Listen. There's not a soul in the realms who may live their life without giving the gods their due. It's either the God-King and his allies, or the Dark Powers. And *those* gods, they'll laugh as they devour your soul. These words are not empty dogma, boy. They are the only answers. Especially in tainted lands like yours. Your people's pagan beliefs gained you the eyes of the Dark Gods. They see you. They want you. Your customs and souls reflect the corruption in your lands.

'During our journey, did you think my words empty jest? We came to save you, but salvation is no simple feat. Even for your sister, or your parents. Reclaimed savages may dress in our merchants' gingham and go to temple on the proper days. They can make the offerings, speak the prayers. But your hearts are difficult to change. You're rooted to your ways. The Five sense that – and they hunger. Can a pagan's soul be saved without a censor? Perhaps, in other realms. But not here. You killed those nomads, Heldanarr Fall. *You*, not another. Now help your sister pay penitence for their destruction, as the church guides us to do.'

Elene's zeal-stricken eyes did not leave mine. Beneath her words, I sensed the truth. Ambition and scorn, cloaked in altruism. Greed, glazed in the honey of a cleric's sermon. That was what the Azyrites had come to do, was it not? To teach us a lesson in everything. To peddle costly salvation from the curses they had brought.

The censor was no boon. Merely a tax, as Varry herself had said. A bribe to the hammer-handed god for protection he would not provide. My father's corpse proved that. His death-mask, tucked away in the nook of our home, proved that.

I sneered. I was no fool. 'You despise us.'

'No. I pity you.'

Fury welled in my heart. Nothing could change the way Elene felt about us. Not faith in Sigmar, not his false absolution. Not my accented Azyrite speech, not my adherence to Yrdoval, not even my respect. I had shed blood to save Elene's skin, but we were still nothing to her. No, worse – we were *savages*.

I stormed towards her and jerked her raiment out. Gem boxes clattered to the ground. I ripped a sputtering jewel from one, sashed it, then tossed the box.

Elene clenched her teeth and shoved me. 'Why, you revolting–!'

I shoved her back, throwing her to the mat I had made for her. 'Cancel the censors or don't.' I shook another precious Izmenili from its box, an electric current tingling from it through my palm. 'I'll pay your God-King's bribes with this.'

Elene went red. She glanced around until she found courage and a rock. She rose, raised her weapon. 'Those are for the ordination! Not ashfoot heathens!'

I batted the rock from her hands, pumping my fist into her gut.

She heaved, breathless, then toppled. She landed hard, sputtering, tears silver in her eyes. Her wrist blushed where she had landed on it, sprained.

But she rose again. By now the chipped edge of my dirk quivered between us. I had drawn it without thinking. I regained control of myself, brandishing my blade.

'You tried to cast a spell on me in the Ashwilds. Now this. I didn't tell Varry, but I will now. Raise a weapon against me again and–'

A meteor hurtled into my side and ripped the words from my throat. The world turned over; I slammed down.

Varry. She wrested my dirk from my white-knuckled grip, tossed it aside. She pounded her wrapped fists into my chest and temples. I shielded myself, as I could. Her strength could have toppled towers.

When she relented, I staggered away. She breathed hard, her leg wraps and heat skirt drenched with the water she had dropped. The pails she had lugged up the tall hill lay overturned, their contents spilt. The wasted water steamed on the ground.

Varry marched to Elene. 'Sister, I'm sorry. Can you–?'

Elene swatted at Varry's hands, still fighting for breath. 'Away!' she gasped. 'Away, godless ashfoot!'

Varry went pale with horror. Elene glared at us, then spat. She gathered her skirts and stormed to our hovel.

Varry's chin trembled. Her eyes glistened, ready to ignite. I knew those fires would take me with them.

'Varry.' I ached, bruised by her blows, but seeing my sister's pain felt so much worse than that. 'She–'

'Go!' Varry shouted, shaking. *'Go!'*

I hadn't meant to hurt the priestess. I hoped I could explain. But stewing over the censors these past few days, Varry's patience had been worn thin. Now I had shattered it.

I tried to move words around my tongue, like wet ash. I wanted to say so much, but nothing could fix this. Varry cupped her hands over her brow, bowed by the sheer burdens of life, by Elene's humiliating insult. *Godless*, she'd called her, and *ashfoot*. After all the gentle love Varry had showed that worthless priestess and her faith.

Tears seethed behind my eyes. I wouldn't show them, nor apologise. I wasn't wrong. But I couldn't control myself. How empty and vain all my years of yearning to curb my feelings felt then. I couldn't even bridle the heat in my heart. I was shaking.

And I was ashamed. Varry's pain was worse than my own.

I kicked mud from my feet and retrieved the pails Varry had dropped, then the yoke. I affixed the pails to the staff, heaved it up, then descended the bluffs, leaving my sister alone with her shame and overtaxed love.

True night never came to the Pale of Bodshe. Hours after sunset, the sky's wrathful red became mercurial blue, the dusk colour of polluted aether and placid seas. Often the Cursed Skies roiled behind the firmament like a disturbance beneath ocean waves. I recalled Elene's tales of the Mortal Realms and imagined other-worldly leviathans prowling beyond the heavens, hungering.

A dull glow smouldered on the horizon. At eventide, flickering eclipse light danced over the leagues around us, as if the rim of our realm was on fire. Bodshe existed in this sleepless fugue, never able to surrender to dream's release, unwilling to cede reign to the darkling night.

Our well sat in a saddle between our jagged hill and its neighbour. I never wondered why this ancient settlement's inhabitants had abandoned it. Yonder, Cardand's Burning Valley was easier to traverse, more hospitable. Here, good aquifers were rare.

I gathered a coiled rope beside the well's stacked stone wall. I lowered the pails, filled them with steaming water which stank of eggs, then set them to cool. A drop of Aqua Ghyranis could purify the brimstone taint. We had at least ten thousand.

Then I remembered the censors. I shouted, kicking the dirt. I slid down against the wall and stewed in my shame. Control was all I wanted, all our people had ever wanted. Before the reckoning of ages, the Yrdun had founded empires which had spanned the Pale. Ancient Cardand, and Lost Bharat. Yrdoval was once the Pale's iron law from one smoking coast to the next. Vengeance, Hospitality, Sanctuary – these were the tenets of our great kingdoms. While the barbarian God-King still taught his obsequious subjects to clothe themselves and conjure fire, our people had chiselled cities into Aqshy's crust. The Yrdun had united the Pale's Beltoller tribes into a mighty nation. Bharat's Holmon duardin delvers outmatched the Khazalid Empire's finest architects and engineers. Ushara warborn protected Cardand's marches across the Pale.

During my years as an Ashstalker, the Sun Seeker battalions' Azyrite veterans boasted of the accomplishments of the

Agloraxi mage-kings. Those sorcerous lords had raised spiralling towers that wounded the heavens, delving sprawling citadels into the crust of Aspiria, like the one that became the Azyrites' Brightspear.

Those same veterans had scoffed when I told them the truth: the Agloraxi had fortified Aspiria to protect their hinterlands from *us*. Such an invasion never came to pass – the Yrdun were too divided.

The Azyrites mocked my claim. They spat. They could not bear the contemplation that Yrdun ashfeet had once made tremble the Agloraxi masters of the Parch. They could not handle the truth.

I was young, but I knew enough of people to know Azyrites were no better than any of us. No length existed which mortals would not cross to deceive themselves, if it meant protecting their sacred ideas. But we were superior. Most Aqshians gave in to the heat of the realm, as if passion made them stronger. Only the Yrdun resisted Aqshy's heat and mastered the flame within. Against serenity, fury was no boon. In lands of fire, only the iciest hearts should rule.

Control was power. Power, freedom.

My fingers balled into fists. Then I chuckled, loosening them. Perhaps I was wrong. I did not sit in Candip's gilded halls. The peoples of these lands did not pray to the old Yrdun gods or speak our tongue. When the daemons had come and darkness had fallen across Aqshy, Bharat had been lost, and Cardand had been broken. Then the Azyrites came.

In centuries past, conflict had cursed the Great Parch, riding in on the storm winds of the God-King's tempest. The ancient tellings still cast shadows across my heart. Stark lightning had lacerated Bodshe's Parchward skies, it was said. Screams had echoed in like the snare of thunder on darkened horizons. War had cursed the realm, war like the Pale had never known.

But those wars did not reach Bodshe. Only the Azyrites did,

first in trickles, then in flows. Pioneers and missionaries brought architecture and education. Trappers and merchants brought endless, blinding custom. They purchased land for their keeps. They chained the greatest mountains in the sky.

They promised so much, but they took more than they gave. What Palers had once stewarded with prudence and loving care, Azyrites and their pet Capilarians exploited with the resistless want of wildfires.

Now they thought us savages. Now Carnd-Ep was Candip. Now my people were vagrants in our mothers' mothers' lands, and the Azyrites were kings. The Pale had been broken by its new masters, like the uncanny equine steeds ridden by Candip's outriders.

Perhaps this appraisal was unfair, for I knew not if the oral tellings were true. Where was I, in the beginning? I was nowhere. I only knew what I knew – what I had heard with my ears and seen with my eyes. I knew the blue bloods in Candip preferred custom from their own kind and closed their gates to mine. I knew the Yrdun were once proud and powerful and now we scraped burning filth from cooled earthfire to barter to sweating merchants in the city they had stolen.

A quirk of fate. An accident of history. This had enriched Sister Elene's people and enslaved mine. The truth was a landslide, and it had buried us alive. We couldn't claw our way out of it.

The night my father died, Varry always said, our mother disappeared in a flash of lightning. Silly, to think she had ridden out on thunder to the God-King's mythical realm, as Varry believed. In the back of my mind, sometimes I pretended it was true. But in my heart I knew she'd abandoned us. With our father in bloody pieces, certain we would starve, my mother had run. We were too much, her twelve daughters and sons. Despair had bested her; I knew its touch well.

I resented my mother's memory. But I had also learned her

lesson. Control was a blessed shield I would have done much to acquire – but nothing which might have hurt Varry.

I sighed and rose, coiling the rope by the well. I hated that Varry had misunderstood me, hated that I'd lacked the courage to speak truth. But now I held my own reins. I was ready to apologise and ask forgiveness. And what came, would come.

I turned to leave. Then I saw them.

Warborn. Twenty or so, heaped upon each other, an ugly disarray of broken limbs and twisted necks. Blood stained their heat shawls a brutal shade of brick-red. Their sand-iron blades were scattered and broken, save the rough-hewn lance stuck in the sand, the slender head pierced atop it.

The mouth lolled open in the half-light, the eyes rolled up. Bony piercings and worked metal discs studded the dead nomad's blister-black flesh.

My nose wrinkled. I hadn't smelt them for the brimstone. Ushara, dead, on our lands. Impossible.

I approached, low, dirk drawn. My offhand was achingly bare – my second dirk still lay on the hilltop. This had been an Ushara war-party. They must have been close to the others I had killed, to have been able to track us. But I couldn't understand. Varry and I were Ashstalkers tried-and-true, capable of hiding our trail as well as any hooded aelf-wanderer or Ushara savage.

Elene. She would have left a trail.

Yet what had killed these warborn? And when? I crept closer to examine the mess of tracks surrounding the heaped corpses. Man-blood, black under the roiling skies, coagulated in hoof-shaped craters.

My heart dropped, and ice rushed into my belly. Not just for the hoof-shaped tracks, nor the presence of the Smoulderhooves beastkin which the tracks signified.

The blood of the dead flowed uphill. It trickled up the hoofmarks in red runnels, winding up the scree-covered slopes. Worms and snakes of gore slithered up the cracks of boulders, towards the abandoned settlement and the little moon and the place I called home.

Bile rose in my throat. I knew well the magicks of Aqshy and the mutability of time. Impending slaughter had its own eerie gravity.

I shifted, sand grinding under my heels. Then I hissed all the curses of my people and bounded up the ridge.

CHAPTER FIVE

I crested the hill and my heart leapt in joy. Varry stood over the corpse of an ungor, unharmed. Her shoulders heaved, her sickle-edged, Hammerhal-forged falx hewn deep into the beast's carcass.

I slid my javelin from the dirt, hurled it. Even without my throwing thong, the dart flew true, catching another ungor in the belly.

Varry swivelled, tossing my second dirk to me. I snapped it from the air. 'More below,' I said.

Varry paled. 'They're searching for ways up.'

I nodded. Then I heard them. Howling, bleating, baying – a bloody herd of the feral beasts. Behind the ungor my javelin had lanced, our hill's broken bluffs seethed. The stench of blood and ordure rose with the beasts, repulsive and unsettling. Too many to stop. Too many to fight.

Varry's eyes flittered to our little moon. The metalith bobbed on its cordage.

I understood. 'I'll cut the moorings.'

'I'll get the priestess.' Varry raced off.

I meant to tell her not to bother but the gor-kin were already here. These were bigger. One gruesome brute tossed back its horned head and brayed, its breath steaming in the air. The others saw me and snorted and pawed at the dirt.

I charged in, skirting two gors before I slid under the third. I dragged my dirks along its heels, severing its tendons. The thing squealed and thumped to the ground.

I raced on to the cords. I swiped my blade across the braided rope and it snapped. I doubled back over a piled stone wall, but a beast intercepted me, howling. The rotten offal reek of its breath was choking. A skirt of human leather resembling a flayed face flapped at its groin.

I probed its defences. It stayed low. I thrust a blade into the socket of its eye, driving it deep. The dirk stuck fast so I left it, sprinting to the second mooring. Once Varry found damned Elene, she could cut the final rope. Then we'd drift into the night, derelicts in our own lands, but alive.

Except Varry would not find Elene – because Elene was here, crouched and quivering beside the wall, in our ash-garden. The damned priestess had been relieving herself when the beasts came. *In our garden.*

I clapped. 'Up the ropes, heinous woman!'

Her eyes flashed. 'The Izmen–'

I tore a handful of the electric gems from my sash, lobbed them at her face. I clapped again. 'Move!'

She scrambled up, bumbling back the direction I had come from. I scoffed. What could those gems be worth, that she would die for them? Surely not her life. Avarice was a curse, mastering the worst in us.

I sashed my dirk and clambered up the spell-treated rope. Then I got a view of our hilltop. My stomach turned.

Beasts filtered up the slopes, filling the abandoned settlement. Braying and snorting, growling and drooling. Bellowing, hissing, ravaging – hungering. They hacked at ruined statues and toppled crumbling columns. Their hideous stench purged the sulphur cut in the air. In their dark tongue, jackal-headed gors snarled commands to their underlings. The beasts were wet and sweaty, mutants of every size. They cast goat-eyed gazes across the temple of my home, searching for prey. For us.

Beside the last mooring, Varry stood over the spilt entrails of another beast. She locked eyes on the priestess. Elene bungled through our hovel, her arms overflowing with jewel boxes.

Scorch Elene. I slid my dirk's edge across the rope. The cord snapped. I swung, then slammed into the rugged face of our little moon, eating a mouthful of dirt. The metalith wobbled, as ready for freedom as I.

But Varry had crossed the hilltop, to Elene. Now beasts encircled them both. They growled with devious appetites, cleavers and chipped-iron axes outstretched on their mange-scabbed arms. Varry's falx licked out at them, graceful and efficient, opening bellies, severing limbs. That could not last long.

I let go, plummeting. I hit the sand and grunted. Roaring, I charged into the heaving masses. I threw myself upon the largest of them, driving my dirk down its spine. I levered until its neck popped and its head flopped down. The beast toppled like a felled tree.

Varry, bleeding and huffing, cried, 'Held!'

'Left!' I said.

We fought, as we never had before. We called out foes, guarding each other's backs. I heard Varry. Varry heard me. Calamity rang in my ears, even as my head thudded with confidence, the hubris of my affection.

This was what we were made for. For this, the fates had joined us in common parentage. Blades shinked and rang. The air grew rancid as the beasts' press thickened. They fought as grubby individuals, none willing to sacrifice themselves for the others. That was our advantage – selflessness. Between us, Sister Elene screamed, hands clapped to her ears, her gems scattered in the bloody mire.

A creature bunted its horned head into me. Varry's falx arced through its neck. Another gor yanked her hair. I plunged my blade through the soft part of its jaw, into the roof of its skull.

In my life I have learned one lesson above all others: ages pass in the violence of a moment. Queens may be crowned, and kingdoms may fall. A substance beyond time burns when our lives are at stake. There is no finer way to live forever than in the pan-flash of battle.

Yet even eternity must end. I fought with everything I had, breathless and swinging until my muscles creaked and my lungs heaved. Then I fought harder, until I was febrile and mad and no longer sure of anything. I should have been dead. Had Varry not filled the spaces I left open, or quickened where I lagged, I would already have been a corpse.

'Sigmar!' she bellowed. 'Sigmar!'

It was not a battle cry. It was a summons.

Lightning flashed above, and the world became red and white. In delirium I wondered if Varry's story of our mother was true. Her falx scythed down another beast, and another, and another. Her vocal cords frayed with her God-King's name. Beyond the ring of our foes, the horde of hulking monsters pawed at the sand, snorting and chuffing, cautious. A wall of corpses separated us from them. Could we do this? Could we win?

Then a long maul lashed out and smashed Varry in the skull. Her head snapped back. She went down the way mountains fall, limp, cracking the ground. Blood drooled from a seam in her brow. But she was alive – still alive!

I roared, plunging my dirk into the ribs of the gor that had struck her. I twisted the blade, shifting its bones. Its triumphant howl became a tormented shriek. I enjoyed this sound.

But Varry. I yanked my dirk free and released it, then fell to her side. I lifted her lolling head. The corners of her eyes dribbled insensate tears. Blood oozed from her brow. Beneath the red, the white of her skull gleamed.

The beasts seized their chance. Elene wailed for me to fight – but I was not here for her, or any of them.

As the beasts swarmed in, I shushed Varry's whimpers. 'Breathe,' I sobbed. 'I can't let you go.'

And I didn't. Not as the beasts took us, nor as they dragged us down the craggy hill's hot shingle slopes. Not as we were wrapped in mildewed nets and tossed into a chariot's splintered bed. Not as their tusked abominations pulled us into screaming deserts and the end of my world.

CHAPTER SIX

I have said battle warps the reckoning of time. It is in us, I think. We are mortals of dust and clay, but some higher sickness within us worships the narcotic transcendence of violence.

Just as battle shrinks eternity into instants, agony may bloat moments into forever. These are not the same. Any mortal who has lived knows the difference. And any who have died have felt the solace of oblivion. Suffering is life's curse. Not that pain of the flesh, but the hurt of the heart. When we truly suffer, time does not pass at all. We linger.

Even now, of the days following our capture, I remember little and will say less. The horror lacks concept. Encompassing all the Mortal Realms in my feeble hands would be easier than relating what I have lived. Filling the gulfs between the stars with the blood I have spilt would be simpler.

But in this prayer, I shall try.

I have seen many things, but I never saw the bones of children until the day we came to Lurth. What remained of it.

Lurth was a hamlet in the marches of the Cardand, within boglands near the River Losh. The settlement was known for its drawled dialect of Azyrite and spiced jerkies of wing-leather dried in the heat of Hysh. Varry had traded for this, when she was able to. She had known I liked it.

Lurth was also known for its religious zeal. Church faith was unusual in Bodshe's hinterlands. When Cardand was conquered, many Yrdun turned back to tradition, seeking virtue in the past. But some, like Varry, had looked to our occupiers and the future they brought with them. Lurth's faith in Sigmar had been a bulwark.

Then the Smoulderhooves had come.

The chariot ceased rocking. We were pulled from its bed. I carried Varry in my arms, stumbling and squelching through a thick morass beside Elene as the beasts flogged our backs. At our feet, steaming mire had reclaimed Lurth's old irrigated paddies. A grove of red granite tors rose ahead like the weather-worn turrets of an ancient castle. In the flat saddles between the tors, decrepit buildings leaned precariously. Behind us, Lurth's boglands stretched into haggard forest. Spectral wildfire danced in the trees' foliage. Cardand's looming ridgelands rose faintly in the distance.

We stumbled from the bog onto harder ground, then up a steep slope. We passed through a rickety gate in a plank palisade smouldering with grisly flame. I knew little of magic, but whatever rites supplied the fire of Lurth's palisade had clearly not been refreshed for weeks. The flames billowed and wheezed, coal-black and sick. I remembered Candip's palisade well enough to know how dangerous those flames were.

In the hamlet, we staggered along a raised path. Chewed gristle and tattered clothing blanketed the charred peat. Heads and gnawed-clean ribcages were piled up around corpse heaps in the village commons. The hills of the dead were mudslides, stinking of blood, buzzing with clouds of corpulent flies. From some of the carcass piles, greasy smoke poured into the sky. Dying wretches moaned and writhed within the gruesome mess, suffocating beneath the weight of their dead kinsfolk.

The beasts whipped us up a switchback, onto the greatest tor, then locked us into a cliffside pen at the top. Below, Lurth was an island of carnage, divided from the fens by the burnt gash of its palisade, which crackled hatefully beneath the tor. My back bled and stung, but all I could think of was those charnel hills in the commons, the palisade of greasy flame – and Varry in my arms.

I collapsed against the pen, which was wickered from wood scraps and corded mortal hair, then dragged Varry onto my lap. She still breathed. Elene, blank-eyed, shuffled through the mortal chaff crowding the pen. The others were like us: duardin and humans and aelves of every stroke and colour. On the other side of the enclosure, the Pale's rarer peoples loitered lonely against the red granite of the cliff. Cat-eyed and scaly telantr, or beings with splayed-out wings instead of arms, or with crowns of antlers for hair.

They did not bother me. Nothing did. I existed in a place between life and death, between reason and madness, a nether-space no mortal should tread. Passing through the Ashwilds and blighted deserts, days had come and gone. We'd had no food, no water. No rest, to mark the passage of time. I was a gheist in human flesh, a revenant walking.

But I could survive, if only Varry did. Empty eyes blinked in the bruised sockets of her skull. Ragged breaths fluttered from her lips. Blood drooled from her brow, and the sight of it filled my stomach with lead.

I lifted my eyes to seek help. What a useless endeavour. No

help could be had from these other lost souls. Over the hours, the beasts took us, one by one. Captives pled and screamed as loved ones were torn from their arms. Moist-eyed lovers kissed each other farewell, and parents assuaged their red-cheeked offspring all would be fine, because – *Sigmar!*

This sickened me. They knew what was coming. Soon we would be on the beasts' feasting boards. If they were bold, they would have spared their kindred the horrors awaiting them. They would have killed them themselves, rather than lying and pretending everything would be fine. It would have been a mercy.

Even as this thought stung me, I knew I was like them. I would never let Varry go. Not until the beasts chopped me apart and ground my bones to meal. I sneered, disgusted with them. With myself.

Then I saw her. A woman with all the ages in her eyes, sitting across the pen. The cut of her face was mine, painted red. That was not the ash-ink filth I mixed, but traditional Yrdun sun-daub. I had not seen it in years. Meditative she was, her back against the bare rock, her legs crossed. Black rags hung from her scrawny shoulders, their tattered ends tossing in the breeze. She was young, thinner than I, but looked older and sturdier than time. Her teeth were dyed black and she was soon for death, from the edge of a cleaver or the withering of hunger – but so were we all.

This woman regarded me as if through a prism. Then she beckoned.

I ignored her. I bent and kissed Varry's clammy brow. I didn't know what to do for her fever, her wounds. I spit saliva into her lips, hoping moisture might help. Then warm rain pattered against my shoulders and the back of my head. The drizzle was not water, but red gruel, thick and stinking of iron.

Blood rains.

Blood soaked my soiled heat wraps. Blood sullied Varry's wan skin. Blood puddled on the ground like quicksilver, beading like maggots on my skin. The droplets wriggled in search of my veins. I flung them off. The blood rain continued, until the burnt-stone stench of it burrowed into the soil of me. I turned and vomited.

Below, in broke-neck Lurth, the beastkin heaved and howled. They revelled in the rain, worshipping the sky's unseen slaughter, braying to their grisly gods. The trumpet screams of the beasts' sacrifices rose like a black salute. The crimson rain was a torrent, each drop a spattered leech, difficult to breathe through. I covered Varry's face and peered up.

Then I felt it. Then I saw it.

Then, Aqshy's fires take me, I understood what it was.

The Orb Infernia, Aqshy's red moon, scudded over our heads like a curse. As the moon penetrated the realm's atmosphere, a halo of grievous fire ignited around it, like one of Sigmar's heavenly meteors. The moon blasted across the sky. Fire spilt in its wake, blood pouring in its trail. I shouted myself hoarse trying to ignore these horrors but couldn't dispel the moon's vision, its horrifying blare. This was a nightmare to haunt gods.

Yet worst was not the flames, or the blood, or the cackling pagan beastkin in the bogs below.

Worst was the daemons.

I saw them as clearly as if I gazed through an Azyrite voidscryer's crystal glass. Hordes – no, *seas* of them – writhing in the second red sky. They piled on each other like wild dogs, snake tongues slithering from jaws which fell down to their chests. Horns curled over their heads like ancient crowns.

Bloodletters. I never knew they existed before this. I thought them myth.

They slaughtered each other, chopping outsize cleavers at their fell brethren, gambolling in the feast of violence. The victors cavorted higher in the sinking fields of damaged flesh – only to be cut down by others. I witnessed this hellish scene and remembered the grape-treading girls in the vineyards north of Candip.

Within me, a horrible thirst awoke. The daemons' invitation resounded in me. In my bones, like blight in my marrow, polluting me. They looked down upon Aqshy, meeting my horrified gaze and summoning me to slaughter.

How I resisted! Yet I never refused. Some sickness afflicts us mortals all. Any who have felt the urge to strike another, know.

The damned moon carved through the sky, blazing and blaring. Then it shrank towards the horizon. The madness receded, and I mastered the nascent Chaos in my mind.

'Ice,' I chanted. 'Ice.'

Below, the beasts rose in raving cheers. Just as the rains diminished, I heard her voice.

'Held,' Varry murmured.

I blinked in disbelief. She looked at me, conscious.

'Held,' she repeated, her voice a threadbare rasp, like the desert's whispers at night.

Then she became lighter. Her back lifted from my legs, hovering over my lap.

I felt lighter, too. I glanced around. I was levitating. So were others. Frantic, I cursed, searching for something to grip. The fell force of the Orb Infernia's passage would carry us with it. The red moon's rain had ceased. Now Aqshy's had begun.

Corpses from the piles in the commons speckled the sky, trailing the shrinking moon. Yowling captives gripped each other or the pens. Fell gravity dragged the weakest of them free, to join the cursed moon's cometary tail. Beasts rose from Lurth, pulsing in ecstasy, braying as they were stolen for slaughter.

I held Varry close, gripping the pen. Her pendant legs dangled beyond her. Others sailed from the tor's top into the bruised horizon, trailing the moon. To save themselves, many captives released their loved ones. Those who remained clawed at the stone and the pen and mud, desperate to hang on, weeping and wailing with regret.

I would not let Varry go. She slipped my grasp, but I snatched the strap of her waterskin.

'Varry!' I hissed through clenched teeth, cables of spittle hanging from my teeth. She croaked, half aware, likely thirsty. We just had to hold on. This, too, would pass. So would everything.

The wickered wood cracked, scraping the mud. Not now, I thought. Not like this. My knuckles white, I held on.

Then the strap snapped. I slammed down. Mud soiled me.

And my fingers were empty.

I scrambled up. 'Varry!' I stared at the sky, but she was gone. The Orb Infernia, too, blazing below the horizon, nothing left but the long trail of its tributary slaughter, and even that fast diminishing. And Varry–

I did not know. I didn't know where she was.

Tears pooled behind my eyes, rippling like far-off seas. Panic scrabbled up my innards, a lonely man clawing at the walls of me. I tried to think. Others wept, but they had been weeping from the start. Elene ambled around the enclosure in a daze, her sullied raiment stained the many shades of torment.

For all this, the scrawny, cross-legged Yrdun woman still regarded me, her eyes askance. She nodded, as if all was right in the realm. But nothing was right. I glanced at Varry's waterskin and its snapped leather lanyard, rocking in despair. Nothing remained of her, nothing but a memory.

The same was true of me.

'Heldan.'

My mouth was swollen and dry. I had no idea how much time had passed. My heart ached, my mind was blank.

'Heldan. Heldanarr Fall.'

Elene crouched beside me. She had lived. For strength, perhaps. Or for Sigmar, blessed be his name, protecting all the things that were his. My eyes wandered Elene's face. Beneath the brittle glass of her courtesy, the woman I loathed was still there.

Elene's throat bobbed. 'Water.' Her blood-caked nails scrabbled at the leather of Varry's waterskin. 'I need water.'

I blinked. 'Water.'

She nodded.

After Varry was taken, I was emptied. All the insanity around me might as well have been mist over my cairn. But as the priestess spoke to me, I returned to life. 'Water.'

Elene stroked her licked-dry lips. 'Please. I'm dying of thirst.'

Her words kindled within me. Then the fire's embers died. The ashes frosted over, bewitched by a strange spell. Some might have called it hate. Others, anger. I called it something to prove.

I gave her the waterskin, then watched her drain its dregs. She sighed with relief.

'Enough?' I asked.

She nodded, grateful. 'Thank you.'

I seized her arm, pulled her closer. 'It's not enough.'

Our fellow captives' attention drifted towards us. Elene made to ask what I meant. But before she could, I crammed a fistful of coagulated gore into her mouth.

She gagged, turning her chin. 'Enough?' I asked. 'No. You're thirsty.' Another fistful.

Captives murmured in the blood-muddied corners of hell. Others shouted. Beneath their putrid fear, decency skulked, lending them courage. I had only hate.

I gritted my teeth and pushed Elene's face into the ground. With her open jaws I carved tracks in the liquefied mud, ignoring her pathetic gags.

'Drink!' I said. Hospitality was a pillar of Yrdoval, so I would be hospitable. She had saved my soul.

Hands scraped my shoulders, or blunted claws. The other captives – the fools meant to stop me.

With all my strength I pushed. I shoved Elene's pulsing head into the pen, until her face bled. 'She needs more!' I screamed. 'She's thirsty!'

They all shouted. I didn't understand. But the more who came, the more the others were encouraged. Soon the crowd of them besieged me. They wouldn't stop me. Where were they, when Varry fell? I held on, pushing Elene's spasming body against the fence, defying all. Strength I didn't know welled within me.

Then the pen gave. The wickered wood teetered over the edge and scudded out of sight, smashing against the palisade below. The others shouted to pull back, but the crowd's mass and hysteria pushed the closest of them over the edge. Laughing, I slid wide-eyed Elene over the edge, too. She slithered off the blood-slicked stone, silent for the first time in her life.

Sickening cracks echoed from below, like falling fruit. Bones, smashed. Bodies, broken.

As the others retreated, I cast my bristling gaze upon them. I must have resembled a daemon, then. Coated in blood and mire, staring them down. Judging. Fathers and sons. Mothers and daughters. Lovers and friends. Different breeds, different peoples, different ages – but all of them the same. They had clung to each other as the priestess had clung to her gems. Yet when the time had come to cling lest the realm take their loved ones away, they had let them go.

What paltry lives, theirs. What meaningless deaths, so unlike Varry's.

Now they feared... what, exactly? A fall and the palisade's fire? A death of their own choosing? I couldn't understand. Was it life they clung to? Their lives were not precious. And why live at the beasts' whims, when they could die by their own?

Insanity and naked pain raved in the darkened nooks of me. I was still burning from my sister's death, still unsatisfied by Elene's. I knew what awaited us – in the heat of that moment, everything was clear. I did not think twice before I hurled the first of them from the cliffs.

They tried to defy me. But I was stronger than them. Half-blind with madness, agile in the clench, fast in my grip. Some cried out to their gods; others, to the gors. To the gors! The beastkin entered the pen, snorting and barking, and the captives crowded around them for salvation. They were all so pathetic.

All the creatures surrounding me worshipped gods. I worshipped nothing. The nothing of my life, the nothing of my past. The nothing in my heart and the nothing of my sister's death. I prayed to nothing for the world to end. Then I flew to my feet and ran.

I tackled a gor. Weight and force slid the braying giant over the edge. I swept the legs of a second, but a third thrust its scrap shield into my chest.

I levered its spiked maul from its weak-fingered grip, then crushed its skull. I threw myself into the crowd. The beasts meant to keep the captives alive, as livestock. I meant to save them.

More beasts entered, yellow-eyed and stinking. As they filled the pen, more panicked captives tumbled from the enclosure. The animals must have known they had lost control. Perhaps they didn't care. Perhaps they lacked the sense.

Then the largest of the gor-kin loomed closer, like a gargant from the heathen legends. Smoke plumed from its split nose as its goat-eyes passed over me. Its nostrils flared, and its groan rumbled through me. The creature's chipped battle-axe drooled thick flames limned in midnight's shadow. A trick, I thought – just a coat of oil and an errant spark.

Yet instinct and intuition told me that axe carried a darker blessing. My flesh was here to feed that weapon's boons.

But I would honour no gods. Not with my life, not with my death. I howled and charged, parrying the raised axe with my stolen maul. I leapt and thrust the beastlord's crown of horns back, then bit into its throat.

Warm blood welled around my teeth. I wrenched my head back and tore off a flap of fur-covered meat and pulsing artery.

Then I laughed. Ungors dragged me from their dying master, blood spilling from its neck. Its meat fell from my teeth, and I laughed. I laughed as I was thrown to the ground, laughed as my head was held still, tribute for another's axe. Tears of wounded joy bled from my eyes. At least they knew: mine had been a life worth ending.

Then war horns sounded. The thick-nailed grip of the Smoulder-hooves beasts relaxed. Gunfire rippled on the other side of Lurth. Even from here, Aqshy's crust shook beneath the drumbeat of three hundred trampling hooves.

Cavalry. I had been an Ashstalker with the Sun Seekers of Candip, and I knew well the horns of the Derders, the applause of their pistol volleys, the earth-shaking percussion of their charge.

The Azyrites had come.

The gor-kin in the enclosure snarled to each other, then rushed to join the rest of their brayherd beneath the tor. In the peat bogs beyond Lurth, soldiers in sun-coloured livery marched. Candip's bright banners marked their lines, fluttering in a dead breeze. Derder cavalry trotted forward in knee-high swamp waters, blue-coated men on foreign steeds, firing pistols to keep the beasts at bay.

Battle was joined below, and I rose to my knees to worship the slaughter in the sky. Scarlet light smouldered on Bodshe's sunset horizon amidst clouds of black smoke. In the boglands around

Lurth, the rainbow meadows of Sigmar's armies manoeuvred to quell the beasts. Candip's host was here – and with them, true salvation.

But they were too late. Varry was gone, gone, gone, and she was not coming back.

CHAPTER SEVEN

The Battle of Lurth went the only way it could. The forces of Candip had taken the time to encircle the hamlet. For the beasts there could be no escape.

Artillery in the forest beyond the peatland blasted Lurth. The stagnant bog waters rippled with each volley. At every deafening crump below, beasts' limbs pinwheeled through the air. In the bog, a lively drum and flute march sounded off from the battle lines of Freeguild halberdiers and arquebusiers. The grizzled Azyrite soldiers wore thick platemail and livery the colour of the sun, and their high-spirited battle march lent dissonant dignity to the undignified enterprise they had come to undertake. They advanced against the cornered beastkin as an unbroken, spiked wall.

Deprived of the element of surprise, caught off guard in the wake of their revels, the beastkin were little more than animals corralled for the slaughter. They surged out into the bog against the lines of Candip's host, but each wild pulse was thrown back.

As the soldiers crowded the beasts into the killing grounds between Lurth's tors, Derders harried them from the steaming fens. The mounted Derder pistoliers hailed from Golvaria, where their strange equine steeds ranged. They wore light armour with belts and bandoliers for their pistols and powder. Since they were Company mercenaries rather than Freeguilders, they wore navy coats and azure half-cloaks instead of the Sun Seekers' orange and yellow. I thought their advance too brazen until I glimpsed the spear and halberd lines bringing up their rear. The Azyrites' execution of the battle was rigorous.

Candip's host closed, shock troops in the vanguard. Militia and line infantry covered the flanks, tightening the noose. Harried by crossbow riders and Derder pistoliers, the Smoulderhooves' numbers turned against them. A hunch-backed bray-shaman with mossy horns and foggy eyes tried to rally its panicking brood. The shaman thumped its gnarled staff against the loam, ravelling spells of syphilitic magic into the humid air. Then a bright mage of Hammerhal cast a fireball, immolating the shaman and ending its futile show.

When the slaughter began in earnest, I joined the killing. I slew beasts with my hands and my teeth and their own battered blades. I could hardly fight with axe or maul, but any real fighting had ended when the Derders' horns had sounded. My toil was little more than patient butchery, chopping into a distressed herd of cattle. The beasts were packed tight, hardly able to lift their shields in the press, peppered with shot and arrow. When the Smoulderhooves had despoiled Lurth, they had heaped the village's dead and dying innocents in the commons. When we were finished, we did the same.

Soon, fly-ridden corpses and mutant blood carpeted the battlefield. Two dozen wild-eyed Candip mercenaries circled around me. I slavered, wild-eyed and broken. *'Varry,'* I growled. Everywhere

I turned, the soldiers' blurred silhouettes reminded me of split fangs. The realm had swallowed me whole.

I almost continued fighting, almost got killed for it. The soldiers thought me a beast like the others. That day, I was.

One of the Derders saw through my blood-drenched coverings and shattered sanity. Weapons holstered, hands raised, he soothed me.

'Easy, man. *Easy.*'

I relented. Then a wall of exhaustion crashed into me and I toppled into him. The Derder guided me to the muddy yard of a desecrated croft and left me to recuperate.

For a long while I sat alone on a hot granite chopping block between a home's plank wall and a dilapidated farmer's fence. Chickens roamed the yard, pecking at the mud. Of all things, *chickens* had survived Lurth's slaughter. Not Varry, not the beasts, not me. Chickens.

The Derderman picked his way back through the mud. He was an officer, judging by his stripes and brass spurs. He tilted back his half-helm, shifted his gorget, staring. His lopsided moustache hung to his chin, thicker than my thumbs.

'What?' I said.

'Nothing. Just wondering who pissed in your oats.' He offered a tin cup. 'Someone told me to give you water and bread. But I've had the water and I've had the bread, and there was no reason to make you suffer any more than you have. So here. Coffee magic, brewed from roasted Ghryan beans. Drop of nectar in it, too. Enjoy.'

I drained the cup's steaming contents. The bitter black fluid scalded my mouth, but I felt better than I had.

He offered his hand. 'Name's Micaw Boskin.'

I stared, then gripped his hand. He shook hard, in the manner of Azyrites.

'I'm Heldan Fall,' I said. 'You're, what? A Freeguilder captain?'

Boskin spat. 'Candip's Freeguilds are all gutted. I wear the blue. And I'm no captain, neither, because according to Sigmar's Law, captains receive frankly disappointing stipends. So I'm a qual, and the ladies and gents who nearly spit you clean through are from my gord. And quals and gords, as you perhaps know, make much more barrel than captains and companies.'

I almost smiled. *Qual* and *gord* were Yrdo words. They meant captain and company. Whoever filled Boskin's flask, he had mocked their ignorance of Bodshe's ways right on his unit charter and officer's commission.

He sipped from his own steaming cup. 'Lords and ladies, all it takes is a drop, eh? A little salt, citrus and nectar, and coffee's better than a stiff ale or aged wine.'

I leaned against the plank house, hollow, searching for words. All that emerged was a croak. I was empty.

Boskin seemed to understand. 'The beasts are dead and gone. To the last braying kid. We gotta take you out soon, with us. The priesthood's dousing and burning the village. They'll make Lurth ash and char by evening.'

More Derders passed. Boskin greeted them. They raised their arms or tilted their helms in salute, then eyed me with a breed of contempt.

When they were gone, Boskin leaned on the farmer's fence. 'I was supposed to be a lord, you know. My grandfather's lands were stripped by House Se Roye, so my father lost the titles. Fall from grace, some might call it. I call it a crime. But I like riding with the Derders. Telling them what to do fills my flask. Playing cards with them empties it. But they aren't like us, are they? They still got grace. They grew up reading books, real ones, with wood covers and leather bindings. You and me, we've seen mother flies birthing maggots, haven't we? We've picked the worms from our plates.' He sipped more. 'I like my gord because they fill my flask. But they never wallowed in the mud a day and they don't even know it. One day I'll buy back the land my grandfather settled, give it to my kids. Then they'll be like those soldiers. Fat, reading books, real ones. I'll probably hate them, too. Your kind, ashfoot? You don't get chances like that.'

I flinched at *ashfoot*. A dull flame within me stoked to life. 'Get out of my face.'

'Easy. Just wanted your attention. Call it charity, from the goodness of my heart.' He coughed. 'Commander wants to see you. She wanted all the captives, but it's only you and a painted woman left, and she's half mad. The Lady Lellen doesn't waste her time on poor men, friend. Take it from me.' Another sip. 'When you meet her, make an impression, and soon you might be rich. Charity. That's all. From the goodness of my heart. I'd want someone to tell me.'

I gazed at my feet. Remorse tingled up my spine. 'All of the others are dead?'

'Yeah. And too bad, since the one we came for's dead, too.'

'The priestess. Sister Elene.'

'That's right. A damn shame. Not really, I don't care. But I do like you, friend. I'm glad you're alive.' He straightened, brushing off his sleeve. 'Come on. Commander don't like waiting. Or gambling, or drinking, or smoking, or anything else worth doing in these petty little lives of ours. Ah, she does like going to chapel. Makes a whole show of it. Me too. I love going to chapel, if she asks. Mind your step.'

We marched across the yard. Overhead, smoke from the first fires of Lurth's crematory streaked the crimson skies. 'Lady Lellen Se Roye,' I said. 'Your commander?'

'That's right. The Right Honourable, of House Se Roye, and the Company, et cetera, et cetera. All those titles, but she doesn't think to share. Well, scorch it, neither would we, eh? Lords and ladies,

I hate her guts. But if she asks, tell her I go to chapel. Come on. Mind your step.'

Boskin's words raised a question I had dared not ask.

The other captives. They were innocents, as I suppose I had been. Would they have lived if not for me?

Perhaps. Candip's host had marched even as I shoved Elene's face into the mud. Even as she slid over the edge, as her body snapped against Lurth's palisade with an echoing crack. The other prisoners had died as Candip's horns sounded or in the moments after. Before battle was joined, after our beastly guards had fled. I'd finished the captives myself.

It had seemed right, then. Brutal, certainly, but underlined by mercy.

Perhaps. Perhaps they might have lived. That is my answer. *Perhaps.*

But perhaps is a long word filled with uncertainty and the realm is cruel. On that day my sanity was as short as the span of my arms, or the length of my life. I tossed them from the bluffs to spare them the misery that awaits us all. They prayed for the deliverance of their gods; I gave them the deliverance of death.

That was what Varry had got. Sharing it with the others felt like kindness.

Perhaps they would have survived. Perhaps they still would have died. Or perhaps they would have endured and seen what the world has become.

At any rate, I saved them from you.

I followed Boskin into the Freeguilders' camp. Blood-soaked peat squelched underfoot. Years ago Varry and I had served with the Sun Seekers of Hammerhal, the only Freeguild in Candip. Here I recognised none of the units around me, only the atmosphere.

Soldiers of any breed were easy to recognise, laughing, jeering, drinking, belching – especially after battle's end. Some precious few brooded, but most were thrilled to have lived. Soldiers were the same wherever one found them, in Freeguild markings or in mercenary livery.

On our way to Se Roye's camp pavilion I glimpsed the battle's aftermath. Beast carcasses were piled high, then put to the flame by soldiers and sanctioned pyromancers. Candip's war-dead, much fewer but more diverse, lay in neat lines. As officers identified them, scriveners scribbled their names in parchment logs.

Now the Azyrite rearguard had come as close as they could to Lurth's bogs. Derder outriders and foot battalions had cleared the grounds up to the river beyond the burning blue of the woods. I could smell the rich fecundity of the Losh's waters, even beyond the trees' spectral fire.

I halted near a line of caged carts parked near the Azyrites' baggage train.

Boskin turned. 'If you want to fill your flask, you really ought not keep the lady waiting.'

I shrugged his hand aside. 'I know them.'

'Who?'

'*Them.*' Men and women, stuffed into the back of the caged carts. They were dirty and wretched, roped together by the wrists, all the realm's scorch in their eyes. Yrdun, or Beltollers. The heat of their glares told me. The cut of their faces. Their hair, the colour of their skin, the broken light in their eyes.

I almost thought I saw Jujjar leering in the back, silver studs pocking his chiselled cheeks over his beard. Jujjar, who had gifted my dirks and Varry's falx. Jujjar, who had watched out for me in the Ashstalkers.

Boskin dragged me away. 'I'll bet you do. And if the bailiffs see you, you'll soon join them.'

'They're my people.'

'Yes. Ashfeet, like you.' I scowled, but Boskin shook his head. 'I don't mean evil in that. But bailiffs get paid by the head, and we do love our pay.'

'What?'

'You Reclaimed are all bandits and poachers. You all hunt on Company grounds in Cardand, call it tradition. And you all pick maggots from your food, just like me. So trust me. Unless you want irons clapped on your ankles and wrists.'

I glanced back, but the land's lay blocked my view. 'Why are you helping me?'

'Charity,' Boskin grumbled. 'That and the goodness of my heart. And maybe there's better ways to make a drop, today. Now come on.'

The pavilion was a city of its own. Tents towered into the dimming sky. Lazy smoke unspooled through vents from kitchens, or maybe forges. In an aviary on a long mast, messenger crows fluttered to and fro, scripts wound to their legs. Their droppings painted the canvas below; I wrinkled my nose from the waste's ammonia stink.

Swords clanged as soldiers trained, making me wince, even as I marvelled. This was a castle of curtains. I imagined its cool halls within, its courtyards and turrets and thrones fit for queens. I almost expected gates, but there was only a canvas flap guarded by four warriors. The guards wore spiked helmets, mail skirts, harem pants. Star-studded lamellar covered their chests, but their heat wrappings were like mine. Only their haughty poises gave them away as Capilarians.

I knew of the Cossery Guard. Alone of all Bodshe's Parcher companies, this storied regiment was allowed into Ulcarver, for they guarded its inhabitants. Cosseries were not Freeguilders, but they were fierce and expensive and they could give any of

Hammerhal's Greatsword battalions a run for its akwag. The flame-edged swords on their backs made that point clear, each sharp and heavy enough to cleave a duardin in twain. In Lurth, they had unleashed a magnificent slaughter against the beasts.

Boskin saluted them. The Cosseries ignored him, checking me for weapons. Their suspicious eyes crossed my bloodstained wraps, sizing me up. Capilarians have always unnerved me. My people resisted Aqshy's heat, but Capilarians gave in to it entirely. The indecency was dreadful.

Boskin led the way into the pavilion, in truth the fortress I had imagined it to be. Armouries and provisions filled some tents. Others were scaffolded with mountain timber and banded iron reinforcement, shelters in case of bombardment. Perfumed servants bade us follow in polished Azyrite I hardly understood. The air was as cold as another realm's glaciers. Boskin was as out of place as I.

Soon we arrived to the heart of the drapery and surfeit. A sweeping table of wood – foreign timber, precious and flammable – served as this chamber's long spine. A beautiful brazier of worked steel anchored the table's centre, unlit. Tongues of naked flame danced in the air around the tent's ceiling, casting the court in a flux of light and shadow. It was all so excessive.

'The Honourable Lady Lellen Se Roye,' Boskin muttered. I realised an introduction had been made, but he was already gone.

I swallowed pooling saliva, blinking away the dry in my eyes. I pretended to relax. I was too cold to feel at home, but not just for the air. Lady Lellen was ice incarnate.

She sat at the foot of her endless table, bent over an armrest. Dark hair framed her ebony features and poured down her shoulders. One hand and a quill sketched restless lines into her table's patina. Her other hand stroked the ascot of her suit. Rings encrusted each of her fingers.

The Lady Lellen Se Roye, of the Se Roye Company, of House Se Roye. She was Candip's viceroy-regent, who had formed our Ashstalker battalion, then disbanded it for reasons unknown. She alone was responsible for Candip's prosperity.

Years ago, I had seen her from afar. She had been difficult to look upon for long, like the blazing sun in midday's swelter. As much as I wanted to hate Se Roye for what she represented – as much as I should have envied her – I had only ever admired her.

Maybe that was wrong. But Varry was dead and I had nothing else. In that moment that couldn't last, I was smitten. Lady Lellen represented to me what a person could be when they had everything they deserved.

Lellen pinched powdered chewleaf from a tin and packed it into her lip, then regarded me.

My heart raced. 'I am Heldanarr Fall, seventh son–'

'I was told.' She leaned forward and lowered her quill, lacing her fingers. 'I heard of your valour from my Cosseries. They say you fought as they did. Burning with spirit, nothing held back.'

I felt my cheeks flush. 'And you have… many fine carpets. My lady.'

She chuckled, though I didn't know why. 'Yrdun are proud. They say your hearts are frigid, to fight the fire in your veins. That's how I know I can trust you. Creatures of cold logic see with cold eyes and think with cold minds. I can trust you. And you, me.'

I swallowed, then nodded.

She smiled. Then I glimpsed the bleeding sadness in her eyes, like a gash left to fester. 'I'm also told you knew the priestess who died in the pens,' she said.

I kept my countenance frosty. 'Sister Elene.'

'They say a butchery began in those pens, just before my army's attack. You told them this?'

I blinked. 'Yes.'

Lellen held my gaze. 'You were all meant for the beasts' revel. You were cattle. Livestock. I know the beasts' ways. I wish I did not, but my position's one of burden. Beasts do not waste feasting meat.'

She saw the truth through the glass of my face. I raised my chin.

'I can trust you,' she said. 'And you, me.' Her smile must have ached, a mask like my own. 'What really happened up there?'

I unburied the truth. 'Before they took us, my sister and I found the priestess wandering the Ashwilds. My sister swore to take her to Candip. That's what we were doing when the beasts came. They tracked Sister Elene's scent from the wastes, to us.'

Lellen nodded. 'Where's your sister now?'

I couldn't find the words for that. Where *was* Varry? Grasping for the answer to this question was like reaching for the Blood Moon, or the corpse cloud flocking behind it.

I hadn't spoken a word, but Lellen still understood. 'She's gone.'

I swallowed again. 'Yes. Gone.'

Lellen's shoulders slackened. 'Elene belonged to the Daughters of the Unberogen, Sigmar watch her soul. She wore the cloth, thus her name was given to him. But when Elene was born in my mother's manor in Hammerhal Aqsha, she was Elene Se Roye. And she was my sister.'

My face smoothed.

'You didn't know,' Lellen said. 'Now you do. So tell me – why did she throw herself from the pens? What happened?'

I searched for words. 'Better to die at the hour of our choosing than be gutted on their altars.'

Lellen's brow flattened. 'Yes. So it is. I always thought Elene a coward. But maybe that was it – cowardice. Or maybe I was wrong, maybe she was braver than I thought.' Her eyes sank. 'If it was courage, it was poorly timed. Or I was a poor sister. I don't know.'

I watched, trying to feel.

She looked up. 'Heldanarr Fall – if you feared punishment for your failure to protect Elene, take heart. You did your people an honour. And mine. If Elene stood behind you, so will I.'

Lady Lellen shouted through the dyed fabric walls. Crystal goblets were brought in on a silver platter by a boy in heeled shoes. Ice bobbed in the goblets, chinking on the crystal, which was foggy with cold.

Lellen raised her goblet. 'To sisters.'

I imitated her, drinking as she did. My presence here felt like an accident of fate, or a dream before waking. The icy liquid melted down my throat, crisp like foreign magic. This was the dew of another realm's snow. I could taste the winter in the water – the relief.

Lellen lowered her goblet. 'Consider your sister's censor paid. Elene was coming from Hammerhal Aqsha for a momentous occasion. Honouring your sister's death as I would honour mine seems auspicious. I like Sigmar's auspices, friend Fall.'

'They died in the service of Sigmar,' I said. 'They need no censor.'

Lellen brushed tears from her eyes. 'A censor still seems fitting, yes? These were no common martyrs.'

I didn't know how to react, smelling as I smelt, stained with blood both mortal and accursed. I had eked out a living in endless dolour. I had feared how censors might annihilate our meagre wealth. Here Lellen purchased them on a whim, for the sake of repute.

She summoned her equerry, whispered into his ear. He left.

'A full cask of Aqua Ghyranis will be dispersed to you from our stores. And a crystal decanter, with my seal. That's enough for your sister's censor with the church, and to live in Candip for as long as you draw breath. You belong there, no matter your heritage. Not in the Ashwilds. Not in the wastes. Not one who fought for Elene.'

My jaw fell open. I didn't know what to say, to any of it.

Lellen gestured to the shadows. Armour clinked, and a Cossery emerged. Just like that, the dream was over. I had to leave. I had been fortunate for even these scant moments of Se Roye's attention. The drinks and her sympathies were the privilege of lords.

Had I let things end here, perhaps I never would have learned the truth. Perhaps I would still be rotting in Ulcarver's effete luxury, attending Sigmar's mass on temple days. Chanting meaningless invocations, to a god who did not care.

But *no matter your heritage* echoed in my head. I shook the Cossery's hands off. Like an electric shock, surprise flickered through Lellen's countenance.

'The beasts must be slain,' I said. 'All of them.'

The Cossery gripped my arm again. Lellen bade him stay. 'That's not lost on us.'

'They killed my parents. Now my sister. And yours.'

'Yes.'

I clenched my teeth. 'I served with the Yrdun Ashstalkers. We were oath-bound to Hammerhal's Sun Seekers and later disbanded by your order. Give me charter, lady. Give me the waters to raise a regiment of Yrdun. We'll hunt the beasts to the ends of the Pale. We'll put them to blade's edge.'

Her eyes narrowed. 'That can't be done.'

'Yes it can. It would be easy. It'd be nothing at all.'

Lellen furrowed her brow. 'Nothing at all…' She cast her gaze down the mile-long table before her, delicate muscles flexing in her delicate neck.

I sensed her perfume and winced, waiting for an answer.

'My retinue numbers one hundred and twenty Cosseries,' she said. 'Never more, never less. Our Derders are three thousand on a good day, a sober day; I squeezed five hundred riders into this march. Their other units patrol the outlands and Candip Plain. As viceroy-regent, I also command Candip's foot. Oh, I have foot – entire battalions, tens-of-thousands strong. Sickle-armed militia, sand-eating swordsmen, babble-tongued auxiliaries of every cut and colour. But that's foot. Foot can't chase the beasts down, friend Fall. Foot protects our holds, or musters for sieges.'

My chest swelled. 'Ashstalkers could do it.'

'So could the Sun Seeker battalions,' another woman's voice boomed. 'But Se Roye refuses to deploy them.'

My gaze shot up the table. A cloaked giant loomed at its head, her metallic face glimmering in the faint light of the tent's pyromancy. I hadn't seen her until she spoke. I had confused her for the tent's draped wall and shadows.

She stepped forward, the force of her movement rattling the table's brazier and unnumbered chairs. Breathless, I scuffled back. She was enormous.

Lellen grew irate. 'Will you ever do a thing I ask? Of course not. You're chosen. Chosen to stick your nose in others' business. Quiet while the little people talk, Ildrid Stormsworn.'

'I am not yours to command,' the cloaked titan said. She lowered her hood, revealing a full-faced helm. Her stern mask was bronze in the tent dimness. Over her citadel shoulders, the sun rose – in truth, a spiked halo of worked metal. Beneath her billowing cloak of fine fabrics, I sensed lurking mass, like a lavamander's as it snaked beneath the earth.

This woman affixed her unblinking gaze on me. I held the black void of her eyes, as I could.

Lellen's good humour evaporated. 'No, Lord-Imperatant, you're not mine to command. But neither are the Sun Seekers. Perhaps *you* should answer Heldanarr Fall's question, Stormsworn. Why won't Hammerhal send troops to cull the Pale beasts? Why won't your Stormhost? Why won't Hammerhal's Saddlebagger vagrants lend me Demigryph Knights to do what needs to be done?'

The Lord-Imperatant's head turned, armour creaking, until her monumental attention fell on Lellen. I thought she wouldn't speak. Let contempt alone be her answer, if the judgement in her gaze didn't wither Lellen altogether.

But she spoke.

'First, because the Freeguild demigryphery is expensive to maintain and must be employed accordingly. The preylands here are not enough to sustain high-tempo campaigns, so the demigryphery marshals are rightly jealous with their beasts – just as I have advised them to be. A camelry would suit you better, should you ever spend your wealth on the waging of war instead of the accumulation and guardianship of more treasures. And that, I venture to guess, is the real reason you will not raise this man's skirmisher battalion. That is the question he asked, Se Roye. None of this folly about the demigryphery.'

Lellen shot me a self-satisfied sneer. 'Didn't I–?'

'You speak of Hammerhal as if they ignore you, Se Roye,' the titan interrupted. 'Hammerhal's conclave sends no forces because you wish to supplant them. A woman of your stature should have known better than to challenge Hammerhal.'

Lellen shrugged. 'They can't see the greater good. For their avarice, Stormsworn.'

The titan made a meaningful pause. 'Greed is only the half of it. If all the armies of Sigmaron were yours to command – if all the Stormhosts marched at your whim – you would still not be able to cull the Smoulderhooves beasts. For you, Se Roye, are a fool.'

Lellen sneered at me again. 'What Stormsworn doesn't understand – which *any* reasonable mortal might – is that Hammerhal's demands are excessive.'

'Hammerhal's demands are inexorable,' the titan said. 'Now leave the manling out of this. Speak with your eyes straight.'

Lellen scoffed. 'Friend Fall, allow me to introduce Lord-

Imperatant Ildrid Stormsworn, of the Hammers of Sigmar. They call her the Refuser. Because she refuses everything I ask of her. Isn't that so?'

The Stormsworn giant was soundless and still. Then: 'I refuse the enemy. What does that make you?'

Se Roye tossed her hands. 'You never talk, except when I ask you not to. Enough, let's close this matter–'

'I have shared my counsel often,' the Refuser said. 'And I have been loud. That is my role here – to provide counsel, not commands. Now you beg my guidance in jest and expect this savage's presence to stay my tongue, or that his plea will move me to change my position. His plea is to *you*, Se Roye. The business of Sigmar's cities is a mortal matter. I am here to help see the God-King's will done. Hammerhal shall send their armies when you concede the brightstone owed to them.'

Lellen's fists slammed the table. 'Let them empty my vaults? My whole damn reservoir! Fires on us all, Refuser, your Stormcasts could end this in a day! Where are your saints? Where are the Hammers of Sigmar?'

Stormsworn shook her head. 'You would drag Stormcast Eternals here to eradicate errant gors? You insult us. That task is fit for your mercenary dross, or the Freeguilds you refuse. Or' – Ildrid nodded to me – 'the forces he has promised to raise.'

I glowered. I didn't like her disdain, or the feeling I was a pawn. But I didn't understand a word of what they were saying, either. I was an ant in a palace of gods.

Ildrid leaned closer, anchoring her gauntleted hands on the polished table. The timber whined. Even from here, the Refuser stank of ozone and blue flames.

'What a fool that guides Candip's ordination,' the Refuser whispered. 'People like you make me question the wisdom of mortals. Greed blinds you all.'

'Need guides us. But what do you know of that?' Lellen huffed. 'Nothing! You don't eat or sleep. You don't love.' Lellen faced me. 'That's enough. You understand the gist. Now leave.'

Again, I shoved the Cossery away. 'No, lady. I understand nothing. The Refuser is right. I need only a company of Ashstalkers. Natives, like me.' I pounded my breast. 'A hundred fighting Palers. We could cull the beasts with these numbers, drive them into the wastes. We know these lands.'

Ildrid's black gaze grew heavy upon me. Despite her silence, she was the only one between them who heard what I was saying.

But I needed Lellen's support, not that brooding giant's. Lellen only simpered. For the first time, I glimpsed the falseness in her smile.

'Here's the truth,' Lellen said. 'We could raise your company. I have the waters for it. But not a soul in Candip is comfortable with the idea of your folk under arms. We were at war, you know. Briefly, but war is war. War leaves scars. Many still consider you our heathen enemies. No matter how much time passes, or how many of you the missionaries reclaim. Participation in *my* armies requires a certain pedigree, friend Fall. Dating back to the Tempest, at least, like the dog-loyal Capilarians. My family traces its origins to Azyr. Your roots lead to no such light. I possess authority, yes, but I'm beholden to others' interests. Yrdun, under arms…'

I searched her face, trying to understand.

Lellen shook her head. 'No. I can't see how. And respectfully, your people can't be as tough as you claim. You needed us to begin with, didn't you? To show you the way? Without Sigmar's boon, what would ancient Cardand have become? Dust of the ages. The Great Enemy is numberless and ever hungering. Do you know what threats prowl the wastes out there, beyond the Pale? Not only beasts, but mutants and witches and marauders. Some are already here. More shall come. Given Candip's burdens, my resources are stretched thin.'

'I don't understand.' I blinked moisture from my eyes. 'You said I have your trust.'

Lellen finally rose. She rested her hand on my shoulder. Her bejewelled rings prodded through my sweat-stiffened heat shawl. Her fingers were heavy with them.

She looked me in the eyes. Besides the death of a sister, I know of no blade which cuts deeper than the sympathy of a foe.

'Let me put it simply. The beasts are a minor threat. Their eradication is no priority. If Candip's armies tried protecting everything within the Pale – why, we'd be protecting nothing at all! Do you see, Fall? Do you see why I can't raise the Ashstalkers?'

I nodded. I did. At last, I understood.

CHAPTER EIGHT

Boskin met me outside the pavilion. He took Se Roye's chit, then departed to retrieve the akwag I was promised. Candip's host kept their akwag in a silvered steel tank dragged on two brass beds by twenty aurochs. I, a native, was allowed no closer.

Lellen had promised a crystal decanter of Aqua Ghyranis. Boskin gave me a beaten flask, half-full, cloudy with groundwater. He gripped my shoulder, hiding his silver and gold teeth with a frown. 'They fleeced you, mate.'

My eyes lowered to his bulging waterskin. 'You fleeced me.'

His eyes widened in false offence. He denied it. He made great talk of his charity, the goodness of his heart. But I didn't care. As far as I was concerned, the censor was a bribe for Candip's church. A censor could not bring Varry back. A censor could not heal her absence. Of wealth, I had no need.

I rejected Lady Lellen's offer to return with her host to Candip. Their great army departed Lurth's burning ruins piecemeal. The main force marched, camp followers in tow. Then the baggage train, guarded by tremendous mercenary regiments.

Last, Boskin's Derders, escorting the prison carts I had seen. Plumes of Aqshian sand marched up behind them into the smouldering sky as dusk fell. An impressive sight, that army. But I would have liked more than an impression.

When the great host was gone, I was alone. The mad Yrdun woman with skin red and rags black had disappeared. I journeyed home, away from the smoking pillars of Lurth's ruin, tired, hungry and bruised. The flask's waters were still potent with Aqua Ghyranis, enough to grant some semblance of life. The Derders had given me a steed whose rider died in Lurth's slaughter, but battle had exhausted the alien creature. I named her Micaw Boskin and walked her back, planning to slaughter her for her meat.

On the slopes of our hilltop, around the savaged ruins of our home, the little moon orbited in crippled circles. Our hovel was toppled and burnt, the grounds torn apart, our hoarded magnure scavenged by beasts or thieves.

I didn't care about that, either. Strange, how time had changed everything. Days ago paying the warborn's censor was my greatest worry. The two stones of magnure had been precious. Varry was alive. And now...

I tied Micaw up. I went through the motions of life, stacking stones from our toppled home into a fire pit. I started a fire with the mat I had stuffed for Elene. I meant to slaughter the steed then. To roast her meat, to eat in silence.

Instead I burnt everything. Our pitiful belongings, our trinkets and clothing. The furniture we built from cactus wood, the baskets we wove from river reeds. I found one of my dirks and Varry's falx and almost burnt those too, then changed my mind. Steel was steel, even Hammerhal's. And I was beginning to think I'd need it.

The fire did it. I stared at it, mystified, as if gazing at a distorted reflection. The flame was me, I was the flame. The flame was the truth, beyond my control, raging for more, even after I'd fed it everything that was ever mine.

Nothing at all. That's what I was to Lellen and the Azyrites. That was what my sister had been. Candip's estates and country manors were something. But not us, not our parents' croft, not the so-called poachers in the caged carts. I guessed they'd been captured after hunting their traditional prey-grounds. Lands stolen by Azyrite lords, cut up and parcelled out on parchment. The beast-kin never bothered the Azyrites until they took their priestess. Now that Elene was dead, the realm was as it had been.

I ambled down the hill to the well we once clawed from the rock. I lay down on the hot scree and stared at the hilltop and its flames. The horizon glowed like a city's rim at night. The mercurial sky rippled with the power of its latent curse, a maverick light.

My mind travelled the ash roads of our past. Years ago, after our parents were gone, nobody had come for days. I had been too young to remember much, but I remembered Varry. When soldiers finally came – tax collectors and their escorts – Varry bore me in her arms to the cart which would carry us to Candip. My only other memories were my yowling belly and the passing Ironweld cogforts, coughing acid smoke into the virgin skies.

No system in Bodshe existed to deal with the orphans of the war dead. Tractor guilds took some of my brothers as labourers to clear debris from Candip Plain. Ulcarver's stables took another, to brush the ordure of creatures from barns finer than any abode he had ever dwelt in. Of my sisters, Varry said little. One swore fealty to an aelf Wanderer, then disappeared. Another married a cooper. Within the year, our family was scattered to the eight winds. Only Varry and I remained together.

We lodged in Candip's lone poorhouse. When that filled, we were relegated from the safety of Candip's crevasse to the ruins of Cardand. My sister toiled in lime fields, digging out the bones of dead Cardand to line the purses of Sigmar's merchant vultures.

I remember how she staggered into our room one night, face sooty, shoulders bent. The air was hazy with brazier smoke. But in chalked hands still scabby from her excavations, Varry clutched a miserly box of stale crumble cake. A gift, to me, from Candip's bakeries, for my naming day.

Thrilled, I had cried in blind joy. Nothing had ever been given to me before that.

I delved deeper into the past. Once, my Azyrite had been accented and coarse, difficult to comprehend. Varry found a costly tutor willing to teach Yrdun pupils. The pedagogue claimed to have taught in Ulcarver – an obvious lie now that I remember it.

Back then, I thought myself the luckiest boy in the realm. Then Varry learned what this tutor had been teaching me. *I'll teach you myself*, she'd said, her eyes watering, her cheeks roses. As it turned out, the tutor's rates had not been worth her lessons. We had gone hungry for those rates; Varry had indentured herself to field labour for them, for a chance at a better life.

Then, long before we became Ashstalkers, Varry had asked me of my dreams.

'I want a bathhouse,' I said, in Azyrite.

Stitching my years-old shirt, she paused, then resumed, unwilling to waste the flickering light of our precious kerosene. We had no pyromancy. Only a chipped lantern and a fraying wick.

'What kind of bathhouse?' she asked.

I held my hands as far apart as I could. 'A *fine* bathhouse. With new soap, and clear water. We'll have a place customers leave their brushes and rags, so they don't need to use others'. When they come to wash, they know they'll leave clean. New soap. Clear water.' I grinned. 'They won't have to share!'

After that Varry spoke no more of dreams. In Ulcarver, Azyrites had as much water as they pleased. Soap was a commodity, much of it crafted with the lime Varry chipped from Cardand's husk. In Ulcarver, none shared brushes or rags.

Only we. Only the Yrdun.

I remembered all this and thought, *I should be angry.* But after all this time, all I felt was shame. Shame for not being good enough, for not deserving the things Azyrites threw away like rubbish, like nothing at all.

I balled my trembling fists. Who had made things this way? Not me. Azyrites had brought nothing but suffering into my life. They went where they pleased, with promises of salvation and acts of indignity. They took from the Yrdun and made paupers of kings. They took territories from the beasts, and decades later we died for it. The Azyrites came to Bodshe and took, took, took. They gave nothing in return. They peddled magic we couldn't use and technology we didn't want in return for faith in a god that hated us.

What Azyrites took, they did not relinquish. Now they had taken Varry. Soon they'd take me, too.

I climbed back to the hilltop. The fire raged, but its touch was my baptism. The little moon was gone, its last mooring eaten by the flames. Let it be free, I thought. Nothing else is.

I gathered what I needed. My dirk, Varry's falx. Two javelins and a throwing thong cracked by the fire's heat. By chance, I found my father's death mask. According to tradition, death masks must be entombed in the cairns of the dead, to scare away fouler beings. But years ago the beasts left nothing of father. Varry and I had cherished this last piece of him.

I clutched the mask, my face sinking and sore. The red-hot metal knifed through my hands. Its twisted grimace gnawed at my soul. Flames billowed around me, but the heat and pain were a medicine. I was cured. Or soon, would be.

The horse, Micaw, whinnied in stark terror. Flame had devoured parts of its long hair. Linger, and soon the flames would take us both. I almost killed the steed then and there, as a small mercy, like my mercy in Lurth.

Yet courage stayed me. Control was all I had ever wanted. Control and the freedom of flying mountains, before the Azyrites had enslaved them. This terrified horse had been a slave, too. If I could find freedom for myself – even the freedom of vengeance – surely I could find it for this alien, equine thing.

I cut her tether and flew onto her back. In terror and rage, she screamed. She galloped from the fires, down the hill, absent of caution, devoid of fear. I struggled to hang on.

We rode from the blazing hill into the bandit darkness. The inside of my father's mask burnt like coals on my face. The truth smouldered in my heart, though I did not yet know it.

Soon, I would. But first, vengeance.

CHAPTER NINE

The Pale of Bodshe knew two seasons. Flame, and Smoke.

In the Season of Smoke, hell's heat relented. Ash drifted from the heavens like manna. Crops were planted and watered, weeded and harvested. These harvests sustained Bodshe's peoples. But during the Season of Flame, life was a contest of endurance. On the hottest days, a mortal striding Bodshe's surface might burst into flames if they lacked shade or spell to protect them.

I set off after Candip's host when the sunlit skies had reached full flame. At dawn, oceans of fire simmered above, slow-boiling like sludge, scabbing Bodshe's soil with their heat. Mirages distorted the horizon. Molten metal glistened on far-off mountains, and stone hissed underfoot.

To defy the heat, Se Roye's host would have to take Cardand's unterways back to Candip. The ruling Yrdun houses of Carnd-Ep and lost Bharat had constructed the unterways at the height of their power, when the Holmon delvers were our thralls. Cardand's unterways ran beneath the Burning Valley and its outlands like the threads of a spider's web. They led to a nexus in ancient Carnd-Ep, now Candip. As for what had become of Bharat, none alive now knew. The lost city's tunnels had disappeared with it.

On a high shelf in the sunken corridor of an unterway I crouched, staring along the ribbed passage. The roots of charred trees bored through the sandstone ceiling. The hanging roots choked certain passages into bottlenecks. I could see through my mask, but breathing was difficult. It was my nerves, gnawing at me from within.

Ancient delver runes pulsed on the old stone below, shielding the unterway road from the earthfire's touch, but many had begun to decay. Some of the tree roots smouldered eerily. Exposed earthfire glowed around them, morphing, stinking of brimstone.

Soon they came: the Derders and the prisoners they guarded. Qual Boskin rode at the head of the snake, biting into an apple, looking anxious. He should be pleased with himself. He was a rich man. Why he had pretended to care about me, I couldn't know. We humans were a peculiar breed.

Mounted Derder pistoliers trotted alongside what felt like leagues of supply wagons. Some dozed in the saddle, others played cards. A sturdy woman, likely Boskin's lieutenant, cleaned her pistols but kept an eye on the road. If only she had thought to look up, she would have seen me.

The caged carts with my captive brethren trundled at the back of the Derder column. The carts were spare, packed tight. A pair of Derders brought up the rear. I waited until they passed before descending. Just as I reached the tunnel road, harsh cries echoed back from the vanguard. The spicy smoke of kindling wood wafted my way. Before the Derders came I had spent an hour prising the golden delver runes from where they were hammered into the stone. Now the unterway's unchained earthfire had ignited the column's carts.

I took an easy breath, cast a javelin, then another. They whistled through the air, first one, then two, catching the clueless rearguard in their backs with the sound of rope snapped tight.

I approached and cut their throats to put them from their misery, then sent their steeds off. The captives in the cart – Palers of every stripe and colour – bustled to the cage's gate, hissing for me to hurry. In the dimness ahead, shouting Derders tried to extinguish the flames billowing from their wagons with sand and blankets. Boskin, cursing, called up water from the stores. I worked my dirk into the cart's lock, trying to prise it open.

A bald man pushed his face between the bars and leered. He was hatchet-nosed, bug-eyed, gap-toothed. He extended his wrists.

'Cuts our bindings, please,' he said. 'We can manages the locky-locks. But no rushing. You has plenty of time.'

I slipped my dirk into the cords at his wrist, pulled. The rope binding the captives went slack.

'You see them?' I said. 'How much time?'

The bald man furrowed his brow. 'Two seconds.'

A dismounted Derder bustled around the rear of the wagon. He saw me, then his dead comrades.

I stumbled back, parrying his wild swing. Smoke thickened the air, penetrating my lungs with each breath. Our clashing steel raised the cries of more soldiers.

Then another Derder turned the corner. 'Daggott?'

The cage door swung out, smashing into her face. Beltollers and Yrdun stampeded out and crushed her beneath their feet. They prised my own foe away and trampled him to death, too. As they hurried from their prison, I pointed to the dead Derders.

'Take their weapons. Move up the train with me, and cut their draught beasts free. Put the wagons to the flame if you can, but stay low. You'll inhale less smoke.'

'But how do we get out?' a stark-eyed Beltoller asked, shivering like it was cold.

I pushed a plundered pistol into his hands and cocked the hammer for him. 'You fight. The exit's ahead, close to hill shade. Fight – and live.'

The man stared at the pistol. 'I don't know how to fight.'

I glared, then pushed him aside. 'Then learn how to die.'

I went to my knees, crawling below the cart. The tunnel's hard ground grew warmer as flames rose ahead. Frantic Derders shouted, their boots prancing past me. Panic had mastered them.

The first shot rang out from the captive I had armed. Cries of alarm reached us. The freed prisoners cut loose the steeds and aurochs pulling other carts. A crook-backed woman made to sever the horses' tails, but they were already spooked. They galloped up the passage, crowding the tunnel and tossing Derders from their saddles, then trampling them.

Feet scuffled past me. I crawled onwards, blinking acrid smoke from my eyes. The freed captives dragged other pistoliers down and freed their sabres from their scabbards, hacking them apart.

I reached the next cart. The prisoners had already cut their bindings. I helped with the lock. Behind the rusted iron bars, sweat gleamed on Jujjar's bearded, nail-studded face.

I froze, astonished. Jujjar, my old friend, a comrade sturdier than any other I had ever known.

A dark-eyed woman with faded grey paint around her eyes surged to his side, swatting at my hands. 'We got it, Yrdun-son.' She worked stolen keys into the locks, from the coach driver she had strangled. Prisoners piled behind her, eager to escape.

My death mask shocked Jujjar, but he regained his poise. 'Which way to the exit?' he said, in Yrdo.

'Ahead,' I answered. He did not recognise me.

He nodded. 'Hurry, Yron.'

'I'm not your dog,' the dark-eyed woman – presumably

102

Yron – spat. She popped the cage door, then beamed. 'Keep moving up. We'll do what we can. Find Tul. You'll want to free him.'

I liked Yron. She was clever, quick. 'Tul?'

'Her master,' Jujjar said. 'Three carts ahead. Alone in his cage.'

Yron leapt down, retrieving a sabre. By now, she shouted to be heard. 'Tul. The Exalted Champion!' Captives poured out behind her. 'We fight for him. You will, too!'

I didn't linger. I crawled on, the sheer chaos covering my advance. Dust and smoke choked the air. Desperate mortals bustled, shaking the carts. Pistols fired like thunderclaps. Bullets pinged off stone, or thudded into wood. Blades hacked flesh and clattered off armour. Death's sickly reek grew stronger, more nauseating than the smoke.

I emerged from beneath another cart. The draught animals were already cut free. Before me, a dark blur trotted her steed in a figure eight. Boskin's lieutenant, guarding Tul's cage. I knew it was Tul by the size of him. His muscles were mountains. Scars from old fires gnarled his face. He shared his cage with none.

I baulked. A champion, indeed. Exalted for what, I hoped never to learn.

'LET – ME – OUT!' Tul roared, rocking his cage.

I loped forward. Boskin's lieutenant raised her pistol, but I slid below her steed, chopping my falx into its slender legs.

The horse whinnied and crumpled, almost crushing me. I rose to finish the Derder.

She emerged first, then shoved the muzzle of her pistol into my face and fired.

My head rocked. My ears rang. The world was a struck bell. Nauseous, I toppled in the spinning darkness.

Then I shook off my daze. My father's metal mask had protected me. I expected to die, then, but when I peered up, the Derder woman gurgled, drowning in the blood spurting from her neck.

Someone had knifed her – and saved me. I glanced around, but I glimpsed only shadows. Derders struggling, captives fighting.

I slammed my dirk's blade into the lock of Tul's rocking cart, hoping to shatter the old iron. Tul's mountainous arm burst through the cage's bars. He seized my throat.

'LET – ME – OUT!'

I choked and stared at his black teeth, his red eyes. What I saw in them, I could not fathom. Oceans of blood. Skies of hate. *Chaos*.

Then the cart rolled over. Tul released me just before his arm snapped. I tumbled, rolling to a stop beside a dead horse.

Before me, lambent in the gloom, towered a monster from myth. The titan – Lellen's so-called Refuser. What had her name been? Ildrid Stormsworn. The Lord-Imperatant. She had tossed Tul's cage over like a child's toy. Now she strode towards me, an omen. Reflected firelight blazed in the metal of her stern war-mask. Flames devoured her cloth mantle until its smouldering rags sloughed off her golden armour.

I dried the sweat on my palms, backing away. Ildrid Stormsworn was a sunshine fortress. Each plate of her burnished metal armour lay seamlessly over the next, refulgent in the dark. I had seen something like her in Candip, once. The spinning rings of the Azyrites' enchanted orreries hovered in the heights of the city's rift. The same hands which had designed those, had forged Stormsworn's armour.

But where they were slender, she was thick. They were light, and she was mountainous. What army of serfs must be required to don such miraculous armour? What cranes must be needed to lift each plate in place? Digging holes for oceans might be simpler. Building cathedrals, a less monumental task.

Yet this question was no riddle, and the answer was simple. She never took it off.

'Heldanarr Fall.' The Refuser's voice was louder than the carnage, ringing like a tolled bell.

So she remembered me. 'Refuser,' I said.

The long haft of her warhammer slid down her hands. Its head thudded to the road, shaking the stone. My gaze sank to its head, broader than my chest. I could not fight her. I could not win.

For all this, she did not kill me. She asked a question instead.

'What song does the sun-man sing?'

I blinked. The question was part of an old nursery rhyme. I couldn't make sense of it, but I knew the answer. It floated in my head, as simple as counting to three.

Bile pooled in my throat. I shuttered tears from my eyes, coughing. The air was smoke, impossible to breathe. 'What?'

Ildrid raised her hammer. 'I shall save you, heathen child.'

Tul howled forward, veins swollen in his neck. His black teeth were bared.

'BLOOD!' His meteoric fists smashed into Ildrid's helm. 'DIE!'

Ildrid staggered, then recovered. Tul hammered her again. Their earthquake blows shook me in my bones.

I refreshed my blade grips before a hand jerked me back.

Boskin. He nodded to the grappling titans in the smoke and anarchy. 'That there's a dead man.' He pointed to the nearest stair, covering his face with the crook of his elbow. I hadn't even noticed the exit for the smoke.

I glared at Boskin. He held a knife, still bloody. So *he* had killed the Derder. His own soldier, no less. For what? To save me?

I bared my teeth, shoving. 'Thief! I don't trust you!'

'You really ought to, friend. Unless you fancy dying.' He clucked his tongue and dragged me after him. 'Nah, scorch me, I'll make the choice for you. Come on, now. Mind your step!'

We rushed from the smoke-filled unterway up the timeworn stairs to the realm's scorching surface. Others staggered up behind us. Captives, frightened Derders, flaming horses, all withering in the heat. We raced for the refuge of the nearest shade, the crags.

We ran for all we could, arms flying, sand buckling beneath our feet.

I had survived – I should have been exultant. Instead, dismay chipped at my glacial calm. Stormsworn's words echoed in my ears. That question: *what song does the sun-man sing?* Without hesitation, I had known the reply. What curse was that? What spell?

Beyond the bluffs, the infinite banner of the realm's vaults rose. I knew these crags, these skies. We reached the shade, then a steep precipice, and the valley opened before us.

Below, Cardand's bones swept out across the Burning Valley. The Losh and its tributaries gleamed like red ribbons. Deep within the valley's bleeding carcass, Candip was a pale slash, a buried city. Mountain metaliths peppered the horizon above it, chained to the valley floor like beaten dogs. The sprawling tracts around Candip's burning palisade – Candip Plain – resembled a sun-polished scar.

Beyond the palisade's blazing stitches, tremendous cogforts trawled Candip Plain. They marched along like ants spitting smoke, loud even from here. Closer up, I knew they bristled with guns and sapped the courage of the free. Their soldiery hurled refuse at children. They beheaded the goats of passing shepherds' flocks for a chuckle, then promised worse to those who opposed their march of progress. I knew the Azyrites' abuses. How I knew.

As I took the sight in, everything caught up with me. Varry, the unterway. The Refuser. So many reasons existed not to do what I must do. So many obstacles lay between me and my desires. The cogforts, Candip's armies. More foes from beyond the Pale, like Stormsworn.

Yet I did not start this war.

'Micaw!' I searched for my steed. *'Micaw!'*

Boskin cupped his hand over his brow. 'Right here. Look. That the little girl we gave you over there?'

I glanced over, confused. We had not emerged where I left my steed. But Yron, Jujjar and the others had.

My horse was tied up in the bluffs – Boskin's 'little girl'. The freed captives from the unterway held her steady, pulling her reins. One struck her on the nose and raised his axe.

I scrambled their way, skirting the perilous bluffs. The valley floor yawned below me. Sunlight singed my skin, curling the ends of my hair. I tackled the marauder, yanked the hatchet from his hands. Micaw whinnied – the horse, not the man. She stank of sweat and terror. Her burns had only just started to heal. Now these ingrates meant to butcher her.

Another prised me off, crowing about his hunger for horse meat. I killed him. His spilt guts moistened the sands, steaming. I put myself between the horse and the mortals and raised my blades.

'She's off limits!'

Jujjar forced himself forward, his haggard face contorting. 'Away, you blind pigs! This man gave us freedom!'

'And so did I!' Boskin jogged into the circle, prodding pistols at the crowd. He leaned in. 'You named her Micaw? I reckon that's good!'

'I was going to slaughter her,' I said.

'Well. That's disconcerting. But you didn't. I reckon *that's* good, yeah?'

'Why's this Golvarian outrider still breathing?' Yron shouted.

In the day's light, I saw her clearly. Her temples were shaved scalp beneath a filthy war braid. Her grey eyes were masked with Beltoller sun-daub.

'Someone kill the Derder,' she said. 'Bring me his tongue to burn.'

Yron's tribesman raised a looted blunderbuss, pulled the trigger. The hammer rasped against the firing plate.

'Ah, pitiful.' Boskin seized the gun, then filled its barrel with powder from a horn. He retrieved what looked like a wasp's nest from his baldric, then rammed the tissue down the gun's muzzle and passed it back. 'Give it a load and another wad of tow to keep it in. Pebbles'll do, ten or so. Wee ones, like so.'

The tribesman blinked at Yron. She shoved him off, then glared at me. 'You let this blue coat speak for you?'

'No no, I speak for myself,' Boskin said. 'Your champion here owes me his life. So yes, he's letting me live.'

Yron seethed. 'Our champion's in those tunnels. You would know, Derder. You caged him.'

'Ah, the big bloke. Right. He's dead.' Boskin nodded to me. 'Meet your new champion.'

No one said a word.

Boskin glanced between us. 'You're their champion, aren't you? It's how you ashfeet fight. Why else go to all this trouble?'

The savage with the blunderbuss returned, cranking the cannon's hammer back, taking aim – but the handful of grit he had shoved down the barrel spilt out.

'Ah, see.' Boskin raised his pistol, to shoot him. 'Forget the second wad of tow and it all falls out.'

I snapped Boskin's pistol into the sky. The shot discharged, thundering across the valley.

Jujjar eased the other man's blunderbuss down, disarming Yron with a look. 'I want to hear him out.'

Yron simmered but folded her arms and listened. All eyes turned to me. Tensions were high; our blood, hotter than the hills. All around me stood Yrdun and Beltollers and Boskin, with nothing in common. Who was an enemy? Who was a friend? I could not tell.

But I could not achieve the ends I sought alone. I needed fighters. I needed to sway them to my cause.

I pointed out at Candip. Wind howled over the Burning Valley, the bones of my genesis, the labyrinth of a dead kingdom older than the ages and as wide as the world.

'There lies our enemy,' I said. 'The Azyrites, in the city that was ours. Fight with me, to make it so again. Help me make them remember who we are. Help me finish what they have started.'

None answered. Doubt was a poison, deep in all our guts. I knew its ache well.

Yron raised her salvaged sabre, picking at nicks in the blade. 'Yrdun. Tul always had us kill Yrdun.'

'Tul is dead,' I said. Boskin was right – the Refuser would have killed him. He'd had fire, but she'd had ice. The ice always wins.

Yron stilled. 'The gods demand champions. Champions require glory. What's yours, Yrdun-son? Mercy? Your rage in the tunnels? You're not a champion. You're as mortal as we are.' She spat. 'No. You're not fit to lead.'

Her tribesmen agreed. Sur-Sur-Seri, Hullet, blue-skinned Rock-wrists. Once, the Beltollers had been the Yrdun's vassal-thralls. But in those days, even thralls could be kings. Some of the greatest Yrdun houses were forged by our warrior-thrall dynasties. Yrdun vassalage had resembled the feudal ties of Azyrite lords – not the indentured servitude those very lords had forced upon our people with their piteous wages of akwag.

I said all this, chipping at Yron's certainty. Boskin, chortling, clapped my shoulder and agreed. I shrugged his hand off.

Yet still he spoke for me. 'Listen, folks. This man saved your lives. He went toe to toe with a Stormcast to do it. That's you, bear-hair. And you, ashfoot. I reckon all that warrants open ears and open minds.'

My brother and sister Yrdun murmured agreement. I decided, then, I would not kill Boskin.

'What do you intend?' Jujjar said. He didn't recognise me, but I could hardly reveal myself now. Here, the alliance of Jujjar-the-stranger far outweighed the affection of Jujjar-the-friend.

Before I could speak, Yron scoffed. 'He's Yrdun, like you. Of course you'll hear him out.'

'No one's asking to hear *you* out,' Boskin said. 'I motion for you to shut up.'

Yron turned. 'Why has nobody cut out his tongue?'

Again, the others murmured agreement.

Boskin blanched, regarding me. 'Man, I don't really go to chapel all that much.'

The bickering went on like that, louder and faster, a storm's swell. Others added their voices until the calamity exhausted me. Their passions blew through them like wind through tall grass. They were tedious. They were fools.

'*They'll come for you!*' I said. I don't know if it was my volume or my mask, but they fell silent. 'Return whence you came, the Azyrites will hunt you down like dogs. We have second lives now, all of us! Let us use them!'

I sheathed my blades and faced Yron. 'We are dead mortals walking, Hullet-sister. We have one choice. Bring the fight to them, in the homes they stole from us. On our terms, Beltoller. *Ours.* The past is gone. Our fathers and mothers, dead. We are not Yrdun and Bel-tollers, not any more. We are Palers! Fight with me. Let us rewrite the names of our tribes together, in *their* blood. We are equals before this enemy. But to equal *them*, we must first defeat them.'

Yron flickered. 'Equals, now. Allies, now. But when you have your glory, what then? What will we become?'

My hands dropped. 'Friends. Family, if you'll have me.'

'Friendship won't save us from the Azyrites, or anything that awaits us. You don't walk the Path. How can I trust you?'

I had no answer for that. For ten breaths – the time it took to live, or the time it took to die – silence ruled us.

Then Yron's eyes narrowed. 'Who is *he?*'

We turned. The bald man with bug-eyes and gap-teeth danced behind us, reaching down his ragged tunic.

'Coals, in my shirt.' His voice broke like a child's. The strange fool shook out the draff of dying embers, then sighed. 'That's better. I's Cillus. Hullo.'

Yron backed away, shaking her head. 'I won't do this. We fight for the gods. More than that, we fight for our tribes. I won't replace Azyrite masters for Yrdun. We've no need for new masters. The gods ask enough.'

I was no leader. In my heart, I did not want to inspire Yron's loyalty. I preferred the fidelity of a few over the half-faith of many.

'Then go,' I said. 'Go wherever your useless gods command. Be their slaves, die at their will. But be gone.'

Yron's face flickered. Maybe that wounded her, that I hadn't bothered to convince her. I knew well the ache of rejection. To not be good enough.

Then she hardened. So did I. She beckoned her warriors and they filtered from the shaded crags, beneath the eaves of the ridge-line, away.

CHAPTER TEN

By the time we encamped, Hysh had set and the sky smouldered. Overhead, weather-worn temples and the crumbling walls of their prayer halls loomed. Roofless hypostyles lined the ruins, their pillars marching into the darkness, their painted geometric patterns devoured by time.

I could not imagine what life must have been like to have existed in the age of the Yrdun's glory. What had we done to become so great? The Azyrites possessed their magnificent despot. What had we had but a Realm of Fire and the will to defy it?

Sporadic laughter pierced the night. The toppled remains of the temple's shattered vaults covered the grounds. Cornerless rock, splintered timber, ancient mortar reduced to sand. Ash blanketed this graveyard of hope. The reek of sulphur cut the air, and the redolence of cooking meat.

As the others ate stray dogs, I remained apart. I stroked Micaw's strong neck. She nuzzled my arm, whickering. Maybe she knew I had saved her. I supposed that absolved me for nearly killing her.

Boskin approached, impossible not to hear. He cursed, his spurs scuffing stone. He might have been quieter on horseback. He plopped down beside my campfire chewing stringy meat.

'I'm Micaw. Please don't call her Micaw. You'll confuse me.'

'The name fits her better,' I said.

'Right. Fine. Then I say that makes us square.'

I glared. 'Return my Aqua Ghyranis. Then we're square.'

Boskin pouted. 'Why do you think I took it?'

'I saw your skin. Bulging at the seams.'

He chuckled. He didn't even bother denying it. I respected him more for it.

'Speaking of names,' Boskin said. 'The others don't know yours, do they?'

I had almost forgotten I was still wearing my mask, so accustomed I had grown to its weight. Despite the stinging sweat, I couldn't bring myself to take it off. The mask was a part of me, like my father's gheist returned from the dead. My anonymity was a shield – but also a blessing. No one had cared about Heldanarr Fall and his sister. But the mysterious nobody I had become was different. Powerful.

'Oh, I get it.' Boskin's eyes gleamed. 'So you've got a secret identity. Good for you, friend. I'm great with secrets.'

Jujjar slipped beside the fire, far quieter than Boskin had been. 'What secrets?'

I turned and joined them, relishing the char aroma of meat across the camp. 'Boskin's secret. Why he's helping us.'

'Mm.' Jujjar nodded. 'I want to hear this, too.'

Boskin glanced between us, chewing his moustache. He prodded his knife in our direction. 'I was supposed to be nobility, you know. Se Roye stripped my house of our titles.'

'You told me. But that explains nothing. Why betray them for us?'

'Don't you see?' Jujjar asked, in Yrdo, looking at me. 'That's it. He wants his title back.'

I scowled at Boskin. 'Greed? You fight for us because you think we'll make you a lord again?'

'Course not! I also owed the other captains a few barrels from a few bad hands at cards. Debts were going to be called back in Candip, sure as the realm turns.'

Jujjar looked at me. 'Greed.'

I nodded. 'You won't be a lord, Boskin. Not now, not ever.'

He shrugged. 'Call me a gambling man. I think you'll change your mind.' He leaned back. 'And maybe I just hate Miss Se Roye's guts.'

I narrowed my eyes. I could have killed him, then and there. No one would have lamented his fall. Yet he had saved my life. That I could not forget.

But lordship? The word made me writhe.

Boskin sighed. 'Maybe this isn't the time for this discussion. Point is, I've earned your trust. I saved you. And I can do you one better.' He leaned in, eyes glinting. 'I've been embezzling Se Roye Company nectar my entire career. That's all yours, if you'll take me. But you have to take me.'

'How much?'

'Barrels. Casks. Basins and pools and reservoirs, and not far. I'm an industrious swindler. It's my most admirable trait.'

I cocked my head. 'So why not just pay your debts?'

'I'm not paying them *anything!*' Boskin shouted, trembling. 'They all owe me! All of them!'

Avarice. The chink in Boskin's soul, the poison that made good men go bad. I swore to remember the lesson.

I nodded and pointed to Boskin's waterskin. Dew beaded on the leather, summoned by the heavenly cool within. Boskin blushed. He rose, securing the skin with Micaw's tack.

'He's Sigmarite,' Jujjar said, in Yrdo. 'A Reclaimed vulture from our city. And worse, a Golvarian Derder turncoat. A traitor's trust is worthless.'

'Oh, but I was betrayed first,' Boskin called over. 'Me, my father, his father. Doesn't that deserve some vengeance?'

Jujjar grimaced. 'He speaks Yrdo?'

I shrugged. 'He speaks Yrdo.'

Jujjar scattered sand into the fire. 'Stranger,' he said. 'I won't ask why you wear that mask. It's morbid, stomach-turning. But you saved me and I have a feeling you won't take it off, so let it be. You should know, if you really want to fight this war, we'll need more warriors.'

I nodded. Jujjar had always been the most reliable of Candip's Ashstalker battalion. He had always demanded more for us from our Azyrite commanders, never satisfied with their compromises. Now he had intuited his place at my side, to provide counsel. I had feared needing to compete with him for his warriors' loyalty, but Jujjar had no aspirations to command. Innate leader and peerless warrior he had been, but the bandit fog in his eyes told me his days of sergeanting were over.

I glanced at the other fires in the camp. 'Will yours stay?'

'Those scraggle-necks won't be enough. Even fattened up, plump with slaked thirst. And they need training. But first we need more fighters.'

'You must know somebody,' I said.

Jujjar vacillated. 'I know many. Down hard dogs, bowl belly beggars.' He sprinkled sand from his dusty fingers. 'People like me, like the others you saved. But we'll need something to offer them. No one fights for free.'

I was almost afraid to ask. 'And you?'

'You saved us from Candip's gibbets. You have my blade, and theirs. And the pretty talk on the cliff, that fine speech – that didn't hurt. But if we want fine warriors, we'll need more than fine words.' He glanced in Boskin's direction. 'We'll need his waters.'

Boskin tramped back. 'Already said I'm in. Don't stare at me like I owe you something. Weren't me made you go poaching. Weren't me sentenced you to death.'

'They aren't poachers,' I said. 'One cannot poach on lands stolen from their ancestors.'

Boskin chuckled. 'Ah, man. Yes. Yes you can.' He peeled back his sweaty sleeve, revealing a poacher's brand on his arm. The ugly scar was half healed by time. 'See? It's the ones with the gallows who get to say.'

Jujjar stared. 'You hunted your forefathers' lands? Why weren't you sentenced to death?'

'Because I'm not an ashfoot,' Boskin said.

I slid my dirk from my sash. 'I'm cutting out your tongue, now.'

Boskin's hands shot into the air. 'Sorry, sorry. Old habits die hard.'

I fought my anger down, then sashed my knife. 'Stop saying it. Stop saying the word. Next time–' I pointed at my mouth.

Boskin nodded, glum.

'But it's the truth,' Jujjar murmured. 'We *are* ashfeet, stranger. And… we *were* poachers. I got so tired of looking at their hunting grounds from the commons. Tired of not having what I deserved. The times you speak of, when Cardand was ours…' He gestured encompassingly. 'The past is dead. We are what they made us – what we made ourselves.'

My heart thawed, and my anger guttered away. Poor Jujjar. Proud Jujjar, who always seethed at the way Ulcarver's blue bloods had spoken to us. My soul sang for my grief at what my friend had become. To hear these words from him was like swallowing razors.

'Heard you talking,' Boskin said. 'You need warriors, yeah? So use my nectar, like he said. I have so much. So, so much.'

'Very generous,' I said. 'For someone who won't ever be a lord.'

'Well, you know me. Charitable, good in the heart. I'll even fetch it for you. I'll be back before you miss me.' He kissed the air.

I turned to Jujjar. 'Give him warriors. I don't want him alone.'

Jujjar shook his head. 'We need them, to get word out. These parts of Cardand crawl with strange foes. Alone the buzzards would take us.'

'I can do it with a steed,' Boskin said. 'Suppose, that girl I gave you, with the handsome name.'

I loathed the idea of sending Boskin off alone. He could take his akwag and flee. Or betray us to the Azyrites for a greater treasure. Yet he had earned some measure of my trust. This matter of his loyalty... it exceeded the reach of my arms. I could either trust him, or not. But I could not dwell in this in-between.

'Fine,' I said.

Boskin shot to his feet. 'I'll get her dressed!'

Jujjar watched him prance off. 'You really trust him?'

'He's earned his chance. Let us see what he does with it.'

Jujjar grunted.

'You doubt my decision?' I asked.

He shook his head. 'Not at all. The world is not right. How can I doubt your decision, if everything is wrong? Look around you. This place, and those others who follow you – we're tied together, by our hunger and hope. But our ties are nothing. Our common blood and common tongue? Nothing. We did this to ourselves. *We* let this happen. Most of our people, in Cardand, in Candip's canyon... they wouldn't spare a glance for one of their own. You've seen Candip? Seen its poor, legless and dumb, dragging themselves bloody across market squares?'

I nodded.

'Then you know. Those of ours who received Sigmar's sanctuary could have helped them but did not. They don't care what happens to their own kind. The world is wrong, but it's the world our people made for ourselves. We let our crippled and starving crawl through the stone streets of our dead cities, until they wither and dogs gnaw at the ends of their fingers. Azyrites don't do this to each other. Only we.' He shuddered. 'I don't doubt your decision. I doubt nothing. We deserve the world we have made.'

I longed to remove my mask. To dry the sweat on my skin, to rinse away the crust of blood and old sun-daub. I wanted to show Jujjar my face and tell him not all was lost.

But I couldn't. Who was Heldanarr Fall? A mortal, and one he had known well. Fragile, vulnerable, human. Not this death-eyed menace who had defied the Derders and freed him and given him something to fight for.

Jujjar was right. Nothing remained to our people – not even our ancient bonds. All we had was vengeance, and my mask had become the face of it. I could not take that from him. I would not take it from myself.

'I need to call you something,' Jujjar said. 'What is your name, stranger?'

Boskin tossed Micaw's saddle down, then fiddled with its straps. 'Legends don't have names. That fellow stood against a Stormcast and lived to boast of it. You oughta have a deed title.'

'Stormcast.' I marvelled at the word's elegance.

Boskin froze. 'You don't even know, do you? You fought her, survived – and you don't even know what she is?'

I glanced between him and Jujjar, who looked amused.

Boskin's eyes twinkled. 'Here's to hoping you never find out. So, speaking of names, what do you think of this?' He paused for effect. 'The Drake of Bodshe. Got a ring to it, hasn't it?'

'No,' I said. 'Drakes are twaddle from missionary stories. They aren't real.'

Boskin pursed his lips. 'The... Wild Flame?'

He went on like this, with more and more of his idiocies. Jujjar mocked him each time. I couldn't help but chuckle.

But Boskin was a mortal of Aqshy. Anger thwarted his embarrassment, and his cheeks reddened. 'Well, how about Heldanarr Fall then, eh?'

We fell silent. Jujjar's gaze drifted to me. Recognition stirred in his eyes, twisted by bitter sadness. 'That's how you knew me,' he said. 'Held Fall, where have you been?'

I battled back my insurgent feelings, but there were too many to master. 'It's been a long time.'

'Hasn't it,' he said, staring.

I turned on Boskin, twitching beneath my mask. 'Great with secrets, was it?'

Boskin hefted Micaw's saddle over his arm. 'Right, well. Maybe I misspoke. I'll leave you two to it.' He tramped off, avoiding me for the rest of the night.

Boskin departed to retrieve his stash of Aqua Ghyranis before daybreak. After he had revealed my name, I'd considered holding him but baulked. We needed the waters. I needed to take the chance.

Meanwhile, I glimpsed more and more of Jujjar's old self. We spoke of old times long into the night. He pledged to keep my identity a secret, agreeing I could better serve as a symbol. Our old friendship changed that evening. I don't know if it was the shared meat or Jujjar's diminished bitterness, but he grew easier in my presence.

This was how brotherhoods were born. Not spun in the womb, but forged in good times and bad. I decided to forgive Boskin's slip – if he ever even returned. As Hysh crawled higher in the sky, the bilious fear I had misestimated the Derder's motivations seethed in me.

But Boskin did return, guiding Micaw and a kempt cart filled with clay casks and greenwood barrels. Akwag sloshed in the containers, so cold it steamed.

'Told you I'd bring it,' Boskin said, greeted by the others' cheers. His untrimmed moustache covered the corners of his grin.

I pretended his return had no effect on me. But inside, something lifted. *This is possible,* I thought. What *this* was, I did not yet know.

For three days, we put the word out for volunteer fighters. When the time was right, we gathered at a night market deep within Cardand, in an old unterway junction ridden with sand-fleas and aether-snakes. Eventide breathed rebel life into the shaded ruins. Impoverished Yrdun and Beltollers emerged from their abodes in the crannies of the fallen kingdom, to seek or offer what custom they could.

Not all in the night market were locals. I recognised Capilarian indigents and beggars whose ancestors might have once fought worlds away, on the Arad Plains or the bloody battlefields of Flamescar Plateau. I disliked what they represented, but I did not judge them. Sigmar had enslaved all the Parch, not just Bodshe. They were the same as I had been.

In Ulcarver's taverns, never-ending draughts of ale poured from vats the size of ogors. But in Cardand, we Yrdun preferred night markets filled with children and petty commerce. Smokeleaf clouds billowed from low tables like incense. The chatter was deafening – and invigorating. This was a place of life.

We conducted our business by the flickering light of a half-spent wick and salvaged candle wax. Jujjar vouched for the open eatery's proprietors, a family who served us cooled devil-meat and brined vegetables. I despised smokeleaf, drinking no firewine, only sandy water. I needed my head clear.

Many warriors had come to answer my summons. Each had a turn at our table. Jujjar and I negotiated their part in my cause.

With each pact sealed, Boskin disbursed akwag with the same dropper and proofing plate he had used to embezzle the splendid waters.

The more people I spoke with, the more I understood what had brought them here. Word of my attack on the Derders had spread throughout this side of the Burning Valley. My mettle had lent my countrymen faith in my cause. As for their akwag, most wanted the waters sent to their kin in the Ashwilds, which we arranged. For the rest of the night, Varry and the family I had lost were on my mind. We were all of us the same.

The number of our sworn brethren grew through the evening, but none recognised me. Few commented on the death-mask. Some asked to see my face.

I didn't know what to say, but Boskin breathed life into a lie. I was no living man, he said, but a ghost, back from Shyish, to see justice done. Who else dared defy the Stormcasts? Only another immortal. Only a revenant champion. The effect was solemn and delicious. Like me, few knew the word Stormcast. We had all heard old legends, nothing more. We were naive.

Yet some were not. And as Boskin spoke of Sigmar's Eternals, I did not miss how they whispered of taboo and raised their cowls, shielding their faces from the stars.

Adure was an old Ashstalker like me. Her sun-daub and heat cowl marked her as blood of a different tribe than my father's. The tribes were older than the kingdoms of Cardand and lost Bharat, a relic of the Yrdun great clans.

She carried a strange weapon I had noticed on others. A cannon, like a reversed battle-axe, its wide stock embedded with black shards of crystallised earthfire.

'What is that?' I said, in Yrdo.

'A fusil of Hammerhal, remade into a maul-axe,' Adure said.

Maul-axe was our word for our macuahuitl, a heavy club edged with obsidian teeth. I liked the clever adaptation, but the fusil's forged barrel and firing contraption annoyed me.

'Can you throw?' I asked.

'Javelins?' Adure shrugged. 'I haven't in years. My mother taught me.'

Later, Jujjar asked what that was about.

'We cannot use those fusils,' I said.

'Candip uses them. They're strong. Loud. They frighten enemies.'

'And give positions away. And the powder, and shot... how would we get it? They're too costly. Too much trouble. Javelins are quiet, reusable.'

Jujjar eventually saw reason. I had no intention of fighting as Azyrites fought. Azyrites had dictated too much for too long. They would not dictate the terms of my revenge. Hammerhal's steel was acceptable, but handguns were too much.

Night went extinct, and the revels of our union abated. I found Jujjar stewing at the night market's edge, beside a shattered wall which stank of urine. He looked bitter again, like all the realm owed him tribute.

Then he saw me. 'What do we fight for?' he asked. 'To restore our people? Or just to make a point?'

I had not fully answered this question for myself. After Varry's death, I had thirsted for revenge, to fill the gulf within me. But the power to change the past did not exist; I craved the power to change our future.

'Both,' I said. We spent the remainder of the evening in silence.

My words were only sparks, then, bright but forceless. Yet they were true. So were the flames they finally bore. I did not want to just kill Azyrites. I wanted to exorcise them, their ideas. I wanted them gone, and I didn't care what followed.

CHAPTER ELEVEN

Eighty of us walked the low road back, once the largest of Cardand's unterways. The roof had caved in, and time had gouged divots in the cobble like gaps in teeth. Cold stars and distant moons shone above. I felt emboldened, knowing Sigmar's eyes watched us from his heavens but did not see. He was too arrogant.

Boskin nursed a bloody nose, a consequence of his flagrant advance on one of our new fighters, a woman already wedded. The Derder stumbled, then cursed, lifting his boot.

'What now? Someone couldn't hold it, that it?'

I glanced down, nostrils flaring. 'That,' I said, 'is a man's liver.'

Jujjar whipped his blades out, as did others. We all smelt it: bile and blood. I passed Micaw's reins off. Ahead, dark shapes littered the toothless roadway.

Corpses. And one of them still moved.

I didn't recognise Yron until I was upon her. She dragged herself from the site of the massacre, barely lucid, a deep gash in her brow.

I crouched. 'Yron. Who did this?'

Her eyes slid up to mine. 'Bloodbound,' she croaked, her breathing ragged. 'Still here.'

I had hardly opened my mouth when a hurricane pounded out from the roadside. The titan ploughed me into an ancient wall looming behind me – then *through* it.

Brick broke. Crumbs of mortar showered us like volcanic pumice. I rolled over scree, scraping to a stop, wheezing, breathless but alive. I felt like I had taken a cavalry charge.

Inside the darkened ruin, I scrambled to my feet. Panicked cries echoed outside. Jujjar shouted for the others to follow him. My lone adversary loomed before me. This one woman had slaughtered Yron's warriors. I drew my weapons. I dared not underestimate her.

She was tall. Not so tall as Ildrid Stormsworn, yet still looking down at me. Muscles corded her unscarred limbs. A black sleeve of bolted metal covered her torso. She brandished two monumental axes, both as light as feathers in her hands. A high-crested helm crowned her head. It did not cover the blood on her face, nor the heat in her eyes.

And that heat. During the attack on the Derders, I had thought Tul's gaze was red. Yet in this living hurricane's eyes, the Orb Infernia still sailed. Daemons danced, and dead suns gleamed. I smelt the fire in her breath, like roses and pumice and murdered things.

Red, all of it red. Red like the world. Red like me.

I have never felt so close to extinction as in the moment the Seeker found me. That night, I glimpsed the truth, though I did not know it.

Her eyes ignited, flames licking up her brow. Mine widened. Her raw belief was a force, catching fire in her gaze and inflicting fear on me like a curse. For so long I had striven to cage my heart in ice, to bury my hurt. This foe burned hers for fuel.

In all the realms, no surrender exists for such a person. No defeat.

'Ever seen mountains die?' she asked, in accented Azyrite.

My courage mouldered. I shook my head.

'Everything dies.' She flourished her axes. 'You just have to kill it.'

She swept forward, powdering brick beneath her iron-shod heels, scorching the air over my head. I dodged as I could, dancing like a child over coals. I should have felt fear, but all I felt was vacant hope. The witless craven in me had hungered for oblivion since Varry's fall. Now it had come.

Yrdun warriors poured in – my fighters, put to early test. But they were late, distant. The dread fighter's axes clanged my falx aside. Rocked by her force, I stumbled and fell. Then she swept in and lifted her axes for the killing blow.

The husk-dry timber beneath her creaked. Her leg crashed through the wood of the ruin's collapsed vaults. She sank to her hip, caught fast, splinters thick as thumbs jutting into her flesh.

She raised her eyes, and the fire in them guttered. 'Everything dies,' she said morosely, almost amused. 'Just have to kill it.'

At that moment I almost pitied her. Then I raised my falx and chopped off her hands.

Her axes thudded down. Blood jetted from her ragged wrists – unnatural rivers of it, painting the wood and sand red. My fighters surrounded her and hammered their heels into her head. Her helmet fell aside, revealing her jet hair. As the blaze in her eyes died, her consciousness ebbed, sustained only by a wicked strength. But her gaze didn't move from me. To her, I was all there was.

That night she was spared by my command. Questions burned in my mind. Who was she? Who had sent her? Why now? Her ambush could not have been mere coincidence. Not on the night I had gathered my first fighters.

Back on the low road, I mastered my humours. We bound her in old ropes and scavenged chains, then dragged her back to camp.

All that time, she never stopped watching me. And like the oceanic crimson in her eyes, she didn't die.

'You're back.'

'So are you, Yron.'

'Where else would I be? That devil killed my fighters. Almost killed me, too. But if you found me, then the gods must have willed it.'

'So now I'm favoured? Now I'm glorious?'

'Deeds don't lie, Yrdun-son. And blood warriors don't lose, not so easily. You cut off her hands. That can't be just fortune. She lives?'

'Until I figure out who she is.'

'I told you. A blood warrior. Go, cut off her head, take her skull. She wants yours. She wants all of ours.'

'Jujjar says you can't be trusted. That you've had your chance.'

'I liked Jujjar better in the cage.'

'Yron.'

'I don't jest, and I haven't lied. You really think fourteen Hullet marauders could've waylaid eighty of you? I told you, we meant you no harm. We were night-prowling, to raid an outlands manor. But we were weary. The blood warrior came like the wind and trounced us all. Now take her head.'

'She's no Azyrite.'

'You know what she is, same as me. You know who she serves.'

'The Dark Powers. Chaos. Like you.'

'No. Not like me. I seek glory. Through glory, the gods grant power. The power to protect my tribe. Myself. Through glory, my people are protected, even out in the wastes where we were driven. But I'm not like her, Yrdun-son. I'm not fool nor thrall enough to surrender as she has. The blood warrior craves no glory. Only skulls.'

'You're all like that. Like her. You're all mad.'

'I do what I do for their eyes. We all find our own way. The Path to Glory is narrow and treacherous. But I am not like her. Take her head, before it's too late.'

'Listen to you. More delusions, even after your gods sent their true champion to bury you. You live a lie.'

'The gods are what they are. I don't love them – I ask only for their strength. Look at *her*. Look at what she did to my kindred. That is not a delusion. That is a red portent.'

'I bested her. That's a portent, too.'

'But her wounds haven't killed her, have they? Even missing her hands, skull cracked like a nut – *she lives*. And those wounds *will* heal. I've seen darker miracles. *That* is the power of the gods. Kill her, before she uses it against you.'

'All that power, but still fourteen dead marauders and two severed hands. I like my chances better without your gods.'

'I don't claim to know their will. They're gods. I don't trust them. But I want their power, not their love, and so I tread the Path to Glory. You don't believe me. You think you've seen. But you've not seen what I've seen. There's no other way.'

'So why kill her? Why not use her?'

'Because that blood warrior has gone farther than we're meant to go, all for bloody *Khorne*. Has she shared her name?'

'No. She speaks… in circles. But the idiot Cillus calls her Kadd-arar. The Seeker.'

'Well, hells with her name. She's still marked. Defeating her was a miracle – *your* miracle. So take her skull! Earn their favour!'

'I don't believe a word of this.'

'Believe in nothing, that is what you shall become.'

'Agreed. I am nothing at all. Enough, Yron. Cillus'll bring meat. Tomorrow I'll find you, to learn more of this outlands manor.'

'Ah. So you were serious about fighting the Azyrites.'

'I was.'

'Maybe… maybe we should have joined you. My warriors would still be breathing, then. They were my brethren.'

'*Maybe* is a long word. And it does not raise the dead.'

'…Maybe.'

'You're very clever, Yron.'

'Mockery. Stop smiling, Yrdun-son. I see your teeth beneath that mask. You're madder than any of us. What's your name?'

'Hatred.'

'Mm. I think we'll get along. If you'll have me.'

'No one else will. Yron… this Path to Glory. Tell me, where does it lead?'

'In the end? I don't know. I haven't seen. Where do champions roam, when the gods' call takes them? No one's shown me. But…'

'But?'

'I've always hoped it is a path without end, like life.'

'Life ends for all of us, Hullet.'

'No, Yrdun-son. Not for the Chosen.'

Yron and her Beltoller savages had meant to raid a manor in Cardand's outlands, to eke what living they could off the blood and treasure of rural lords.

I thought it a good start for us, too. I needed to test my warband against a soft target, to seize what weapons and waters I required to wage my war of vengeance. The outlands holdings were the best place for this. Defended, but difficult to reinforce. Well-stocked, but not so precious to the Azyrites they would avenge the loss of a single estate. Yet as much time as I had spent in Bodshe's Ashwilds, I knew little of the vast hinterlands of Cardand's rim.

Yron led us there, along winding gullies between the bones of edifices so old and weather-worn I almost mistook them for crags. Ages had worn the smooth ashlar stone into bluffs, weathering the seams to rills. Everywhere we went, ash choked the air. Where sunlight smouldered, sand scabbed into a blistered crust.

Moving up the valley, adhering to the shadows of the ancient towers, I marvelled at my people's legacy. How might it serve us now? Skilled warriors who knew the terrain could strike at their enemies, then slip away in the ruins. Even a host as mighty as Candip's could have no hope of retribution against partisans who knew these lands well.

We could do this. We could fight them.

Tall ridges marked the outskirts of the Burning Valley. Pinnacles, tors and jagged flanks of stone. More ruins adhered to the rocky slopes like meat lining a split ribcage. Slender trees sprouted from their cracked foundations. Groves of bristly rootwood, thick and succulent. The thought of tasting their sickly sap set my mouth watering.

Then fields of smoking rye opened before us, and the gargant drew my gaze.

I stumbled back, raising my blades, my stomach dancing. 'We cannot kill that,' I said. Everyone looked horrified.

Yron, amused, glanced between us. 'I did tell you. Didn't I tell you?'

Boskin strode forward. He'd been inking a map of the lands with Cillus, the gap-toothed fool of strange talents. But for my protection, I suspected the others would have already killed them both. Cillus came from an Azyrite line, and Boskin was Golvarian. Jujjar hated Golvarians. Many did.

Boskin regarded the slumbering goliath in the fields of smoking crop. The mountainous creature leaned against a windmill, its tattered wind sails stirring in a breeze.

'Scorch me, that's Drowsy.' He scratched his chin. 'She hasn't woken in years. Bloody hell, I didn't think she was real.'

Yron grinned, her teeth white beneath her bruised eyes.

'Gomurtha is bound to the Hullet, my people. She'll wake on our command alone. Look. The scar on her belly, the eight-pointed star. Generations ago, that brand sealed our pact. Only the pact can awaken her.'

I forced my eyes from the slumbering behemoth. Beyond, a foreign manor stood perched on a distant hill beside the fields' edge. Smoke rose from metal stovepipes in the squared manse. Beyond that, labourers trudged with stooped backs across terraced stone. They scrabbled in the rock, clawing chalk into wicker baskets on their backs. Their smallness needled through me. It was more than their mere distance; it was the nature of them. We were all small to the Azyrites.

I glanced at the gargant, Gomurtha. Even from here, her putrid musk hammered at my nose. 'You mean to wake her now?'

Yron shook her head. 'Only if you want to die, Yrdun-son. Gomurtha's belly is bottomless. The green waters dull her hunger, but she'll only stir for the pact. That requires promise of a feast. Here, we'd be her meat. We leave her out of this.'

'And what of them?' Jujjar pointed to the terraced crags, the serfs.

'Your people,' Yron said. 'Yrdun. Let them live, I say. We can use them.'

Jujjar's cheek twitched, the studs in his face shifting. 'We should kill them. They're traitors. Working Azyrite manors for salaries.'

'Oh, sure.' Boskin cupped a calloused hand over his brow and stared at the estate. 'I reckon they live like kings. No maggots in their porridge. All gold in their thrones.'

'They're paid,' Jujjar said. 'They live better than us.'

'That doesn't mean they're free,' I said. My gaze swept the jagged lee of the hills. The tenants' squat clay lodgings, the puffing chimneys and trench latrines. I could not make sense of the manor, nor the smoggy grain fields, nor the dozing gargant.

As we circled the fields, Yron explained. The estate was a quick-lime farm. Bones – always in great supply – were imported from the Parch's battlefields abroad. These were buried beneath the terraces, until potent Aqshian magic from a convergence of ley lines transmuted the bones into quicklime. Kharadron airships – arkanauts like Hewer – exported the quicklime to far-off Hammerhal, to its steel forges and powderworks.

Yron said the cruelty of the lady of the manor and her priest-advisor were notorious. Tenants late on the debts they undertook were tossed to the winds or worse. Criminal debtors were gibbeted on a ruined fence on the far side of the smoking fields, withered and lifeless.

'Yours?' I asked Yron.

She shook her head. 'They did not walk the Path. Look at them. Slaves.'

Boskin polished the leather of his baldric with his cuff. 'Not slaves. There's no slaves in Sigmar's demesnes. More likely they just owed debts. Running short on a nectar tally can carry a stiff penalty.'

Flames smouldered in my belly. 'Debt is a crime?'

Boskin shrugged. 'How'd you think the lovely Lady Lellen seized my family's holdings? It wasn't me that wrote the laws.'

The sun blazed high in the sky. We scouted the outskirts of the properties, then encamped in Cardand's ruins. Crumbling ziggurats slumped at our backs, still tall enough to touch clouds. Leather-winged buzzards crowed in the sky.

As I saw it, we had three challenges. First, the manor's garrison. Freeguild veterans in gaudy livery, heavy with scars and muscle and good steel. These could only be dealt with one way. Then, the bright mages. Yron swore three protected the manor. They were college-trained, and all of us knew the calamity pyromancers could inflict on the uninitiated. I had no solution for them, so I acquainted myself with the possibility of losing fighters in our eventual attack. Many, many fighters.

By far my most pressing concern was the sleeping gargant, Gomurtha. I did not for a moment believe Yron's claim about her people's pact with the giant. The gargant's feet could have flattened mountains.

At dusk, Yron and I crawled into the hazy fields, noses wrinkling at the grain's endless smoulder. The crop was a spiced strain of rye, supposedly good for brewing staple Aqshian ales. Crawling closer to the dozing hill, my fingers gripped dark soil, loose and warm like crumble cake. I relished its aroma, yearning to rub it in my face, to eat and be sated.

Bloated, fat Gomurtha was more like living terrain than a mortal being. The patched sails from a salvaged shipwreck mantled the slopes of her shoulders. She had fashioned the keel of that ancient vessel into a crude club which lay at her side. I could not get over her size. I might have camped our warband on her corpulent legs. City gates might have been built in the gap of her lips. Her snores were thunder. The stink of her gale-strength breath made me retch.

'But why doesn't she wake?' I whispered, though we were half a league from the gargant. 'Why doesn't she devour the Azyrites?'

'The pact. How many times do you want me to say it?' Yron rubbed her eyes. 'The first shaman, Hullet, bound her to him, generations ago. But since the first darkness ended, our tribe's always lacked the meat to make her stir.'

'Will she wake if killing begins? Could she smell the blood?'

Yron bit her lip. 'Maybe. Oh, shut up, I know – a long word and all that.' She gestured to the smoking crop. Tendrils of haze drugged the air. 'This smell should cover the meat scent. But who knows.'

'And if someone dies in these fields?'

Yron paled. 'Let's not find out. Gomurtha's legendary, Yrdun-son. She'd gobble us all up for a snack.'

So. We just had to kill the Azyrites on their own lands, before they knew we had come. It seemed easier said than done.

CHAPTER TWELVE

When we returned to camp, everyone was agitated. In my absence, as eventide had broken, Cillus had wandered to the gates of the Azyrite manor. Only Boskin had noticed he was gone. Only Boskin defended him now.

'He's not a traitor,' Boskin pleaded, ignoring the others' shouting. 'Just a little light in the head.'

Cillus slouched cross-legged in the dirt, oblivious to the others' calls to kill him. They thought him useless. I had been keeping him as a retainer for his ability to complete minor tasks with single-minded efficiency. Cillus was a fool, yes. But not all fools were traitors.

'What was he doing?' I said.

'Looking for iron. That's all. Says the prisoner who sent him for it. Kaddy.'

I shivered. I remembered what Yron had said, that the Seeker was too dangerous to let live. And only Cillus had known her name. That could not have been a coincidence. She was trying to use the fool to escape.

I had to kill her, I realised. Day in, day out, Yron still insisted on taking her head. Nobody had forgotten our meeting on the low road. Kaddarar's continued existence unnerved the warband, and I hadn't got a word from her about her purpose. If she could manipulate Cillus, it could not be for anything good. Perhaps I should have killed him, too. Fortunately for Cillus, I had a soft spot for the shunned and the spurned.

The next evening, I approached Kaddarar. She was chained to a broken pillar where we were bivouacked, in a derelict market. My fighters were scattered in the gallery around her. The raised shelf where I slept overlooked their campfires. The air tasted of dust.

Kaddarar sat cross-legged on the warm stone behind Boskin's cart. The open wounds on her arms reminded me of serpents split in half, gruesome but clean. I had hoped gangrene would solve the dilemma of her existence for me. Why I was reluctant to kill her, I could not say, except perhaps I hoped she would be useful. Perhaps.

'Feathers and soap,' Jujjar said. 'That's what I smell. Not the slightest stink of rot. Those wounds should have killed her. From bleeding, or blight.'

My skin prickled as I watched her. 'Her blood doesn't flow for us. Nor does it rot.'

Kaddarar opened her eyes. A bone-chilling smile curled her dark lips, sweeter than lilies. Then her lids closed. She lifted her chin, exposing her throat.

Yron reached for my blade. 'I'll do it. Her god demands it.'

'No,' I said. 'She killed your fighters. You don't owe her or her god.'

'Then maybe I just want to kill her. What's wrong with that?'

We lingered, our torchlight dancing across Kaddarar. Her muscles engrossed me, topographical, like a detailed map. Her black plate cuirass, rigid and bolted with brass, absorbed the light. The sheen of her jet hair shimmered.

'I won't do it,' I said. 'I won't kill her.'

Yron's lips hardened. Her painted eyes puckered into pinpoints. 'Coward.'

I swivelled. 'And what do you know? You're their pawn, too. I'm not. I won't give in. I won't sate her god's blood thirst. I won't sate yours.'

After a long stare, Yron relented. She bowed her head, then strode away.

'Have her moved closer to my fire,' I told Jujjar. 'I'll watch her myself. And, Boskin – don't let Cillus near her again.'

Jujjar, displeased, nevertheless saw my will done. He sulked off and shouted for hands. I watched him go, trying to understand what drove him. I often felt as if he thought I owed him some kind of special obedience for our friendship.

Boskin scratched his neck and started away.

'Wait,' I said. 'You brought Cillus back from the manor. Why didn't they follow you back?'

'Told them he was my horse's groom.' Boskin tapped his skull. 'Said he's soft in the head. Acted real lordly about it, too. I have a knack for that. It's in my blood.'

'And they just let you go?'

Boskin chuffed. 'What were they gonna do? Send for the Order of Azyr?' He grinned. 'Don't you get soft in the head, too. We got Cillus for that.'

'Soft in the head?' I seized Boskin, pushed him into a wall. 'Who's softer in the head? The fool at the enemy's gates or the fool who follows him?'

Boskin tensed. 'Easy, man, easy. You're right. Apologies.'

I released him, beating back a swell of anger. 'Go. Do as I said. And don't leave Cillus alone with the others.'

Boskin smoothed the rumples in his sun-faded blouse, then straightened his gorget. 'There's one more thing. When I got close,

I saw the guards and the bright mages. They were all drunk. It's all these country types do, drinking. The smoking rye from the gargant's field – they brew ale with it. A strong sort. They like having a good time, methinks.' He shrugged, turned to leave. 'Might be a good way in.'

Firewine was the poison I needed. Endless caravans shipped the foreign liquor from Candip's distilleries across Cardand. I thought of raiding for it, but Boskin suggested just buying it. This was faster, quicker and perfectly sanctioned.

After parting ways with a fat merchant on one of Cardand's low roads, I couldn't stop beaming. Commerce had always been the Azyrites' secret weapon, the golden thread tying their scattered civilisation together. To turn their prosperity against them, even in this small way, amused me.

We returned to camp with six casks which barely fitted on Boskin's cart. I disguised myself as a caravanner and rode out to the quicklime farm alone. Once I was out of my fighters' view, I removed my mask, relishing the air's touch.

The impressive manor was a towering edifice of brick and unblemished stucco. The watchman at the estate's outworks checked my cargo against his register, a parchment scrap bound to a leather cover.

'Where's the salted fishes?' he asked. 'And the aurochs flanks and waloe tubers? Where's the sanctuary vegetables?'

'I don't know,' I said.

He scratched his scar-nicked brow.

'I don't know, do I?' I said. 'But the accounts are paid, and I can't bring this damn drink back to the vathouses! So what do I do? Pour it out? Hand it to ashfeet? The wet-thumbs in Candip'll have my neck if I have to ride back out here once your quartermaster sorts out your logs.'

The watch stared at my cargo. 'The accounts're paid? On all this?'

I nodded, casting a furtive glance across the estate's grounds. Forty soldiers lounged, ate and trained in the manor's courtyard. Around twenty more likely walked the grounds. The pyromancers were nowhere to be seen.

Higher on the terraces, my people toiled.

My knuckles went white on Micaw's reins. White like the rocks my people clawed through, white as the dust on their faces and the blisters on their hands.

The sentinel disappeared, then returned. 'After long consideration, we've elected to accept these here paid-for libations.' He extended his register and a quill. 'Make your mark. Be off. Sigmar speed you to safety.'

That night we waited around the smoking fields, in irrigation wadis carved from drained channels of earthfire. The rye's fumes were soporific, heavy. We took turns keeping watch, our heads bobbing like toys. I'd considered waiting in our encampment in Cardand's ruins, but Kaddarar's new pen was by my fire. Every time I passed her, she watched me. With that bone-chilling smile, like all was right in the world.

I checked Micaw's tack, then my blades. I didn't enjoy this subterfuge – I wanted to name myself to my enemy, then rip out their throats. Being forced to resort to this ploy with firewine was exasperating. I craved for the Azyrites to know we were better than them, craved to scream it in their faces.

The prospect of losing lives was not what had made me careful, though that consideration was not meaningless. This would be our first fight, like Uolter's rebellion in the ancient lore. Uolter was the first *Maal* of Bharat, and like him before Bharat's uprising against Cardand, I had yet to prove myself. I had shown my courage in the unterways, and my father's mask had made me a symbol, but the others needed more than that to follow me. I must become a champion. I wanted to prove it to myself, too.

As eventide fell, the bright mages made party tricks of their sorceries. Flames gouted into the air, joined by laughter and praise from the drunken soldiers. I could almost smell the firewine fumes from here. Their drunkenness was repellent.

Gomurtha's distant snores shook the earth. The dead glow of Aqshy's horizon silhouetted the darkling hill of her in the smoke-filled fields.

'How'll we know when they're drunk?' Jujjar said. 'They look drunk now.'

Boskin chuckled, oiling his visor's hinge. 'Never been drunk, have you?'

Wounded pride crossed Jujjar's face, pulling at his piercings. 'I don't drink your people's poison. So no, I wouldn't know.'

'They aren't drunk yet. Just a little sipped. Give it time.'

'Quiet, both of you,' I said. 'When they sleep, they're drunk.'

Boskin passed a flask. 'Maybe you should try some, Jujjar. Might make you more pleasant.'

Within the hour, the time came. Watches remained awake, but many of their lanterns had guttered out. They were too drunk to light them, too clumsy to patrol the grounds, too inebriated to fear their mistress' reprimand.

The tension in my chest made the air feel thin. At least they weren't too drunk to die. I mounted Micaw, then drew my sister's falx.

'Move,' I said.

From the moment we attacked, we painted the lands red.

I killed the first myself. The watch from earlier in the day, with the trade log. He turned at the drumbeat of Micaw's gallop. Then the scythe of my falx cleaved through his slack-jawed mouth, splitting his skull in twain. Later, Boskin would call that the cleanest slash he had ever seen, all the more impressive since I had never fought on horseback. I had spent days practising with sheaves of rye on the far side of Gomurtha's fields, but skulls are tougher than grain.

The manor's guard billets were built of Ghyran timber, something to do with Candip's convoluted trade with Hammerhal Aqsha. The Azyrites had at least been clever enough to wrap the timber in enchanted silk and soaked hides, then cover the garrisons in earth. Our flaming brands were useless.

Instead we entered the billets and slit the soldiers' liquor-moistened throats, or ran them through on their straw mats, or crushed their skulls. When the shouting began, nothing could be done. The soldiers were inebriated, clumsy, their weapons out of reach. Few had the sense to rise for their blades, and these stumbled against us. Our butchery was efficient, almost tedious.

But drunk or not, the pyromancers – the vaunted bright mages of the Azyrites' Collegiate Arcane – were lethal. Each carried a caged flame at their waist from which they cast their devilry. Fireballs immolated four of my fighters. Walls of inferno marched up across the manor grounds, dividing us, scaring my warriors.

'Ya!' I drove my heels into Micaw's belly, and she leapt across the flames. We both knew fire's touch. We no longer feared it.

She galloped across the sands. Closer, the bright mages were vulnerable. I cut one down, then Micaw trampled his body into pulp, his cage into twisted steel.

Behind me, foreign syllables made my ears perk. A pyromancer's robes billowed like the flames in her hands. Spell-fire etched runes into the air.

I turned Micaw as the heat from an errant blast brushed my coverings and kissed my father's mask. I saw the world through his face, by the light of the mage's panicked fireball. But my father's grimace warded me. So did Micaw's speed.

I cut her down like a dog, circling around, shouting orders

through a voice roughened by strain. My raiders regained their composure, but the guards' resistance was forming, too. They were collecting into a battle line.

A feeling scratched at the walls of my insides, like ants in my bones. A slipped footing; a lost grip.

'Brother!' Jujjar cried, pointing to the fields. 'The last mage!'

I saw her. She tumbled through the smoking rye, towards the mountain of sleeping Gomurtha.

I cursed. She meant to wake the gargant. She meant to kill us all.

I spurred Micaw onwards. We tore through the unmowed crop. Drunk, slurring, the pyromancer's meteoric flames lanced over my head. She hurled her last fireball at Gomurtha just as I rode her down, nearly combusting us both.

'No!' I screamed. Azure flame chewed a hole through Gomurtha's sail-stitched clothing, and the flames spread. My eyes grew into moons.

Fire. Oh, the fire. I felt it on my cheeks and in my eyes, burning in my soul, below the horizon. I had never had faith in anything but the flames of Aqshy and my need to defy them.

But faith was useless. Faith cured nothing. It was the fire I wanted, burning Gomurtha, awakening her. Fire was everything I wished for, and nothing I could escape. Despite what it would cost me, at that moment I wanted everything to burn. A wretched sickness in me longed for the gargant to stir and devour us all.

The flames guttered where Gomurtha's drool had moistened her rags. Then the gargant's eyes slid open like a river crocodile's. She blinked, twice, the wet thud of her eyelids echoing through my core.

Then, she returned to her slumber.

Panting, I trotted Micaw in a wide circle, astonished. I peered at the somnolent hill. Gomurtha slept soundly. Her snores rumbled through me like the breath of the entire realm.

Tepid fascination trickled in my veins. All my planning and preparation, yet only chance had saved me, saved us all. A fluke of fate, the accident of Gomurtha's unnatural drowsiness. The eight-pointed scar on her belly glowed.

In the end, I controlled nothing. I rode back to the manor's slaughter, annoyance aching up my bones.

The enemy was broken. Jujjar and Yron led marauders into the half-defended manse as Boskin and others finished what few soldiers remained outside. Those with fusils, like Adure, hadn't fired a shot. They hadn't needed to.

In the manorial chapel, a retinue of duardin in corded metal armour defended the estate's cowering mistress, who was still in her slip. The duardin were Holmon delvers, mercenaries exiled from their hill clans. Dour eyes glared at us through the grilles and slits in their helmets. Radiant beads clicked in their plaited beards. The oil on their long spears and broad axes tickled my nose. They must fight like castles, I thought. Low, sturdy, never reaching farther than they should.

A priest stood before them, a hammer in each hand. He was not soft, not as Elene had been. He was rough and cruel, or so Yron had said. But I had seen the meagre lives of the manor's workers. As far as I was concerned, Yron was right.

'Surrender and die,' the priest growled.

I laughed. My warriors, too. Even the cruellest of enemies can be proud and strong. A lifetime of war had forged this iron priest and the duardin fortresses behind him. They were strapping, and fought well. Were there more than eight of them, they might have even won.

We killed them all, then set the manor aflame. As the fires rose, I wandered the smoking corridors. Wooden stanchions hissed and cracked. Half-dressed servants piled from the rooms into the courtyard. In the chapel and kitchens, I drove out bevies of terrified labourers who had taken refuge. My warriors pillaged everything. Fine fabrics, jewel-studded treasures. Leather-bound tomes with iron corners and buckles and words I did not know.

In the manor's vaulted undercroft, my fighters glugged mouthfuls of akwag from deep basins, then soaked their sleeves and carried drippings away like that. Yron was wise enough to gather those she could to ladle the cold waters into skins and flasks, to heave off with the rest of our plunder.

They did not get it all. Yron shouted for me to leave before the flames took us, then cursed and left without me.

I remained, drinking my fill. Flames roared and crackled, yet I drank. I had no need for riches, so I used the Aqua Ghyranis as it was meant to be used. For healing, it was said.

But the akwag did not heal me. My chapped lips went smooth, my scrapes and bruises disappeared, but the hole inside me remained. I drank until I saw the light of the water's magic, until its radiance wriggled in my eyes like bright worms. I drank until dregs remained, spotty with sand, grease and blood. I drank and I drank and still Varry was dead, my people broken, my family gone. Pain possessed me. I could not exorcise my past.

I staggered outside, sooty and scowling, my belly stretched full. The terraced hills surrounding the manor glowed with dawn's rebel light. Hysh burgeoned in the sky, warming the sands. Choking pillars of smoke marched into the air. Afar, Gomurtha still slumbered, her miasmic breath poisoning us all.

My fighters herded the manor's surviving labourers together. Yron and Adure argued over their fates. Yron desired to make them our thralls. Adure wanted blood sacrifices.

'They must be bled!' Adure cast back her cowl. 'They're traitors! They worked for Azyrites!'

I guided Micaw closer. My horse sweated from the night's efforts. 'So did we, once,' I said. 'We won't kill our own.'

Adure scoffed. 'Our own? They aren't ours. Look at them. Reclaimed dogs, every one of them.'

She was not wrong. I heard the prayers on their lips, for sanctuary and succour. I smelt the fervent reek of their despair, the vanity of their faith. Whether Yrdun or Beltoller, Parcher or half-blooded Azyrite, these pathetic folk worshipped Sigmar.

But so had my family. So had Varry. I would have protected them. These I should have, too.

So why didn't I challenge Adure? Sloth. Moral cowardice. The culmination of all my uncertainty, like lost footing, or an oil-slicked grip. Cruelty is the sum of all our frailties. Weakness, fear, spite. Suffering had made me weak, not strong. I did not speak to save those innocents because I was a coward. I did not stand against Adure's bloodthirsty demands because I lacked courage and control.

I looked over the huddled fearful. When Cardand had fallen, not a battle had been fought. This was the story of all my people. *We had not fought* for each other. My parents had tried, but look what had come of it. Even Varry had fought for Elene, not me. She had died – for an Azyrite.

Yrdun, Beltollers, Azyrites. Where had they all been when I had needed them? And now that they needed me, why should I answer? Jujjar had been right. We did not fight for each other – and I didn't care.

My lips hardened and I prepared to leave, then stepped on something.

A severed hand. Its fingers twitched at the touch of my toes. I lifted my foot, fearing to hurt it.

I raised my eyes. Beyond, stoop-backed Cillus scrabbled in the dirt, snatching scraps of discarded metal and riven flesh into his arms, plopping them into a looted wicker basket on his back.

'They drops it, I picks it back up,' he muttered. 'Drops it… picks it back up.'

I peered at Adure. 'Leave them be,' I commanded.

Adure froze. Then she laughed, joined by many others. Even Jujjar chuckled.

Adure raised the toothed stock of her fusil, preparing to execute a captive. 'I'll leave them for the crows.'

I lurched forward, drawing my dirk. She was quick, but so was I. I dodged her bladed fusil, catching her wrist in my hand. I slashed her belly.

She gasped. Her follow-through had raised her arms higher. I pushed them above her head, and her entrails slopped out onto the sand, warming my feet.

Her fusil clattered down. The light in her eyes guttered and she toppled, groaning as she died.

The hushed hiss of thirty blades touched the air. My fighters had drawn their weapons against me. I realised, then, how many of them knew each other. They had not known me, nor fought for me. Only Boskin's akwag brought them on. Only my thirst for vengeance.

I faced them. The grimace of an Yrdun death mask is meant to scare away the Nighthaunt gheists, lest our fallen be stolen for the cortèges of the dead. Yet it did its work now, striking fear into the hearts of the phantoms surrounding me.

My phantoms, I told myself. My warriors.

'Who agrees with Adure?' I said, in Yrdo.

None moved, or spoke. They were cruel and frail. I was neither.

I pushed past Jujjar, ignoring his furious scowl. 'They won't be thralls, either,' I told Yron. 'Let them go.'

Bemused respect shone in her painted eyes. 'Yes, Yrdun-son.'

I pointed to our pillaged stores of Aqua Ghyranis. 'Take what waters you can. But any who take the Azyrites' treasures shall meet their ancestors in Shol. Leave the rest for these indigents.'

My warriors hesitated, then nodded. Some, impressed, murmured stronger assent.

I staggered away, awaiting no questions nor challenges. If any of them disobeyed me again, they knew what would come of it.

CHAPTER THIRTEEN

Before returning to camp, I stopped in the hill flanks. I hacked down armfuls of furry rootwood, then dragged them to our encampment. I meant to crush the wood and drain its sap, to taste, to remind myself sweetness was not yet extinct in the realm. Then I'd mix the rest with river water and wash in it.

Back at camp I tossed my harvest down, ladling river water from our casks into a dusty basin. I peeled off my soiled clothing, rinsed blood from my skin. I brushed dirt from my nails and ash from the corners of my eyes. The water rinsed away my bitterness, my hate. I mixed the last dregs with ash and let it sit. I would make sun-daub on the morrow.

Then I sighed and sat. Below, my raiders filtered back to camp, so I rose to give them orders. Some had brought tapestries from the manor's walls, for sun-tarps. Others helped Yron lug pillaged casks of akwag to our stores. They had all obeyed my injunction. That pleased me.

I dumped the used washwater at Micaw's hooves, to evaporate

at sunrise and keep her cool. Grimacing, I returned to my place. Exhaustion pulsed behind my eyes. I felt like years had passed without a wink of rest.

This day, I would sleep well. And if my fighters tried to kill me in my slumber, they would fast learn I was no sleeping gargant. As my gaze wandered the crumbling walls of my world, sleep took me.

In all this time, I did not notice that Kaddarar and her chains were gone.

Voices woke me at dusk. Below, my fighters stowed our gear for travel. We intended to set out for another outlands manor. Eventually I hoped to increase our stores of waters and recruit more fighters. When we had the strength, we would strike Candip's holdings in Cardand. But all in time.

I rose, leaning against a pillar, watching below. Boskin handled our stores and restless Micaw. Yron supervised the remaining warriors. Jujjar stood sullen with the day watch. Some prescient Ashstalker had stolen the surviving steeds from the enemy's scorched manorial stables. Others prepared them for travel.

My raiders' shoulders tensed beneath my eyes. Some glanced up, offering respectful nods. Yron planted her fist over her breast in tribal salute. I returned the gesture. They were mine, I was theirs, no matter what Jujjar might have said. Let there be no more doubt as to whose command this warband would obey.

I turned to don my mask and froze.

Kaddarar held the mask in the crook of her elbow. She brushed her healed wrists over the rictus metal, the virgin flesh whispering against its charred angles and curves. Her arms should not have healed so quickly. They had not been sutured. No poultices had been applied. Hardly a day and a night had passed. This was unnatural.

She dropped my father's face into the perishing embers of my fire. Pendant chains clinked uselessly at her side.

'I know you,' she said, without a whiff of deceit. Her crested helm sat against piled rubble. Her heavy-lidded eyes were crystalline, like red quartz. This was not the thoughtless champion I had broken on the low road. This was a woman oracular and fearsome, like a storied Maal from lost Bharat.

I met her eyes fearing what I might see. Another verging massacre, or another blood moon in red skies. But no matter what I saw, I would not give Kaddarar the extinction I knew she sought.

'You don't know me a whit,' I said.

A dead wind tossed jet hair into her eyes. She blew it aside. 'You think there's so much to know?' she asked. 'You, half-marked, same as us all. Your dead parents, your dead people. You're never different.'

'You don't know me.'

She raised her handless arm, gesturing to the smoke on the horizon. 'I know what you did out there wasn't wrong. You killed your kin. But Azyrite, Yrdun, Parcher – it matters not from where the blood flows.'

I inched forward, stooped low. I snatched my mask from the embers. I danced back, brushing white ash from the metal. I donned the mask.

'It doesn't hide who you are,' she said. 'I assure you. Quite the contrary.'

'But I'm not hiding,' I said through clenched teeth. 'You were. Before I cut off your hands. You're a snake without fangs, writhing in the sands. I could crush your head with my heel.'

She looked down. Iron stakes hung from her pendant chains. We had hammered those nails into the stone, at an angle. I glanced to where we had kept her. She had shattered the stone when she jerked the chains free. No mortal should possess such strength.

She looked up. 'I'm not sure you could.'

I scowled. 'You drink blood. You worship the Smoulderhooves' god, the red daemon – Oxhead. I know your kind.'

'Don't insult me. I'm not a beast.'

'Look at you. That's all you are! Who sent you to kill us?'

Exasperated, she exhaled. 'Nobody sent me.' Then she paused. 'Well, Godeater sent me. To kill you, I thought. But now I think it was for something more. Listen. I freed myself hours ago, at dawn. I could have killed you then. I could have killed you so many times. You were *so* killable.'

'You want me to ask why you didn't.' I touched the handle of my dirk, which I'd left sashed through the night. 'But I know the answer to that.'

Her eyes bunched with contempt. 'Oh, so lethal. So cool. No, boy. I could have killed you *so many times*. You sleep as a child sleeps – a very killable child.'

Her words gnawed at my patience. 'Why're you here?'

'I told you. Godeater sent me.'

I drew my dirk, hurled it between her legs. It stuck in the stone. She looked up. 'That was actually quite impressive.'

'Who is Godeater?' I said.

'My god. Khorne-Godeater, on the brass throne, under red skies.'

I sputtered. 'Sounds a lot like Oxhead, Seeker.'

'That is repellent,' she said. 'I don't care what those creatures worship. The beasts sense the Dark Powers better than any of us, but they don't understand them for what they are. Gods. *Gods!* Not forces, not spirits. GODS.'

'Gods, and your Godeater,' I said. 'So poetic.'

She stared. 'I would have said *vile* but to each their own.'

'You talk so much.'

She nodded. 'Yes. The word for that is *garrulity.*'

I quietened. Eventide's breeze whispered through me, heralding night's coming cool. Kaddarar, unarmed in the most literal sense of the word, was nevertheless dangerous. No mortal could have yanked those chains free. No mortal could have healed so swiftly.

But I had not expected such... restraint. Such *garrulity*. I relished the word's shape on my tongue. The Seeker transfixed me.

'So, your Godeater told you to find me.'

She nodded: a gracious, pernicious gesture. Her eyes never moved from mine. 'So he did.'

'He should've told you to watch your step.'

She examined the scarred knots on her arms. 'Yes. That would have been nice to know. But he works in mysterious ways.' She lowered her arms, then her voice. 'He'll see. Then he'll know.'

'You killed Yron's fighters. Why not me?'

'Whose fighters?'

'The marauders. On the low road.'

'Oh. The wildings.'

I nodded. 'You must answer for that.'

She blinked. 'They walked the Path. They knew its ways.'

I had imagined Kaddarar like Bharat's legendary Maals, but she could not have been more different. Long ago, Bharat had defied the nightmarish hordes that had assailed the Pale of Bodshe, as Cardand had. Those hordes had conquered the Parch. The heraldic darkness that followed had been called the Age of Chaos. Varry had enjoyed preaching how, when the darkness came again, only Sigmar could save us. I'd thought it all hollow myth.

But Kaddarar was one of those fabled monsters in the flesh. A warrior who had heralded the dark. Yet she was no monstrosity of dagger-teeth and sickle-claws. She was human. A killer, certainly, the same as many of us. But nevertheless – *human*, with hair like spilt rock oil and sun-blotches on her tan skin.

Her red eyes fell. Wind made her jet hair dance over her muscled shoulders and bolted cuirass. The breeze brought forth her gentle smell, like pumice and cactus flowers at night. Days of captivity, unwashed – yet she smelt nice.

'I couldn't understand why,' she murmured. 'I answered Godeater's call, but he abandoned me. I came for the skulls, as he commanded. Then he nearly let you take mine.'

She was… crestfallen. I almost pitied her.

'He does not care for you. All gods are masters. All mortals, slaves.'

Her lips bent. Her crystal eyes glimmered behind the blowing strands of her hair. 'How very rhetorical. And maybe – just a bit – correct. I pondered this mystery many nights, why he abandoned me. I have wandered for years. Across fields of glory, over seas brimming with elder things. I could count the years of the little lives I have ended, and those centuries would fall short of the time I have spent wandering. Godeater sent me to seek out the greatest skull of them all. So I have sought.'

'If you seek tribute, find the Ushara. Their warriors will play your games.'

'But that's just it. I didn't understand. Godeater didn't want tithe. He wanted a champion. He wanted *you*. Long have I sought you, Godeater's Son. But in the end it was you who found me.'

I stared for a long time, my neck tingling. 'Whence come you?'

She darkened. 'A floating city, like a marionette. With long strings pulled by a wicked god.' She waved. 'That was before the Khul rose. I don't even know what the lands are called any more.'

'Aridian,' I said. 'You're a berserker. I thought the Azyrites had exterminated your kind. I thought they wiped you out before they came here.'

'Far from it. We're the same, you and I.'

I shook my head. 'We are not the same.'

'You fight the usurper. The false God-King. As do I.'

'I fight *all* gods. You worship them.'

She grew grave. 'I worship the death of gods. That is Chaos. That is Godeater, who will take all skulls before the realms die.'

'You lie. Bodshe teems with Azyrites, yet you attacked us.'

'This again? You walk the Path. So you know its ways.'

'I walk my own path.'

'That is *the* Path. There is no other.'

Her sophistry annoyed me. I narrowed my eyes. 'Give me a reason to believe anything you say.'

This, she had been waiting for. She raised a trembling arm. 'Let me serve you, Godeater's Son. Through me, the gods have chosen you. Now I must guide you. I alone am fit for it.'

'Guide me for what?'

'Your final trial. To prove if you are a skull – or skull-taker.' She blinked, clearing the fog from her eyes. 'I'll kill your enemies, too.'

'I don't trust you.'

'Good. Don't. Because the time will come when I kill you, or you kill me. That is the measure of our lives, Godeater's Son – those we kill, and those who kill us. Until then let me be good to you. Let me serve you until our time comes.'

'Our time,' I said.

She nodded, like a gladiator saluting her own imminent annihilation. 'Murder brings mortals very close.'

I had nothing to prove to Kaddarar or her god. Yet I could not deny the solemnity of her vow. Her eerie smile – a killer's smile – felt brittle and perilous. Like a budding flower's life in crags of ruthless stone. I pitied Kaddarar, because she wanted this – *bad*. She feared my rejection as a child might have.

My scowl evaporated. In my chest, my irritation warred with her lurid beauty. I was loath to acquiesce to Kaddarar's request. Her zealous drivel drove me mad. But she had been a fine warrior, which I was in need of. And she possessed a certain charm, unvanquished by her danger – or even enhanced by it.

As I debated accepting her offer, her eyes followed mine to the ends of her arms. She must have sensed the arc of my thoughts.

'Send Cyloth,' she said. 'He can fix this.'

'Who's Cyloth?'

'The Azyrite. With the bald pate, and the witch's nose.'

'Cillus?' I asked. Could the fool really not pronounce his own name? Or had Kaddarar said it wrong?

She nodded. 'Yes. Cyloth.'

'Your hands rot in a distant ruin. I won't send him or anyone back for them.'

'What?' she said. 'No. How do you get anything done? Cyloth was enthralled to Hashut's breed, the dark-hall duardin of the hell forges. He's trained in their arts, as fine a curse-wright as they come. He can forge me new hands.'

'Even if that is possible' – I felt out my words as I spoke – 'I don't trust you. You tried to kill me. And you *did* kill Yron's kindred.'

There. Her smile, evil and delicious.

Kaddarar stepped aside. Behind her, the heads of four dead Ash-stalkers were stacked into a pyramid. Sand and dry blood encrusted their rolled-up eyes and lolling tongues. Cracked vertebrae and spinal tethers hung from their ragged necks. She had torn their heads clean off.

I blenched. Assassins had come for me as I slept. What were her words? A very killable child?

'They came one at a time,' she said. 'I gave them the glory they sought.'

I was confounded.

'Let me serve you,' she said. 'If anyone will give you the gods' peace, it shall be me. Until then, I would see how far down this Path you will walk.'

'The gods' peace.' I shook off my confusion. 'I would have called it death.'

'You really are rhetorical.' She sucked on her lip. 'Perhaps. That's all I shall say, Godeater's Son. *Perhaps* you're meant for something more. Perhaps. But perhaps is a long word filled with bad odds, is it not?'

I shuddered. Then I summoned my warriors. They tensed when they glimpsed Kaddarar.

'She's ours. One of us. Spread the word, then bury these traitors.' If mutineers had sought to kill me, they must have been angered by Adure's execution. Kaddarar had excised their treachery before it could flower – but they were still Yrdun. They deserved cairns for that, if nothing else.

When my warriors departed, I faced Kaddarar. 'I'll send Cillus, or Cyloth. Whoever.' I held my breath, then exhaled. 'Don't make me regret this.'

'You will. Or I will. One of us will.'

No matter how cryptic she wished to be, I sensed her relief. I had accepted her service. For that, she was glad.

We broke camp by nightfall, Kaddarar among us. I couldn't help but watch as she mingled with the others, scaring them. She relished their fear. She danced around it with her long words, her *garrulity*. It all felt so human. So charming–

So dangerous. I was alive for the first time in days.

CHAPTER FOURTEEN

Kaddarar roamed free. I trusted her less than anyone. But same as Boskin, she had proven her intent.

It felt foolish acting on instincts I didn't trust. At the same time I felt certain a commander's faith might inspire a warrior's fealty. The two formed a circle, a closed chain. I hoped the freedom I granted the Seeker might earn her true devotion.

Still, I hedged my bets. By night and day, my Ashstalkers kept silent watch on the Aridian berserker.

The days became weeks, and Cardand's outlands became our hunting grounds. My war party prowled the Burning Valley's rim, sacking holds and farms. We pillaged weapons and waters, building our strength. We developed our battle tactics for the day we would take on Candip's forces. Beyond the extraction of revenge, I had no final aim. We murdered toll collectors, piked their heads. We attacked caravans from near and afar. Millers on the Losh and its tributaries we left alive, but their wheelhouses we toppled and burnt. What loot we couldn't carry, we left for the vultures, the riffraff, like us. We kept our distance from Candip's crevasse and the well-fed armies there. Most importantly, we never stopped moving.

Our victories were never flawless, yet all triumphs possess their minor perfections. The outlands estates' garrisons often possessed strong outworks. They watched their outskirts and patrolled their enchanted hillock-palisades. They were fierce.

But the warband I was forging consisted neither of petty bandits nor mere marauders. We were Yrdun Ashstalkers, bred for the brutality of Bodshe, wise in the ways of our enemy. They had trained us, before they had thrown us away. What advantages the enemy possessed in equipment and drill, we overcame through spirit and ingenuity. We dictated where, when and how we would fight. We ceased using ploys like the firewine, because they were not necessary. The sun was always at our back, always in the enemy's eyes. We needed little else.

More Yrdun joined us. Ashstalkers, and outlands brigands. I was careless with their lives, when I could afford to be. My conscience was a pendulum swinging between extremes. In times of boredom, I stopped murderous scraps between my fighters. In times of frenzy, I ordered dozens to their deaths. My warriors fought when they needed to – *died*, when they needed to. But what I needed changed every day.

You think I didn't care? I did. That was the problem. I had lost so many people – my parents, Varry, myself – and I refused to tether my heart to anything else I might lose. My warriors were not those labourers we had freed at the outlands manor. I owed them no sanctuary, nor hospitality. In the life that had been inflicted upon me, only one thing was certain: nothing lived forever. To this truth I inured us all.

Where Azyrite properties burned – where the piked heads of foreign lords and greedy merchants reddened the sands – the word *Ashstalkers* was whispered, half from reverence, half from fear.

Beltoller brethren and Parcher sellswords came seeking employ. Jujjar despised them, but I accepted them. Yron instilled in them respect for her gods and regard for me. She was useful, though I lacked her faith. But at least she made her intentions clear. Yron craved power and its seedling, glory. To her, faith was a tool. Soon our foreign warriors began to wear her face paint and war-braids, carrying their necks as straight as hers, praying to her gods. I tolerated this.

Boskin's understanding of the mysteries of logistics was his own path to glory. None other could tend to Micaw or our pack animals. None other could organise our provisions or the watch set over them. When our war-party numbered over two hundred souls, only Boskin could predict our needs. He calculated how much of what pillage must be taken, and what we possessed in excess. He named this secret art *mathematics*. I have never been wise in the magics of the realm.

During our little war, as I came to know the others' names and humours, only three souls defied my understanding. Kaddarar, of course, was the first.

Jujjar, my friend, was the second. After our first raid he grew as mercurial as Bodshe's Cursed Skies. I healed this as I could, hearing out his dissent or agreement, keeping him and his counsel close. Yet his moods changed as often as the stars. He acted as if the realm owed him something – as if *I* owed him something. I could not understand what he expected from me.

Cillus was the third – or Cyloth, or whoever he was. The bald, gap-toothed fool never fought in our raids. He roamed the corpse-scattered killing grounds, collecting flesh and metal scraps, murmuring his ditties and rhymes. *They puts it down, I picks it up.*

The fool found time to cobble together punch knives for Kaddarar, their blades as long as my arms. Once, while battling at our side, the Seeker stopped and consulted with Cillus. She tramped away when our clash with the enemy had reached a fever pitch – just when she was needed most. Hours later she trudged back to our camp with a stranger's liver, his lover's bloody kerchief, the molars of thirteen dead wilding aelves, and wolfsbane which had blossomed under moonless skies. She gave all this to Cillus for his curse-wrighting, then disappeared.

I permitted this. Kaddarar was a wild force I no longer wished to chain. As for Cillus, I could not decide whether I should regard him and his craft with pity or fear. Each time he caught me watching him, he pointed to his face and mine, then offered a crooked, honest smile – a *child's* smile.

The day came when I realised I adored the simple fool. After that, I kept my distance, watching him no more.

It is strange to look back upon the past and realise I was happy. In the joyful days of the little war, our enemy did not yet understand us.

Neither did I. I understood nothing.

The Season of Flame guttered into the Season of Smoke. The rebel rains came, stinking of brimstone, vitalising the lands. In my youth I'd thought I had seen bizarre things with Varry, but the labyrinthine skeleton of the broken kingdom concealed countless wonders.

Once we uprooted a burning bush for forage and a djinn emerged, begging to grant our wishes. I knew the legends of their caprices and forbade this, but one fool defied me. She haunted us for days after, begging for succour as the djinn devoured her soul. Soon only her shadow trailed us, but even that withered and disappeared. Three days later we crossed another djinn wearing the shape of her, which offered secrets in return for sanctuary. None so much as looked at her.

Another time, I glimpsed the reflection of a drifting mountain in an ancient stepwell. Blue spirit-fire burnt on the metalith's slopes, but only in the water's reflection. I could not decipher the meaning of that azure flame, nor its appearance at dusk and dawn. After the djinn episode, I didn't want to. Not knowing felt better. Safer.

Then, beneath one of Cardand's ruinous high roads, we passed a column of sellswords and silk merchants. Each trader, sergeant and camel was frozen mid-stride, or beside their carts, or still in the saddle. Their eyes were sealed in delectable slumber. As we debated killing them and pillaging their wares, Kaddarar urged us away. We retreated to the surrounding ruins.

Between the pillars beneath the high road, drifting out from ruins between red palms, a colossal head appeared. It floated under the high road, towards the sleeping merchants. Dark smoke billowed from fissures in its cracked wooden mass. Its eyes were smouldering husks. That restless gaze flittered over the sleeping soldiers and merchants, as if reading words in the wrong directions.

The spectral head moved from one mortal to the next. Staring at this eater of dreams, I thought of father's death mask. I wondered if others looked on me and feared me as I feared this creature.

The devil's head departed, and we emerged. But the sellswords, the traders – they were gone. Save for the camels, every mortal beneath the high road had been transmuted into the strangest of things. Rusted needle beds, or drippings of fly-ridden tallow.

That night, sitting with Kaddarar at a campfire, I caught a whiff of her fear. As we ate the meat of the camel we had slaughtered – we had captured the rest – I asked her to explain.

'Why did you warn us?'

She skewered a hunk of seared meat on her punch-knife, tore a chunk from it with her teeth, then chewed. 'Those creatures leave no skulls for Godeater. They leave nothing.'

'What was it?'

Her glittering red eyes found mine. She chose her words carefully. 'Mortal Realms exist beyond Aqshy. But there were other realms before ours, too. Mortal cycles come and go, but the winds of magic are endless. Some beings survive from one cycle into the next. That swollen head was one such creature. Things like these are *powerful*. They're worthy of fear – even among the Chosen.'

I recalled the ghostly devil's head, the doomful smoke billowing around it. I remembered its lawless eyes, unwriting everything they saw.

For a long time, Kaddarar ate in silence. 'People whisper Sigmar wasn't always a god,' she said. 'Many gods are like that – like those heads, older than time. This is the source of their power.'

'What of your gods?' I asked. 'What of Godeater?'

Kaddarar's lips flattened. 'I don't know. I don't.'

That night siege rains fell, hammering at canvas shelters we had raised in Cardand's ruins. The rain stank of acid and burning copper. The roads became mud.

As we waited out the rains, Yron spread rumours. She told the others of totems and rituals which could protect their souls from creatures like the devil's head. She told them of her gods and her twin bulwark: glory and faith.

Totems, prayers, sacrifice. I had been tolerant before but forbade these absurdities. I loathed the idea of any power greater than my own. I scorned superstition. But despite my efforts, in the following days I discovered the mutilated carcasses of long-tongued lizards, or desiccated songbirds. My warriors began to wear necklaces of tiny skulls, tying icons into their braids. Even Jujjar participated, painting goat eyes on his eyelids. He wore bracelets of beads baked from clay gathered at the estates we had plundered.

I could not punish them all. The weaklings craved belief in something bigger than themselves. They were desert ash, tossed around by the Parchward winds, going to places that could only abuse them.

Even Kaddarar mocked them. Kaddarar – our living evidence of the gods' power and their fickle favour. 'Want is a poor fuel for faith,' she said. 'Faith is what the gods want. Not this. Not desperation.'

Even now, years later, I say all faith is desperation. Not a mortal in the realms worships the gods for nothing. Once I had been certain this was why my people, vagrants from cradle to cairn, made for a stronger breed than the Azyrites I had met. Our desires were enormous. Our wants, unsated. In our starving childhoods we had amused ourselves with toys built from refuse. We had struggled to fill our bellies and asked for nothing from the divine. Yet Azyrites like Se Roye and her broad-backed Freeguilders had been born in castles. They beseeched their God-King for trifles – and their God-King provided.

They were weak. We were strong.

Or so I had thought. My warriors' totems and pathetic rituals scrubbed this weary falsehood from my mind, and weeks passed before my scorn faded to indifference.

The River Losh gave shape to the Burning Valley. When I was a child, my mother had told me the river rushes were planted by mythical tree-folk, the *syrwanedd*, children of the Everqueen. She had said the syrwanedd heard their mother's song in their hearts.

Then the day had come when roiling night blacker than the Cursed Skies covered Bodshe. The sun's fire had dimmed, then settled and did not rise. The Everqueen's song faded. Her children were lost. So they came to the Losh to sing their own song. Their fingers sank into the mud, forming roots, and their desolation became them. Their bones became the rushes, their tears the silt-red currents. Whenever I cupped the Losh's waters to my lips, I remembered my mother's story. I thought I could taste the bitter vestiges of the tree-folk's grief.

Under my watchful eye, Jujjar sloshed through a current of knee-high water. Tall rushes blanketed the riverbanks. The mud stank of fecundity. He tossed a meaty toad from his javelin to my feet.

I accompanied Jujjar on his hunts, when I could. Among the others I was unapproachable and anonymous. I did not wish to damage their reverence for me, nor remove my mask. But alone with Jujjar, life was as it used to be. I was human, and we were friends.

Jujjar skewered another toad. 'The Azyrite fool has a tent. Brings it with him wherever we go. He works on something, day and night.'

'The Seeker thinks he'll give her hands again,' I said.

Jujjar brushed sweat from his eyes. 'You believe that?'

'They believe. I don't wager on miracles.'

'Let's kill them both,' Jujjar said. 'Hang them from Cardand's road signs as examples.'

I chuckled. 'If we killed everyone you wish to kill, we would have no warband. It'd just be you and me. Perhaps you miss your cage.'

Jujjar scowled. 'The man who caged us sleeps in our camp at night,' he spoke, in Azyrite. 'You let him live. Not me.'

'I gave him sanctuary.'

Jujjar hurled his javelin. A toad screeched. Then he swivelled.

'What're we doing? This war's supposed to be for *our* people. *Our* vengeance. Now foreigners walk our camps. Traitors and fools and pagan fanatics.'

'We fight,' I said. 'We take our revenge together. Those traitors and fools and zealots deserve it as much as we do.'

Jujjar halted in the current. He agreed with few of my decisions. After I had killed Adure, he had not spoken to me for days.

'I doubted once,' he said, conquering his reticence. 'I thought our people failures.'

'I remember.'

'The old stories tell of our failings. But they also tell of when the great clans became the great houses. We lost our way. That is what broke Cardand, Held. That is how Bharat was lost. I always thought, what fools they were. At least we know better. But we don't. We're just like them. We enact our own extinction, even now. When will we take what we deserve?'

I crossed my arms. 'I see you've been planning a talk.'

He thrust his javelin into the mud. 'Yes. I have. Because I *believe* again. In us – because of you. Once I was your mentor, and you've always been my brother. Now listen to me as your friend. Give us what you promised, Held. Banish the outlanders. Return glory to the Yrdun. It's only us. Only you, only me.'

Before I could answer, distant song drifted to us through the rushes, over the burbling waters. The lyrics and haunting tune brought me chills. But the ghosts of the syrwanedd had not risen from the riverbanks. I recognised the words, the tune, the flutes and drums and lockstep beat.

Azyrites. An army of them.

We abandoned Jujjar's toads and slogged from the silt and rushes back to our camp. This close, the marching hymns of Azyrite battalions could mean only one thing.

They had come for us.

CHAPTER FIFTEEN

Word of our tireless depredations must have reached the ears of Lellen Se Roye weeks ago. I had assumed her retaliation would be vicious and immediate – these outlands estates were ultimately beholden to her precious Company. When it hadn't come, I had grown complacent. I had thought Se Roye had lumped the outlands into that category of *nothing at all*, like the Ashwilds she wouldn't protect. But now the times of fat and plenty were over.

Six full regiments of mixed mercenary and Freeguild companies with Ironweld support had come for us. Their heavy guns unlimbered across the river. Thick-hulled steam tanks smashed through brick-strewn ruins, tearing down walls for their firing positions. Blocks of infantry deployed, screened by clouds of Derder outriders.

Worst of all, the screeches of well-fed demigryph wings echoed across Cardand. This was an enemy we could not beat.

'Withdraw,' Jujjar said, our fighters hustling around us to break camp. We stood in a crumbling ziggurat overlooking the river. 'This is a battle we cannot win. We have no choice.'

Boskin agreed. 'That's an elimination force. They're here to make a point.'

'So are we,' I growled. The Azyrites concentrated at the river fords, utterly contemptuous of our presence. All this time spent dreaming of vengeance. Now the day had come to enact it and I didn't even know what to do.

Yron's neck stiffened, her grey war-paint refreshed in anticipation of the slaughter. She glowered. 'You're all joking? Has victory made you weak? We've grown fat off easy pickings and lazy triumphs. Now the chance for glory marches across the river, and you want to turn and run?'

'They outnumber us,' Jujjar said. 'They're trained for this. Us, we're skirmishers, raiders at best. Our fighters can't form battle lines. If you need to die for your gods, do it alone.'

Yron spat. 'Slander the gods, but it's not me wearing warding circlets. Death got you all scared, is that it? Death was always part of the bargain. There's no glory in flight.'

She glared at each of us. Clearly, few agreed with her.

Then her lips smoothed. 'You damn Yrdun. Crowing about the fate of your kingdom, and now this. Know what happened to my tribe when your kingdom fell? We fled to the wastes beyond the Ashwilds. You know nothing of the nightmares breeding out there, or the strength it takes to kill them. I'd rather die than turn my back on our enemy and our gods. I'd rather die than lose their eyes. Only *their* strength protects my people, Yrdun. You cowards never did.'

Jujjar twitched.

Yron faced me. 'I cannot return to my people without glory. If you think you can turn and run, you're as stupid as you are craven. The Azyrites will come for your lands. Run, you'll find your place with my people. And if you think we'll be kinder than that army on the Losh, we'll swiftly rouse you from that fancy.'

'You speak Azyrite?' Boskin asked. 'They'll kill us, understand? They'll burn our corpses in the fields.'

Yron's eyes flashed. 'Then *so be it!* So be it.'

Kaddarar loomed over us all, quiet, beautiful, hungry.

I pointed. 'What say you?'

Her red eyes simmered. Her black hair billowed. 'Everything dies,' she said.

Yron stamped her approval. Jujjar jeered. Boskin chuckled. But only I heard the Seeker's unspoken words.

Somewhere in the ziggurat, Cillus' laughter cracked out like thunder. Men and women fought over water and scraps. The first Azyrite skirmishers waded over the distant fords, clearing the crossing.

This was a test. Whose, I could not say, but I wanted to pass. I met Kaddarar's eye and craved her approval – then the thought of that craving brought me disgrace. Whatever I did today must be for myself. Not for her, not for the others, not for the gods. *Myself.*

I gazed out at the heat-blurred ruins, at the tiny banners flapping beyond the river's red ribbon. What might Varry have done? She would never have been here. She would never have done as I prepared to do.

My eyes meandered along the river, through Cardand's shattered stone bones. 'There's another ford. Two leagues yonder.'

'Damn the fords!' Boskin said. 'Let's slip out the rear. Make them chase us.'

'We're not running,' I said. 'We fight.'

Yron lifted her chin. Kaddarar's lips curled into that pernicious smile.

'I want our fusils here,' I said. 'The rest with me, to the fords. Blades and javelins only. Leave the weakest to hold this temple, with guns. Fire everything, save nothing. Give ground if they assault. But make them think we're holding.'

'A last stand,' Jujjar said.

'A feint, you fool,' Yron corrected.

Boskin craned his head. 'Those Ironweld guns'll pound us to dust.'

'Only a handful will remain,' I said. 'And you, and Kaddarar.'

He narrowed his eyes, wrinkles sprouting in his face. 'You saying we're expendable?'

'I'm saying there's not enough of you to kill.' I grimaced beneath my mask. 'These old stones have withstood the ages, Boskin. What's cannonry to that?'

Boskin peered at the river. 'Reckon we're about to find out.'

I faced Kaddarar. 'Only give ground if you must. Hold. Until you hear my signal.'

She nodded.

'I don't understand,' Jujjar said. 'You flee to the fords and call that fighting?'

Kaddarar rose over Jujjar, grit crunching beneath her ironshod heels. He backed away from her, looking up.

'The Godeater's Son will attack their rear,' she said. 'He will be the hammer. We are the anvil.'

Jujjar scoffed. 'Brother, are you mad?' he said, in Yrdo. 'Two thousand of them! Two hundred of us! And the heat! The Season of Smoke is dying. The Season of Flame returns!'

'The high swelters are still weeks off,' I said. 'The march'll hurt, yes. We will thirst. Some may die. But that is just part of our advantage. Today we achieve the impossible. They'll never see it coming.'

Everyone fell silent. Then Boskin grinned, loading his pistols, his lopsided moustache hanging over his gorget.

'Ah, the impossible. Man, why didn't you just say so?'

Blessed are the furious, for they shall inherit the realms.

A priest of Candip's cathedral told me that. For so long, I

thought the words senseless and hollow. All war is travail and battle. All battle is misery and luck. Fury is passion, and passion must be reined in. A good warrior's heart is ice, her hands frigid. In the hacking butchery of the press, champions are less useful than farmers. The moil of slaughter is like scything down grain.

But the priest was not wrong. As our remaining warriors snapped off scattered fusillades, I led the bulk of my fighters through Cardand's ruins. We snaked along the Losh. Aqshy's heat hammered us. I did not mount Micaw, not yet. The others ran, and so would I. I needed her strength for our charge.

We crossed the fords, then circled back. Exhaustion overtook me, and nausea swelled in my chest. Time ran like molten nickel. But each moment I thought of resting, I looked around and saw my fighters close behind me. They followed me, to death and glory. I could not let them down. I dug deep into the core of me, for fuel to keep going. I found no ice – only fury. Fury at the life I had lived, at the occupiers who had forced it upon me. Fury at my sister's death and the Azyrites' wilful neglect.

We arrived with haggard breathing and burnt-dry muscles, but our envelopment paid off. For the Azyrites, we had indeed accomplished the impossible. We smashed through their pathetic rearguard. Then I mounted Micaw and gave the order to topple their artillery into the river.

But the Ironweld gun crews were adept and swift. Their clever captain, a gruff child of nobility with a broad-brimmed hat, turned half his ordnance against us. The remaining pieces pounded my warriors in the ziggurat, just as Boskin had predicted they would. The ziggurat held for now, but I needed to close the noose. Artillery held my reserves at arm's reach. I needed to relieve the pressure on them.

As Helblaster Volley Guns turned on us, we dithered before the black hole gazes of their muzzles. Each weapon was a marvel of cast metal, like pipe organs loaded from the breech. Their captain implored his frantic crews to fire, but their hands were shaking. Our presence had shocked them. That panic would not last long.

I hacked the captain down, circling before the Helblasters on Micaw's back. Before the Azyrites' wall of cannonry, I urged my warriors forward, but their courage flagged.

I knew then we had failed. Jujjar had been right. We were not prepared – *I* was not prepared.

Then, a miracle. Our youngest fighter surged forward, a boy with malice lining his eyes, and courage. His wild war cry spooked the crew of the closest volley gun. They fled, and he closed, locking his sweating hands around the gun's steaming barrels. He pushed. Shoving and howling, the boy sent the unlimbered gun disappearing over the edge of an escarpment, into the Losh. The crashing cacophony of its impact echoed back, and all our fears fled us.

We charged. After destroying the artillery, we smashed into the Azyrites' rear. At the same time, Kaddarar led a doomful charge from the ziggurat. That open road should have been a killing ground, but our storm of javelins sowed confusion among the Azyrites. Attacked from both sides, they must have feared they were outnumbered.

Confused, their serried ranks melted into an ungovernable rout. If their Freeguild demigryphery had been there, things might have been different. But the host's naive commander had sought to embark on a long flank, as I had. His knights went the wrong direction up the river, where no fords existed for miles. The Azyrites did not know these lands – because they were not theirs.

Order. That is the great lie of the Azyrites and their God-King. At the Losh I showed them the truth, one I would soon discover for myself.

Slaughter is a thankless task. We cut down enemy soldiers as farmers scythe down wheat, as miners dig for ore. We plucked hapless crewmen from bogged-down steam tanks and tore them limb from limb. We severed hands heavy with rings and filled the Azyrite baggage train's carts with them.

These days, when the smallfolk whisper of my massacre on the Losh, hoary drunks and educated cynics doubt. They mock the figures as an exaggeration. Two hundred savages could not have defeated a trained army ten times its size.

Let them whisper all they want, for we alone know the truth.

The priest of Candip was not wrong.

CHAPTER SIXTEEN

In the highlands over the Burning Valley's rift, my champions hunkered in the knots of a massive whitewood tree. The tree jutted from the craglands like an ivory spur, a mountain in its own right. Beyond, the rugged horizon basked beneath the void's lonely blue.

I wondered if the Azyrites had discovered their dead on the Losh. The charnel heaps of them, handless, hopeless and blind. I hoped it would awaken terror in them, as it had in me.

Victory conjures many feelings. Yet hiding in that exultant tapestry is a silver thread, grim and caustic, a worm in the soul.

Shame.

The Losh was the first time I made a river run red with the blood of my enemies. That shamed me. My execration for the Azyrites shamed me; their ignominious deaths shamed me. Every moment of the slaughter on the Losh had brought me pleasure – and I was ashamed of it. Every true warrior knows of what I speak. To look upon the broken body of one's foe, to see one's hands and blades reddened with their extinction – this is a sobering feeling.

At the Losh, when the smoke and screams cleared the battlefield and we knew we had won, we had showed not an ounce of magnanimity. We had butchered the Azyrites' camp followers. Cooks, smiths, laundresses, engineers. Their children we had spared as tribute to Cardand's merciless wilds, to survive or not by their own strength and will.

That was justice. And more than was given to me.

But now I suspected we all felt as I did. The Losh had made us from stalkers into slayers, from vultures into wolves. But we'd had no time to ponder the river's fresh crimson and its ripples in us. We'd been forced to take flight. If Candip had mustered her army following a handful of scattered raids on outlands manors, I couldn't imagine what her response would be after a triumph as terrible as the Losh. The demigryph orders still roamed, too, and I would not furnish those knights and their beasts with our tired meat.

So we had fled to the rocky brim of the Burning Valley. Minus the smattering of our honourable dead, we had found refuge on the whitewood. We were battered, bloodied, hungry. We were proud. The enemy would not underestimate us again – that was some minor jubilation.

But it was daunting, too. The Azyrites knew what we were capable of. New futures now opened before us, like savannahs prowled by mythic beasts and perils unknown. I didn't know where to go from here, or how. I couldn't say which was worse – the shame or the uncertainty. Nothing was so frightening as victory.

We had no grain for porridge, no water to wash with. Boskin had had the foresight to load up our akwag on the pack animals, but our other provisions were gone. Our bellies were empty, our spirits low, our humours festering.

So when the silence on the whitewood finally chipped at my calm, I ordered a feast. Soon we had no pack animals but much meat. The aromas of charcoal and seared flesh permeated eventide's coolness.

Yet even with this, I knew joy could not burn without bellows and fresh air. Once I had detested my fighters' friendship, but now they were my killers. If they could kill for me, then why should I not live for them?

I wandered the massive whitewood boughs and the campfires we kindled in their knots. I extolled each fighter's courage; they gloried in my praise. Where I walked, revenants returned to life. I learned much from them. The freckled youth who saved us against the Helblaster battery was called Marder Mosh. His twin sister teased him as we spoke. Intrigued, I prised at the mystery of their past, as commanders perhaps should. I wanted to know.

This continued through the night. For the first time, the warband was one. One force, with one purpose, and one mind.

By the time I returned to my retinue, exhaustion peeled at the corners of me. Yet I owed them as much as the others. Yron, Jujjar, Boskin – the day had taken a toll on us all. Even Boskin had nearly been killed when a mutineer tried to siphon our akwag and flee. He had shot her dead after she slashed at his arm. He called this wound his patents of nobility.

Boskin brandished his camp knife, charred meat on its tip. 'Earl Boskin. That's what you'll all call me from here on out. Royal quartermaster. Yeah?'

'You're not an earl,' Jujjar said.

Boskin shrugged. 'Baron then. Or... Supreme Qual. Point is I'm a lord. You aren't.'

Yron prodded. 'You haven't the belly for lordship. You need a belly, a great belly. Round, hanging over your belt.'

Boskin swallowed a chunk of meat. 'Oh, milady. I do what I can. Our vittles aren't so sumptuous, but I'll try, yes I will.'

Jujjar tossed back a bottle of firewine, scowling. He had always abhorred liquor. Yet after surviving the impossible, the time seemed to have come to re-examine his old spite.

Yron raised a beaten chalice she had pillaged on the Losh. 'Jujjar is pickling himself.'

'All he speaks of is titles,' Jujjar sneered. 'Titles, titles, titles. What do you fight for?'

'Lovers,' Boskin said. 'Plunder. Like any good lord. Or lady.'

Yron chuckled. 'To lovers and plunder.'

'Aye.' Boskin gnawed at his grilled meat.

Jujjar shook his head and grumbled.

My mouth ached from the falseness of my smile. Somewhere, somewhen, my friendliness had slipped away. Fellowship had exhausted me.

'There'll be no more nobility if we beat the Azyrites, Boskin,' I said. 'Even for you.'

'Well, even your people had great houses.' He pinched the air. 'Just gimme a wee one. An itty-bitty one.'

'The great houses failed us,' Jujjar said. Firelight gleamed on the studs pocking his bitter face, like an insect's many eyes.

Yron faced me. 'What else would you do? If we win?'

I pondered, then shrugged. 'I'm not sure.'

Jujjar leaned back. 'Give them what they gave us.'

'Maybe not all of them,' said Boskin. 'They aren't all feasting in Candip.'

Meat hissed and spat over the flames, but no one said another word. Tribal hymns rose from another of the whitewood's nooks. I gazed at the welkin over Cardand. Beneath that star-punctured void, Candip was a distant conflagration, a band of lurking light beneath the blurs of chained metaliths. On the Losh, life had felt so final. Now all was unwritten.

Boskin waggled his knife. 'You ever wonder how things might be? Were we in their place, and them in ours? Kaddy calls you

Godeater's Son. But what if you were the God-King's Son? What would you do on their side of the valley?'

'Against you?'

Boskin nodded. The others watched.

It was an ambuscade of a question, as surprising as they came. But what would life have been like, raised by Candip's lords, or in the palace-keeps of Hammerhal? Who would I have been? The Yrdun would have been strangers. I wouldn't have seen the injustices against them. I might have even felt as Elene Se Roye had, that Sigmar's serfs – *my* folk – had come to enlighten the 'savages' of Cardand. The realm would have seemed so different.

The silence lingered, allowing my mind to wander. For a breathless moment, I was no longer a disgraced Ashstalker on a nickering horse with reddening eyes. I was a knight stroking the neck of his crooning demigryph. I was a broad-shouldered man banqueting in castle halls, not this unwashed wretch who had gnawed at the ends of boiled bones. I could smell the perfume. I felt serge and silk on my soft, soft skin. My family was alive, even prosperous.

Why hadn't life been like this? Who had made it this way? It wasn't the Azyrites. They had scavenged the carrion of our kingdoms, but they had not broken them. Who was really to blame?

'I would have killed you all by now,' I said.

The others nodded, chuckling.

'I was thinking just the same thing,' Boskin said. 'If only Se Roye knew what imbeciles you all were.'

Yron laughed so hard she couldn't breathe. Boskin thought she was choking. She slapped his hands, shooing him away. She rolled over, breathless with laughter, pounding the wood.

The night continued like that. Later, swaying with the liquor that filled his belly to his eyes, Jujjar pulled me closer. 'Your sister, Varrianala,' he said. 'Where is she?'

The night's joys had felt invincible, but Jujjar's question finally vanquished them. I brushed him off and departed to rest. We'd all earned that, and the others seemed to think I had most of all. But Jujjar's question echoed between my ears.

Varry. Where was she?

Jujjar did not know she was dead, but it was not her death that disquieted me. All the folk of Aqshy knew life did not end after death. In Shol, called *Shyish* in the elder tongue, myth spoke of black pyramids and the gheists of the gracelessly dead. Maybe Varry was there, wandering fields of grey asphodel, seeking our father as Kaddarar had once sought me. Maybe she awaited me in peaceful repose. Or maybe daemons had devoured her soul and spared her the torment of forever.

Maybe, maybe, maybe. All those maybes, and not one which could fill her absence.

I searched for Kaddarar. Our victory owed as much to her as me or Marder Mosh. The Seeker had led the charge from the ziggurat, into enemy lines bristling with halberds and handguns. I understood the nature of her god and hoped the day had quenched her thirsts.

Yet she had not celebrated with us. Since I had attended to the others, I decided the Seeker deserved the same. And I wanted to see her face.

I couldn't find her. But Cillus was by his canvas tent at the base of the whitewood's trunk, tucked in its titanic roots, toiling away. Micaw whickered at my approach. I stroked her mane and kissed her brow. Cillus worked in the light of a potted furnace, worrying at dark metal with sooty fingers.

'Kaddarar?' I said.

'She sleepses. New hands. Very tired.'

'New hands.' I chuckled. 'You're mad, you know.'

He huffed on his metal, burnished it with his sleeve. 'I thinks so too.'

I gazed at the object of his attention. The black iron breathed in his hands, its surface rising and falling like the breast of a sleeping babe, glowing with strange heat. The metal reeked of blood.

Cillus prodded at it with bare fingers, then turned it over like clay. His eyes scrunched.

I would never understand him. 'That for her too?' I asked.

'No. For you.'

I groaned. 'I don't want your curse-metal, Cillus.'

'You doesn't choose.'

I glowered at his defiance. But when I looked into his eyes, I saw only the honesty of a simple man.

I crouched. 'I do choose, Cillus. *I* choose. Not you, not anyone else. I alone choose. And I choose no.'

Cillus clucked his tongue, as if belabouring the obvious. 'Their eyes is upon you. You doesn't choose. They chooses.'

'Scorch their eyes!' I slapped the back of his head.

Cillus grinned, biting his tongue. 'Yes.'

My hackles rose. 'So you know the Dark Gods' will?'

'Mm.'

'Even Godeater?'

He glanced up.

'So? What does he want?'

Cillus' eyes flittered. He moaned, as if I had asked a question without answer. Then he returned to his labour.

Chills ran up my neck. 'Cillus.'

He looked up again. Knowing, seeing, brooding. Thinking, musing, weighing. He hoped I would understand without him speaking a word. Because there were no words, I suspected. Not for this.

Then, he farted.

I recoiled. 'Damn fool.' I stumbled off, alone.

Thus the night ended. So did the magisterial wonder of Chaos.

At that time, I thought I already understood you from everything everyone had told me. Kaddarar, Yron. Even Elene, in her fearful way. Years would pass before I discovered the truth in Cillus' quiet. You were never the god I loathed. You were something less. Something more. A beginning, but also an end.

CHAPTER SEVENTEEN

Things changed after the Losh. Azyrite caravans moving between Candip's outlying fiefs disappeared. So did the toll collectors and millers, the wandering tinkers and menders. Lords ransacked their own outlands estates, then returned to Ulcarver in Candip with their doors, shutters and chattel. Often we broke down the barricaded doorways of a country manor only to learn from the vagrants who had become its stewards there was nothing left to take.

I left this dross of humanity to their windblown existence. We could still pillage the estate fields and livestock, I thought. But always the kine were slaughtered, their meat spoilt, their bones broken, their hides rent to shreds. The fields were smoking barrens, burnt to char. Nothing was left for us.

Fair markets dotted the Burning Valley. These Azyrite bazaars gravitated around their rural churches, with little worth taking and nothing worth guarding. They began to disappear, too. When we tried to raid them, we found the Azyrite hamlets emptied, their wares removed. The destitute and lamed smallholders left behind told us Candip's soldiers had come with a decree to relocate to Candip. Trade in Cardand, it seemed, was now forbidden without a market charter. Such charters required Se Roye's seal. All were issued in Candip.

This was a new kind of war, one I had not expected. Major commerce had always taken place in Candip – wool, hide, steel, enchantment, wine, often traded wholesale. But smaller lots and finished goods – clothing, shoes, implements, provender – were once commonly sold in Cardand's settlements. Without the local merchants, the valley's rural economy stagnated. We had nothing to pillage and nowhere to replenish our stores.

After the Losh, Se Roye had changed tack with a drastic wind. We had made war on Azyrite lords and seneschals, but their smallfolk had been our lifeline. Food became precious. Even our silent allies among the Yrdun and Beltollers could offer no succour nor sanctuary – they barely had enough to feed themselves.

Meanwhile, displaced refugees filled Candip's defensive tracts. In the light of their burning palisade, under the aegis of their gun-bristling cogforts, camps emerged, overcrowded and disease-ridden – but under Candip's control. Beyond those tracts, heavily armed Azyrite patrols surveyed the low roads and high roads to Candip's largest fiefs: walled castle-towns which could not, need not be abandoned. The Azyrites were constricting us.

I was astonished. I'd known Se Roye was shrewd, but I'd thought her ilk too greedy to cut their incomes and suffocate their holdings' prosperity to defeat wretches like us. This seemed out of Se Roye's character, or at least the one I had imagined for the woman who once reminded me of the blazing sun of midday's swelter. Yet it was utterly effective. Our provisions dwindled. I considered turning our blades on our miserable kindred who remained in Cardand's ruins. But that was what Se Roye wanted. To make me

desperate, to divide my warband from those we depended upon –
to turn the Yrdun and Beltollers against us.

We could have taken what we needed from those who remained
in the valley, beyond Candip's aegis. We could have chalked it up to
necessity. Yet such a solution would have solved today's dilemma
at the price of tomorrow's curse. I could not ruin our reputation
amongst those who had suffered as I had. We were brethren in
suffering, if nothing else. This bond was more sacred than blood.

So I changed tack, too. I sent foragers into the craglands rim-
ming the Burning Valley, into the heat-blurred Ashwilds. The
Season of Flame was upon us. We needed secure lines of provi-
sion before the realm turned against us, as it always did.

My foragers returned with handfuls of scrawny tubers or the
meagre carcasses of ashfawn and stray ungors. We boiled this
meat in reeking water, living like wastrels.

Of all the souls I sent to Whittale's End, none returned.

Whittale's End was a hamlet ten leagues from scorched Lurth.
Saddles and gulleys filled the country between there and Candip.
The Azyrites possessed easy traverse to the hamlet, if they desired
it. But I had heard no word of their passage. If they had killed
my foragers, I couldn't fathom why they would bother to protect this place.

With those I trusted, I pondered my options. Our fire blazed,
and we chewed on pitiful nourishment. Soaked saplings of willowy
cacti. The husks of winnowed grain, stewed into thin porridge.

Yron stirred her broth. 'Might be other marauders. Tribes prowl
the Ashwilds. If times are hard there, they might have come into
the valley. They could have killed our people at Whittale's End.'

'They're not our enemies,' I said.

'Says you. Friendship is… relative. Glory matters. Glory comes
from any victory. Those tribes will see you as a rival.'

'Parchers, too,' Boskin said. 'Wars up there something fierce. Hammerhal's enemies flee that city and follow the Paleward Winds. Crossing seas and deserts and mountains is nothing if it means fresh prey. Look. Here comes one now.'

Heads turned. Kaddarar mostly kept to herself, rarely speaking, and then only with Cillus – yet here she was. She had removed her armour, and a snug surplice hugged her impressive figure. A cord of sinew bound her kempt jet hair behind her skull. She was...

Pretty. Beneath the armour and the helm and the flames that war lit in her eyes, Kaddarar the Seeker was beautiful. A blade-wife, with siege rams for legs and a wyrd impenetrable to my knowing. But fetching.

Jujjar gaped, but not at her beauty. '*That* is your fool's fabled craft? A curse-wright, I'd heard. But I could've made you better hands with the rubbish in Candip's gutter!'

Kaddarar glanced at the ends of her wrists. Her punch-blades were gone. Two uneven lumps had replaced them, coal-black and rocky, like clubs.

She shrugged. 'They're not finished. You summoned me for counsel.'

Yron scowled, her neck stiffening. 'No one summoned you.'

Kaddarar turned her red quartz glare on Yron. 'Still pretending to walk the Path, I see.'

Yron snatched her axe. 'You don't scare me, Bloodbound.'

Kaddarar's nostrils flared. She cocked her head. 'Then why do you stink of fear?'

'*I* summoned her,' I said, interrupting their petty dispute. 'If you have counsel, I'll hear it.'

Kaddarar's gaze stabbed at me. 'Stop doing what the enemy wants you to do.'

'*Pah!*' Jujjar stalked off, muttering all the curses of our tongue. I gestured. 'What do they want me to do?'

'Distract yourself with frivolous matters. It's the city, Godeater's Son. The city must be your target. That is where your blood tithe lies.'

'We can't take Candip.' Boskin avoided Kaddarar's gaze. 'Not with two hundred. Unless you brought a host with you, Kaddy.'

'Two hundred is more than enough. The gods give their blessings to the worthy. So *prove* your worthiness. Through sacrifice. Bargain for their power, and they shall provide it.'

Yron's eyes flashed at me. 'Heed nothing she says.'

I waved. 'We've nothing to sacrifice. That's the problem.'

'You have the only thing worth sacrificing,' Kaddarar said. 'It matters not from where the blood flows.'

Oh.

The fire crackled. I couldn't believe my ears. No – I certainly could. Kaddarar was a fanatic. But to sacrifice good warriors' lives? For what, meagre boons of strength? War flames in the sockets of my eyes?

I shook my head. 'I'll not enslave myself to your Godeater. I won't walk your Path. There must be another way.'

Kaddarar gazed long and hard. In her face, I saw much unspoken. Disgruntlement, ire – but strangely, no malice. I had seen this look in Varry's eyes before, too. I braced myself for calumnies, for accusations. *You're hiding behind your warband,* she would say. *Behind your father's face. Cowering in Cardand's outlands…*

You are craven.

Instead, Kaddarar turned and left. 'How do they get anything done?' she grumbled, disappearing into the terrain and the burnish of sunrise.

Boskin raised a finger. 'Here's an idea.'

'If it's sacrifice, you'll be first on the fires,' Yron said.

'Nah, queen majesty. I'm with the king on this. Gods ask a bit much. They don't give half as much as they take.' The Derder brandished an oil rag in one hand and his dismantled pistol in the other. 'Suppose there's foes in Whittale's End. We do have to fight them, yeah?'

'Not for the gods,' I said.

'Right. But if it is marauders – and we can all agree it's probably not Freeguilders or mercenaries, since there's nothing there worth protecting – maybe you can make liegemen of them? Add their strength to yours, yeah?'

I looked to Yron.

'It could work,' she said. 'All tribes respect strength.'

'And strength we need,' Boskin said. 'Kaddy wasn't wrong about that, was she?'

Flames danced in the crevices of our burning logs. 'You know the Ashwilds marauders?' I asked Yron.

'Some of them.'

I nodded. 'Then let's do it. You'll come with me. No more wringing our hands over this. Boskin, stay here, keep the warriors disciplined. I don't want harm done to locals. And see that Jujjar stops souring.'

'Quite a task there. But I'll give it a go.'

Boskin finished cleaning his pistols. Yron departed to gather warriors. The stones in the firepit hissed, and my hollow belly whined. If any in the warband slept that day, they were stronger than I was. But then, it was not for strength they slept.

At dusk Yron and I marched with forty warriors to deal with the menace of Whittale's End. We kept to low ground so we wouldn't silhouette ourselves against the sky. The journey was long but easy. Azyrites didn't fight the way we fought, so I anticipated no ambuscades.

Still, I imagined threats behind every boulder. Aelvish Wanderers who might waylay us, or a sudden charge of the mythical duardin slayers who wore nothing but the oath-runes they pounded into their flesh. The Azyrites' legends played games in my mind. Kaddarar was right: Lady Lellen's ploys had got to my head.

Soon jagged gullies gave way to smooth stone channels. I left fighters at the mouth of this traverse, who watched Micaw. My steed snorted, loath to see me go. After the Loth we had grown closer. I stroked her muzzle, wondering if the loss of innocence had brought us together. I admired the scales bulging beneath her hair, the reddening shade of her pupilless gaze. I kissed her and we parted ways.

One by one we moved in the shaded channels, walking on raised slabs between rifts of long-hardened earthfire. Burgeoning flames in the sky roared like distant thunder. The lands' smell reminded me of a Candip bakery, crumblebread rising within an open oven.

'What?' Yron asked.

'Nothing. My stomach, playing tricks on me.'

Yron grunted, running her hand-axe over the wall. 'See these?'

I glanced at the relief carvings clicking beneath her axe-head. They were ancient images captioned in indecipherable cuneiform.

'The Azyrites' legends,' I said. 'Whittale's End was their first settlement in Bodshe.'

Yron craned her head at the wall, her war braid dancing with each step. 'I thought they stole everything they had.'

'Not everything. You've seen what they build.'

'Thought they stole that, too.' She faced me. 'How do you know their legends?'

I touched my mask. Yron knew me well, but like everyone else, I tended to keep her at arm's length.

But not today. 'My mother told me,' I said. 'She used to tell us their stories. She loved them. Loved their God-King.'

Yron fell quiet. 'Enough surprises for one day,' she said. 'Didn't think you had a mother.'

Mirthless, I chuckled. 'What'd you think?'

'You never take off the mask.'

I halted, letting others move past. 'You, what? Thought your gods sent me? That I was born from ash and blood?'

I saw the wounded faith in Yron's painted eyes. She ran her fingers over her shaved temples, deflated. 'You needn't mock. You smell bad, like us. Eat like us. But... so what if I hoped? That we'd earned it, and they'd help us?'

My face smoothed in sympathy. Yron believed in me. And if I didn't believe as she did, it was only because I believed in nothing.

We continued. The loaded quiet of the hills pressed in on us, and wild birds cawed and shrieked on the horizon.

'Twice I was a mother,' Yron said. 'Both accidents. But my people have no midwives, Yrdun-son. My boys pulled themselves from my womb. They were born champions.'

'Good. Bring them here.'

'They're dead,' she said, a tremor in her voice.

I looked back. 'Forgive me, Yron.'

'It's not you who took them. The shamans told me I was too weak for motherhood. I didn't listen. But at least I could fight. A mother's strength and a warrior's strength. Same, I thought, but also different. I came from the wastes to save my people, Yrdun-son. But I could not save my sons.'

'I understand your pain.'

'No, you don't. You haven't loved. You've not bred. You don't know what it is, holding the realm in your hands, listening to it cry for your dried-up, wasted teat. You've not felt their ash sift through your fingers from the ritual fires. My boys' deaths brought us blood-manna from the sky, Yrdun-son. But I did not wish it.'

Yron had sacrificed everything for her Path to Glory. For her tribe. I understood, then, why she had opposed Kaddarar. I wondered what sacrifices had brought the Seeker this far, to Bodshe.

'I wish it was me instead of them,' Yron said. 'I wish they were here with you, and not me. Whoever you've lost, can you say that? Can you?'

That, I could not answer.

Whittale's End was no hamlet.

'A temple.' I exhaled pure amazement. The settlement spiralled into Aqshy's crust, augured from sheer stone. Arched edifices and carved stairs reminded me of Cardand's ancient stepwells. A union of masonry and geometric perfection, nothing like I had ever seen. Sigmar's lightning sigils adorned the open doorways at every level.

'Something at the bottom,' a warrior growled.

'Something here, too.' Yron retrieved a broken maul-axe, its wood splintered, its obsidian teeth scattered like coins. 'Maybe we were wrong. Maybe the Azyrites defend their holy places.'

'I see none now.' I stared into the temple settlement's depths. 'You smell that?'

Yron nodded. 'The blood stink. Like copper.'

We descended along the pit's shaded spirals, gravel crunching beneath our heels. Whittale's End resembled a tiered strip mine. At the bottom, a second pit lay below the first, carved rifts in the stone separating them. A skylight.

With hands and knees, we climbed down a steep stair, our weapons clutched precariously. A market forum lay in the cooling darkness below the delved temple. Like all of Cardand's settlements, it was abandoned. Trade stalls were shuttered or dismantled. Wares not valuable enough to be pillaged or removed were piled and half-burnt.

The underground forum continued in every direction, into the edgeless dark. Near a branching passage, bodies filled the ground.

Yron wrinkled her nose. 'Ratmen. Grot-kin. Old gods, this is repellent.'

I had never seen skaven before, nor greenskins. Ancient tales told they were no more than diminutive pests, but they were wicked things, bigger than I had imagined. A warrior thrust his javelin into the mangy barrel-chest of one of the skaven, and another hacked at a grot's dagger-nosed skull. The death-reek which spilt from their corpses made me retch.

Yron lifted her boot, looking at her heel. 'Days old. They must have come before our foragers.'

I kicked a ratman over, staring at its scorched fur. 'So they didn't kill ours.'

Yron shook her head. 'But something must have. Either that, or they deserted.'

I crouched, gazing at the massive hammer-imprint which had crushed one of the pestilent ratkin into the stone. 'I do not think they deserted.'

'Godeater's Son,' a warrior called, from deeper in the darkness.

We picked our way to him, to a simple Azyrite shrine. Gold candlesticks covered an altar, each topped with a melted-down lump of wax. On the altar's dais, electricity crackled in silver fili-grees, the last of its power now fading.

As I surveyed the scene before the shrine, I inhaled sharply. Whatever had killed the rats and greenskins had killed our people, too. For here they were, the dozen of them, laid out in the carnage like diamonds in the chaff. Death extracted a gruesome toll on the mortal form, but these were not the broken piles of torn flesh those disregarded skaven and grots had been.

My dead warriors had been washed. They smelt of oils. I could not see what wounds had killed them – tight linen bandages swathed their torsos, limbs and heads. Their mummies were knelt before the altar as if in prayer. Their heads were bowed, their hands clasped. They were still.

We gathered around them. My stomach turned at the stink of incense burning in sand-filled vases positioned amongst the dead. As a boy, I had seen this ritual before, at funerals in the outskirts of Cardand. My mother used to promise I would pass from the realm with such ceremony. Elevated, transcendent.

The others circled, rattling blades against stone statuary in the shrine, or prodding our dead as if to awaken them. One collapsed into pieces, and his head rolled to my feet. Great care had been taken to reassemble him into the prayerful pose.

Yron turned. 'I don't understand.'

I did. At the Losh we had desecrated the mountains of our enemy's dead. We had severed their hands and crushed their flesh into dust and rubble. We had reddened the river with the pieces of them. We had laughed.

Whoever had avenged them here, they had committed no such horrors. They had honoured our fallen as they might have honoured their own. My warriors had been Reclaimed – in death, if not life.

And that putrid magnanimity gnawed at the core of me.

CHAPTER EIGHTEEN

I stormed back in anger and shame. The scene at Whittale's End was insult to injury. It was pure scorn – my own or another's. Someone was taunting me. Someone was *mocking* me. All I wanted was to tear them apart.

When we returned to the site of our encampment, my warband was gone. Then I saw the bodies. Corpses, mostly Candip mercenaries, their jackets thick with battalion sigils and regimental markings.

We followed this grim trail deeper into Cardand. I buckled from hunger, but rage filled me. The old kingdom's ruins clawed up around us like mountains.

Soon the trail of the dead led to a wondrous stepwell within the ancient city. It was a pit like Whittale's End, as if the negative space of a ziggurat had been carved into the hard earth. The tiered stairs descended to a deep basin of olive water which stank of algae. A dark doorway led into the stone near the water. The stepwell seemed paltry compared to the delved temple of Whittale's End.

Where had Cardand's ancient masons learned the arts behind their elder works? I dared not ask.

A picket line of Ashstalkers let us through. My fighters washed in the low basin, drinking their fill, or dozing on the stone stairway. Others stirred and cheered at our arrival. As they laughed and bantered, sputtering hot meat turned on bent spits over timid flames. The warriors sipped milk-white tea and tore hunks from marching bread pillaged from the mercenary dead.

I handed Micaw off to Boskin to be watered and fed. Kaddarar sat on the upper lip of the stepwell, her muscled torso enshrined in her breastplate. She kicked her heels against the stone like a child. She was eating. Her coal hands gripped a human femur. Her fingers – eight to each hand – ground as they moved around the bone like a spider's skittering legs.

Beside her were the chains that had once bound her. They were coiled into piles, ending in the reforged heads of her old axes. Cillus' savant hands had worked them into bladed mauls. Together with the chains, they made for wildly long flails. The heads were slick with gore, their nooks and crevices studded with chips of bone.

Kaddarar ripped a hunk of meat off and passed it to me. I had been angry, then afraid, but the sight of food pushed all that away.

I snatched the meat from her disconcerting fingers, then wolfed down a bite. 'What happened?' I asked through a mouthful.

'Azyrites came. We killed them.' Kaddarar swept her arms across the camp. 'And now, we have meat.'

I stopped chewing. I peered at the fighters deeper in the step-well, already sharing food with the other arrivals. I glanced at the femur in Kaddarar's hands, imagining how it fitted into a human hip socket. A gruesome surfeit – but satiating. Once cannibalism might have disgusted me. Now I felt only relief. We had been hungry and no longer were. It seemed simple.

Kaddarar related what had happened. The Azyrites had fallen upon our camp. Jujjar and Boskin had meant to stand and fight, but Kaddarar had seized command. Of all things, she had ordered a fighting retreat. Each time the mercenaries had closed, my warriors had broken their formations with a javelin volley and an unexpected charge. Then our fighters had faded into the ruins and the Azyrites had pressed on, mistaking each flight for a rout.

This had continued until my force had whittled down the enemy force to nothing. When the running battle reached the densest part of Cardand's ruins, too thick to navigate without a local guide or the night's leering stars, Kaddarar's moment had come. She had set upon the last of the enemy, killing them all.

She tore another hunk of meat off and chewed. 'Or, almost all of them. But soon it'll make no difference.'

I marvelled. 'You did well. But I thought your god despised deceit?'

'He does.'

'So? What was this?'

Kaddarar stopped chewing and ruminated. 'I'm not sinless. I'm not perfect. But... they say it matters not from where the blood flows. When the Azyrites came, something told me it matters not *how* it flows, either. A voice, from a tall tower of dark light.' She raised her glimmering eyes. A string of jet hair fell into her face. 'A visitation. Godeater spoke to me.'

I chuckled, a conspiratorial smile cracking my lips. 'Survival. That's what I call that.'

Kaddarar regarded me. For a moment, I felt close to her. As close as two mortals could ever come. In that moment, I knew I'd done right not to kill her.

'I look forward to the day one of us kills the other,' she said.

I sighed and continued eating. Our grim meal tasted better

than expected, salted as it was with triumph. 'You make this all up as you go, don't you?'

'Not at all. Everything I do is preordained. I obey my god's desires.'

I grunted. 'You mentioned enemy survivors. How many?'

'One.'

I raised a brow. If Kaddarar had let a messenger get away, she was cleverer than I thought. Let the Azyrites spread tales of what we could do to them. Let them *fear* us. But then, if she had let one escape, we couldn't linger.

Kaddarar anticipated my concern. 'He didn't get away.' A wicked secret blazed in her eyes.

I furrowed my brow. 'Out with it.'

'I thought so highly of you,' she said. 'I forgot you are as I once was. Mortal. Frail. But I smell bloodlines, Godeater's Son. Yours is rich in iron and shame.'

'And vanishingly rare. I'm the last of my line.'

'No. You aren't.'

I gnawed on a string of human gristle. 'If you really smell my bloodline, you'd know it leads only to Shol. My family's dead.'

'Yes, yes. I know your story. Your burnt croft, your dead family. So tragic. How cruel the realm is.'

'I don't jest,' I said. 'You don't either. My father's dead. My mother's likely dead by now, too. And my brothers and sisters—'

My brow smoothed. They could not all be dead. Kaddarar was serious. I recognised the heat in her eyes – the hate by many names.

'Impossible,' I said.

'He thinks his family is dead, too. Says beasts killed them.' That pernicious smile flowered on Kaddarar's dark lips. 'So tragic. Just like you.'

I tried to remember my siblings, but youth and misery had

buried my past where it could not be found. Still, some things could never be forgotten. Kinship – and love.

If a brother of mine lived, I would do anything for him.

'He's in the water house,' Kaddarar said. 'Deal with him. Or I will.'

Reverent eyes turned as I descended the stepwell's many stairs. Warriors nodded. Some saluted, like Yron. The stepwell basin stank of algae and washed-off blood. Bile rose in my throat, and my heart thudded in my ears. I couldn't fight the poisonous feeling of my own vulnerability. Kaddarar might have mentioned her discovery to the others; Yron could have related our intimate exchange during the journey to Whittale's End.

For so long, I had striven to make my warband fear me. Could they see who I really was, now? Mortal, through the rifts in my mask and the cracks in my soul? With a brother to love, and family to cherish?

The dark doorway at the well's bottom led into an enclosed pumphouse where the prisoner was bound. Ironweld devilry chugged within a nest of cogs and belts and sputtering engines. A furnace powered the contraptions, its flames wheezing with foreign magic. The chamber reeked of sweat and moisture; contradictions seemed to define the dank cell. Fire and water, Azyrite and savage, love and hate.

After I sent the guards away, I had to squint to see the man tied before the furnace. He had freckles and dyed-bright hair. Such dyes were common among the Capilarians in Bodshe, but this man was no Capilarian. His face was cut like mine, his three-day beard coarse like the stubble I shaved.

Yrdun, through and through. My eyes settled in the dimness, and I stared at my cruel reflection.

'You,' he sneered. He was beaten but unbroken. The same could not be said of his ribs or the bones in his swollen cheeks.

'Me,' I said.

'You're the devil they seek. No – devil's a big word for a small man. Brigand king. Heathen. Godeater's Son. Eater of broken meat and human flesh. Sigmar save you, for we won't.'

My lips set into a hard line. Then I removed my mask. In the dim glow of the furnace, surprise flashed in his brown eyes.

'So you are mortal.'

'Aren't all brigands and kings?'

'They say you came from the Cursed Skies. That you were sent to destroy us.'

'The gods wouldn't try so hard.'

'Not your gods. But I'm still right. You're half a man, with half a life. You're not worth the fire in your veins.'

'I would have your name,' I said.

He spat in my face and laughed. The sputum dribbled down my cheek. My eyes wandered over his wasted livery. I stroked his captain's badge.

'Halberdier,' I said. 'Battle line. Candip won't miss you.'

He flinched, eyes blazing. I saw pride. This man – my brother – thought himself more than nothing. One could always smell hubris miles away.

'Tell me what I wish to know,' I said, 'and I'll send word to Candip of your death. I'll tell them you fell with honour.'

He huffed. 'Kill me now.'

'I will not kill an Yrdun-brother.'

He froze, as if daring to hope. 'My name is Tayler Reiriz. Of House Reiriz.'

'Nobility?' I scoffed. 'But you're Yrdun.'

'Our tainted heritage means nothing to the God-King. My father adopted me when I proved my constancy. I saved him in battle against the Kruleboyz clans of Tithamat.'

That was a sobering thought, and it caught me off guard. All

Varry and I had ever known was the Azyrites' indifference. To consider one of our brood had been given a home by my sworn enemy rocked me to my core. Had his Azyrite family loved him, too? Had he loved them?

And if he had – had they deserved it?

I recalled the scene at Whittale's End. Our dead, honoured with Sigmarite ritual. Insurgent hate crawled up the cracks of me. What did it matter if they had loved him, or he them? In the end they had made a weapon of him to use against us – against his own kin. Like everything in the Pale, they had taken him from me. And now that I had him back, I was supposed to… what? Be grateful they had been kind to him?

Generosity came easily for those who had only ever washed in clean waters. If they had shared a shred of their wealth for charity, that did not make them good.

I forced ice into my veins. I doubted Reiriz even remembered our true father.

'What of your blood kindred?' I asked.

He sneered. 'Drake's mercy, what is it with you heathens and my blood? I told the berserker already. They're dead. As you'll soon be.'

I paced, surveying his bruises and tattered livery. He had good arms and legs. He was well fed. 'Why did you attack us?' I asked. 'Foot regiments can't overtake us. You should've known that. Candip's been starving us. Between you and me, it's worked.'

His jaw hardened. 'I know it's damn well worked. I know what you're eating out there, too.'

I sighed. 'Reiriz. Give me reason not to kill you.'

He paused. 'It's the Stormcasts' plan. Scorched earth.'

'The Lord-Imperatant,' I said. 'Ildrid Stormsworn.'

Reiriz seemed surprised. 'The viceroy-regent seeks to smash you and end this war, but the Refuser forbade it. We were sent out without the Stormcasts' knowledge.'

Now I was surprised. I had not expected division in Candip. 'You send heavily armed columns out to your fiefs, too. They patrol the roads. What of them?'

Sweating, Reiriz hesitated.

I tapped my foot. 'Reiriz.'

Shame twisted Reiriz's face into a glum frown. 'Those patrols are sanctioned. To keep you off the roads and unterways, away from the lesser keeps. But Lady Se Roye tires of the Refuser's strategy. Candip's revenues suffer, and the people hunger. I'd thought she was right. We all did.'

The flames in the Ironweld furnace hissed their secrets. Tireless moisture dripped in the dark.

'You're my brother,' I said. 'The berserker smells the common blood in our veins.'

Reiriz raised his eyes. 'That's impossible.'

'It's outlander sorcery. Don't try to understand it.'

'No – I mean my brothers and sisters are dead.'

'Yes. And our father fought to protect us, and our mother, too, with a pan and a knife before Sigmar's lightning took her. It's the same story. We're one in blood and bone, heart and soul.'

Reiriz shook his head. 'Your blood's thin. Your soul, too.' He spat again, a forceless spray. 'My only sister was Greve Reiriz and you tore her limb from limb at the Losh. Wild dogs, eaters of men. You're not my blood.'

I shoved my face into his. 'Look. At. Me.' His breath stank of hunger and a parched throat. 'Look.'

Silence drained Reiriz. Beneath the grind of Ironweld machinery, I could have sworn I heard his blood roaring in my ears.

'Whatever they call you,' I spoke, softly, 'they're your masters, as they would be mine.' I brandished my mask. Acid rains had pitted the metal, and arid blood stained its grooves old green. 'This was our father's. Our true father's, forged to protect his soul from the Nighthaunt. But after he died, we had nowhere to leave it. The beasts had gorged on his flesh. You know the story. I see it in your face, you know.'

Reiriz's eyes flickered, naked and weak. He didn't want to believe. But the truth was volcanic. The truth could not be stoppered, its victims could not be saved.

'You didn't know,' I continued, growing hopeful. 'You didn't care. Maybe you even forgot. But I didn't. So know what my warriors do not, Reiriz – family started this war for me. I fight for family. I fight for *you*.' I gripped his quivering shoulder, so much like mine. 'Fight with me, brother. Live. I'll send word to your house. If your honour be precious, let it be saved. But I'm your blood, boy. Not them.'

He gazed at my hand, then me. 'You don't even know.'

I winced. 'Know what?'

'The Lady-Imperant. She says you've all been led astray. That you can be redeemed and Reclaimed. That you *will* be, in time. The Lady Lellen called it nonsense. But… it's true. You don't even know what you're doing.'

'I told you exactly what I'm doing.'

'No. You call me family. If you truly believe it, then listen – it's you who must turn.' Reiriz's hot breath pumped into my face. 'Only Sigmar's grace protects these lands. I've seen the horrors of Khul's Ravage. I've seen what the greenskins did to the wretches in Tithamat. I've seen how lesser liches steal your people's bones from your cairns to make into wights. Powers like those you fight for will destroy what we've built. And I do mean *we*, heathen. The Azyrites and the Yrdun reclaimed the Pale of Bodshe together. It was a hard fight, and few have forgiven the damage inflicted by your kin – including my father. But look at how this has changed. I'm his son, now. We are not enemies. There's a better path to what you seek.'

I backed away. 'No.'

'*Please.*' His eyes were wide and earnest. 'If you think yourself my family – then end this! The people suffer. *Our* people, for we're all the same. The innocents of Candip, the Parcher smallfolk. My sister – *oh*, Sigmar's mercy, do you know what you did to her? Do you even remember?'

Coldness washed through me. 'I–'

'Don't do it to me too,' he begged. 'Please. *Please*... brother.'

I paced, raking my fingers through my hair. Against my stone certainty, the torch of Reiriz's defiance had been hopeless. But now his words were pickaxes, chipping my convictions apart.

His forge-bellow breaths stirred the stagnant air in the pumphouse. 'I won't turn,' he said. 'Kill me if you will – my censor is paid. But don't do to me what you did to Greve. Don't make me a sacrifice to your Godeater. She was my sister... Greve, oh gods, he doesn't even know what he's done!'

Reiriz sobbed. His wrists pulsed against his bindings. The knots at his wrists creaked, glistening red. My feet were somewhere far, far away, scuffing the stone. I almost raised a hand to comfort him but stopped myself. He was wrong. He was *wrong*.

'I worship no gods,' I said. 'I make no sacrifices. I am–'

'*Then why have the blood rains come?*' Reiriz roared. 'It's you! You did it! You're damning us all!'

CHAPTER NINETEEN

I ordered my fighters to stay clear of the pumphouse when I left. 'Let the Azyrite starve,' I said. 'Let him eat his faith.' They chortled and nodded.

Words were the fellest poison. Reiriz's ran in my veins like quicksilver, hardening into lead, burdening my once guiltless conscience. I had walked into that dank chamber with purpose and scorching fury. I had emerged a feckless warrior in doubt.

I made Cillus inform the others I would not be disturbed. I climbed the stepwell, then clambered up Cardand's bones to the jagged pinnacle of a broken tower. Through the cityscape's dead teeth, the Paleward winds assailed me. My heat wrappings snapped from my wiry body like pennants. The winds whipped the breath from my lungs.

Distantly, the world seemed unchanged. Metaliths were chained to Candip. Cogforts pumped exhaust into the wounded skies. Closer, the same. The redolence of charred flesh wafted up from the stepwell. The laughter of my warriors echoed.

Yet *everything* had changed. I had told Reiriz I fought for family, but the chance to prove that impetus had come and gone. Knowing what fate had awaited my brother, I had done what I must to maintain my warriors' esteem while respecting Reiriz's last wish. To have let my Ashstalkers devour his flesh would have been to let them devour mine.

But I should have let him go.

Cillus scrabbled onto the tower landing. 'She doesn't listen, never listens!'

I hurled sand at him. 'Be gone.'

A mountain loomed behind Cillus, casting her shadow on us both. Kaddarar kicked the fool aside. 'Go, Cyloth. I have blood to spill.'

I rose. 'No, Cillus. You'll bear witness.'

Paralysed with indecision, Cillus paced in the corner. 'He picks it up, puts it down, puts it down, picks it up–'

Kaddarar strode closer, her chains uncoiling, her mauls thudding to the stone. The day's battle damage to her bolted cuirass had already scabbed over. Her unholy hands crunched tight around her flails' chains.

'You killed him,' she spat. 'For *mercy.* You thought to hide your cowardice. But Godeater knows.'

I bared my teeth. 'Come on then. Come on!'

Kaddarar's eyes smouldered, wisps of smoke rising from them. 'Where's his meat? Give me his *meat.*'

'This is not about meat,' I said.

'No. It's about why we do this. Me, the others – *our* purpose is clear. What do you fight for?'

'Family,' I said. 'I gave him a clean end. Threw him in the furnace.'

Her eyes twitched and snapped. She lurched closer. 'Family? That's it? Family?'

I flourished my blade. I was eager for blood, eager to forget. 'Come on!' I shouted.

She shook with rage. 'What's *wrong* with you? I have tried to show you the way. You don't listen! You *never* listen! Do you really treasure family more than the gods? More than Godeater? Family is *nothing!*'

I pointed. '*You're* nothing! Your gods are nothing! The Five, Sigmar – all of you! All curses, all shame! They've made slaves of you and you love it!'

She grimaced, calming, but only for a breath. 'So little you know.'

'I know I can't control you. Or your gods, or the Azyrites. So let's put an end to the myth we were ever on the same side. Let's finish this.'

'Control?' Her eyes contorted in disdain. 'You're that foolish?'

I thumped my falx's hilt into my chest. 'I control what's mine. I control myself. Why shouldn't I? Why should I give the gods anything at all? Reiriz was my brother. Mine.'

'Nothing is yours. Nothing is mine, or anyone's. You should know that by now. Where was your family when the beasts came?'

I clenched my teeth. 'By my side,' I growled.

'No. Your father died running to save his mistress. Your mother abandoned you because you were worthless. Your siblings scattered to the eight winds to save themselves. And your precious sister–'

'*Shut up!*' I dropped my falx, struck her jaw. I had thought I was strong. I had expected her to go down. But striking Kaddarar's jaw was like punching stone. She didn't budge, then butted her head into mine. The world flashed like fire.

Then I was on the ground. Kaddarar crushed her knee into my chest. The febrile heat of her cursed hands scalded my neck as she pinned me to the stone.

'Godeater told me the truth,' she hissed, fire spitting from her eyes. 'Your sister died for a priestess of Sigmar. And when she went, it was with an empty head and drool on her chin. She wasn't thinking of you, boy. Not when the red moon destroyed her body. Not when the gods devoured her soul.'

I groaned and squirmed, but Kaddarar's grip was fast, her rugged fingers spidering around my neck.

'You were supposed to learn,' she said. 'Maybe I was too easy on you. That was my mistake. I'm not perfect. But Godeater will forgive me with this sacrifice. I'll do better next time.'

'*Kadd–*' I gurgled.

'I… AM NOT… KADDARAR!' she roared. 'You mock me as a mindless orruk, warring for the sake of *war!* But I fight for something bigger than you – something bigger than *me!*' Her shoulders heaved with anger, but for another moment she found her calm. 'I was Khotara, heiress to mages and kings. And when Chaos came, my masters thought my sacrifice could save their little lives. *That* is family, boy! They offered me up to the Khul like *meat.* The Khul took me. Then they took my family's skulls and the racks of their ribs and their flanks. For *that* is our value, Fall. Cattle is all we are. Family is just a closer cut of meat.'

Choking, I reached for my blade. Kaddarar slammed my arm.

'The Khul showed me the truth,' she said. 'I learned it again at the Burning Skies. You wanted family? *I* was your family. And Cyloth, and your drunkard kin-brother, and that wilding woman. Even the grubby pistolier. Where is our *meat?*'

She struck me. I groaned.

'WHERE?' she screamed.

She struck me again. My mask fell from my face.

She huffed. 'Look at you. Just another skull.'

Kaddarar had mounted me; her bloodlust ached from her thighs into my belly, a deadly heat. I felt her thirst for blood on my tongue, even craved death myself. I wanted to blame Godeater, as if his curse had overcome our senses. But this was us. This was what we were.

The Dark Gods could only amplify what already existed within us. They had not changed Kaddarar; they had only given her release.

Black flames spilt from her eyes. Her disgusting hand scooped up the coiled chain of her flail. She whipped it back, preparing to crush my head.

I bucked her. Her maul struck astray, cracking stone. I bucked again, then snatched my blade.

Kaddarar rolled aside and swung. I could not parry her flail, so I ducked. The maul carved over my head and walloped stone. I slashed my falx down her armour. She howled as if she had felt the blade in her flesh.

Another slash, and I could have toppled her head from her shoulders. I'd have ended this deadly game once and for all.

But Kaddarar froze, and so did I.

A bald wreck of a man writhed beneath the head of her flail. A half-digested meal of human pieces stewed in a puddle around his split belly. The stink of Cillus' gore and bile was sickening. His eyes flickered with failing life. Mortified, he scooped ruptured innards back into his torn sides, stuttering: 'I drops it – I picks it back up.'

Kaddarar's chest heaved. Something in her loved what she had just done – I could all but feel the thrilling heat of her pleasure. But she was not as mindless as I had thought.

Regret. That was it. Kaddarar, or Khotara, or whoever she was, had slaughtered armies. Yet after she killed a simple man she hadn't meant to – her *friend* – the fire in her eyes mouldered into forceless smoke.

She straightened, blinking the fumes from her eyes. Her evil hands loosened. I peered at her face, but she turned away.

She knelt beside Cillus, who still muttered his ditties. Her evil fingers caressed his bald pate, then snapped his neck. I had known of Kaddarar's strength, but the careless ease of that kill unnerved me. He had been her friend.

'Blood for the Blood God,' she whispered. 'Skulls, for the Skull Throne.'

Kaddarar stood and departed. Beyond the tower pinnacle, Hysh ensconced itself into the rugged horizon. Once the Seeker was gone, I sensed alien moisture in the air. I glanced at Cillus' corpse.

Beside him, where Kaddarar had knelt, dampness blotted the sand, as if from spittle, or an errant tear. Then just like that it was gone, sapped away by the heat of Aqshy.

I couldn't say why Kaddarar hadn't killed me. Control, or lack of it. A fondness shy of love; a respect short of reverence. But after she left, I wished she had. My solitude was a state worse than death.

For days I remained beside dead Cillus. I was half-cooked meat, scorched outside, raw within, soon to be putrid and unclean. The Cursed Skies dulled the days' merciless swelters and lent me peace in the nights. I saw no one and spoke nothing. I wasn't ready.

Ashstalkers broke my solitude to ask for orders. I ignored them until they left. As for why they had come, I was baffled. The warband had its meat and water. Our stores of akwag were abundant. The enemies that had discovered us were defeated. Was none of this enough? A foolish question, for I knew well it was not. My own desires could never be sated.

The second time they came, they tried to drag Cillus' bloated body away.

'Leave him.' The words wheezed from my thirst-cracked throat.

They ignored me, muttering in Yrdo between themselves. I listened and learned they were worried about me. They were Yrdun, like a second family, but that word had lost its sacred aura. I wanted to be alone. For a mere handful of days, I had wanted nothing in the realm to change, but they would not even allow me that.

As they lifted Cillus' arms and legs into the air, I blasted from the sandy stone and slashed the closest warrior's throat. He tried to seal the wound with his hand, but black blood spurted from between his fingers. He toppled, gargling and dying on the stone.

The second drew her weapon. *'Godeater's Son!'*

My blade chopped through her maul-axe. Then I gripped her hair and threw her from the jagged pinnacle. She careened from the broken tower, screaming. She smashed like an overripe fruit in the stepwell below.

Ashstalkers gathered around her. They lifted their veiled gazes to me. I stared hatefully, then retreated and sat beside Cillus and the corpse which had joined us.

Over the next day, oblivion filled me. I coveted death. I dreamt of my fighters' rebellion, that they might free me from the existence I clung to. I later learned Yron had warned them to keep their distance from me during this time. She told the fighters I was conferring with the gods – that the Dark Powers bickered amongst themselves for the privilege of granting me my first blessing. When I heard all this I thought it ridiculous. But I look back now and I see maybe she was right.

Kaddarar had been right, too. Family was nothing. This revelation pained me to admit. But all truth is pain.

So. What did I fight for? I had loved, surely enough. I had hated. I had tried to burn the world, and in some ways I had. But all that was wet ash in my mouth. Even Yrdoval and its greatest pillar, Vengeance, were not enough.

My mind travelled the ages. Cardand hadn't been the only Yrdun kingdom of Bodshe. During the Age of Myth, Lost Bharat had become the greater of our people's domains. For centuries the lost city's war-chief Maals had struggled with Cardand's great houses for supremacy. The nature of those wars was lost to time, but it was said that after the Agloraxi withdrew from the Pale of Bodshe, only Yrdun dared threaten Yrdun. No one else had been able to.

But why? Perhaps our twin kingdoms had disagreed on the nature of Yrdoval. Perhaps they had disputed claims to power, like Azyrites and their pedigree-obsessed aristocracies. But before the end, in the moment that mattered, neither Bharat nor Cardand had been able to save themselves. How their war had concluded, none remembered – for Chaos soon rose ascendant.

As Aqshy drowned in blood, Bharat was lost forever. Through providence and skill at arms, Cardand eked on, broken by the Dark Powers but alive. What a bitter end to our people's glory. But what intrigued me was that the war between Cardand and Bharat had never mattered. It had not mattered what started it, or why. It had not mattered what they had said, or thought, or believed in. It had only mattered what they had done, and what they had not done. And at the moment of truth, they had not acted to save themselves.

That moment played out again now, between me and the Azyrites. History was a chain circle, linked to itself. History was a serpent devouring its tail.

Cursing, Boskin scrabbled up to my pinnacle. He was overloud, stinking as Golvarians do. His leathers were unbuffed, his skin unwashed, his armour unburnished. As he ascended, the Paleward Winds gusted. A sandstorm was coming.

'I'll kill you,' I warned him. I assumed he had come to talk about Cillus.

But he made no mention of the fool. He peeked out from the landing below mine, his pistol raised.

'I know you will. But see, I've got charm and class, owing to my roots in nobility.' He cocked his pistol's hammer. 'I'll fare better than those other two did.'

How I burned inside. How I smouldered. 'All you do is run your mouth,' I spat.

'Well, maybe I like talking.' Boskin chewed on his lopsided

moustache. 'There's matters need attending. Three things. First, nectar's down to dregs. Second, your horse – which you'll remember I gave to you, before you stole my name for her without asking – now eats human meat.'

I gave an arid chuckle. 'You object?'

He leaned against the stone, his pistol still aimed at me. 'Well, it doesn't really seem wise feeding her our kind, but what do I know? I've only been around horses my entire life.'

I faced him fully, shifting my crossed legs. 'Boskin.'

His pistol inched higher. 'Yeah?'

I had mulled a certain matter in my solitude. I desired Boskin's opinion. 'Those columns from Candip, patrolling the low roads and high roads. Heavily armed, heavily manned. They don't move supplies. So what is it they do?'

Boskin blinked. 'They're presence patrols, guarding the ways to Candip's fiefs. Satellite columns move around the main forces. What're you on about?'

'What are they for?' I asked. 'Keeping us off the low roads?'

Boskin brightened, as if realising I hadn't known the self-evident. 'Satellite columns. That's how an army advances into hostile country. It's usually Derders or whatnot making the circuits. But footsloggers can do it.'

Boskin was good for more than logging provisions and grooming horses. He had been an officer; he possessed an Azyrite's military education.

I gestured for him to show me. Boskin moved pebbles on the ground, diagramming with them, his pistol still raised. 'Attack a column, let's say.' He tapped a pebble. 'It sends a signal up. Smoke, horns, lightning – the signal depends on the general and the magecraft available. Another column sees the signal, they converge around it. They surround the attackers, then annihilate them.' Boskin reoriented all the pebbles around the first. 'The noose closes, the enemy dies. End of story. A real delight, this. It's how Hammerhal Aqsha moves armies through the Flamescar Plateau.'

'So they're not hunting us,' I said. 'They're baiting us.'

Boskin shrugged. He squinted as another gust kicked up sand, then spat grit from his teeth. 'Both, probably. They probably assume we'll fight like marauders and try to hit them. Fair enough, I say. That's what we did up to the Losh.'

I considered the size of Candip's host, then compared that with the scale of Cardand's geography. 'One column requires how many soldiers?'

Boskin whistled. 'Oh, lots. And not just troops. Supply lines have to be perfect. Candip's likely stretched thin. Unless they got reinforcements from Hammerhal, which I doubt. Se Roye hates the Freeguilds, because they're loyal to Hammerhal's conclave. She prefers units she can control herself.'

I stood, sheathing my falx. Dust and gathered sand poured from my shoulders and legs.

Boskin relaxed. 'What's this?'

'We march for Candip,' I said. 'Dusk. Pass the word.'

'But, the city–'

'Is undefended,' I said. 'Think of how many roads and unterways are in Cardand. Think of how many of Candip's fiefs dot this valley. Se Roye has been sending these columns and satellite units across the entire Pale. The city's forces have to be overextended.' I sneered with sick pleasure. 'We can bring the fight where they'll never expect us.'

Boskin holstered his pistol. 'Blind me. A raid, right at their heart. In and out before they know it.'

I shook my head grimly, relishing the cut of sand as it whipped through my heat wraps. 'They will know when we've come, Boskin. And they will never forget.'

He nodded, biting his lip. 'There's one more thing. Kaddy. She's gone. Last night. Said nothing when she left.'

My countenance grew as still as the metal in my mask. After our argument, Kaddarar had departed for good. She must have lost faith in me. The only thing that surprised me about that was how much it hurt.

I dismissed Boskin, who hustled down the crags to spread the word. I moved behind him with far less verve, shielding my eyes from the growing sandstorm. Kaddarar didn't matter. Let her chase her gods' desires. Let her find what she sought. For I sought another prize. After the Age of Chaos, Cardand and Bharat had gone extinct. They had weakened themselves warring over... what, ideas? Beliefs? It didn't matter. Because when their greatest challenge had come, those beliefs could not have saved them.

I would not repeat their mistakes. I would not surrender to despair. My beliefs did not matter, nor my fears. Only my actions did.

I would bring my foes low. I would make a point to the ones who had started all this.

CHAPTER TWENTY

The sandstorm abraded all. Gale-force grit penetrated my mask, so thick I could hardly breathe. We had awaited the full cover of the storm before we advanced. Now it stripped away the Azyrites' advantage of observation on Candip Plain.

After slipping past the cogforts trundling across Candip Plain, we found ourselves in the overcrowded refugee camps closer to the city's Burning Palisade. We entered unnoticed, spreading word among the locals of our arrival. They provided us with the patrol routes of Candip's watch. I sent out my Ashstalkers and waited in a cramped square.

The haze of sand and violent winds decreased visibility. Tents with tattered sides surrounded us. I spat a wad of sand-muddied saliva. Behind me, my warriors waited in stubborn silence. Micaw pawed at the ground, steam pluming from her nostrils before it was stolen by the sandstorm.

Besides my warriors, hungering natives filled the crowded camp. They were refugees and plaintive poor, subsisting in squalor and penury, drawn to the rumour of my presence. What a sight we made. Se Roye's stranglehold decrees had brought us all here. When I looked at them, I no longer lamented the violations of Se Roye's people against my own. Everything the Azyrites had done had made me stronger. Soon we would all have vengeance.

Six silhouettes resolved from the sandy blur. They dragged a Candip watchman, his legs limp, his spirit broken. Refugee children shrieked and giggled in the storm, running circles around men and women with swords. Wide-eyed parents seized their oblivious children and dragged them into the nearest tents.

Yron and Jujjar threw the watchman down at my feet. Misery filled his eyes. Blood encrusted his chin.

'Did you learn something before you cut out his tongue?' I asked.

Yron's neck stiffened as she wiped her knife clean. She wore a linen band to protect her eyes from the sandstorm, like a blind swordsman from a fireside legend. 'The cogfort garrisons don't leave their positions in sandstorms,' she said. 'The upworks garrison keep to their cover. And you were right. The city doesn't have the numbers to stop us once we enter.'

Jujjar grunted and spoke. 'He also said the next column is scheduled to return tomorrow. They're usually late.'

I looked upwards. I glimpsed a vague roiling beyond the seething sandstorm. The Cursed Skies burned.

Yron noticed. 'We bear the gods' blessings, Yrdun-son. The time is come. Will we go through with this?'

My warriors touched their totems for luck. Their pathetic superstition wasn't totally worthless. Even if the totems lacked power – even if the Cursed Skies didn't bless us – the warriors believed in both.

High morale. That was the real magic. And our numbers didn't hurt.

I signalled. My warriors stalked into the sand-ridden hell to scout the way into Candip. They teemed at the edge of my vision before disappearing into the storm. Then I faced the others. The refugees, Yrdun and Beltoller miscreants armed with cudgel and knife and staff. They shifted anxiously, awaiting my word, their chests filled with pent breath. They wished to join me. They only required a nudge.

'I would stoke your misery into loathing,' I spoke, loud so they could hear me over the storm. 'I would kindle your loathing into hate. I would tell you what the Azyrites took from us, and from our lands. I would brush away their lies and reveal the truth.'

I paced before the first rank of rabble, meeting each wretch's eyes. Then I shoved myself into their midst. 'I would tell you of the city they stole from us.' I gripped the shoulders and arms of the men and women around me as I passed. 'I would guide you to the halls they stole from your mothers' mothers. I would pour for you the waters they wrenched from us. But I need not do any of this. For you already know!'

The crowd murmured assent. Sporadic cries of support rang out.

I was trembling now, thrilled and incandescent. 'We clawed out the riches of our lands for them! We slept on gravel as they wiped their boots with silk!'

'Hear him!' a young woman said, a cruel heat blazing in her eyes. Others joined her cry.

I paused and surveyed them all. 'Oh, so you agree with me?'

When their deafening answer filled my ears, I laughed and raised my falx in the direction my fighters had gone. The crowd parted for my blade, and for one brilliant moment I felt the control I had always craved.

'Don't tell me, you wretches!' I screamed. 'Tell the Azyrites!'

The roaring crowd of them bustled into the sandstorm, towards Candip's upworks. I was surprised at them – surprised at myself.

I had come here to raid Candip, not instigate a rebellion. But I was far, far from displeased.

Shoulders heaving, I lowered my blade. I searched the sand-blasted tent city for Micaw.

Then I saw Jujjar bending over to slit the watchman's throat.

I rushed to his side and pulled his arm back. The sentinel was just an ordinary man, conscripted into Candip's watch after the city's men and women had died at the Losh. We had already extracted what we needed from him, and removing his tongue had been excessive. Yron had no doubt done that for her ritual flames.

Jujjar grimaced at me. I ignored him and regarded the watchman. Time would not heal his wounds – time would not return his tongue. *Let him live,* a sickness within me whispered. Not mercy, but a breed of cunning and spite. I wanted the world to hurt as much as I did, and the sickness inside me whispered how it might be done. I would let the man live. I would let him infect the realm with his pain.

I gave Jujjar this order, a command which rippled through him. He cut the man's bonds and kicked him into the sand. The man just lay there, insensate from shock.

I threw my leg over Micaw's back, taking care not to prod myself with the spines on her flanks. As I settled, Jujjar came beside me.

'Something to say?' I asked.

Jujjar stroked Micaw's neck. Then he planted his hand on my thigh. 'A good speech,' he said, in Yrdo. 'Tell me, Held – what are we fighting for?'

I might have chuckled. 'For all the things we deserve.'

The glint in Jujjar's eyes told me he was well versed in the contents of that bitter ledger. 'We'll all get what we deserve before the end. Maybe not today, or tomorrow. But the longer I fight with you, the more I see this is the way things must be. Those with no rightful claim cannot be allowed to rule us.' His eyes glimmering, he nodded to the man puling in the sands. 'He is Azyrite. He deserves death.'

I ignored his objection and prepared to ride.

Jujjar pulled at my leg. 'Held. Would you fall on your sword?'

My eyes wrinkled behind my mask. 'What?'

'I would.' A pained smile bent Jujjar's lips. 'I would plant my blade in the sand and fall on it when the time comes. I would take my life for the Yrdun. *That* is why we are strong. We are willing to do things the Azyrites would not.' Jujjar patted Micaw again, then released my leg. 'Thank you for reminding me of who we are.'

I watched as Jujjar trudged after our motley army into oblivion. He stopped to kick the watchman's head into the sand, then disappeared into the vicious haze.

Below, the man lifted his eyes to me. Tears streaked his face, red trails where Aqshy's sand stuck to them. Blood and spittle dribbled from his tongueless jaw. Through the gusts, through the grief, I sensed the roots of a hate as white as mine growing in his belly. I buried my pity, then left him to choose his fate.

On the narrow road between mud-walled bunkers and frame-house barracks, Freeguilders gelled into a thin rank. Their thruster swords clattered against the brass bosses of their shields. Their arms gleamed in the sorcerous light of their burning palisade. They smelt like polish and lantern oil, but the sand had got between them and their clothes. How they squirmed.

They were the Bronze-and-Blues, a foot regiment of swordsmen with brass helms and good steel and livery as blue as their blood. Bright orange scarves billowed from their necks. Once they had been chartered with Hammerhal's Sun Seekers. Now they were Candip's mercenaries.

'Firm now, boys an' garls!' an officer cried. 'Here they come!'

My fighters and rabble coagulated into a loose rank, then parted for me. Lovely Micaw trotted out, carrying me forward, her red eyes reflected in the line of hoarded steel before us. Smoke eddied from her nostrils.

The Bronze-and-Blues retreated a foot at a time. 'Hell's face, it's the Godeater's Son! The Godeater's Son is here!' The soldiers glanced to their neighbours for courage. I let them have that, but nothing else.

We broke their ranks with javelins, then closed with maul-axe and pillaged steel. All the courage in the realm could not have saved them. We were too many, too angry – too wicked.

Nobody came to help the Bronze-and-Blues. The tongueless man's tidings were true, and my gamble had proven correct. Candip was nigh undefended.

I had planned for heavy losses battling Candip's vaunted Demigryph Knights to enter the city. I still remembered the Refuser's conversation with Se Roye about how they were often stabled in Candip. This was the sole reason I had encouraged those indigents crowded onto Candip Plain to join us – that they might soften the Azyrites' monstrous cavalry charge. The knightly orders were supposed to pounce when we revealed our presence. As our rabble tore the Bronze-and-Blues apart, I held most of my Ashstalkers in reserve.

Yet the knights never came. Across Candip's upworks, their stables were empty. I assumed they were on the march with Candip's scattered hosts. This fortune was more than providence or chance – it was justice. The demigryphery's absence in Candip at the moment they were needed most was nothing but the long girdle of the Azyrites' cruelty closing in on itself. They had wronged us for years; now the crows had finally come home to roost.

My remaining Ashstalkers joined the combat, and I gloried in the tumult. When the bloody work neared its end, I surveyed the sand-blurred killing field. My blade glistened with the black sludge of accreted murder, but I left it unclean and tightened my mask. The enemy soldiers had known my face. If my notoriety had become a weapon in this fight, I would not relinquish it. I would harness it to its fullest.

The Kingdom of Cardand was a relic, a ruin in the past. When the Azyrites had usurped our people's ancient domain, they had levelled tracts of Cardand's surface into Candip Plain. In those defensive barrens, they had raised their mudworks and precious palisade. To keep my people out, they had unleashed their trundling cogforts which bristled with guns and shook the earth.

But beneath the plain's surface, the true city loomed like buried treasure. Carnd-Ep, the illustrious heart of Cardand's unterways, once safeguarded by Yrdun hosts and earthfire canals which had protected us from mining ratmen and snivelling grot-kin.

We descended from Candip's upworks down pyramidal tiers of stairs into the city. The stairs reminded me of Whittale's End and the ancient stepwell. As the sandstorm's roar faded into a far-off whisper, the stink of burning torch tar replaced the dry storm-winds in our parched throats.

Then, the city Carnd-Ep had become unfurled before us. Candip, cursed be its name.

It was an underground crevasse. In the base of Candip's forever rift, Azyrite towers loomed. Gaudy edifices of white deco masonry lined the cliffs of the crevasse, capped with haughty domes of beaten metal. In the canyon's wrinkles and cuts, orreries and blinding suns floated over tent-draped agoras. The whole city gleamed like an underground sunrise. The crevasse wended on and on, a scar in the realm, a city as edgeless as time. Once, Candip had been our home. Now it was sanctuary for soft-handed tyrants.

Distantly, pillars like gargants held empty metal piers aloft: skyquays for the Kharadron airfleets that entered from the port tunnels. Those merchant ironclads belonged to the likes of Hewer Durandsson, but now the wharves were empty. The airships had taken flight before the sandstorm. Truthfully, I was glad Hewer and his kind were not here. I would not have wanted him to see what came next.

We coursed into the city's rift, into its streets. Above, Candip's chains stretched from the canyon's base to monumental metaliths hovering in the deep. Bodshe's fettered mountains swayed with restive might, each a city in its own right. More metaliths lay above, hovering over Candip Plain, their colossal chains running through the ceiling of the covered canyon. And those *chains*. The iron in each link could have armoured legions. At each chain's base, chugging Ironweld devilries enslaved the metaliths' ceaseless stirs, transmuting Bodshe's native power into a cruder electric fuel. The sound of their mammoth motion groaned through the canyon, tickling the roots of my teeth.

As a child I had never believed in miracles until I'd seen this all for myself. I had accepted it then, as children do. Now it hurt to behold; I could not understand it. The Azyrites' hunger for *more* never ended. Hubris was their disease, power their affliction. Soon we would cure them.

The city's screaming inhabitants cleared our way as we surged down Candip's main boulevard to the unfinished cathedral at its centre. The glorious edifice jutted out over the city's heart, a centurial labour still under construction. Bridges and buttresses soared over the cathedral's stone hive. Pillars, domes, keeps. Timber scaffolds and gantries towered where construction was ongoing. The cathedral was a tumour, defiling my people's heritage.

So we gutted it. With flame. We ran like barbarians through its half-built corridors, spilling the entrails of its servants and builders and monks. Scattered war priests emerged to defy us, and we gave them the martyrdom they craved. We shattered altars, strewed treasures across pristine masonry. We crushed their holy chalices and ground saints' relics under heel. A pathetic friar shielded a flock of church novices from me, his arms shaking as he pleaded for their lives. I cut him down, hewing my falx through his clavicle to his midriff. The shrieking novices fled and were soon chased down.

As flame roared in the cathedral halls and devoured its scaffolds, we ran wild through Candip's streets. Hundreds of my warriors, the unwashed riot of our kindred. Some were eager for pillage, others hungry for vengeance. We raged through the clothiers' district and the alchemists' ward. We burnt the tanners' houses and spread the hellish reek of their craft. We set frame houses aflame, shattering counting tables and scattering mongrel coinage. Let only Bodshe's native stone remain. Let it run red and gold with the Azyrites' treasures.

For all my worst intentions, little of the blood we shed in Candip was blue. This was not from our restraint. By the enemy's prescience or their selfishness, Candip's halls had been stripped of their gentlest Azyrite class. Beyond the cathedral clergy and isolated pockets of mercenaries, no foreigners remained. I was enraged. I could not understand what holes the Azyrites had crawled into. Candip was populated by tens of thousands, yet all the Azyrites were gone.

So we satisfied ourselves with the gristle of those who had attended to them. No matter their heritage, any who had found refuge in Candip were leeches, fat with their own people's blood. The Reclaimed Yrdun and Beltollers of Candip had enriched themselves through their treachery. They were not like us. Not like me.

I felt havoc in my veins. I wanted this war to never end. I wanted to show Reiriz he had been wrong. I wanted to prove to whoever had honoured our dead at Whittale's End that we could never be Reclaimed. We were pagans and savages – the animals we'd been made into. For the first time in forever, I felt unshackled. I drank my fill of freedom, measuring it in quarts of the enemy's blood. Yet the more we killed and the freer I became, the less it felt like enough. Control was mine, but it no longer satisfied me.

I gritted my teeth and redoubled my efforts, butchering all who resisted. I hoped to heal my pain with the feeling of third-class flesh beneath the edge of my blade.

I was so lost, so barren, I couldn't see the trap I'd fallen into. I couldn't feel the tears in my eyes.

When we came across Ulcarver's cast-iron gates, my lips wore an arid smile. *Of course* the district's wealth had been guarded – and *of course* those guards had deserted at the first sign of woe. Akwag was a meagre potion for loyalty. Blood and common hatred were thicker.

A mob of wretches from the camps on Candip Plain already screamed through the ward. They barged in where they pleased, toppling those who barred their path. The desperate cries of holdout soldiers filled my ears, then ceased as they were killed.

As the anarchy unfolded, I rode Micaw through Ulcarver's knotted streets. Enchanted lanterns flickered over my head. The gutters were red with spilt wine and blood. Amidst the deluge of our incensed rioters, my blooded Ashstalkers concentrated behind me, shattering resistance where it coalesced. A handful of mercenaries formed into a rank on the street; we impaled them with javelins from afar. Others tried to ambush us from alleys; we enveloped them and hacked them apart. How vain those fools were, seeking to resist the resistless to protect what was theirs. Se Roye had once claimed protecting everything in Bodshe would amount to protecting nothing at all. Now *nothing at all* had come for her people's *everything,* but she and her ilk could not let it go.

As savages hurtled through the streets, knocking over carts and shattering crystal-glass windows, Micaw clopped into the court of a splendid manse. I craned my head at the unblemished ashlar stone framing its white-brick facade. Tiled mosaics carpeted the court's garden walks. The mosaics gleamed with strange Chamonite colours, until they were charred by Micaw's scorching hooves.

I dismounted, letting Micaw graze on the meat of the murdered. My warriors tore House Se Roye's seal from the iron-reinforced doors. I pushed those open and entered alone, anxious, even scared. The time had finally come to finish what Se Roye had started.

Within, a moon-eyed servant fled at my appearance. The wide corridors were empty. In the counting room, Aqua Ghyranis rippled in half-empty casks. The whole manse was like that, half-pillaged. Someone had come through in a rush, taking what she thought most precious. Se Roye's flight must have been sudden and desperate. But she could still be here.

I stalked deeper into high-ceilinged halls. My silent warriors sauntered behind me. Half-starved indigents and looting rioters rampaged into the manse after us, tearing all they could apart.

Soon a pair of carven darkwood doors barred my path. Linenfold engravings decorated the panel reliefs on them. They depicted scenes from Sigmarite mythology. Dracothion finding the God-King; the forging of his Pantheon; the Tempest. Disdain wrinkled my eyes. The Azyrites always bragged about the good times. Always ignored the bad.

'Not any more,' I muttered. The doors creaked open at my touch.

A chapel lay beyond, tiny by Sigmarite standards. Three pews lined the nave. Through stained-glass windows in the alcove, I glimpsed Candip's great chasm. Mountainous towers and meta-liths loomed in the city's canyon, limned by the fires I had started. Se Roye's chapel jutted over Candip's crevasse like an exercise in audacity.

Alone of all places in Ulcarver, this chapel was unabandoned – but its sole occupant was not Se Roye.

I smelt her before I saw her, saw her before I knew who she was. She stank of ozone and cold air, lightning in the void. Each of her gentle breaths was a titanic swell, a distant storm. Her armour was gold and her hammer was heavy.

Tension filled my lungs. 'Long have I awaited this,' I said.

Ildrid Stormsworn stood before the chapel altar. The Refuser, Lord-Imperant of the Hammers of Sigmar. All meaningless titles, accumulated like scars from pox. I had not expected Stormsworn. But her presence did not surprise me.

'Good,' she said. 'Then let us begin.'

CHAPTER TWENTY-ONE

I raised my chin, lips tightening, heart fraught. I remembered Reiriz's tidings well. This warrior-immortal thought I could be redeemed. But I would prove I was beyond her god's reach.

My Ashstalkers' feet scuffled up the aisles surrounding the nave, fine carpets bunching beneath their dirty heels. Our untrained rabble froze in the threshold behind us, bearing witness.

The Refuser stared. She was enormous. Her outsize hammer stood perched before her like a monument. Once she had been so still I had mistaken her for the canvas wall of a tent, but now she was restless. Her hammer's heavy head ground upon stone. Restive movements whispered from her warplate and under her heels. Whitewoods did the same, groaning during gales.

'Kill her,' I told my fighters.

'They cannot,' she said, her voice like a pealing bell.

I urged them on, but they withered under Stormsworn's glare.

'My positioning is flawless,' she said. 'You cannot outflank me.'

I masked my annoyance with poise I did not feel. 'Amusing. For an immortal about to die.'

'But you are not yet immortal, Heldanarr Fall.'

I winced. 'So. You remember my name.'

She nodded. 'Do they know as well? Or do they all use that loathsome calling, Godeater's Son?'

I loured. 'I've heard stories of your kind. Forged by the God-King's own hands. But you're devils. Thunder golems, with lightning blood and starlight blades.'

Then I turned to the others.

'Everything dies,' I said, gesturing them forward. 'You just have to–'

'Varrianala Fall,' the Refuser said. 'Do they know her name, too? Or your father's? Your mother's? Do they know you had fifteen brothers and sisters and a crib with three legs?'

Her questions sucked the air from my lungs. 'Eleven,' I said. 'Eleven brothers and sisters.'

'Fifteen. Four died within their first year, but they still lived before that.'

I growled. 'Sigmar told you.'

'No. Sigmar says nothing of you. Sigmar does not know your name or your family. Only your sins.'

I gritted my teeth, gripping my weapons' hilts until they creaked. Then I relaxed and fell into a pew.

'You want to talk?' I said. 'Let's talk.'

'Godeater's Son–' an Ashstalker hissed.

'*Shut up!*' I shouted. The warrior withered. I would not let the Refuser take my victory from me with her words. I wanted complete control.

I faced the Refuser again, wrinkling my nose, admiring her sheer size. She looked as terrible as that day in the unterways, but I didn't believe the legends. Stormsworn was big, yes. Her weapon mighty, and her armour a castle. But divine? A demigod? Ages had passed since the sight of her armour had conjured orreries in my head. Behind her stern-faced helm, beneath the realm of her warplate, I suspected Ildrid was like me. Human – nothing at all.

'Last we met, you did not know me,' the Refuser said. 'I am Lord-Imperatant of the Hammers of Sigmar. We are Sigmar's Chosen, reforged by his will. We protect his flock and annihilate his foes. We are strong. We are many. We are here.'

'One of you,' I sneered. 'Alone.'

'We are never alone. Sigmar is with us, always.'

I glanced up. Banners and blessed pennants festooned the chapel walls above. 'Where is he?' I asked. 'Clinging to the rafters?'

Ildrid's silence was more scornful than any retort she could have spoken. The night in her eyes might have bored holes through mountains.

'Maybe you thought he was in the cathedral,' she said. 'In the sanctuary, hiding behind the chancel like a coward. Sigmar is my heart and soul, you simple boy. I take him wherever I go. Our blades speak his name – our hammers brand it on his foes. Cast our temples down. Kill our faithful, if you dare. You cannot destroy what Sigmar stands for any more than you can destroy me.'

I raised my chin again. 'We killed your priests. Strewed their guts over your holy things.' I tilted my head. 'But I guess that's nothing.'

I cherished the silence which followed. First blood.

Stormsworn inhaled deeply. The candle flames on the walls stirred. 'How can you do something like that and believe your cause just?'

I shook my head. 'I don't think it is just, Refuser. That's the point.'

'Enlighten me, child.'

I leaned forward. 'I met my brother the other day. He'd gone to your side. Before I killed him, he told me you think us victims. You think we can be Reclaimed. But we've nothing left to redeem,

Stormcast. Nothing left to save. You took it all already. You, your people – your god.'

'You are wrong,' she intoned. 'There is someone here worth saving.'

I chuckled. 'Sounds like an article of faith.'

'Yes. It *is*. No one else believes in you, Fall. But I do. Because only I know what you are.'

Beneath my mask, my smile bled out. I'd thought this a contest of will. I'd hoped to break Stormsworn's hollow message before I broke her body and the tabernacle and the reliquary against the wall.

But she wasn't jesting, or taunting. She was serious. She believed. In what? In me?

I straightened. 'You spoke of when last we met. But when first we met, you didn't even notice me. Now I'm someone, is it? Now I'm worth something?'

'Yes.' The mail beneath her warplate tinkled with a near indiscernible shudder. She hid her feelings well. 'Often we Stormcasts forget the people we once were, and those we came from. But I have a better memory than most.'

'I have a good memory too,' I hissed. 'I remember washing in dirty water and eating tossed meat broken on your tables. But you I won't remember. Your god doesn't know me? So be it. I'm not surprised. He doesn't even remember his own dead slaves. Lightning didn't come for anyone we killed today, Refuser. Just fire and steel. And it won't come when we slaughter you, either. I know what the Cursed Skies do to you creatures.'

She waved a hand. 'A minor impediment.'

'Minor.' I whiffled. 'I hope the daemons of Chaos eat your soul. I hope you remember who fed you to them. Anything else before we finish this?'

'Only an offer,' she said. 'A pact, to save your soul.'

I groaned, then roared. I pounded my fists, shaking the pews. A kneeler fell onto my foot; I booted it back into the pew.

'Redemption? You really think I'll stop? This far down the hole?'

'Yes. Because you have no idea how far down this hole goes. You are misguided, Fall. Lost. You are a victim.'

I forced myself to laugh. I wrenched it from my chest like consumption. 'Whittale's End. That was you.'

She nodded.

A chalice clanged on the stone to my right; an Ashstalker started. She had been toying with possible plunder on a table of offerings to Sigmar. The others cursed her, then hushed and held their breath and watched me.

Focused on Stormsworn, I hardly noticed them. 'Did you redeem the bloodreaver, too? That brute from the unterways, Tul? You make him an offer? A pact?'

'No. I crushed his skull beneath my boot. But he was not Heldanarr Fall.'

The pew creaked as I shifted. 'My name doesn't scare me. *You* don't scare me.'

'Only because you do not know what to fear. I know so much more than your name, boy. I know why you fight, and why you shall lose. I know what it will take to save you.'

'Enlighten me,' I spat through clenched teeth, my blood seething. Let her have her say. Then I'd kill her ideas with her.

The Stormcast Eternal lifted her hammer. She let its head thud against the stone. The chapel shook, and dust trickled from the vaults overhead. 'Lellen Se Roye is greedy and selfish,' Ildrid said. 'Her ambitions are endless. Her rulership damns the mortals of Bodshe to a fate worse than death.'

My jaw slackened, but only for a blink.

'Candip is the jewel in her crown,' she continued. 'A domain with which Se Roye hopes to challenge Hammerhal, once Candip's glory flowers. This may come to pass. Se Roye is shrewd, clever and faithful. But she is short-sighted, without a shred of empathy. The costs of her ambitions have become unacceptable to the rulers of Hammerhal. She has built her majesty and wealth in the name of Sigmar, yes, but on the broken backs of your people, on the emptiness in your bellies. I have come to judge her reign, to broker a settlement with Hammerhal Aqsha. And my judgement, boy, is Sigmar's judgement. Se Roye's petty rivalry with the Twin-Tailed City must end. It damages the God-King's designs and war plans. Her ambition has pitted you against us. But before I can resolve this conundrum, you must cease this madness.'

I was speechless. I had expected none of this.

'I knew you would come here,' she said. 'Because I know what drives you. Revenge – but against Se Roye's greed, not the God-King's designs. I do not think you are wrong, Fall. Your means? Certainly, and this butchery demands atonement. But what drives you… the grief… I understand this. The things that mortals like Se Roye do for the sake of wealth and power boil the blood, do they not? They are all the same. Short-sighted. But they have not seen what I have seen. They do not know.'

A chill ran through my bones. The Refuser's unsettling magnanimity smacked of power greater than me – greater than us all.

'Why are you here?' I asked.

'I told you. By Sigmar's command. By his wisdom and grace. I will smooth out the conflict between Candip and Hammerhal and eliminate the obstacles to Candip's ordination. But first I must deal with you. I do not wish to kill you, boy. Trust that I will deal with Se Roye, and lay down your arms.'

'You'd betray her?'

'I couldn't care less for her wishes,' she said. 'That woman disgusts me.'

Disgust. I tried to reconcile the word and its place on Ildrid's tongue. She was one of them. Even worse – an exemplar of their god and king. How could any of this disgust her?

Stormsworn raised a shaking fist. The heavy metal of her gauntlet rattled on her iron hand. 'Se Roye *will* be taught her place. In time, Hammerhal's arrogant lords, too, whose petty bickering obstructs Sigmar's true aims and exhausts my Stormhost's strength. But I am thankful. All of this brought me here, to you. I had meant for us to meet sooner, but Se Roye thought she could beat you without me.'

'The Losh,' I breathed.

She nodded. 'Lellen has little in the way of patience. Her impulses have served her too well. She was eager to protect her incomes in the outlands. She lacked the stomach or head for a real war – the bitter grind of it.'

I recalled Reiriz's words. 'You're the one who bled us dry.'

The Refuser nodded. 'When Se Roye failed, she turned to me again.' She swept her mighty arm around the pristine chapel. My Ashstalkers all but recoiled, shaken by the shadow of her gaze. 'Now look where I have brought you.'

I gritted my teeth so hard they might have splintered. 'You didn't do this. I did. Me.'

'So eager to prove you are free. But you control nothing, boy. You are like Se Roye. Short-sighted.'

'I *will* win.'

'Maybe. Today, or tomorrow. But your triumphs would be fleeting. Candip's fate has long been ordained. Even without the realmgates, Sigmar's wrath would come for you. A Dawnbringer host, to erase you from the face of Aqshy. Stormcast Eternals, to purge your taint from the sands. Sigmar's crusade never ends. You merely delay the inevitable.'

I tapped my blade against the pew. 'I'm not seeing redemption here.'

'Redemption is not a gift. You must earn it. You have this one chance because you still reject the Great Enemy. But only one, and you must seize it now – or I shall force it upon you. I told you I have seen the touch of Se Roye's hands upon Bodshe. I promise you now that will be corrected. But not like this. Not with slaughter, and flame.'

I couldn't believe my ears. 'How could we trust you? After everything the Azyrites promised? After everything you stole?'

She hesitated. Then she crossed her heart, stroking the breast of her cuirass with her gauntlet. Her armour's radiant metal rasped. 'I do not ask you to believe in Sigmar. I ask you to believe in me. Because you cannot survive in these realms without believing in something, Heldanarr Fall.'

Her gentle oath unseated the core of me. 'Who are you?'

She lowered her arm. 'I am Ildrid Stormsworn, blessed by Sigmar's hands. But in another life, I knew your mother. She loved you once, in a way she thought she understood. And the way she loves you now, the woman whom she once was would not recognise. But she *does* love you, Heldanarr Fall. More than you realise. I know of you because of her.'

Eternity breathed in the hell of battle. I felt it now. My heart thudded behind my eyes. I held it in my miserable hands, felt it beating upon my calluses.

'The God-King is cruel,' Ildrid said, 'but he is merciful too. He brought us together as one final kindness for your mother's faith.'

'My mother left us to die,' I said, battling back the tears brimming in my eyes.

'Your mother took up a pan and a knife to protect you and your siblings' lives. She invoked the twelve names of salvation to save you from the beasts. You do not remember. You were not there when Sigmar took her. But if she still remembers you after what she has endured, you must remember her, too.' Ildrid's breathing quickened. She inched forward, her toes protruding over the altar's dais. 'You have to. You *must*.'

I grew still, fixated and bemused.

Then I understood.

Silence ruled us. If I weren't gripping that pew's timber, I feared I would fly from the chapel, into Candip's stone skies, the way my sister had been taken by the blood moon. My mother was *gone*. She had left us to starve and had let Varry die. She had cursed us to live alone in Aqshy's fires and the sands of wasted time. Nothing the Refuser could say would change my mind.

Ildrid must have sensed that. She reached up and slid her helmet free. The blessed metal whispered over the bound hair beneath.

I expected a stranger's face. Or thrice-cursed Elene, mocking me from after death.

But it was her. Not as I remembered, but her nevertheless. The unblemished flesh of her face was burnished gold, like her armour. Her eyes were the same black midnight as the pitted orbits of her mask. Yet even remade into this radiant idol – even cursed by Sigmar's boons – she was the same as she had been. This woman had borne me into the realm and nursed me at her breast. She had sung nursery rhymes and pinched the youthful pudge of my cheeks and rocked me to sleep.

And she was braver than I was, for I still hid behind my mask.

'Tell me,' she spoke, in perfect Yrdo. 'What song does the sun-man sing?'

The question from the unterways. She had asked us so many times in our youth. Tucking us into bed on the mantle of our croft's stove, or lulling us to sleep with more senseless rhymes of Sigmar's glory.

Unthinking, I stroked the beaten metal rictus of my father's dead face. Control was a lie. I was mortal and had forgotten. My breathing grew ragged.

'My warriors,' I whispered.

'Slaves to Darkness,' Ildrid said. 'I cannot vouch for you all. Not after your atrocities. But you I can save, Heldanarr. The others must be culled.'

Around me, terror filled my fighters' eyes. They feared what was occurring before them but dared not intervene. They inched away from the altar, down the aisles, piling against each other at the doors. Yet epiphany turned within me, slow and inevitable, like the grinding gears and cogs of the Ironweld's clockwork engines in Candip.

'They're my people,' I said.

'Sigmar's faithful are our people. Faith binds us, freeing us from the fetters of blood. You are your mother's son, Heldanarr. Consecrated by her hand. Sigmar saved you, at her plea. Now she shall protect you again.'

My fingers balled into fists. 'Sigmar took everything from us.'

'Yes. That is the way of the realms. Where will you stand at the end, Fall? Where?'

'Free,' I said, even though I knew that wasn't enough.

'Freedom is what I offer – through *faith*. In me, if nothing else.' She raised her hand. 'Trust me, Fall. Trust the woman your mother became.'

I gazed at her hand, at the offer it held. I almost reached out to take it, to graze her fingers one last time.

Then I drew my blades and sidled from the pews.

Ildrid exhaled. She cast her black gaze across the chapel and her arm fell. 'Well, then. I suppose you must be taught a lesson.'

'No one's coming to help you,' I said, sounding braver than I felt. My eyes flitted to the vaults. 'The Cursed Skies reign.'

Her golden countenance flickered. Her face was so similar to her mask I almost forgot she had removed her helm. '*That* was your ploy?' she said. 'You thought the Cursed Skies would protect you?'

'Sigmar's lightning cannot strike. Not today.'

Ildrid pounded her hammer against the stone. This time, the entire manor trembled. Banners hanging higher in the chapel fell from their nails, billowing to the floor. The vaults creaked as forces unseen moved on the roof.

'I would not have allowed any of this to occur were there any chance of failure,' Ildrid said. 'My chamber arrived three weeks ago.'

Behind me, timber crashed. I turned just as a Stormcast titan plummeted from the broken ceiling, crushing the rabble at the doors. More Stormcast Eternals pounded to the floor of the chapel, splitting pews. Broken shingles rained down behind them. Each was a behemoth like the Refuser, each as terrible as the monster my mother had become.

And they were fast. One swept her blade out before her, scything down a pocket of wretches. Before she had followed through on the blow, her other hand snapped out to intercept a screaming Ashstalker's strike. The vice of her fingers snapped his maul-axe, then she snatched him in the air and crushed his skull. His brains squelched through her armoured fingers. She flung these grisly drippings to the floor and moved to her next foe.

This all occurred before the first of us screamed.

Behind, Ildrid's steps quaked closer. I swivelled and stumbled, snapping my falx and dirk up between us.

Then a lone blur shot forward. Marder Mosh – the boy whose valour had saved us at the Losh. His maul-axe cracked into Ildrid Stormsworn's thigh. The weapon's obsidian teeth chipped; splinters jutted from the haft.

Beneath his soiled tawny hair, Marder's eyes widened. They shot to me.

'Go!' he cried.

I glanced across the nave. Three Stormcasts with halberds and opulent capes swelled closer. One kicked a pew from his path. The heavy timber juddered ten feet and pinned Marder to the floor.

Stormsworn towered over him, raising her hammer. Then she hesitated and glanced at me. 'Turn away, son. I do not want you to see this.'

This was Mosh's moment of sacrifice. In the days I have brought to Bodshe, my banners have grown heavy with the gore of friend and foe that drenches them. But it was never my strength and heart that had raised them up. At least, not mine alone.

I sprinted to the chapel's alcove as the liquid crush of Marder's extinction echoed in my ears. I threw myself through the stained glass, away from Stormsworn, into the city I had set on fire.

CHAPTER TWENTY-TWO

Shattered, we plunged: the shards of a stained-glass wall and a stained, glass man. For the time it took to blink, for the time it took to die, crystal shivers chimed in the air around me. I remembered Varry slipping from my grasp. I recalled the cloud of the dead trailing the Orb Infernia and the weightlessness the blood moon had summoned.

Then I thumped to the road and my head snapped against the ground. Broken glass showered the stone around me. I saw midnight and stars. Pain twinged through my shoulder, more discomfort than agony. Nothing broken. Nothing but me.

Candip quaked with the passage of demigods. Down the winding road, Stormcast warriors pursued my fighters and the wretched knaves who'd heeded my call. They threshed down those who resisted, or pinned them against masonry and broke their backs. Others – Yrdun and Beltollers, warriors and wretches – scuffled against each other, corralled by lines of Freeguild soldiery.

I understood, then. To bait us into her trap, the Refuser had let Se Roye's mercenaries die. Through a smoky haze I glimpsed a pack of beast-cavaliers in gun-metal mail. The Demigryph Knights fought like daemons, riding down the crowd of savages who resisted them.

Azyrites were everywhere, descending from Candip's chained metaliths in flying Ironweld pinnaces. More Stormcasts soared through Candip's yawning chasm on sharp pinions of frozen sunlight that could have gutted swine as easily as they bore the immortals aloft. The flying Stormcasts' arrows lanced through the captive sky, battering Candip's cityscape, spearing my men and women, then exploding and scattering human drizzle. Distantly, Freeguild artillery resounded across the crevasse-city, pummelling the districts we had overrun. Fusillades of gunfire applauded in their wake.

A trio of Stormcasts marched up the street, towards me. Their only words were the hiss of their blades and the percussion of their hammers as they hewed down all in their path. They offered no battle cries, no war chants. They left their fury sheathed. We were not worth it.

Far above, Ildrid Stormsworn loomed in the jagged sill of Se Roye's chapel alcove, glaring down. She seemed to be judging the distance. Soon she'd blaze down like a meteor, cratering the road with her fall.

Then Yron's voice rang across the street. 'The Godeater's Son!' she shouted. 'Protect the Godeater's Son!'

Before I knew what was happening, half a dozen warriors dragged me up and away. Half a dozen more remained behind to buy us time. Thunder followed – the Refuser's crash to the stone – but by then we were gone.

I found my feet and ran. Wailing was the city, and tribulation. Every alley, every lodging, every dome. The stink of Candip's fires choked us. Bodshe's crust shook beneath the feet of its conquerors.

Each ragged step brought another twinge of pain in my shoulder, but my legs pumped onwards. What fuel burned to keep me going, I did not know.

Yron glanced at me. 'Boskin,' she panted. 'Boskin, past the plain. He'll have a plan. He always has plans.'

Boskin, yes. He was still in Cardand, beyond Candip Plain. He was far-sighted, always prepared for contingencies. If we got to him, we could escape. He had probably already stowed our supplies and gone into hiding at one of the old camps. I dared not let fester my old doubts about his loyalty. My mother was alive, in the service of the enemy. Any more betrayals would have shattered me. If we reached Boskin, we could retreat to the craglands. We could lick our wounds, regain our strength.

Lost in these fools' dreams, I felt cold and naked and small. I was in my mother's hands again, pulled screaming from her womb. Where had she been? Where was she, when Varry died?

Over the buried horizon, murderous celestials swooped down, then rose anew with Ashstalkers in their grip. Those heathens who resisted tumbled back down to the canyon floor. As they cracked down on tin roofs, their bodies made the sounds of fruit falling from trees. Jujjar couldn't be among them, I prayed. To whom? I didn't know. What a useless medicine for despair prayer was, I thought – even as it gave me hope.

Our flight brought us to a long alley, a straight slash through the city's rim. The puddly brick road was wide enough for two chariots, leading to a plaza and an unterway.

Our escape. I halted at the alley's mouth to regain my breath. Yron led our stragglers past shuttered storefronts and walls of peeling broadsheets. Two dozen fighters passed, no more. More must live, somewhere. I didn't consider the alternative.

I turned to bring up the rear. Then a scaled abomination sailed down from the sunken sky. The whole street shook with its impact.

Dust and sand billowed out from under it, and stone crumbled beneath its claws like cake.

All the fires in me guttered and died. A Stardrake blocked our way, mere legend until now. It was massive – it should not have existed. But there it stood, a scaled colossus with a crown of wicked horns and fangs longer than I stood tall. The beast turned and screamed. Oiled parchment windows split, and shutters flapped from their securements. I recoiled, fluid trickling from my ears.

The monster crushed the closest fighters beneath its claws. The golden knight on its back yelled, and then starfire smouldered in the drake's jaws. Pent heat, from a divine furnace. I dived for cover behind a horse's trough.

A jet of purest light blazed from the beast's craw across the alley. Stone became glass. Flesh dusted away. As with earthfire, the heat's merest caress blistered my skin. My wrappings curled into charred parchment and my mask seared my face.

When the light faded, I rose. Tongues of electricity snapped and spat in the glassed street. A grisly nothing filled it. Yron was nowhere to be seen.

I looked upon that creature as one looks upon the end of the world. I had nothing which could harm this living castle. No siege equipment, no hero's sword. This was my end.

Behind me, Ildrid strode from where we'd emerged. Her retinue's lockstep march accompanied the gentle thud of her heels. Her warriors – those with halberd and mantle – stood like her. They watched me as she did. Like they were all my many mothers.

Ildrid raised her mountainous arm and they halted. Up on the leviathan, the shining templar tightened his long reins. The monstrous drake beat its wings, rising to other battles. The gust bowled me down and it disappeared.

On my hands and knees, I gazed up at the Refuser. I'd come

here to defy her kind. I'd come to prove a point. But in my desolation I croaked the only words a small boy could, deprived of his mother for so long.

'Where were you?'

Ildrid stopped. She wore her helm again, the mask of metal. 'I was far away, child,' she said. 'But I am back. And I will not leave again. Praetors – take him.'

Her retinue marched forward, their capes beating and snapping in the wind.

Then the nearest praetor halted and his head jerked left.

A shadow overcame us all before Kaddarar landed. She smashed the glassed stone between the praetors, cracks spidering out from her impact.

Everything happened at once. She whipped her head back, her helm rolling free, her jet hair flogging out. She ripped her muscled arms forward. Her chains uncoiled from her hands, then lashed out. Her bladed mauls chased after them.

Their twin heads slammed into the closest Stormcast Eternal. Blood sprayed from the warrior's ruined helmet. He exploded into a pillar of living light, dashing into the stone skies. When I blinked away the flare, Kaddarar was in the thick of it. She raged between Ildrid and her retinue, drumming strikes against their armour as if they were gongs. The Stormcasts met Kaddarar head-on, but she pushed where they pulled, staving aside the hafts of their weapons with her arms.

Yet Kaddarar's rampage was not invincible. Twice Ildrid drew her blood, and where that tar dribbled it caught aflame, burning like ritual fire.

'It's too late for you!' Ildrid roared between strikes and gust-like breaths. She whispered an Azyrite spell, and a nimbus of light glowed around her hammer's head.

Kaddarar howled her defiance, her chain-mauls juking and

flailing like two awful serpents. The flames in her eyes were stark scarlet, a colour more compelling than all the God-King's gold.

But the Stormcasts were judicious and utterly in control. As Kaddarar's blows rippled through them, they staggered or slid back, allowing another to fill the gap. Boots rasped over the stone, and blades barked – but none fell. The Stormcast Eternals were gears in a terrible clock, moving in perfect synchrony, counting down the seconds to Kaddarar's annihilation.

I had yet to overcome my shock. Only Micaw's heinous roar brought me back. I glimpsed my dark steed galloping down the slash of ruined road, her hooves trailing black fire. Had she always been that big? Her muzzle slavered like a wolf's maw.

I glanced back. I should have taken that time to mount Micaw and escape – the others had given their lives for that. And no matter why Kaddarar had left me, she could only have returned to save me. Before foes like Stormcasts, even Kaddarar's mad assault was mere vanity.

But then the slow-moving mass of an epiphany eclipsed my reason. It was like falling beneath the shadow of a metalith crossing deserts, or the shade of an entire realm. None of this could be real. Immortals, monsters, Stardrakes. Yet here they had all collected, mythology given vicious form – and I was their living witness.

A key turned within me like a sword. The wound it left behind opened my heart to revelation: I could not win this battle. Not alone.

Red bled over my eyes. Red, the colour of my life. Crimson dappled the dead street, reflected in the others, in the ugly light of their inner flames. Everything became engorged, bloated and ripe. Everything begged from me a savage harvest. Brass light gleamed from perforations in the world, in all the places things might be severed. In the Stormcasts' necks, or across the smalls of their backs. On Kaddarar, too, and in the seams of the buildings' stone. The light did not discriminate. It did not lie.

I felt its spirit in me, too – an exalted radiance and relief. A wicked high pulsed in my ears and pounded in my belly.

How senseless. How *maddening*. Someday, when all the realm's violence and pain dissipated like smoke, things would be better in the ashes. I was certain of this.

But today was not that day. I rushed towards Kaddarar, and wisdom old and new slipped from my grasp. Fire, blood, shadow – these became me as I battled the Stormcasts at the Seeker's side. Darkling dreams, and glorious red. My red, our red, your red, shining in dark light from a tall tower, so unlike the redemption my mother had promised.

CHAPTER TWENTY-THREE

Where is the realmstone?

Ildrid had shouted this question as we had galloped from Candip's flames. I barely remembered Kaddarar at my back, and Micaw's bucking gait. But Ildrid's parting words were star-fire, branded into the substrate of my soul.

Heldanarr, where is the brightstone of Bodshe?

Nothing had answered her, nothing at all. Now I was burnt to ash, seeing things which shouldn't exist. Strange visions immolated me. Fields of charnel fire, and mountains of broken iron. The hellish reek scorched smooth the passages in my nose. Blades screeched, axes on distant grinding wheels. The noise lacerated the tunnels in my ears.

This, I realised, was the Realm of Chaos.

Across grim fields, dead Cillus wandered. Hunchbacked and bald, muttering ditties. He loped across the dormant carnage, stooping to pluck chipped femurs and snapped hilts and lengths of shattered chain. Beyond him loomed a titanic throne and its lurking tyrant, both far too enormous to take in with my eyes. Hills of skulls rose around the throne's base. Endless, leering skulls.

Beyond all this, a distant city gleamed with dark light, fleeting yet forever.

Cillus tossed his morbid harvest into a cauldron strapped to his back. 'They drops it, I picks it up.'

'What?' I rasped.

Cillus looked at me. He lurched closer. He was long-limbed, big-headed, horns sprouting from his swollen brow. His teeth became yellow bricks in the drooling mess of his mouth. His eyes swelled like black beacons and he stank of spoilt milk.

'They drops it, I picks it up!'

I staggered back, but he closed the gap.

'They drops it, I picks it up!'

I turned and ran, but Cillus chased me, his footsteps drumming through the realm.

'THEY DROPS IT, I PICKS IT UP!'

Those words thundered in my chest. Of the delirium of our escape from Candip, I remembered nothing but this hallucination. I dared not remember more.

I gasped for air, sagging half-conscious over Micaw's broad back. Kaddarar trudged beside us, the tallest woman I'd ever known.

She squeezed my arm. 'They're almost here.'

My head lolled. Blurs closed around us. Mirages, or vultures. I blinked until they resolved into Freeguild skirmishers. I craned my head around. We were in the Ashwilds. That seemed even less plausible than my visions of Cillus' damnation. We must have ridden for an entire day.

'Flensing Men,' I croaked. That was what we had called the *Linzimen* of Hammerhal Aqsha. They had been Candip's only other skirmishers besides the Ashstalkers, notorious for the hides they took. They claimed lavamander pelts protected them from Aqshy's heat. But that never explained why they flensed their foes, too. Brigands, bandits. Blood of my blood.

Kaddarar's blazing eyes swept the enemy. She was unafraid. 'They'll come,' she murmured. 'They swore they would. They'll see and they'll know.'

They have come, I tried to speak, but the words were nothing more than a feckless rasp. The Flensing Men debated which of them should attack first. They craved Sigmar's eyes but knew the first to approach would die at Kaddarar's hands.

Eventually the matter was settled. They closed in together.

Then the sand beneath them churned. A sinkhole, like a lava-mander's emergence.

The Flensing Men staggered back. The slowest were swallowed by the rift. After the ground disappeared, only a ribbed passage remained. An unterway – but summoned, not built. Its stone shimmered like the craw of a living volcano.

Warriors surged from the passage, each a whirlwind, each a storm. They fell upon the wide-eyed Freeguilders with maul-axe and javelin. They were human and aelf and duardin, people of every cut and colour. They wore shale-grey armour bolted into gruesome plate, sewn with dried sinew into skirts of shivering mail. Their brutal helmets reminded me of the Seeker's old crested helm, but sharp and swept back, with spines rattling at the nape.

The butchery which followed was simple and honest, and the newcomers didn't pursue those Freeguilders who routed. Instead they worked their serrated knives through the necks of the fallen, collecting heads with rolled-back eyes, or scalps if the skulls were too disfigured.

A champion among their number approached, a twisted breed of knight. Her armour pattern was familiar, her colours, her weapons. Something about my unexpected saviours tingled within me, oh-so-familiar.

Kaddarar grunted. 'The Godeater's Son. As promised.'

I almost scoffed, but I was too weak. Of course Kaddarar had saved me only to sell me. She would never have acted to save my life. I was only ever her lost sheep, to guard and then slaughter.

I was weak, broken off, unable to escape. But I could at least look the champion who'd come to buy me in the eyes. Brass trim lined her armour. Not an embellishment – just reinforcement. Beneath the angles and granular metal of her nasal helmet, beneath her crest of spines and murdered things' feathers, sun-daub oozed from her savage eyes into her dyed-black teeth.

I knew her. I had seen this emaciated woman in Lurth, sitting in the pens like a mad ascetic.

'What tribe…?' I said.

She answered in a lilting Yrdo dialect. 'Yours, brother of Cardand. I am an Yrdun-daughter of Bharat. You, I'm told, are heir to our legion. Returned to us at last.'

Kaddarar couldn't understand our tongue. 'He's the Godeater's Son,' she said. 'I'm certain.'

'You seemed less certain before,' the champion of Bharat answered. She lovingly stroked my crown. 'But he has a fine skull. Succeed or fail, he'll do.'

CHAPTER TWENTY-FOUR

In Candip, after the revelation and the red faded from my body and mind, half a man remained. He was spent, fading like coals in a cold brazier. But after a draught of something thick and spiced seared down my gullet, I returned to life.

A cup was pulled from my lips. A stranger's words echoed in my ears.

'Swallow. There he goes. Good, good. He's ready, Maal. I'll get the axe?'

Blood swam to my head. I stirred, the place of my presence registering in a soberer mind. I sat upon a cold dais in a long forest of pillars and gloom. Hard to see anything in that twilight. No pyromancy illuminated the hall – only torchlight sconces and scorching eyes. Eerie geometric patterns had been carved on the floor. I caught a whiff of burning coals. Around me, a thin crowd of armoured warriors circled in the dimness like sharks in the deep. Two murmured amongst themselves, and one of them cackled. He removed the decapitated head of a Flensing Man from his belt, lifting it into torchlight to admire its morbid leer.

My sluggish eyes centred. A woman in ragged black raiment sat cross-legged before me, two yards away, on a folded carpet. Fresh sun-daub painted her eyes. She gazed at me askance, as if trying to see through a prism, to see me in a different light.

She was the crone-maiden from Lurth, the armoured champion who had saved us from the Flensing Men. Between us lay porringers of spice-encrusted meat swimming in red oil. Rice, too, fragrant with green herbs. I'd never seen rice before. I'd only heard stories of its service in nobles' feasting halls. The herbs I recognised. Common weeds.

'Have you ever seen flames devour a man?' the woman asked, her teeth dyed black, her gaze still sidelong.

'I speak our tongue,' I said. She'd spoken Yrdo in the Ashwilds. Lilted, strange Yrdo.

'Ah. You hardly spoke. I feared you only knew the common tongue.'

'What tribe are you from?' I asked. 'Where are we?'

'Bharat. On both counts.' She stared. 'Ever seen flames devour a man?'

I coughed, then tested my arms. My shoulder was healed.

Then I sniffed and smelt moisture. I reached out and poured unclean water into a clay cup before me. I waited for the sand to settle and pounded it back. My throat cooled.

'The Sigmarites burn our faithful,' the woman said, still looking through the prism. 'Immolation is a simple craft, with their spell-magic. But I speak not of pyromancy. I speak of low fires, with wood and hay. Have you ever seen flames devour a man? His joints go first. Then he tumbles apart. The wise tell the future in the way your limbs land. Try this some time.'

'Burning?' I said. 'Or being burnt?'

She shrugged. 'That depends on what you're worth.'

I glanced around. A circle of the Ashwilds warriors surrounded us, still clad in their shale armour. My falx and dirk rested on an amber cloth before me.

My eyes surveyed the feast between us. I couldn't recognise the cuts. 'Mortal flesh?' I asked.

'All flesh is mortal. This? This is your horse's meat. Your cursed, damned horse.'

I digested the words but nothing else. Then I reached for my blades.

'I only jest.' She raised her hands. 'This is common swine. Pork. I stole it myself, above. I jest. That's all.'

'Amusing.' I examined my dirk's notched edge.

'This is Bharat's custom. Humour is our greatest trial. You and yours forgot the old ways, but not we. We search for weakness, for those who laugh. They always give in to Aqshy's fire. Understand?' She pounded her breast. 'We excise laughers from our number. No ice in their hearts.'

'I laugh often,' I said flatly. 'I'm very humorous.'

'Oh.' Her eyes fell, then widened. 'Oh! That is very good. Humorous indeed. The Seeker vouched for you. Perhaps she was not wrong.'

'She'd laugh too, if she saw what I saw now.'

She leaned in. 'And what see you?'

I looked at her and hardened.

She nodded approvingly. 'You are very good at this. Yes, very humorous. I shall use that later in another trial. You're like the old kin, like us. Cardandish humour was once renowned, it is said.'

'Wait until I show you how we kill.'

She considered my words. 'Less humorous. A little too subtle for me.'

She explained more, perhaps to thaw my frigidity. Bharat had survived, she claimed, through rigour and cruelty. They couldn't let the wrong ones in. They couldn't take chances as I had. Because

I, she said, had been fortunate in my company. Her people would have usurped me in the many moments of my frailty, but mine had stayed with me unto death.

She said if I failed her people's trials they would spill my entrails and burn me in low fires. She would read the future in my limbs' falls and polish the char from my skull before adding it to her collection.

'You're a liar and a witch.' I spoke Azyrite. 'Bharat's gone. Dead. Dust of the ages, ash from the flames.'

She pointed to the red tar on her face. 'Who else would–?'

I slashed at her eyes. She rolled back, just out of reach. My dirk threshed loose strands of hair and nothing else.

Then I was gone, barrelling past the loose circle of our audience, legs pumping me through the temple murk. I tumbled headlong towards a wound in the wall, a passage. Two warriors guarded it. They wore shale armour and carried axes. They moved to stop me and I struck once, then slid over the gritty stone. I ignored the clank of a tall helmet and loose head toppling to the ground behind me.

As the woman shouted for the others to stop me, I hurtled away into torchlit corridors. They reminded me of unterways – they *were* unterways. But instead of weather-worn sandstone and foreign hexes chaining veins of earthfire, they were smooth, painted, well-lit – the capillaries of a living city. I didn't know this place, but it couldn't be Bharat. Bharat was lost, to time and an age of darkness.

Then I barged out onto a promenade overlooking a crevasse, like Candip in miniature, loud with life and bright as day. Vaulted ceilings covered the soaring heights. Carved walkways jutted overhead, criss-crossing the gorge. Another promenade ran parallel to mine, and railways ran through the levels below. Down there, from rusted pens and unclean butcheries, the rank bite of aurochs dung and the fresher tang of their halved carcasses wafted up. Between them, lean mortals from every breed and nation guided hulking metal beasts in thick barding, which dragged laden carts over the railways. I'd never seen such juggernauts. They snorted, trudging tirelessly, fell light aglow in the seams between their armoured plates.

Around me, smoke coughed from furnaces into the closed skies. A ceaseless clamour assaulted my ears, ringing and clanging. Metal screamed as it was tempered in barrels of oil in forges. Half-naked warriors wrestled in sandy paddocks below the promenade, barking as they trained in the dirt. They grappled, pounding fists into each other's bellies, grunting and cursing.

This place was the nativity of violence. The scale took my breath away. It was as if some god had hammered a dirty ratkin sprawl into a fortress, then tempered it with fire and blood.

Warriors stormed from the passage I had just left. They saw me and I was off again, pushing through crowds of thralls, of warriors – I couldn't tell which. They were all half-naked, carpeted in scars, lean and leering. I didn't care who they were. I didn't care what wasteland kingdom had usurped Bharat's legacy. I just wanted to escape. As I flew through another knot of corridors, a needle of light pierced the gloom ahead. Daylight, outside.

I ran harder, grinning at the ease of my headlong escape. Had I the breath, I would have laughed at my captors' incompetence. Long, and loud, and low, the better to mock the custom of Bharat – of 'Bharat'.

Then I reached the end and slid to a halt. Daylight, yes. Outside, not quite.

Because beneath this precipice of smooth stone plunged an endless abyss of ivory skies. Red cirrus striped the great nothing, like fresh blood in old milk. I couldn't believe my eyes. Then I looked up.

The world was upside down. Half-familiar craglands stretched into the capsized horizon. Molten stone dripped from the earthen ceiling of this world into the infinity below. Cyclones danced along the rocky vaults, throwing brimstone sands down into the abyss. The city hugging this upturned ground was also reversed, but recognisably Yrdun. The stepped terraces of ziggurats marched down into the bright gulf. I stood in one such tower.

Beyond the reversed city loomed a distant mountain like the base of a titanic bowl. A liquid red ribbon sliced into the abyss from its apogee, its nadir. Below that mountain, a red storm reigned. I felt as if I was watching the breast of Aqshy give suckle to hell. Nothing could sate the realm's burn.

I glanced around, shameful panic swelling up the cracks of me. A whole realm stretched out before me, turned on its head. The bottom of Aqshy – the base of the world.

'Maal, here!'

They'd found me. I choked down my panic and pivoted, blades locked into my fingers. A crowd of barbarians closed in.

I saw them for what they were, then. Yrdun in their hearts, wearing outlanders' shells. Foreigners, speaking my tongue, wearing my people's legacy armour. I hadn't been willing to admit it. But the truth is a siege ram, and it takes us by storm.

'Where are we?' I demanded.

The woman in black rags pushed through her warriors. She was a diamond in the coals. She bared her ink-black teeth. 'Kaddarar, calm him. Please. Now.'

The others made way. Kaddarar strode forward with regal dignity and a knower's scorn. When she saw me, she offered her pernicious, venomous smile. Whatever I had thought of her and her god, I would be lying if I said her appearance did not bring me joy.

She crossed her arms, her curse-hands grinding into eight-fingered clubs and tucking into the bulges of her muscle. 'I'm not

talking him down. That's the whole reason he's here – to talk him
up. He's the Godeater's Son. Let him have his kills.'

Vexed, the woman in black rags clicked her tongue in disappointment. She extended her bony hand, and a helmed head dripping
gore and spinal fluid was placed in its grip.

She tossed it to my toes. It belonged to the warrior I had slain
not minutes ago.

'Your trophy,' she said. 'To do with as you wish. Rigour and
cruelty, Fall. Didn't I say?'

I looked up. 'He was one of yours.'

'Sometimes the wrong ones get in. But they do not stay long.'

I couldn't see through this woman. I didn't understand what
she wanted.

'I'm not laughing.'

'Good. This is no jest. I thought you an unlikely Champion,
but I'm warming to the possibility I was wrong. Come, brother.
There are simpler ways to see your city than this. Blood, and the-
atrics, and rolling heads.' She clicked her tongue. 'You make this
all so tedious.'

Sweat beaded on my brow. Finally, I lowered my blades. 'Where
are we?' I asked, for the last time.

'I told you, Fall. Bharat, beneath Aqshy – the place where all
blood flows. And, I dare hope, your kingdom.'

Her name was Tominer. She was a Maal of Bharat, one of the last
of the fabled oracles who had once given counsel to kings.

The warriors of Bharat answered to none but the Maals. Tominer
could direct them, but her rulings were not orders so much as
spiritual counsel. She was a priest among the lay, a chaplain among
the sergeants. If Kaddarar's eyes were burning quartz, here smouldering, there blazing, then Tominer's gaze was burnished brass,
always reflecting some sourceless glow.

Her retinue escorted us back through the Hell-Mills, the place where Bharat prepared for war without end. We took a different route back to the feast, metallic suspension decks rattling beneath our feet.

Below, the blood-stricken skies. Above, endless earth. Reverse-ziggurats loomed in the monstrous horizons. Forests of chains hung pendant from Bharat's ceiling – its ground? To behold this mysterious city's unceasing industry unanchored the core of me. I felt as if I was in Aqshy's choppy outer seas, rowing without direction or fathom. Bharat was massive, as grand as any unfulfilled dream, populated by mortals with callused hands, oiled hair, sooty skin. They were nobody, like me.

We arrived where we had started, in the murk-ridden temple. We partook of the feast prepared for us. Flinty-eyed heathens from tribes I couldn't name gathered to watch us.

As long as I had lived I had been told Bharat was lost. And it had been, in the second sense of the word.

With a sedate tone and a subtle bend in her lips, Tominer told me Bharat's story. The sorcerous passages which had brought us here – the tunnels which opened in the Ashwilds – were realmgates. They were the first and truest of the Yrdun unterways, anchored to feylines, concealed by their magic. At the dusk of the Age of Myth, scryers and Maals had sensed what was coming. They had closed the gates with elder magic. Darkness fell, and with it had come its sister, turmoil. The old kingdoms had been broken.

But closing the gates had not been enough. Chaos found subtler ways into the city. As Cardand's great houses resisted the power of Chaos through skill at arms, Bharat was forced to harness it. Tominer spoke much as Yron did, of our people's need for glory to earn the Dark Gods' favour for the boons they provided. Against Chaos, Chaos was the only shield. It was a circle. A snake devouring itself.

Bharat did not cave to the worship of Chaos in a single night. Predators whittled it apart and scavenged its fiefs. Mad-eyed marauders despoiled its villages and temples, or abducted its maidens and firstborn sons for rites unknown. Faced with extinction, the city's war chiefs and house kings made the only choice they could. They gathered their people at the top of their mountain, *Asharashra*, and prayed for salvation to powers they did not understand.

Whatever came to pass there, it saved the city. Pagan hordes with pin-eyes and dagger-teeth retreated. Raiders who had blanketed the seething darkness with their torchlight departed in search of easier spoils. Long-horned things with long tongues and long swords disappeared. So did their predations.

After all this, Bharat's lands turned on their head. Bharat's great leaders never returned from Asharashra.

'Only the Maals remained,' Tominer said, speaking Azyrite for Kaddarar's benefit. 'They opened the realmgates again, to send the faithful to the Pale of Bodshe.'

'For what?' I asked. 'You were safe. Why leave?'

'To save the others. Your kind. The Yrdun of Cardand, the Beltollers. Bharat's Maals wish to teach those who had remained in Bodshe the truth. To protect them, with the good word.'

I sipped water. 'And what's the good word?'

'The truth. The fourth pillar of Yrdoval, revealed to our people on Asharashra by the powers of the red god, Bloodfather.'

'Khorne-Godeater,' Kaddarar incanted, slurping from a porringer of scalding chili oil. 'That's his name. Not this blood-pappy rubbish.'

I pointed. 'You don't believe it either?'

'Not a word of it.' She tossed her emptied porringer behind her, where it clattered.

Tominer turned her eyes on Kaddarar. I could have cut the

tension between them with a knife. They despised each other. What had brought them together, I couldn't understand. They didn't even agree about their own gods.

'Ignore her.' Tominer spoke Yrdo. 'I've told you the truth. What say you?'

I leaned back, trying to exhale the discomfort from my bulging belly. 'You're Yrdun. But you're not. You're pretending. And I don't like pretenders.'

'Says the man who won't take off his father's face. We're Yrdun. Like you.'

'You look so, with the daub, yes. But not these others. Some don't even understand us.'

Our onlookers blinked, murmuring amongst themselves. Those who spoke Yrdo interpreted for the others.

Tominer gestured. 'We rebuild the old kingdom. This takes time. And blood, in every sense of the word.'

I bit down. 'I see Azyrites. Parchers. Outrealmers from different lands, different seas, different skies. I don't see a single mortal I'd name brother or sister. Not a soul I'd trust to fight by my side. Not even you.'

This, at least, Tominer understood. 'You adhere to the old ways.'

I nodded. 'You said that was good.'

'In some things, yes. In others, no. Ice is good, to chain the fire. But you see the realm with old eyes. Bloodlines and native tongues no longer bind us. Faith, Fall – faith binds us. Look to what Sigmar has done. He builds an empire of shared belief, an imaginary world at best. But that world is a hammer, smashing apart the broken kingdoms of every realm. Bharat must do the same. Bharat must answer Bloodfather's call.'

Tominer led us back to the precipice and the baffling vista. She pointed to the mountain thrusting into the cursed welkin, the storm below. The lone red ribbon gushing from Asharashra's lower peak glistened by the light of an evil sun. Ivory clouds limned in red lightning surrounded the crimson storm.

'When the war chiefs and house kings made their bargain, our people retreated to Asharashra's slopes, there. The holy mountain. They communed with Bloodfather. They still do. For their faith he blessed them. In his name, we spread revelation.'

'The Yrdun are there? Not your orphans and widows, the true Yrdun?'

'Yes. Living under Bloodfather's aegis, in his light. Those of our nation who prove themselves worthy are granted permit to descend the mount and meet our great lord. They face his trials. Those who pass gather as heroes and heroines of Bharat in antici- pation of war, to deliver what was promised to Cardand.'

'We could have used that help,' I said, in Azyrite. 'We've been at war.'

Tominer shook her head gravely. 'Not like the war we await. A last war, Fall. A war which shall never end.'

Kaddarar groaned and thumped away, muttering *daft witch* under her breath.

Tominer's eyes glittered, then returned to me. 'The Seeker thinks the war's begun too. But she doesn't know. She's not one of us. I came from Cardand, like you. I didn't believe until Maal Qulemone showed me the truth. We're all found above, then brought below, desolate until we understand. *We* shall rebuild Bharat, Fall. *We* shall inherit the realm. This is why we took you.'

'Me.' I stared at Asharashra and the silk fire spewing from its crags. Thunder from the crimson storm rumbled in my belly. 'Oh, me.'

Tominer turned her head. 'I searched for you. For so long. I sensed you in Lurth. And even before the Seeker's wanderings brought her to us, and you to her, I learned of your exploits. More than that, I know what they mean. The first Maals told of a hero from Cardand who could raise the Chosen legion on Asharashra. The final legion, for the final war. This is why we need you. This is why I must test you.'

'You want me to worship your god.'

'I want you to lead your people. You're a tome unwritten. You are all of us. Anyone with eyes can see whom the Seeker serves, but you...' Tominer steadied her breath. 'I know of no greater measure of a mortal's will than their defiance of fate. That is you.'

'I'm not looking for salvation.'

'Good. Because we are the saviours, not the saved. All comes from Chaos. To Chaos all returns. The God-King speaks a vast lie, that Order can be made in the universe. He seeks to build an eternity that does not exist. Our duty is to spread the truth. Only one road leads to forever.'

And there it was. 'The Path to Glory,' I said.

'The path to *freedom*,' Tominer said. 'The path to *control*. Only Chaos provides this. Only the Five. Only Bloodfather.'

I regarded her with eyes heavy and cool. If Kaddarar was the sharpened axe, Tominer was the moment of its fall.

'And if I agree?' I said.

'You dwell with your people again, with us. You lead our war-parties, until you are ready for the trial of the Chosen.' She gestured to the abyss, to the breast of Aqshy and its endless cataract. 'The pilgrimage to Asharashra will show us if Bloodfather finds you worthy. But all things in time.'

I nodded. 'And if I disagree?'

She gestured to the abyssal skies. 'I cut your throat and toss you away.'

How laughable. But how I wanted her to try. How badly I wanted to be petty and small and extinguish our existences for the sake of making a point. The defiance of fate, she'd called it. I called it power.

Yet that bitterness warred with everything I wanted. I craved to be among kindred. I yearned to love and be loved. Even if that meant a lifetime of war beside brethren who might better be called foreigners. Even if that meant false oaths to false gods.

Then there were the secrets of the mountain draining into hell. I did not care a whit about Tominer and her gods. Yet if my true people, the Yrdun of lost Bharat, resided upon Asharashra's slopes, I had no choice but to meet them. I would embrace them as sisters embrace brothers. I would compel them to help me finish what I had started. They would understand, because they were family. They would know what I wanted, even if I did not.

Because I didn't. After Candip and Ildrid, I wasn't sure what I wanted any more. I just knew I didn't want it alone.

'I accept,' I said.

Tominer exhaled in measured relief, and I heard a blade slip back into its scabbard beneath her rags.

CHAPTER TWENTY-FIVE

Crimson dye dripped from hanging skeins onto the sands we paced. Rose madder overflowed in baskets by the pen, stinking like cut weeds. For me, Kaddarar and Micaw, these were our accommodations. A dirt paddock on an ancient scaffold, hanging from Bharat's undercity like a vulture's nest.

When Micaw first sensed my smell, she grew restless. Now she circled the paddock, knocking baskets of madder over when she passed too close. Grit kicked beneath her hooves, steaming from their heat. No matter what she'd become, I could only be proud. She'd come a long way from that wretched mare I once contemplated killing. So had I.

Distantly, sleepless furnaces belched rotten-egg gases into the air. Kaddarar seemed to enjoy the smell. Brimstone made her faster, stronger. Each time she launched herself at me, I feared it would be the last.

I rolled. The mauls of her flails thudded the sand where I'd stood, shaking the paddock.

'You're swift. That's good. But against Stormcast Eternals, swiftness is not enough.'

We traded blows. Her flails were hard to parry. She ripped them through the air, and they moved with a life of their own. Swaying like serpents, striking like cobras. I couldn't feel them out. So I dodged back, then rolled away from the walls before Micaw came round and trampled me.

'You said I held my own in Candip,' I spoke, panting. 'Before we escaped.'

'Only because I was there.' She struck again; I moved. 'You had the red haze in your eyes. The oldest boon. *Rage*.'

Then her chains swept my legs. I smashed in to the sand. She could have killed me, if she wished to. Instead she helped me up.

'Rage is the oldest boon,' I parroted.

'Yes. A foundation. But not enough, not by itself.'

I paced, gathering my breath. She prepared to strike, but I raised my hand. 'Can you for once say something useful? Just this one time and never again. Tell me something that makes sense.'

Blackness bled back into her pupils, replacing the glow shaded like the dripping skeins overhead. 'The God-King's chosen are faster than you, stronger than you, smarter than you. Until you receive the gods' boons, you cannot beat them in a fair fight. Or an unfair fight.'

'So I can't beat them?'

She shrugged. 'You're mostly hopeless.'

I tossed my hands up. 'My gratitude. Very encouraging.' I slashed at her throat.

Her stony hands swatted my blade aside with a clatter. 'Accept the truth. Only then can you change it.' She punched me to the ground.

I ate sand, then groaned, waiting for her to crush my skull. She always claimed her final trial awaited me. But if it did, it was not now.

'Insolence,' she said. 'That must be your weapon against the Stormcast Eternals. Sheer audacity. A brass neck.'

I sat up, sucking in a lungful of air, dispelling my nausea. Micaw neighed with amusement, a basso that shook my soul.

'Chaos,' I sneered, a taunt more than an insight.

But the word clicked in her head. 'Yes. Chaos, in its own way. Stormcasts are powerful and cunning foes. Their fatal flaw is that they know this. No matter what they pretend to be, they are not humble. They're arrogant. Hubris is inevitable for the blessed and the false-divine. *Use* this. Do what they do not expect – do what *you* do not expect. Now stand. Practise on me.'

'You think like them,' I said. 'You underestimate mortals.'

She gestured with her disgusting hand, the eight fingers splayed open like spider legs. 'I would not call it an underestimation. You're puny and fragile – that is the truth. All you must do is defy it. Now come and kill me.'

I tossed a handful of sand into her eyes. She blinked but didn't budge.

Instead of following through on my attack, I baulked. 'This is why you came for me? To taunt me?' I scoffed. 'You gave up on me. Then I did what you counselled and you changed your mind and came back. But I see what you are, Seeker. You'll leave again. You're inconstant.'

'I'm constancy incarnate. I was just a little rash. Maybe I was the reason you wised up. Maybe you should be grateful. Because you could be dead.'

'You pledged to serve!' I shouted. I hadn't realised I was angry until those words came out. I forced ice back into my smouldering heart. 'I trusted you. Then you killed Cillus and left. And it *pleased* you.'

Those words wounded her as my blades could not. She lowered her gaze.

'People see us, and they think they know. You, with your mask and hatred. Me, with Godeater's boons. But we're more than monsters. I'm not an orruk, killing for killing's sake. I serve my god as true as I can. But whatever Godeater made me, I am not perfect. I killed Cyloth, yes – but it did not please me. I regret his death. I'm human, Fall. Stormcast Eternals are the same.'

'You killed Cillus and left,' I repeated, standing and shaking sand from my sleeves. 'You would've killed me, too. You're a puppet. An abacus counting heads like beans. Scorch that – you're the damned axe that takes them!'

Her eyes glittered. 'For those skulls, Godeater loves me. I give Godeater what he wants – and he *loves* me. No one else in the realms loves so freely. Cyloth was a friend. But what difference does it matter if he died then or in eight days or eighty years? Cyloth is dead. Soon you'll be too. And when my head comes up, Godeater will love me as much for that as any of the others.' She shook her head, murmuring. 'They'll see. They'll see, then they'll know.'

After I'd had my fill of quiet I spoke. 'You're nothing like what I expected.'

She chuckled. 'You don't know what to expect. You've lived hardly a lifetime. I've existed for centuries. You know what crosses the gaze in that much time?'

'Enough to worship lies. Enough to fool yourself.' I sighed. 'Your god doesn't care for you. He uses you. Scorn me, scorn Tominer and her people, but your beliefs are as foggy as theirs and you won't even admit it. I ask why you came back, you can't even answer. It wasn't for them, it wasn't for me. And I'm still alive, so it wasn't for Godeater. Do you even know? You don't even understand it, do you?'

'*Understand?*' Kaddarar's face wrenched up in pain-polluted wrath. 'Is that what you want? Understanding? I understand, Fall.

I understand why my family offered me up to the darkness. I understand why the Khul killed them instead of me. But understanding helps nothing. I need not understand the gods' wills. I need only accept things as they are. Godeater takes care of the rest.'

My demeanour thawed beneath my mask.

'You want to know why I returned?' she asked. 'I came to kill you. I went to the stepwell seeking your skull. I tracked you to Candip and saved you from that witch-Eternal – *seeking your skull!* I sought you out, Fall. No one else. You're a fruit on a high branch. Only I deserve to pluck you.'

'Wait.' I considered her words. 'You went to the stepwell?'

Her eyes smoothed.

'You didn't know about the attack on Candip when you decided to return?' I asked. 'So how'd you know I was still worthy? Why was my skull still so precious?'

She said nothing. Her eyes grew dangerous, smouldering into evil life.

Oh. *Oh.*

'You didn't want my skull,' I said. 'You came back for me.'

She flinched. Then she shook her flails out and roared, launching into the attack. The time for talking, it seemed, was over.

In all Bharat's uninviting splendour, not a single library existed. Instead, Tominer instructed me to meet her for a lecture on the gods on the slaughter-floor of an abattoir. Here the city's mongrel population handled the meat of creatures abducted from above. Other provisions were stored in ebony casks. Grain overflowed from them, piling onto the floor. Meat confits submerged in their own congealed fat sat in covered basins.

I arrived to find Tominer anointing a warband of Bharat raiders outside. She dragged a long knife across their slate-metal breastplates. Oil trickled from the wounded plate, then ignited. Like that they leapt into the abyss below the abattoir, one after the other, trailing fire. Not a soul looked back.

'Keep the wrong ones out,' I said, in Yrdo.

'I think of it more as letting the *right* ones out,' Tominer answered. 'Let's begin.'

I pointed over the precipice. 'But what was that?'

'You'll soon know. Come, no more banter.'

That eerie spectacle was the most interesting part of the day. For hours, Tominer droned on about Bharat's credos. She and her fellow Maals would not let me march with their people's warbands without proper indoctrination into Bharat's ways. I feigned intentness. I admired the withered youth in Tominer's body, that nest of physical contradictions. Old with new, new with old. Yet she spouted so much nonsense, I couldn't swallow it all. She spoke of eternity and evanescence. She spoke of the Azyrites and their addiction to everlasting order; of their never-ending kingdoms and forever empires; of their false prosperity without end.

Then she stopped. 'When did you stop listening?'

'I wasn't listening for most of it,' I said. It seemed my patience was more fleeting than Sigmar's.

Tominer glowered, then pouted, as Varry might have. Strange to reconcile this soft woman with the one who'd steeled herself to cut my throat and toss me into the sky.

'This is no jest, Fall.'

I wrinkled my eyes. 'Yes it is. Your words stink of aurochs' filth, like these butchers' pens. All of you seek eternity. Not just the Azyrites – you, too. That's the Path to Glory, isn't it? That's the will of your gods. You do what the Azyrites do, trading your souls and pride for power, and in return you live forever. But it's empty life. You're all slaves. Every one of you.'

Again, Tominer gazed through the prism, as if inspecting me for flaws.

I reached out and snapped her head straight, so that we saw each other eye to eye. 'No. Look at me. Say the truth.'

'You wouldn't understand the truth.' She freed her head from my grip. 'You must see to know. Only those who see can face the trial of the Chosen on Asharashra. And you *will* see. This is what I prepare you for – to fight with us and learn the truth, to be worthy of leading our army.'

Her words reminded me of Ildrid's hollow rhetoric about her kind, the Stormcast golems. I shook my head.

'You're all slaves. The Path to Glory is a fool's bargain, nothing more. The gods take everything. What they give might as well be nothing.'

'It's not nothing.' Tominer's eyes gleamed. 'Glory is not currency like Aqua Ghyranis, to be spent and lost. Glory, Fall. What is it? Can you explain it? Can you hold it in your hands?'

'Everyone knows what glory is.' I tossed my hands. 'Glory's glory.'

She bared her black teeth, smiling at my ignorance. 'Glorious is the name that lives forever. To whom does the name belong, once glory is achieved? To us – to you. No god can strip us of our names. They may take our bodies, our souls, our minds – often through the very power they grant. In some ways, you're right. Sigmar's no different from the Five in this. From Bloodfather, or the Great Necromancer of Shyish-Shol. But our names belong to *us*. You shall never lose yours. And if you speak your name loud enough in the time you have in these realms – that name shall echo. *That* is glory. *That* is true eternal life. Glory is freedom, Fall. And with it, one may master the truth of the realms.'

The truth. I spat. I wanted to shove all this specious oratory into a fire. 'You don't look free, Tominer. I don't feel free.'

She grew frustrated. 'No one would be here if they had a choice. All things with time.'

'But we do have a choice. And I've been here hours, and what've I got? Nothing.' I waited. 'Why are you staring at me?'

'I'm wondering if I was this bitter and broken when Qulemone found me.' She brushed reed-thin hands over her lips. 'At least you don't laugh.'

I gazed out over the abattoir. A bare-shouldered butcher lugged the torn rump of a ram from the pens. She tossed it onto a thick board, started trimming it with her hand-axe.

'I want to kill Azyrites,' I said. 'I want to break them. I want them to feel what I feel, to see what I see. If I must believe what you believe to lead Bharat's warbands and do this, I will. I'll do whatever it takes. But at least have it make sense. I won't barter with lies.'

Tominer gazed absently at the grated floor. Blood coalesced and coagulated there, to be collected later in gelled sheets and purged of evils, then floured and steamed into cakes. I wondered if the false Yrdun of Bharat ate vegetables. I wondered if Tominer's gospel wasn't all just calculated deceit, meant to keep its captive nation sated, its commerce flowing, its warlords' gazes fixed on outsiders instead of each other.

'The Azyrites did not break Bodshe,' Tominer spoke. 'They came after our fall. We did it. Bharat's legions. You've heard of the ancient wars in the Age of Chaos. Bharat despoiled Cardand, with iron and flame. Bharat sapped Bodshe's strength. Bharat paved the way for the Azyrites' conquest.'

I blinked, her words sinking their claws into my chest. This could not be true. We were supposed to be one nation, even if Bharat's folk had become little more than a masquerade of foreigners.

But Tominer was not lying. I could see that much. I struggled for words. 'Why'd you tell me this?' I said, in Azyrite.

'The truth will set you–'

I shot to my feet, raking my head. 'You killed us. You ruined us.'

Tominer tugged at my leg. 'I told you, Fall. We wish to save our people. There's no other path but Chaos. None of us would have chosen this if it were not the only way.'

My fists trembled. My breath shortened. 'There's always another way. Bharat could have helped. But it was you. It was always you.'

'No. Cardand sealed its own fate. Their great houses were too stubborn. They resisted when they would have been wiser to submit – to join us. Instead, they opposed us for the sake of their greed, like the Azyrites. They sought to protect what they thought was theirs from those who would have used it for the final war. Cardand wouldn't accept the truth of Asharashra, Fall. That is why we fought them.' Tominer released my leg. 'Bharat did not foresee Sigmar's tempest. If we had, perhaps the ancient Maals would have done differently. But that does not change the truth of Asharashra, or its absoluteness. All must accept the inevitability of Chaos. I didn't when Qulemone found me, but I did before the end. And when your time comes, Fall, you must accept it too. That, or–'

I stormed off. 'Scorch you,' I said. 'Scorch your truth.'

'Where are you going?' she asked.

But I did not answer her question, for she had answered none of mine.

CHAPTER TWENTY-SIX

After I had told her of Tominer's revelations, Kaddarar sat with the unbearable patience of one who had seen it all.

'Don't tell me you agree with her,' I said. 'I swear I'll kill you.'

'You couldn't if you tried,' she growled, eyes smouldering. 'But no. I don't understand. Their belief in the gods is too complex, too sophisticated. Mine is more primitive.'

'You're all primitive.' A breeze pushed through the red skeins on the drying racks. Dye dripped on us, a red rain, moistening my hair. I remembered the Orb Infernia, then. Varry, slipping my grip. Nearby, Micaw gnawed on a rack of aurochs ribs.

'I like primitive things,' Kaddarar said. 'Like axes. There's nothing to axes. They're simple. But guns, fusils, muskets… they're too much. Ideas can be like that. If they're too complex, they become difficult to handle.' She gazed at me. 'Don't do what the witch does, Fall. Don't twist things to make them fit.'

'That's the problem. I think it does fit. Look at this place. The bottom of the realm.' My head sagged. 'I don't want them to be right.'

Kaddarar scoffed. 'Aqshy has no bottom. This is a primordial flameworld your old kings must have stumbled upon. And that absurdity about your people? Your war chiefs and house kings dwelling in paradise on the mount? That is pure fiction.'

'So where are they?'

She shuddered with contempt. 'Who knows? Who cares? Dead now, or living a lie. There's no paradise in the Mortal Realms. All things are simpler than they seem. Even Godeater's message. I often say we're either skulls or skull-takers. But the truth is, we're *all* skulls. Even the skull-takers.' She huffed, then rose. 'Don't let the witch complicate your purpose. Remember yourself. Tell her what you must, to get her warriors to fight with us. Now, stop fretting, little fool. Stormcasts do not fret. Stand and fight.'

I stood. 'Tominer called me fortunate in my company.' I gave my falx a swing. 'She said her own people would have usurped me in the moments of my weakness.'

Kaddarar whipped her chains, kicking up sand. The heads of each flail skipped along the paddock and beat the air. I slowed my breathing, anticipating their motion.

But the Seeker halted, her flails skidding to a stop. She raised a curse-hand, flexing each of the eight fingers, like coal petals on a stone orchid. The blossom's brutal crunch sent chills down my spine.

'You *are* weak,' Kaddarar said, '*so* weak. But the witch knows nothing. Weakness scars into strength.'

I launched into an attack. For the first time, I caught Kaddarar off guard.

So Kaddarar did not understand. Let her live her life like that, if it pleased her. She'd proven her faith to me. By now I had little reason to think she might break her oath to kill me when the time was right and no sooner. If the Seeker was no friend, then at least she was no enemy. Of Tominer I was less sure.

In the days and nights I spent much time alone. I contemplated what awaited me on Asharashra's depths. I stared at its slopes in a fugue, trying to discern the purpose of the distant masonry and brass edifices. Stone monoliths were suspended beneath the mountain's peak, their engineering as miraculous as it was audacious. The red ribbon coursed from it, into the roiling storm below, eaten by distance and clouds.

My mind would not cease its travels. I thought of those I'd lost and left behind. Yron and Jujjar, both likely slain in Candip's streets. Boskin, who'd either abandoned our cause or been captured and met a traitor's death. Varry, somewhere in Aqshy's orbit. My father, somewhere in the ash and wind. I thought of the halberdier Reiriz and the final peace in his eyes. I thought of my mother, then of the Refuser. But those thoughts travelled far from each other. I could not reconcile them.

Kaddarar told me of how the refugee encampments in Candip Plain were scoured while my warband plundered the city's rift. When the Stormcasts emerged from their lairs in Candip's captive metaliths, they managed to consolidate and eliminate all refugees with rebel sentiments, including the rabble I'd served up as if on fine silver. Freeguilders had dismounted from the cogforts and swept through the camps, erasing those who resisted from existence, then banishing the rest.

To Stormsworn, our war must have seemed over. This reflection gave me hope, for I knew it was not. I yearned to prove her wrong.

The Refuser's trap played itself over and over again in my mind. In the evenings, when the nether-sun below Bharat drifted above the wicked horizon and the world's endless depths darkened, I still heard her black words. Her voice rumbled like thunder, and the void in her soul sang. I remembered her ozone stink, and my nose wrinkled. I remembered her triumphant poise; my belly ached. She was still in me, my mother. I could not part from her.

Ildrid. Mother. This thought should have embittered me, but it was still raw, like skin too close to burning coals. Where had she been, when Sigmar remade her? Where had she been as Varry and I scavenged magnure to sell for dregs? We'd lived in the ruins of a broken hill, subsisting on scraps and fears of tomorrow. Where was mother when the beasts came for Elene and cracked my sister's skull like an egg?

To have lived with nothing would have been enough, if only it had been with Varry. Deprived of her I really had nothing, nothing at all. Again the Azyrites had taken everything, as before. But if Tominer was to be believed, my own people had done the same. Where had the suffering started? When would it end?

When I couldn't push away the poison of my ruminations, Kaddarar came. She forced me to train. She grounded me. We fought often, mouths slavering, the iron in our hands ringing through the iron in our bones. Violence gave me peace. Violence made me strong. This was not just Kaddarar's lessons on the vulnerabilities of the Stormcast Eternals, or Bharat's boonful meat. This was that red haze I had felt in Candip, simmering beneath the surface of me. The blood thirst, the hate hunger. I could learn to use it, I thought. I could be more powerful than Ildrid. Then I would fix the realm.

'What is brightstone?' I asked one day. 'The Refuser asked us, didn't she? Before we escaped.'

Then I dodged, parried. The paddock quaked as Kaddarar's maul sank into the sand. I plodded up the taut length of her chain, dragging her down with my weight. She grunted and ripped the chain up, tossing me.

'You fight like an aelf. That's good, I didn't expect it. But you're too heavy. Ground yourself.'

We reset.

'Brightstone.' She grumbled. 'I thought you didn't remember. The red fog filled your eyes. Brightstone is burning metal. Powerful, coursing with Aqshy's fire. It's more precious than Ghyran waters, more potent than a wronged man's wrath.' She tapped her hands. 'Cyloth used a flake to wright my hands. Your people in this city have some, too.'

We exchanged a flurry of blows. Steel rang on steel, sweat stung my eyes. We reset.

'Did I answer her?' I asked. 'I don't remember.'

'The storm-witch? No. I did.'

'And what did you say?'

She gave a brutal chuckle, brushing jet hair from her eyes. 'Something legendary. Something memorable. I don't know. On the slaughterfields I never put as much thought into my words as I wish. Too caught up in the moment.' We continued. Reset. 'But I got the feeling she wasn't asking me.'

If I was vexed by the idea that something could have been more important to Stormsworn than defeating me – which, apparently, this brightstone had been – then the mystery of why she had thought I might be able to answer her eluded me completely. I'd never heard of brightstone.

Kaddarar seized me by the throat. Her curse-hands squeezed the life from me. I dropped my blades, prised at her rugged fingers. *'Hattaha,'* I choked.

'Curious.' She lifted me until my legs swung. 'You're distracted.'

Ugly noises gurgled from my craw. My legs dangled over damp sand. The Seeker had never done this before.

Then it hit me: my trial had come.

She tossed me into the sand. I gasped, retching for air.

Kaddarar took up her chains. 'Maybe that's why she asked you. To keep you on edge. Clever. Get up before I kill you.'

We tired of restraining ourselves to that miserable paddock. Amphitheatres lay higher in the city's mantle, where Bharat's juggernaut beast-cavalry were said to train. I was eager to test Micaw against the alchemical monstrosities, to see whose curse ran stronger.

As we walked there, Kaddarar aped the locals, mocking and imagining narratives of their lives and deaths. I laughed until my mouth was dry. Kaddarar's contradictions were key to understanding her. She was the slayer, the dormant slaughter, the innocence lost. But she was also a person worn smooth by time and patience and faith beyond my fathom. I'd thought she'd surrendered everything to her patron, Godeater. Maybe she had. But what mattered to me in her remained. Vestiges of humanity lurked in the burnt-out husk of her. Twisted, ugly, bitter – certainly. Yet Kaddarar was the same as anyone. She was the same as me.

'Fools!' Tominer roared.

Kaddarar groaned. 'The witch.'

Tominer prowled forward beside hulking raiders in spined helms and that shale-teeth armour. 'Infidels!' she screamed. 'Eaters of offal, washers in filth! Grin, go on! Keep grinning with your teeth, keep laughing with your lungs! You must bathe in used oils and boast to your friends of cowardice! You scavenge others' kills and claim shredded scalps as your own! You're ogors, on a fast! You're troggoths, writing songs! Idiots! Unlethal! Burnt-down!'

I waved her off. 'Enough. It was just a laugh.'

But Tominer trembled with anger. Her knife shook in her hands. Her warriors glared, weapons out. 'How can two warriors so worthy be such cretins?' she asked. 'Did I not say? To both of you? Did I not warn you? Ice. Bharat needs ice! We cannot risk Bloodfather's blessing with anything less. Yet here you are, like orruks crossed with dumber orruks – laughing!'

I tried to explain, but still Tominer seethed.

Kaddarar looked annoyed. 'More drivel about weakness.'

'Drivel?' Tominer was aghast. 'You think this *drivel?*'

'Yes. I think it high-quality drivel.'

Tominer raised a quivering finger. 'Bharat fights with one credo. This credo is iron. You of all people should've understood. You bear his mark.'

'I do,' Kaddarar growled. 'And so I see things clearer than you. You don't fight with any credo, witch. You and your people hide in the corners of the realm while *we* do the gods' work. Be gone and let us prepare. Unless you intend to unleash your tamed dogs and let us do what we're meant for.'

The warriors drew up around us. Kaddarar gazed at their axes and licked her lips.

Tominer wouldn't let this go. 'This offence demands answer.'

I was incredulous. 'I get it. Our good moods spoilt yours. So accept our apology for the affront. Or make us pay, here and now. But let's be done with this.'

Tominer swivelled, lips twitching. 'Have you heard none of what I've said these past weeks?'

I decided enough was enough. 'I heard all of it. I just don't care. The Seeker's right. We're ready for war, even if you're not. How long have you been here, preparing? I've coloured my blades black. I've reddened my teeth against Azyrites. Meanwhile all of you waited here, all this time, launching meaningless raids – against your *own* people. I could have sacked Candip with a fraction of your raiders. And I'd have done a damned sight more than despoil a cathedral and cut down some guards. We could've smashed the Stormcasts. We could've made them pay. But here you sit, cross-legged and close-eyed, crowing about truth and faith. Where's your Chosen legion, Maal? Where are they? If they're the warriors you claim, why don't they fight?'

I breathed hard, my shoulders heaving. My anger had snuck up on me. Bharat's warriors eyed us, gaining our measure. If they really wished to kill us, let them try. I wouldn't be cowed. Adrenaline pounded the stink of brimstone from my nose and purged the slag from my blood. I was fire, blue-hot and burning. I was ready. And I would not be corralled a moment longer.

'You want to know where the Chosen wait?' Tominer said. 'Go and see. You descend the mount. Today.'

'Good,' I said. 'Let's go.'

Bitter qualm churned in Kaddarar's cold face. 'She's not saying something.'

Tominer sneered, her stained black teeth peering through her lips. 'But you already know everything, don't you?'

Micaw pawed and snorted behind me. I calmed her and looked at Kaddarar.

'I'm ready,' I said. 'This is why you brought me here. To meet the elders of my blood. To lead their army and fight my war.'

Tominer turned that cruel prism upon me, the way the sun rises over battlefields.

'No, Fall. She brought you here to try.'

CHAPTER TWENTY-SEVEN

Nobody had ever returned from Asharashra. None. Not those champions of Cardand who had preceded me, nor Bharat's warriors chosen by the Maals to descend the mount and face their trial. Not a single soul in Bharat knew the fourth pillar of Yrdoval but the Maals and those who dwelt in the mountain's depths.

Not all, Tominer said, were worthy. The fate of the unworthy could be no mystery. Oxhead, Bloodfather, Godeater – the gods' names were different, but their needs were the same.

'Do not look up during your descent,' Tominer commanded.

I nodded. Great gusts battered us from every direction. We stood on a creaking timber platform suspended by chains and fastened between Bharat's tallest reverse ziggurats. A hanging stone road connected our platform to Asharashra's peak, the bosom of this world. Sun-withered scripts nailed to the overhang fluttered in the wind. On many, the ink had faded to nothing.

Below, the bleeding storm howled, masked by bruised clouds, limned with slashes of lightning. I glared out at the red cataract slicing into the damaged skies. Wind disrupted the falls, but onwards the blood coursed, pouring as a morbid chalice might be filled, a cup with no bottom.

I tightened my wraps, secured my mask. Kaddarar pulled me aside. 'You'll stick to your plan?'

'Of course.' I squinted through the gale. I would make my case to the true Yrdun of Bharat. I would win my folk over as only I could. Tominer was wrong. Tominer would see.

Kaddarar peered at me, her jet hair whipping behind her. 'This will be difficult.'

I chuffed. 'Now they've got to you.'

She gazed out, her quartz eyes burning. 'Not them. I sense it. I do not try to read the minds of gods, but Godeater speaks to me now, in words I barely perceive. He speaks of a true trial, Fall. The witch doesn't lie. He will not let the wrong ones in.'

I battled the fire in my heart, keeping myself cool.

Kaddarar returned her gaze to me. 'Do not forget your purpose. They're your people. When they ask you what you're willing to do for this, what will you say?'

'I don't know.'

She gripped my shoulder. 'It must be everything. You must be ready for this. Be certain when you meet them, or you will die.'

I moved to prise her hand away. When I brushed her coal-fingers, warmth radiated through me. My hand lingered. 'What are you?' I asked.

Kaddarar's eyes wandered to our hands. I smelt her, then. The pumice, the night-blooming flowers.

'I don't know. I don't know what I was, what I am, or what I'll become.' She freed her hand from mine. 'I only know what I must be before the end. It does not bring me joy. It won't please you, either.'

The time came. Tominer's warriors crowded behind us, aloof,

half reverent. They murmured between themselves. Some didn't think I would live. Kaddarar joined them, disappearing into a sea of oiled muscle and armour plates.

'Remember,' Tominer said, in such a tone I thought she might be nervous. 'Don't look up before you arrive.'

'Then how will I know if I've arrived?'

'If you don't, then you don't deserve to arrive at all.' Her demeanour cooled. I sensed a trace of bitter admiration in her. 'One foot before the other. That's all. And whatever you do – never look back.'

Micaw trotted down the stone road. I slouched on her back, my head hanging low. The tiles beneath her hooves hissed. Much of me hoped a sudden gust might carry us over the edge into the sky and end all my tedious fretting. Inside all mortals lurks this kernel of oblivion. Sometimes it's quiet. This time it was loud.

A thousand variations of what I might tell Bharat's war chiefs and house kings ran through my head. They were my people, blood of my blood. But they'd also accepted a god who commanded them to war against Cardand. How would we see eye to eye? The task before me was as mountainous as Asharashra. I felt some bitter irony that all my tortuous journeys had brought me to this undeviating stone road, to a trial I could not circumvent.

I rocked with Micaw's movements, my neck aching. I stared at dusted sandstone and Micaw's sweating bulk. Wind, gravity and oblivion tugged at us. Perhaps I was already dead. Perhaps I had fallen in Candip and this was the hell of the God-King's making.

I drew my dirk, dragged its edge across my palm. I relished the cursed steel kiss. The slash throbbed, and blood pooled in my palm. It trickled and anointed Micaw, who shuddered at its smell.

So I was alive. I'd seen fallen warriors bleeding out on fields of slaughter as they panted to no one of their mothers and dreams.

They hadn't known they were dead. I promised I would, when the time came.

The bridge widened. We entered what I guessed was a tiered square. We continued down its steps, a path of paving slabs with disturbing illustrations. The red falls of Asharashra's summit roared over epileptic winds. The cataracts grew deafening. Beneath that torrent, I heard metal shinking on metal. My heart pounded as I recalled the Orb Infernia. I felt like I was there again, the dormant breathing of ten thousand daemons rustling in my ears. The heat moved through my lungs like cattle wire. I craved to look up, but ice defeated my curiosity. I controlled nothing but myself. That must be absolute.

Then I saw the blood. Trickling over the flagstone, up the steps, little writhing worms with their own mind, their own wants. They coalesced and pooled around Micaw's hooves, rippling the wrong way through time, anticipating her steps. I had seen this before. Impending slaughter has its own gravity in the realms.

When we went as far as I thought we could, the wind died. My palm ached, and my heart prickled. I fuelled my bated breath with Asharashra's last gust. Then I unleashed that kernel of oblivion and raised my eyes.

No war chiefs awaited me. No wise-women Maals, no house kings, no Chosen.

Brutal brass arches drenched in gore rose before me. They were gates. Around them, pieces of the dead were heaped – the corpses of my people. Hacked down, chopped up, savaged. Ancient jewellery and primeval helms encrusted the gobbets of them. Picked-clean skulls were embedded into the brass gates, their empty black orbits staring out at me.

I ignored the gates, the skulls – for some of the bodies were drifting away. They rose from the gates into Asharashra's throat, into its hollow heart. Asharashra was no mountain. It was a charnel volcano. My stomach emptied at the sight of its innards.

Our dead. They were mortared in around the mountain's hollow like the cobble fill of a castle bulwark. Corpses – old and new, withered and fresh, whole or butchered. From this carrion collection spewed down the cataract of blood into the storm below, bathing the brass gates in liquid red.

These were Bloodfather's faithful, the Yrdun of Bharat. Without eyes to see, without mouths to scream, without hands to pray. They had been slaughtered to the last, as we had slaughtered the Azyrites at the Losh to the last.

Tominer had been wrong. Whatever had happened in the Age of Chaos, our nation had not survived. It was us. We were the mountain's font. Our gore, the spring of its falling waters. And worst, the truth, swinging down like a headsman's axe. The Azyrites had not broken us. We had broken ourselves.

My eyes dropped to the brass arches, drawn by the narcotic pull in my throat. In the river of red, through the foaming blood and the brass gates, I glimpsed another realm – the Realm of Chaos.

Fields of ash and fire. Broken banners of tarnished gold. Armies, nations, empires. They had slaughtered each other for time eternal, and their ruinous remains had collected here like the trinkets of crows. The plains were soggy with *carnage*, not death. The hills crackled with fire. The world behind those gates was memorial to murder.

And over the hills, silhouetted against crimson skies and red rains, I saw *It*. Not he, like arrogant Sigmar. Nor she, as the tree-folk's mythical queen.

It. The shadow of Khorne upon the universe, the hated syllable of its apocalyptic name resounding in my soul. Bloodfather. Godeater. All the other martial gods, of all the fanatics. They had all been wrong. Khorne was no warrior's patron or guardian of honour. Khorne was the Blood God, the Lord of Slaughter, the moment of murder.

Ildrid Stormsworn had been wrong to think any could triumph over Chaos. We were nothing before this force, whatever we believed in or disregarded. Even the God-King, for all his splendour and hubris, could not resist the resistless.

Despair swelled in me. I stood on the edge of extinction. I glimpsed skulls avalanching down mountains, which could have flattened cities. The fires in those fields were all the conflagrations of Aqshy from every age, and they ignited in my miserable, mortal soul. Here beyond these gates loomed the weapon I needed to defeat my enemies – the blessings of Khorne. I needed only to reach out and take it.

As I wavered, an epiphany crept up on me. Maybe Khorne's terrible shadow had breathed understanding into my wretched mind. Or perhaps I'd known the truth all along, and my despair had finally spoken it aloud.

Yrdoval has no pillars. Sanctuary, Hospitality, Vengeance – these were meaningless. The truth lay in the mountain of my dead nation above. The truth was a flood and I'd been drowning in it for so long I hadn't seen it.

Annihilation. That is the only truth of the realms.

For in the end it is all our destinies.

CHAPTER TWENTY-EIGHT

My mind's eye moved from the fields of ash and flame to distant towers twinkling with wicked light. Through the bloody haze, their gleaming turrets and spires captivated me. Paralysed by revelation, fixated by Khorne's ineffable gravity, all I could do was stare at that distant city and shrink. I was so spellbound, I almost didn't hear Kaddarar.

Her thunderous steps broke the spell. Then, her roar: 'He's mine! *My* prize! MY SKULL!'

I bent and whispered in Micaw's ear, shielding her eyes from the red realm and dispelling its hold upon her. But Micaw wasn't disturbed. It was I who needed the distraction. I reined her in and gazed once more through the brass gates. The longer I looked, the less I could make sense of what I saw. Annihilation ran in my veins and pounded in my chest, shifting the course of my blood. I was inside out, upside down, like Bharat.

But I could not accept Khorne's blessings. I could not worship its bleeding darkness. I turned away. And just as Tominer had implored, I did not look back.

Behind me, in the tiered square which I'd traversed with down-cast eyes, a vacant-eyed army stood at rest. The hardened gore encrusting their armour thawed and trickled to the stone. In the pitiless black glares of their crested helms, embers smouldered to life. The warriors stirred into motion, and the whole mountain gasped.

The Seeker barrelled through them, tossing one aside, shaking stone platforms. Her monumental chain-mauls bounced behind her like toys.

'*My* prize! *My* skull!

As devious life possessed Bharat's twisted legion, the cursed warriors shuddered and turned. Asharashra's Chosen Champions had never returned from their trials because *this* was where they waited. They were thralls. Meant for what? Tominer's final war? I had hoped they would fight for me. They looked more likely to kill me.

Stone cracked beneath Kaddarar as she raced towards me. Chosen warriors lumbered between us, raising their terrible halberds. Fell plate of hell-forged metals reinforced their ancient Bharat armour. Metal-capped antlers twisted from their crowns, spiked and vicious. Hellish fire blazed from the visor slits in their helms.

I spurred Micaw forward. She galloped. We trampled a Chosen, then cantered around in time for Kaddarar to leap into the saddle. The Seeker's weight rocked Micaw forward. She was so monstrously heavy.

But Micaw was stronger than she had been. Grunting, my steed bore us back to the gates, the carved stone slabs smoking beneath her hooves. Whatever curse had blessed her, the burden of our masses stretched her might thin.

The Chosen marched forward. I glimpsed one's eyes through his visor, as unforgiving as the day I was born. The knotted edge of his wicked halberd whispered for my soul. Ringed, toothed worms squirmed from the crooks of his armour.

As this inevitable legion closed, Micaw teetered back, snorting. I dared not look through the hellgates again, nor up into Asharashra, the grisly tomb of my nation. Tominer could not protect us, and Bharat's legion would slay us. Salvation lay in my choices alone.

'The Ashwilds portals!' I cried. 'How do we return to Cardand?'

But Kaddarar's mouth was agape. She stared through the brass gates at the realm better left unseen. 'No,' she whispered, over and over. 'No, that's not right. They'll see. Then they'll know. But not this. No.'

I cursed. My head swivelled to the goliaths lumbering towards us. A tongue lolled from one's outsize jaw to her armoured chest. Another blank-eyed champion chanted words without sound. I felt them in my soul, echoing like forgotten memories. Nothing could be worse than dying here now that I'd spurned that accursed god. Khorne was insulted; Khorne was *jealous*.

Then, another revelation pealed from the bronze bell of my will: I wanted nothing here. Nothing from this god, nothing from this legion. Bharat was a lie. *Yrdoval,* a lie.

But I could still be true.

'Ya!' I kicked my heels into Micaw's sides, my vocal cords blistering. '*Ya!*'

My nightmare steed reared, screaming. She bowled the closest Chosen to the ground.

Then she galloped ahead, to the lip of the stone landing. We hurtled over its edge into the end of the world.

My stomach lurched into my throat. Clouds whipped past. Red lightning slashed around us. The ivory skies parted into carrion flame, and blood rains drenched us. Above, far above, Asharashra shrank away. Below, far below, a mythic vortex blazed.

Micaw screamed again, a gut-curdling sound. Kaddarar moaned – ill, humbled, quiet.

But I laughed. Aqshy's red flames swallowed us, and I laughed. Khorne's venomous truth bled through me – and I *laughed*. I understood something I had not before – a different truth, one I could hold in my hands and speak with my tongue.

Scorch the gods. Scorch the realm. I could win my war alone – like *this*.

As we tumbled into the inferno, this doom of my own making possessed me. I was free.

CHAPTER TWENTY-NINE

We lay beneath a lip of stone in the craglands between the Ashwilds and the Burning Valley. Pools of acid bubbled and steamed nearby. Bleached white trees loomed above us like scarecrow skeletons. Beside me, an oesophageal portal sealed up in the sands. Leather-winged scavengers crossed the skies, cawing.

I stirred, hacking phlegm from my lungs. Sensing my life, the scavengers above departed. No meat today. I almost pitied them.

I lifted my mask and wiped my lips. Then I glanced at the shimmering glass scar which had spat us out. The secret of Bharat's realmgates amused me. I'd seen Tominer anoint her raiders, then watched them tumble like fallen idols into Bharat's flaming skies. I'd thought them suicidal, but *that* was how the portals worked. To rise, first one must fall.

We couldn't linger. I hadn't chosen the place of our emergence, but I knew these lands were dangerous. And Tominer's axes might come for our heads. I guessed where we might find sanctuary among Cardand's natives, but we had to leave soon.

Yet after regaining my bearings, I didn't move my eyes from the Seeker. She was unconscious. I should have left her to die. I would need to kill her, sooner or later, or she would kill me. She'd sworn this. Many times. Instead I waited for her to awaken. Micaw whinnied, impatient, regarding us with a look that could have gutted babes. I cut her loose to graze on wild things between the bleached bone trees.

Kaddarar slumbered, shallow in breath, eyes flickering beneath her lids. Midday's scorch came and went. I had no waterskin, no flask, not even a drop of sullied groundwater. I moistened Kaddarar's lips with my saliva, but she wouldn't stir. Her coma was not corporeal. It was a trance.

Revelation. Khorne's vision had horrified me, but it must have shattered the Seeker. The sight of her god's apocalyptic shadow had changed something. Or perhaps not – perhaps this was only rapture. My eyes wandered her length. For a hardened killer of blistered soul and cursed hands, Kaddarar was beautiful and innocent in slumber.

She awoke at dusk. Hysh sailed beneath the lands, painting the horizon purple. Dusk's death spawned wondrous eventide. Blossoming desert flowers conjured pleasant aromas. The acid pools bubbled placidly.

Kaddarar's eyes found me. 'Good. Still alive.'

My mask concealed my smile. 'I meant to kill us.'

'Excellent choice.' She inhaled, then rose. She reached out, touching my cheek. I flinched and held my breath.

Then she gripped my chin, turned my head. 'You're not marked. You didn't surrender to Khorne-Godeater.'

I exhaled. 'I can't worship what I saw beyond those gates. I'm sorry.'

Her hand dropped. 'It doesn't matter. That was not Godeater beyond those gates.'

I blinked. 'You saw what I saw. The shadow in that realm came from a force mightier than us all.'

'Yes. I don't debate that. But… that was not the presence which brought me to Bodshe.'

'That was *Khorne*,' I said. 'It *was*. I felt it in my soul.'

'Yes. No. Maybe.' Kaddarar shook her head, dazed. She ground her palms into her eyes. She hardly seemed to understand her own thoughts.

I let the matter go and stood. 'It's time. Come. The two of us'll need help to survive. And I want more than just that.'

She blinked the blear from her eyes. Mischief glittered in the red quartz. 'Fascinating. You have a plan?'

I nodded. Much of me feared voicing my designs, as if speaking them aloud too early would banish them like a half-wrought spell. Nevertheless, I spoke. 'We're going to retake Candip.'

'You tried that. You failed.'

'I tried to *hurt* them. I tried to make a point. But scorch me – and scorch my point. Long ago you said Ildrid had distracted me. You were right. I was so bitter and lost, I didn't see. But I see now. It's time to fight in earnest. It's time to take back the Pale.'

Kaddarar brushed her mane back. She straightened her pitted iron greaves, then shook out her chains. Flakes of rust and gore fell from the rattling links.

I glared at her. 'What?'

'Nothing. For once you're right. I'm beginning to think you know. You've seen.'

I might have laughed, but I was too parched to waste my breath's moisture. 'Why's that?'

She stood and trudged towards Micaw's noise. The cursed steed toyed with her desert-rodent prey, tearing its head away. Kaddarar pointed at me.

'Your mask has come undone.'

I reached for the straps, but they were secure. Then I realised I couldn't feel my mask's metal any more. Its touch felt more natural than my own skin.

My hands fell. I decided I didn't understand Kaddarar's abstruse taunt. If she thought I was hiding who I was, she was wrong. A mask concealed nothing if it revealed the truth of the heart. Such masks could never come undone.

I knew of no settlement in the Pale of Bodshe with a name as fitting as Audacity.

In the days of Cardand's prosperity, Yrdun civilisation had overflowed from the Burning Valley's brim. Audacity was a holdover from those times. The settlement's Rockwrists still dared the valley's crumbling canyon walls. They rappelled down the cliffs to bow-hunt four-winged condors soaring over the Losh, or to pluck fragrant ivy-fruit from the cliffsides. They steamed and ate the pits, reducing the verjuice to treacle. A drop of this acidic tar could tarnish your hands for days or fuel two lantern wicks for a week. Twice a year, Audacity celebrated their famous lantern festival, the Lightmoot, when all were permitted to steal their neighbours' belongings. This was the only reason anyone knew of Audacity. They did as we all wished we could do.

Like the Yrdun, Audacity's people carved their living from the bones of Cardand. Itinerant labourers sent their akwag wages home to compensate for the rarity of aquifers nearby. But with its mortals of fighting age moiling for Azyrite lords across the valley – and without Candip's protection – bush villages like Audacity were defenceless.

Now it was besieged. Fat barbarians lugged ladders across ditches to its low palisades. They might have been from Khul's Ravage, but I knew too little of those lands to be certain. How they might be killed was a question much simpler to answer.

Kaddarar and I blazed through the biggest, the fiercest, the fastest of them. As their last champion's dirty nails scrabbled at my shoulders, I shoved my blade down his throat and ended him. I lifted my gaze to the dawn-lit hills, where the other ravagers fled.

'Kaddarar!'

She thundered past me, her mauls thrashing like captive boulders, thudding into the earth in a syncopated beat. 'More of them, praise Godeater. Always more!'

I looked in the other direction. Braying beastkin bounded down the crags towards us and the town perched on the cliff's edge.

Smoulderhooves. The stink of settling blood and the babel of the dying must have attracted them. The beasts groaned and roared. They hefted ugly weapons cobbled together from stolen plough blades, or pounded clubs embedded with human molars against their shields. The largest, a gor-champion with scars lacing its swollen belly, grunted something in its tongue, snapping its bear-jaws in a threat display.

Three dozen beasts, minimum.

'Praise Godeater,' I muttered.

I steeled myself, then flowed in Kaddarar's wake, into a swirling melee. The rugged clay terrain was no impediment; the beastkin swiftly surrounded me. I'd set my eye on the gor-champion, but it had set its eye on me, too.

Micaw stormed down the hillside with unnatural agility, huffing. I caught her reins on the gallop, tossing myself on her back. We circled around, then rammed through the press, trampling and savaging beasts. The lumbering gor-champion stood against me. Just as swiftly, it fell.

After I sawed my falx through its neck, I seized its head by the horns and tossed it down. The lesser beasts before me wavered – I marvelled at their despicable fear. They craved the space to retreat, but we would not give it to them.

I kicked Micaw back into the charge. We smashed through the rabble of beasts. The Seeker filled the spaces I opened, blazing a bloody trail behind me.

The carnage we left in those red clay flats could not easily be called a battlefield. You have seen the floor of Bharat's abattoir: the blood-swamped drains beneath rusted grates, the heaps of gristle and puddled gore. Creatures sheared of their limbs, flensed of their hides, dying beside their butcher's altars. That was what marked our trail.

When death-screams had replaced the savagery of slaughter, I knew it was over. I dismounted and dragged the flats of my blades across a dead beast's mangy fur, cleaning them.

'Kaddarar.'

She came. While Micaw enjoyed her feast of flesh, the Seeker and I sauntered towards Audacity's palisades. Bucket-helmed militia poked out from behind the clenched fist of Audacity's ramparts. Mortals, armoured in the fashion of Azyrites. They stared me down, rattling sand-iron sabres against wooden shields and overturned carts in the entrance. Some cried encouragement to others. Archers begged for munitions and orders. At least none invoked Sigmar's name.

Then an arrow flitted into the dirt at my feet, a better invocation than any god's name.

'Damn it,' I breathed.

Kaddarar lumbered forward, whipping her flails, mutilating the ground she crossed. 'Oh, *excellent*.'

I pulled her back. 'No.'

Another arrow snapped against Kaddarar's cuirass and fell broken to the ground. She glanced down, then at me. 'They disagree with you.'

'Leave them.' I pushed past her. I was certain Kaddarar would one day exact some bitter toll in exchange for her restraint. She was a creature of final equivalence, a balanced equation. Still, restraint I demanded. I had come to Audacity for assistance, not mindless slaughter.

I dropped my blades and raised my hands. The arrows flitting over our heads ceased, and insurgent hope bristled in the locals' eyes. They were lithe and small, but they weren't young. Rock-wrists were a diminutive mannish tribe with periwinkle flesh and indigo blood. Oiled mail gleamed beneath their cloaks, smudged blades shaking in their hands. Only fear had turned them against us. And what fear.

'Why aren't you in the outlands?' I cried out. Now that I was closer, I glimpsed a shade of prosperity in Audacity, and the full ivory of bared teeth. The Rockwrists were healthy.

'The Azyrite manors are long boarded up or burnt down!' a woman answered. 'Mine was pillaged. By Godeater's Son, the legendary champion. So watch your step and your words, you ochre-skin oaf. His eye is everywhere – and he *protects*.'

I tried to make sense of that. The Rockwrist woman was half my size, an archer with a jade necklace at her throat and gold clips in her hair.

Then my brow smoothed. She was one of those we'd left behind, the indentured workers we'd set free during our raids, who had once toiled for drops. For so long I'd ordered my Ashstalkers to take only what they needed to wage our war. People like these must have flourished on our unpicked pillage.

I looked around and saw more of the same. Then I tapped the beaten metal on my face.

'Now his eye is here, Rockwrists.'

One by one, Audacity's fighters lowered their weapons. Hand-fuls emerged, then more. Their clogs squelched through the blood-slicked clay. They crowded around me. None approached Micaw, but children in overlarge helms reached out and stroked

Kaddarar's muscled legs, their fingers probing her body's topography.

The Seeker froze, glaring helplessly. She was unfamiliar with the Rockwrists' ways.

'I'm Welwary,' the woman said. She secured her bow, then took my hand and stroked it in greeting. She released me and pointed to a ravager's broken body, the blackened corpse of a beast lying beside it. 'We thought you were like them. Marauder ilk or beasts come to plunder.'

'How do you not remember my mask?' I asked.

'It's been a while. And you're far from the only one who wears one. Blood of your blood, Yrdun-son.'

This was an ancient greeting, an oath of fealty among the old kindred. I'd not heard the phrase since childhood. I lowered my head.

'Blood of our blood.'

Another diminutive Rockwrist girl teetered on her toes to examine me. 'His mask don't look right. It's all ugly and beat.'

Welwary shoved the girl off. 'Don't mind her. *I* know you. I saw you at Hinterspend Cut. I was a girl then, but I know.' She smiled, eyes twinkling. 'I know.'

The sun rose. As Hysh's light conquered the virgin skies, Welwary of Audacity related all that had happened after Candip. Many Yrdun and Beltollers had died that day. Others had been imprisoned, then burnt on Candip's pyres. Yet even in failure, our raid had fast become legend throughout the Pale. Too fast, I thought. Hardly eight weeks had passed.

I dismissed this for Welwary's other tidings. That day in Candip, many Ashstalkers had escaped the calamity. They still fought, even now. To honour my fall, they had taken up my mask and mantle and warred in my name. But the Ashstalkers were no longer freedom fighters, Welwary explained. They no longer waged war against Azyrite fiefs alone. They had become robbers and brigands. They'd raided Audacity twice.

This news seethed in my belly. In my absence, my warriors had done what I had always refused to do. They attacked native Yrdun and Beltollers, Cardand's easiest pickings. They raided country hamlets and despoiled native market-towns. It didn't matter if their victims were Reclaimed or not. The Ashstalkers sought vengeance in my name but had defiled my cause, claiming the spoils of their brigandage would build a new kingdom in Cardand.

What utter delusion. I couldn't believe it, but Welwary spoke in earnest. I twitched with anger, wondering who was responsible. Yron? Boskin? Or another, one whose cunning and cruelty I had not noticed?

Then, vague guilt filled me. I'd had such little faith in my fighters. I'd left them for dead, assuming the Refuser's Stormcasts had butchered them all. For weeks, as I had pranced around lost Bharat's abattoirs, my people – my *real* people, the blood of my blood – had carried on a distorted parody of my fight. Where had I been when they needed me? Could I have prevented their perversions?

The truth at Asharashra's brass gates still curdled my blood and smouldered in my soul. I had rejected Khorne and the Path to Glory because I stood for something greater. But I could not turn from this. The men and women I had led had become the very cancer I'd sought to eradicate, the very parasites I'd meant to purge. They were scavengers, worse than the Azyrites, feeding on their own.

'Ashstalkers,' I said.

Welwary nodded. 'Or so they call themselves, aye. And the one who leads them kills all who defy him.'

I felt a chill. 'His name. Tell me.'

She offered a sad smile. 'Cardand's Reckoning. The Pale Flame. The Last Qual. He's got too many to count. He's building an army.'

I trembled with anger. 'He's a lord,' I said. 'Isn't he?'

'He sure acts like it.' Welwary surveyed the still-life carnage outside Audacity. Her warriors were picking through the remains of the fallen for salvage. 'But he's not you. He'll never be the Godeater's Son.'

Boskin. I wasn't surprised. Once a traitor, always a traitor. Now his bill had come due.

Welwary clapped, a bandit joy bright in her eyes. 'But the gods've mercy! Blood of your blood, bone of your bone, you're back! We won't be afraid any more! You're the Godeater's Son!' She turned back, jumping in excitement. 'I told you all, didn't I? Didn't I tell you?'

They murmured assent. Welwary turned and tugged at my sleeves like a child, still stroking my arm.

'Let us take you to him. He accepts tribute at his palace. Put him in his place, Godeater's Son. Put him in a cairn!'

I glanced at Kaddarar. She nodded.

Then, Welwary stepped on my toes for my attention. The Rockwrists were not known for their respect of personal space. 'But you promise me,' she said. 'You promise when we take you to him, you'll make him suffer. Jujjar-Yrdovaler's a stinking snake. He's had this coming for a long time.'

CHAPTER THIRTY

No, Jujjar. Not you.

I had thought Jujjar would be the last one to betray my cause. I still remembered his final words above Candip. *I would take my life for the Yrdun,* he'd said. *That is why we are strong. We would do things the Azyrites would not.*

And he had spoken true. In the end, he had become even worse than them.

All the way to his lair I wondered what I'd say. I imagined excuses for him, to recast his actions in the light of misguided friendship. None of it fitted. He'd declared me dead, named himself my heir, then preyed on our people in the outlands. Once I thought Jujjar's loyalty iron. Now I questioned my own judgement. I wanted to be angry, but in the end all I could feel was like Bharat. Upside down in the temples, inside out on the mount.

Flanked by Audacity's cloaked Rockwrist rangers, Micaw carried me up a rugged hill to an abandoned hillfort. We marched on an obsidian path, amber flames rustling from cracks in the earth. I dismounted, whispering a secret into Micaw's ear, to keep her good. We'd told Jujjar-Yrdovaler's sentinels we meant to offer tithe and submit to his rule. That lie had brought us this far. The remaining path was mine to tread.

I entered the hillfort with my head bowed, ignoring the warriors lurking in the hall. Far too many were present for all of them to be my veterans. Most of mine had died in Candip's streets. To have recruited so much fresh blood, Jujjar must have been busy. I proceeded but didn't raise my borrowed cowl. I couldn't reveal myself until I had ravelled out the truth. I needed to know why Jujjar had betrayed my cause.

Walls and crumbling pillars rose above. The hillfort's roof had long crumbled. Where a vaulted ceiling once soared, now the skins of slaughtered things were strung up, dripping with tannin. These hides took the edge off the sunlight's scorch, but the day's heat cast a rancid smell over the halls. The Season of Flame had already passed. Much too soon, I thought.

The further I went, the more contented laughter I heard in the hall. At the end of my lonely road loomed an ostentatious throne built from the scrap of kingdoms. I peeked out from under my hood, tilting my head so as not to reveal my mask.

Jujjar slouched on his scrap throne with kingly languor, his own beaten metal mask propped up on his brow. A cloudy bottle of something evil swished in his hands. Firewine. So he'd taken to drinking, too. A wolf's mane of hair had grown in with his beard. Then I looked no more. I didn't want to.

'Brothers and sisters,' Jujjar spoke in Yrdo, thinking I wouldn't understand. 'Another would-be warlord comes to bend his knee and beg sanctuary. Shall we give it? Shall we save the foreign vulture?'

They shouted as many answers as war has names. I teased out their voices, trying to count those present. The number met my expectations. Outside, Welwary and her rangers would be nervous. Ashstalkers surrounded them. This would be their first blood.

I trusted the Rockwrists. They were not the first force I had built from nothing, and this was not my first time daring the impossible. The rest would come down to chance.

Jujjar stroked oils into his dark mane. 'All you vultures smell the carrion on the Parchward Winds. You sail into the Pale for war, then eat more than your fill. When it sickens you, you beg for reprieve. Show your face. I want to see who has come to prostrate themselves.'

'Just a man,' I said, challenging Jujjar to recognise my voice. 'A man humbler than you.'

Jujjar huffed. The firewine fumes on his breath made me wince. 'On your knees when you speak to me.'

'Is it true you fought beside the Godeater's Son?' I said.

I heard him straighten. 'On. Your. *Knees*.'

Elsewhere, maul-axes rasped as they were snatched from stone. I swallowed my pride and fell to a knee. I had to know why. I wouldn't find out any other way.

Jujjar reclined, his fragile throne creaking beneath him. 'I fought with the Godeater's Son, yes. Before he fell. Before the Stormcasts slew him.'

'You don't fight as he fought,' I growled. 'You don't stand for what he stood for.'

From Jujjar, silence, stinging and sharp. 'And what was that, outlander? What did he stand for?'

'His people. Against those who preyed on them. Azyrites, Se Roye. Cretins like you.'

Ashstalkers grumbled. I sensed them circling in the periphery.

'I fought at his side,' Jujjar said. 'So I know what you don't. The Godeater's Son was no godsend. He was human. Like us. Sometimes he was cold. Sometimes, fire. Sometimes, cruel. Sometimes, kind. But he was always lost. Too afraid to go forward, too scared to go back. He was… stuck.'

I gave a guttural chuckle, but my bitter amusement didn't cure my pain.

'You think I insult him?' Jujjar scoffed. 'Far be it. The Godeater's Son was my friend. I wear his death mask because the Storm-casts left nothing I could build a cairn over. And if you're one of these serpent-tongued roamers who claims I defy his will, you're right. The Godeater's Son didn't stand for his people. He stood for nothing at all. What I do now is more than he ever would have.'

'And what' – I gritted the blades and hammers of my teeth – 'is that?'

Jujjar hesitated. 'I build a kingdom. As our mighty people's great houses once did, and our great clans before them. I return our birthright to our people. Whence come you, outlander?'

'A place where the Yrdun have died,' I said. 'Where people like you have killed them.'

Jujjar cackled. 'You think the Godeater's Son was better than me? He killed Yrdun too. He scythed them down in Candip. Priests, Reclaimed soldiers, merchants. He killed whoever served the Azyrites, whoever sucked at their teat. And he killed *us* – his own fighters! He never appreciated anything as he should have. Not his sister, not his warband. Not me. I tried to lead him in the right direction, but he never listened. He didn't have what it took to lead us.'

'And you do?'

'*I* strive for something!' Jujjar roared. 'I know what we deserve!'

I was shaking, incandescent. He was wrong. I had not been evil. I had been a symbol. Warbands had marched and burned at my command, but those we had laid low had deserved it. If Jujjar faulted my judgement, then let him have everything, and then let the realm take it from him. Let us see what might have remained of him then.

'Eight weeks,' I hissed. 'All it took was eight weeks for you to forsake everything I stood for.'

Jujjar's bottle crashed at my feet, smashing into stained shivers. He surged from his throne to me and cast back my cowl.

I raised my head. Jujjar recognised my bloodshot eyes. The sight of my father's rictus branded horror into his face. The blood drained from his cheeks and he staggered back. His piercings gleamed like stars in the pallid sky his skin had become.

I stood. *'Would you fall on your sword?'* I hissed, in Yrdo. *'Would you take your life for the Yrdun?'*

Arrows flitted into the throats of Jujjar's guards. As his Ashstalkers raced for their javelins, Welwary and her rangers made pincushions of them. They were up on the broken walls, loosing from above, using the stretched-out hides for cover.

Confusion raged in the hall. 'Who let his warband in?' Jujjar screamed. 'They were under guard!'

Kaddarar burst through the cracked doors, two men slumped at her feet. She charged. Her flails threshed through the air, raking ruts in the stone and crushing any who did not flee. After she had killed the sentinels outside, Welwary's halflings had used the time I bought to scamper up the hillfort ruins. Now calamity reigned within the pretender's palace. I strode to his throne and tossed him down.

'Stop!' he howled, to someone. As if I would listen – as if his gurgling warriors could choose not to die. 'No!'

'Yes.' I seized Jujjar, slapped the mask from his crown. 'How long before you betrayed me? Eight weeks, Jujjar. I was gone eight weeks!'

Jujjar's eyes were spinning. 'Eight weeks?'

Welwary and the other Rockwrists scuttled to the floor,

bowstrings drawn taut. A handful of Ashstalker old-bloods dropped their weapons, falling to their knees, even as fighters from Jujjar's camp rallied at the hillfort's threshold. They faltered before Kaddarar. She held the doors.

'Eight weeks.' I spat. 'It'll take me less time to clean up your mess.' I raised my dirk. Other Ashstalkers lurched at us, but Jujjar stayed them.

'Stop!'

'Kill him,' Kaddarar barked from the fort's jagged threshold. She snapped a moaning woman's neck, glaring at me over her shoulders. 'Kill him or he'll do it again.'

I meant to. To cut Jujjar's throat out, or slit his belly and let his guts slop to my feet. But staring at his drunken face, I couldn't. I still saw my friend. The man who had walked into Ulcarver with me all those years ago and suffered the same insult as I. The man who had stood by my side as I fought a hopeless war. The man who had come to Candip with me to die.

Jujjar cried. It was pathetic. And it should have been futile, given all he'd done. He'd preyed on the same folk who had given us succour, people who spoke tongues like ours and who had eaten the same boiled bones as we.

Yet here he was, still alive, heart still beating. I raised my dirk, willing myself on.

'Give me one reason,' I said, tears brimming in my eyes. 'Anything.'

'Eight years, Held,' he said. 'It's been eight years since you left us.'

CHAPTER THIRTY-ONE

Eight years.

Eight years, and Jujjar had risen like a star and fallen back to the realm. Eight years, and my fighters were his, now once again mine.

Eight years, and Candip had never become a City of Sigmar. Eight years of bickering and politics had kneecapped Se Roye's ambitions. Candip remained Bodshe's premier power, but eight years of war unleashed by me had made their existence precarious. For eight years, foreign warbands had sniffed blood on the Parchward Winds and flocked to Bodshe in droves. Eight years of hollow war and shackled peace, eight years of others continuing what I had started. Eight years of fire.

In these eight years, Cardand burned, and the Stormcasts hunted. In Bodshe, across the Ashwilds, smashing many, ignoring others. What the Refuser wanted, Jujjar couldn't say. He called it a great mystery.

But I knew Ildrid. I knew what she wanted.

My time in Bharat had been as warped as the world. Perhaps

my own ire had mangled the course of time. Whenever I recalled Bharat's hell-mills and Tominer and Asharashra, it all felt like the long rays of lantern light on a damp evening in Candip, blurred by rain and the tears of my childhood.

Then I shook off the rain and dried my face and realised eight years had passed. Eight years I was gone, and none had forgotten me. Not my allies, not my foes. Neither had I forgotten them.

At dusk we marched. My mercy towards Jujjar embittered Welwary and her folk. I deprived them of their petty vengeance, which I finally knew was no virtue. Jujjar and his Ashstalkers had married cause to ours. But they were bitter, too – even the old-bloods who'd fought by my side. That is the mortal equation, I see now. Bitterness becomes us all. I speak from experience, not hyperbole. I had spilt Adure's belly for mere defiance. I had killed brethren who had come to comfort me and remove Cillus' corpse. I was bitter, too.

What I'd left unfinished in a cathedral's ashes, now I resumed. I dispatched messengers to herald my return and Jujjar's submission. The heralds were to seek fresh meat, in both senses of the word. We required provisions. We also needed fresh hands for blades and war.

When our messengers returned with crowds of volunteers, I could hardly conceal my astonishment. Ildrid had broken me in Candip – yet the very fact of my defiance had stoked a fire across the Pale. When the children of eight years of yore learned of my return, it roused them. As with the periwinkle Rockwrists of Audacity, my ancient exploits had aged in the people's memory like wine, sweeter in remembrance than in its bitter fermentation.

Not only Yrdun and Beltollers came. Parcher migrants, too, and Jujjar's allies and subjugated warbands. Even the mongrel bastards of the Azyrites answered my call. I never gave rousing speeches for them. I simply greeted them myself, seeking the measure of them. They all seemed to understand what we fought for. Or better said, what *they* fought for. And that was bigger than any of us.

But what was it? Not the Yrdun. We had moved beyond that. Jujjar's words had dispelled the last vestiges of my love affair with my nation, the myth I had built around them. The horror beyond Khorne's brass gates had already fractured that foundation. The rest of it toppled like bricks.

Freedom we wanted. For freedom we fought this war. And of all the obstacles between that freedom and us, the greatest was the force that welded us together.

Spite.

For each other, for our enemies, for ourselves. Spite like Welwary's and Jujjar's, spite like mine. I nourished this spite. I feared nothing else might hold us together. Spite had started this war, so let spite end it. Let it divide us from our freedom until nothing remained, nothing at all. And when there was nothing, let that be freedom enough.

Gradually, an army grew within the broken kingdom's bounds. This was not the warband and rabble with which I'd struck Candip. This was a swarm, a host – a legion. We built our numbers and our stores, pillaging lay water and akwag. We raided merchants and robbed toll collectors but let those wildings who pledged allegiance chase their tribal traditions. My scouts plied the lands, returning with word of rivals and beasts. My spies sifted through forty dozen night markets between the city's ruined ways for rumours of Ildrid's Stormcasts and Candip's allies.

Barbarian warlords filled Cardand, but I'd not forgotten about the true enemy. Lellen Se Roye, the viceroy-regent. And the titaness Stormcast pulling her marionette strings, the single-minded Refuser, on her fruitless quest to hunt, I hoped, for me.

Ildrid Stormsworn, my Mother Fall. Each time I thought of her stung more than the last. Old bones are only gnawed for so long before they're ground to marrowless shards. She was a demigod. But where had she been when we suffered? I couldn't contemplate it. Nothing more could be gained from my grief but misery, so I tried to forget.

Of Candip, the tidings never changed. Se Roye's host rarely left the city, except to retaliate. Some of the city's fiefs had fallen in my long absence. Their refugees and martial remnants collected in the crevasse-city to skulk like rodents, an infestation. The crevasse-city was resupplied from Hammerhal Aqsha solely by merchant airlift. Kharadron duardin, other Hammerhalian commerce guilds.

I'd known Kharadron. Their contracts were never cheap. Hewer Durandsson had always been generous to Varry and me, but that was an exception. A gold-ache haunted the duardin heart, a sickness afflicting Holmon delvers and Kharadron arkanauts and the mythical slayers in equal measure. To afford their fees, Se Roye's treasuries had to be hurting. And to exhaust so much wealth for the sake of mere existence, she was either obsessed or a true believer. Equally the Hammerhalians must be magnanimous, to set aside their ancient dispute with Se Roye for the sake of aiding her against us.

I could never have done such a thing. To attain my desires, I would have burnt the world.

Eight years, and so much had changed, and so very little.

My heart ached to see Jujjar so far gone. Maybe the firewine had done it. Or the years of bloodshed following our divorce in Candip. Any who murder and claim to be untouched by it are false. The greatest movers of butchery in the realm are just as much moved by it. Jujjar had been as I had been – glacial of heart, loyal to old lies, slave to the desires which mortals dare. But war had changed him, as it had me. I could not forgive him.

Yet eight years I was gone, and he had stayed. He'd fought a different war against new foes. He knew things of our lands and her assailants which I did not. The time had come to deal with these barbarian rivals. No one could help me but Jujjar.

We were in a proper tent, with proper maps and a proper brazier. Welwary slept on a peasant's pallet, her dirty dark blue feet hanging over the side. She whimpered from nightmares. Outside, my growing army bustled beyond the tent's coarse fabric walls. The stink of mortal excrement wafted to us from latrines dug by captives' forced labour.

Everything felt eerie and wrong. I was Se Roye, a cheap imitation of her, playing her game, speaking her words. Outside our camp, Kaddarar's singing echoed across Cardand. She sang to the Burning Valley of all the things she would kill, belting out each word. She sang of Azyrites and savages, of songbirds and sophists. She sang of me.

I had posed Jujjar a question, of how Candip might be taken. He finally answered.

'If you don't forge true power, you'll never take the city.'

I brushed my mouth. At least he spoke his mind. Jujjar's bloodshot eyes did not meet mine, nor did he speak our tongue. He hadn't had a drink in days yet stank of crapulence. The space between us spanned a table and a hide map. Nothing I could do could bridge that indomitable distance.

'Explain,' I said.

'This isn't the little war you left behind. Things are different. Candip and her fiefs have forty thousand mercenaries and Freeguilders. The Stormcasts number a fraction of that, but they might as well double the Azyrites' strength.'

'The Stormcasts are gone.'

'No. They come and go as they please. They're gone for three months, then return right as we slink from our holes. They are unpredictable. None know what they want. Meanwhile, Parcher marauders hunt the ruins and the wastes, and that encourages the Smoulderhooves. My allies and minions numbered four thousand, minus the warriors your runtlings killed.'

I glanced to Welwary, who still slept. 'Rockwrists, Jujjar.'

He glared. 'Four thousand. They march at your word, as the old laws dictate.'

'Scorch Yrdoval,' I said. 'They march at my word because you are mine. Are you not?'

He bristled. 'I would not do as you have done. I would reinstate Yrdoval. I would fight differently. And I wouldn't tolerate the Parchers you've gathered to your cause.'

Seeing my reaction, he hesitated, then softened.

'You're my friend, Held. That's why I speak candidly. With your two thousand volunteers, then the outlanders and savages, we have… what, fifteen thousand? But there's the beasts, too. Countless, in the wastes. They'll never submit.'

I shook my head, frustrated. These numbers were beyond anything I'd ever imagined.

'Who reckoned this?'

'Me. Over the years. As I did what you could not.' He levelled his gaze. 'You'd be a fool not to heed my word. What I've done – what you've condemned – I did for good reason. I had to prove my power. That is the Bodshe we live in. I would've preferred the Azyrites and barbarians destroy each other if they had the belly for it, but the Azyrites have not fought since Candip. They are dealing with something else, it seems. It doesn't matter – so are we. You can't break the Pale's balance without more fighters. You must do as I did. Break the will of Cardand's free Beltollers and Yrdun. Force the valley's heathens and marauders to submit. With your outlanders among that number and our rivals cast down, only then can you march on Candip.'

That, I said, was what we had been doing. My fiat was only

forceful as far as I could swing my falx. Each day had brought minor victories which had outweighed our tribulations. Was this not satisfactory?

'Yes. And at this rate, you'll be ready to fight Candip in two decades.' Jujjar stroked a swathe of our map. 'You need a horde. Many warbands, bound to one will. It doesn't have to be Freeguild-strict – marching with banners, in squares. But they must obey you. Other warlords in Cardand seek this, as I did. Champions, sorcerers. Witchfire fanatics. But all of them have something you do not. Their gods. That is an advantage.'

'I'd hoped all this folly with gods and glory was finished,' I muttered.

'You have your own advantage.'

I placed my dirk on the map. 'Pray tell.'

'You're the Godeater's Son. You're a hero, as I wasn't. The people remember Candip. To them it was a victory. And this is your home, and Cardand's folk know it. As for glory and gods, you'll need some of that too. Long ago Yron spoke the truth. Glory is power. Glory's the gods' respect and their boons. I never agreed until I saw it myself. Then I tried to take it. I burnt my enemies, killed those who defied me. Condemn what I did all you like, but now's come your turn. You must play this great game.'

Listening to Jujjar, I didn't feel in charge. I thought I had put him in line. But he was using me, or trying to use me, to fulfil his own ambitions.

A Mukwuk chieftain entered, her beaded braids rattling. As she bowed, the thick trim of her fur mantle brushed the floor.

'*Tulwarak Teyen*.' Godeater's Son.

I bowed, not half as low. I'd sent the Mukwuk to lay a watch on Candip. The Mukwuk were cousins to the Yrdun, an offshoot clan that had long rejected Yrdoval. They were loyal but unimaginative. I trusted them.

The chieftain looked worried. I didn't speak mukwuk well, so she spoke to Jujjar. He darkened.

'What?' I asked, irritated I had to.

'Six days the Mukwuk have sent brethren with knapsacks and blades to an outlook over Candip.'

'I know.' I'd ordered it. I wanted Candip Plain remapped and the expansions to the city's upworks and Burning Palisade noted.

'None have returned,' Jujjar said.

I groaned. Whittale's End, all over again. 'She knows who did it?'

The Mukwuk chieftain spat, crossed her heart, shook her head. Taboo. I didn't need Jujjar to translate that.

'Stormcasts,' I said.

Jujjar nodded. 'Likely.'

My belly emptied. The Refuser. It had to be.

Then my brow smoothed. This was just like Whittale's End. I'd thought the Refuser brilliant, but here she'd reverted to an old trick. She was like a lazy duellist with a death wish, with nothing left to offer but the same flourishes and conceits. I'd learned a thing or two since Candip, but my mother was more human than I'd thought. Slave to bad habits, as were we all.

Then again, I was underestimating her. My own bad habit.

Surely she might've known that? She was Lord-Imperatant of the Stormcast Eternal – the master strategist, the commander. She knew me, as I craved to know her. She was sending a message only I could read.

Why else but to meet?

These thoughts ran along the tracks of my mind like lightning through iron. I weighed my many options then made my decision as I always do: in a rush, all at once, pushing aside caution and shoving Elene over the precipice.

Jujjar relayed my orders to the Mukwuk, who bowed again. She departed to have some brave soul with no fear of death saddle

Micaw. Jujjar watched as I gathered my things. His hand remained on the death mask he'd made for me, at his sash. I'd let him keep it as a reminder. I was his friend, once. In time, I hoped to be so again.

'You know this is a trap,' he said.

'Yes.'

'Still you go.' He scratched his beard, shaking his head. He looked so tired. Eight years, and every minute of it written in the lines of his face.

I stopped at the tent entrance. 'What you said in the hillfort, about me standing for nothing. You were wrong.'

He gazed bitterly. 'I don't think so.'

My jaw tensed. 'How'd you escape? Candip, eight years ago. How'd you get out?'

Jujjar met my eyes. He lifted his sash, revealing a welded knot of flesh. An ugly scar. 'Dragged out, on a litter. Bawling, delirious, half-alive.' He pushed the sash down. 'That watchman, with the cut-out tongue. You let him live.'

'I remember.'

'Know what came of him?'

I shrugged.

'He built a warband. War orphans, widows, widowers – all made into sabrists and musketeers. They fought for Sigmar. They sought revenge. I killed him three years after Candip, but not before he nearly made corpses of us all. You asked how long it took for me to abandon your cause. It was then. I forsook you after I killed him.'

Outside the tent, evening's first stars glistened. I shivered from dusk's unwelcome chill.

'Why?'

'Because I understood what you'd wanted then,' he said, in Yrdo. 'You wanted to do to the Azyrites exactly what had been done to you. You wanted worse. I can think of nothing more terrible than that, Held. Nothing at all.'

CHAPTER THIRTY-TWO

Jujjar's words echoed between my ears until all I heard was their self-righteous ring. He didn't understand. He hadn't felt Varry's life drain away, hadn't watched the daemon moon take her. He couldn't know what I felt, nor how hard this war had become.

I let his words go and focused on other challenges. The thousand and one considerations of building an army had kept me cooped up since my return from Bharat. Dealing with these wearisome matters brought some meagre joy born from tedium, but I still missed our old wanderings. I wished to be unmoored, blowing in the wind, like the vagrant mountains drifting across the sky. Those metaliths still free were paltry compared to yesteryear's. Candip's chained leviathans, anchored by the Ironweld guilds and their idolatrous engineering, now crowded the crevasse-city and its plain. Where Azyrites reign, freedom goes extinct. Much remained unfinished.

What might we have when we were done? Freedom, I hoped. Endless wanderings across an edgeless realm. I would ramble through the world, bathing in clear-water springs and drinking the milk of wild sows. I would sheathe my blades and learn the secrets of strangers' inner worlds.

First, the Refuser. If our looming encounter conjured dread, my anticipation outweighed it. I was ready. Kaddarar had trained me, and my conversation with my mother was still half unsaid.

I think back now and wonder if I was as powerful as I thought. More likely, I was the duellist with the death wish.

Micaw lumbered along sandy switchbacks up cliffside crags. Wind blew, pebbles trickled.

In my childhood, in this part of Cardand, the Arm's Hand had been famous. Youths had dared each other up the megalithic monument's outstretched arm to its upturned stone palm. Furtive lovers had met at dawn between its fingers, to sit and nestle and love.

I'd selected Arm's Hand as our scouts' outlook sight-unseen, working off memory alone. That Stormsworn had anticipated its strategic value did not surprise me. I was beginning to understand how her mind worked.

As we approached the outlook, little lizards scuttled in the shadows. I tensed, relaxed, tensed, contemplating what I might say. My weapons' weight comforted me, like the clement breeze and the cliffside shadows.

Then Micaw crested the plateau and Hysh's fire kissed my sundaubed skin. A great vista stretched out before us, ruled by Arm's Hand and the eightfold winds.

Candip covered the horizon, a scar in the realm, her bound metaliths bobbing in the sky. Cogforts dotted the widened defensive tracts like tossed dice. Lines of slate smoke billowed from them. Like sunset, the Burning Palisade glowed around the city's outworks and upworks. The sight was breathtaking and scary.

Somewhere beneath it all lay Candip's rift, a pustule in the realm. I envisioned its incandescent orreries, the flickering light of its forges. The cathedral would have been rebuilt by now. All my efforts, and yet this war was far from over. It had hardly begun.

Arm's Hand jutted out over the valley's brim. A cyclopean stair ran the tremendous arm's length, to the palm-like plaza at the end of the ascent. The hand was upturned and flat, making offering to the realm. Each finger was a tower prodding at the smoke-streaked skies. The Yrdun had not built this ancient monument. Arm's Hand was older than all Bodshe.

A single silhouette waited at the top, battered by gusts. Not Stormsworn, nor any Azyrite. She was a wilding girl with a stiff neck and war braids.

I dismounted. 'Do as you please,' I told Micaw, letting her reins slap the lizard leather of her neck. I crossed the lonely length of Arm's Hand, counting the steps, watching the sky. When I arrived, Candip yawned below, close enough to grip if only I reached for it. Wind buffeted me, dispelling the lands' brimstone aura, heralding a foetid stink.

My boots scuffed stone. I stared at the woman's back, once my warrior.

'Yron.'

Blood dripped from an iron knife in her hands. She peered over her shoulder, then faced me. 'It's true. You live.'

I lifted my hands. 'I would not call this life.'

Mukwuk warriors – *my* warriors – lay piled around us. One lay on a stone plinth. His ribs were pushed up, the lining inside his disembowelled belly smooth. Flies buzzed over his heaped entrails, at war with the valley's wind.

This whole place stank of death. I preferred the brimstone. 'You killed them.'

Yron cleaned and belted her knife. 'My people killed them. I made use of their remains.'

'This is disgusting.'

'The old rites demand sacrifice. I knew of no better way to summon you.'

I chuckled. 'You didn't summon me.'

'Yet here you are.'

I drew my falx. 'Here I am.'

Her eyes widened, the painted band around them cracking. She raised her bloody hands. 'I'm not your enemy. I sent our warriors away.'

'You're with one of the other warbands, one of these barbarian tribes feasting on Cardand.'

'A sorcerer from Arad, yes. Malokal. His warriors fled the daemon-queen of those lands, for easier pickings. But I'm not your enemy.'

'Aren't you? Here my fighters are, dead. And long I've wondered how the Stormcursed knew we'd come to Candip.' I glanced about. 'I think now I know.'

Yron narrowed her eyes. 'You should know your warriors killed my kin here, too. And as for Candip – the Refuser planned it all.'

'She's not omniscient. Someone told her we were coming. I only shared my designs with a handful I trusted. You were in that number. Do not forget – they found us exactly where you led us during our flight.'

Her eyes smoothed. 'So that's what this is? You think me a traitor?'

'I think you survived Candip, and many others did not. I think you crave glory. And I'm beginning to lose faith in the providence of chance.'

'Jujjar lived. And Boskin. And you.'

'Boskin's gone,' I said. 'Jujjar serves me now.'

She flinched. 'Kill him, Yrdun-son. He's dangerous. You don't know what he's done.'

'Jujjar knows his place. And he's an old friend. You' – I pointed my blade – 'are not.'

My intent was singular, but Yron's look halted me. The scorch of her pain caught in my lungs like fire. Her eyes glistened.

'So this is where my path leads,' she said. 'Me and those who heeded the gods' call. We pulled you, broken, from the streets of Candip. I would've died for you. Because I believed in you, Godeater's Son. Honour is its own glory.'

'Kaddarar speaks of glory too,' I said. 'She said I should kill you if we met again.'

Yron clenched her teeth. 'Do it. We were ready to die for you. We *did* die for you! Then that skull-worshipping cur comes, just as she came on the low road. In Candip she stole everything that should've been ours. *Our* honour. *Our* glory. Did you doubt her? The Seeker? No. Her, with all that time and blood in the Parch, growing fat and strong with the Blood God's blessings. But you think because she stood against Stormcasts and we fell, *we* are traitors. That day I fought them with what little I had. But that was *everything*. For you. Now this glory's stolen from me, as my kin-lives were stolen. Now I'm a traitor. *I'm* who you'll kill. Because I brought you here. Because I used the old rites to do it. Because I craved to see you again. Fie, Yrdun-Son. Fie on me, fie on you. Fie on us all. I was true to the very end.'

My mask concealed the red ache in my cheeks. I faltered, then sashed my falx.

'Eight years it's been.'

Yron looked more tired than relieved. Wind dislodged crumbs of dried grey paint from her face. 'Eight years, and every one of them an age since I've seen what lies beyond the Pale.'

I thought of Asharashra and shuddered. 'We've all gone beyond the Pale, Yron. Say what you came to say.'

My words dispelled the tension in her shoulders. Her neck

stiffened. 'Malokal. A sorcerer-shaman, sworn to the dark oath. He seeks to humble you as you humbled Jujjar. He seeks your submission and Candip's extinction.'

'And, what? You'll betray him to me?'

'I cannot. Eight years ago I would have. But I told you, I have my honour. My tribe is sworn to Malokal. But you deserved the warning.'

'Honour…' I shook my head. 'You could've killed me in Candip. You could do it now. Glory is power – you said that. But *power* is also power. Scorch honour. Betray Malokal to me. I'll be kinder to our peoples than he would, I swear you this. And your gods will not judge you.'

Her eyes held mine. Wind whistled through the great fingers behind her.

'You would,' she finally said. 'And they wouldn't, yes. But I've learned things of the gods I didn't know when I fought by your side. Those who give in fully to the gods are enslaved to them, Godeater's Son. You once asked where this path leads. Now I can answer. Have you seen the monsters spawned from those who surrender completely?'

'No.'

'They're terrible. Cursed. I don't know how Kaddarar has come as far as she has, but I know I cannot follow forever. I'm not strong enough. Before the gods' blessings twist their champions into monsters, they twist their minds around their craving for glory. Power, Yrdun-son. It's their addiction.'

'Like the Azyrites.'

'Maybe.' She exhaled. 'You've always been right to defy the gods. I didn't see. I do now. That is the true Path to Glory, perhaps. Defiance. But I'm too afraid to dare.'

'Join me,' I said. 'Forsake them. Come back.'

She hesitated. 'I don't stand where I stand because I ever had a choice. Honour is all I have left.'

'We all have choices.'

'Says the one whose obsessions guide him.' She smiled forlornly. 'There. I've warned you of Malokal. That's what I came to say. But… there's something else. Is the Seeker still with you?'

I nodded.

Yron's lips hardened. 'I've seen strange things in Malokal's seeing fires. And I've always known the Blood God's will. I think… I think she does not understand who she serves. Not truly.'

Godeater. I recalled the brass gates and shivered. 'She does. I've seen the shadow of her god, Yron. She knows.'

Yron grunted, brushing scabbed blood from her cracked hands. 'Where will you go from here?'

'I'd tell you.' Beneath my mask, I ventured a smile. 'But then there's honour, isn't there? You'd go tell your Malokal.'

'Yes,' she said, proud. 'I would.'

I accepted that. If this would be our final parting, I decided to make the most of it. 'Six days you've been here.'

'Two days. I came when I heard the rumours and realised it was you sending all these Mukwuk inbreds. Why?'

I pointed to Candip and her chugging cogforts, to the blazing gash of the city's palisades crossing Aqshy. 'The Azyrites. The Stormcasts. I wish to know what they're doing.'

She gestured to the corpses strewn at our feet. 'I wouldn't know. Ask the flies.'

I tilted my head. Yron was not Tominer. Were that a jest, she would have laughed.

'Ask the flies,' she repeated.

I raised my brow, then turned. Gnats and flies clouded the stinking entrails of my Mukwuk scouts, buzzing in my ears and eyes.

The winds dropped and I moved swiftly, snatching one from the air. The insect tickled my closed palm and fingerpads.

Yron nudged the air. 'Go on.'

I raised my coiled fingers to my lips, then whispered my question. 'What are Stormsworn's designs?'

The fly's movement ceased. Grimacing, I unclasped my fingers. There it sat in the creases of my hand, fat from its feast of flesh, or maggots in its belly. Its wings hummed in gentle spurts. It danced around on tiny legs, to regard me.

I gasped. The fly's eyes were mortal eyes – white, blood-stricken. Its teeth were mortal teeth, yellowing and rot-ridden.

'Closer,' Yron said. 'Let it answer.'

I raised it to my ear. A fly, sick with mutation, but only a fly – only an aberration. Aberrations could not harm me. Aberrations could not buzz down the canal of my ear and plant their maggots in my brain. Only a fly, and only cursed. Only a monster, in only a tiny way.

I brought it closer. A chill ran up my veins. It said nothing, so I looked at it.

The fly's teeth were grains of sand. Red lightning streaked its pinprick eyes. I stared, until the blackness beneath its glassy pupils swelled up like night. I held all the void in my hands, all the universe. Beneath that black mirror, I glimpsed another fly. Crawling on the glass, creeping into my mind.

A recollection. I found a dying lavamander, once, its neck broken after a clifftop fall. As I waited for Varry, I watched it fade. The creature's neck was twisted so far back it gazed the wrong way. Its vacant eyes were aimed at me, its slit tongue flitting out, tasting the heat in the air. The poor thing still hungered for earthfire. That hunger had killed it. Instinct had dragged it from the stone to the sky, to a place it did not belong. Instinct killed us all.

I stared into the fly's eyes, and this was the answer I heard. *Instinct kills us all.*

I hurled the little abomination into the wind.

'What did you see?' Yron said.

'Nothing.' Just madness.

Yron's eyes hovered on mine. 'Then… I suppose this is it.'

I nodded. 'You won't come?'

'I can't.'

'Next we meet, it won't be as friends.'

Yron gave a grievous smile. 'I was never your friend, Heldanarr Fall.'

So she knew my name. But many knew my name, now. It was not mine any more. It was all the Pale's.

I still had the question that the fly had not answered. Yron, despite everything, was loyal. So if I couldn't have her oath, I would at least have her opinion.

'The smallfolk think Candip was a victory,' I said. 'But the Refuser smashed us. You know it, I know it. So I can't figure out why the Azyrites dally. What are they waiting for? Why didn't they press their victory? Eight years ago, why didn't the Refuser finish us?'

Yron gathered herself. We gazed at Candip. At places we had not come from, to places we could not go.

'Maybe we weren't the victory she sought,' Yron said.

CHAPTER THIRTY-THREE

I could have vexed myself for days imagining answers to the riddles now puzzling me. Maybe Stormsworn was a fool, like Se Roye. Maybe emotion had got the better of her.

But word of my return should have reached her by now. Why hadn't she come? For my redemption? Perhaps she waited for my rivals to destroy me, or me them. Perhaps she was long gone.

Even if Stormsworn waited to the end of time, patience alone would not protect Candip – just as patience would not conquer it. Jujjar had been right. I needed more than an army. I needed a horde. I had never faced an opponent like Yron's Malokal before, but neither had he faced me. And no matter which of our heads eventually adorned the other's tent, after our confrontation, Candip would be closer to liberation. Or, extinction.

In the end I only knew what I knew.

Before returning to my warriors, I set out for Motte Pasheter. Yron had said something interesting before we parted.

'If you want traitors, seek out Boskin.'

Her words stopped me dead in the saddle. 'He truly lives?'

She shook sand from her braid. 'I'm not sure I'd call it life.'

The Mad Earl Boskin held Motte Pasheter, in Cardand's westernmost reaches, she said. Yron had heard word of him on her forages. She'd seen the graveyards marking his demesne and the aftermath of his oathsworn warriors' wrath.

Vassalage, lordship, oathsworn. I couldn't believe these words now crossed my ears. Boskin had taken our old stores of Aqua Ghyranis and built a kingdom in the crevices, the cunning bastard. If Yron had not betrayed us – and if Jujjar and Kaddarar had not – then it must have been Boskin. Jujjar had been right never to trust him.

I surveyed the marches surrounding Motte Pasheter, looking for where a warband might penetrate its walls, or where Boskin's carrion might be gibbeted once I was done with him. The stone keep was undefended. I found no sentinels, as in Jujjar's territory, nor smallfolk who'd submitted to Boskin's power. The whole area was abandoned. The marches reminded me of the ghost stories of the Nighthaunt's phantom corteges, the wraith-kin that haunted curselands in the days when the black sun rose. They terrorised the living, chasing their tortured souls back to Shyish-Shol.

Just the same, some force had depopulated Motte Pasheter's outlands. Desolation haunted their ruins.

The motte-and-keep rose like a wretched tor from a rubble-heaped hill. Its battlements crumbled. Beneath its parapets, untidy brickwork filled in wounds in the weather-worn stone. A moat of stagnant water surrounded the pathetic castle, stinking of ordure. Flies buzzed everywhere.

Micaw's hooves thudded in the sand, breath rumbling from her lungs like distant thunder. I heard shouts and shrieks from within the motte's darkened halls.

I reined Micaw in, craning my head. Boskin staggered between

Pasheter's tall doors, beating the air, berating the torchlit emptiness within. He wore his ragged Derder livery, the armour patched and rusted, his cuffs and hems frayed. His pistols were still polished, and his moustache hung to his chest. He had lived well, and laughter lines furrowed his face. But given what he'd taken with him, I was unsurprised.

He didn't seem the least surprised by my appearance. I dropped Micaw's reins and drew my blades, their metal tongues shinking.

'Hail, earl.'

Boskin raised his hands. 'Now stop. Stop right there. I know what this looks like. And I can guess what you'll say.'

'Not much,' I said.

'You'll ask where I was. You'll ask why I didn't come, when word came 'round you were back in the Pale. Lords and light, maybe you'll even ask if I betrayed us eight years back, at Candip. The subjects say you're on something like that. A warpath. But no, King Fall, it wasn't me. *That* I swear. And you know it's true, 'cause Candip would've just hanged me. I'm a traitor – this I don't deny. But I'm *your* traitor.'

A horrifying smell emanated from within the keep, like bad onions and rotten meat. I retched.

'I can explain that too. But first on the docket, you probably came for the old nectar, eh? I saved it a long time, your majesty. Swear I did. But eventually I used most of it. My subjects, you see. They needed it to flourish. And a good lord provides for his vassals.'

My eyes flitted around. No one was here.

He jerked his finger. 'But. I found something better. Something much better. You'll never need nectar again, not with this. And after I've had my say, should you decide you won't be taking my head, it's all yours.' He blinked. 'Well. Even if you take my head, I suppose it's still all yours. I suppose that's the way of taking heads.'

Micaw nickered. I gazed past the aging Derder, up the stairs, into Motte Pasheter's foetid gloom. Whatever that darkness contained smelt heinous. I couldn't imagine it being more useful than Aqua Ghyranis. There was nothing in that hellish stink I wanted.

After a hard look, I sheathed my blades. I *had* thought Boskin a traitor, but the reality was more prosaic. He was insane.

Boskin tucked his thumbs into his baldric. 'All that time. All those years back. You had no reason to trust me, but you did. Which was poor decision-making, because frankly, I did plan on betraying you. Thought I wanted a lordship, see. Thought I'd invest my nectar in your cause, then take advantage of you when I could. But when the Stormcasts beat you in Candip, blood rains fell. Eight days of red storms, gods blind me. I was lost. And I dreamed of you. So I looked, and I looked. Not that I loved you, but I wanted what you could give. Something like home, I think. Or a duchy. A nice duchy, with vellum patents and suits of armour and horses. I'm kidding. I just missed you.'

I stared, uncertain. His words were mad. His eyes were not.

'Then you know what happened, king? They began to come. My subjects, seeking protection. All the castaways and have-nots. People like us, picking maggots from their plates, who drank the blood rains. They needed a lord. And I realised, then, I've *always* been a lord. Se Roye couldn't take that from me. With you, I always had what I wanted. A liege worthy of me. Me, worthy of a liege. Everything else is horse pie.'

'You're not a lord,' I spoke, as frigid in tone as I was frozen in heart. 'You're a traitor, Boskin. You're the traitor who helped me kill his own men and women for a chance at power. You're filth. Filth like me. That's the truth.'

'No!' he screamed, shaking, his eyes red and wide like bleeding moons.

I flinched. Even Micaw startled. I patted her neck.

Boskin softened. 'No, sir. Just, no. All due respect, I'm nobility, and I've done my part for my people. And since I look out for them, they look out for me, as honest people should. Well guess what? We've looked after you, too. I heard you were back and knew I needed a gift worthy of a king. I told you we have something better than nectar. Have a taste.'

One by one, the torches in his halls guttered out. I squinted into the putrid shadows.

For a moment, hunched creatures lined the murk, growling. Horns twisted, and tongues lolled, with blades wicked, and claws cursed. All of them watched us. All of them hungered.

I shuddered. But the daemons were illusions, a trick of the shadows and light in my eyes. The halls were empty.

Then, as the last torch flickered out, two clay cups drifted from the devoted darkness, as if on tracks. They floated, one to Boskin, one to me. I snatched it but felt no strings, no rails. Just a clay cup of sloshing red.

I sniffed its contents and retched again. Spoilt blood, from pigs or something else.

Boskin glugged his down. I tossed mine to the ground. Where it spilt, brimstone sands bubbled and hardened into ugly tar. The gore was poisoned with enchantment.

Boskin shrieked. '*Whoa!* That's precious! You know how long it took to collect that?' He slashed his arms through the air. 'You know how many people used to live here?'

I looked at Boskin, and all I could do was pity him. All the years he'd lived, the things he had done, and here he was, covering his eyes and his mind like an old wizard afraid of his magic. Boskin could not accept what he had become. He wouldn't even look.

I reined Micaw in. 'Come back with me. Let's put you to better use.'

'Only' – he waggled a finger – 'if you promise to send men

and carts for my stores. I told you, this stuff, it's good. More potent than full-cut Aqua Ghyranis, and better for the bowels. So, promise. You'll send men and carts. Swear it.'

'I swear. Come. Let's go.'

He shut the ancient doors to Motte Pasheter. On the other side, the latch slammed down. No one was there, I reminded myself. Only the force with which he had closed the doors had made the latch fall.

I glanced to the ugly tar mutating in the sand. Then we started off.

Boskin spoke of the Lady Lellen Se Roye. 'You remember her, don't you? She still uses nectar. Plain Aqua Ghyranis. What a bore. Almost pity her, I do.'

'We'll kill her, Boskin. Soon.'

Boskin darkened. 'Shame. I don't hate her guts like I used to. Almost pity her, I do.'

'Why?' I gazed down. 'Charity? The goodness of your heart?'

A troubled look flickered across Boskin's face. For a moment, his eyes welled and his lips grew tremulous. I thought he saw what I saw, then. I thought he saw himself.

'I don't think I'm all that charitable. I don't think I'm all that good in the heart.'

As I rode into Cardand's labyrinth, Boskin sang out of tune. He stopped three times to curse his vassals for their lack of rhythm. I didn't tell him we were alone.

On the return journey, Micaw turned her great neck to gaze at Boskin. Her big eyes remained remarkable, calm. Constant.

I've always wondered how damnation nibbles away at the mortal soul. Of those souls who enslave themselves to gods, I assumed nothing remains. People like Boskin, like Kaddarar, could only be shadows of whoever they were. People like my mother.

But that mortal animus which inhabited them must surely go somewhere. The gods devour souls like river crocodiles wolfing down sows' flesh. Where next?

I had named Micaw for Boskin. She was him, in some way. He was her. As Micaw watched the Mad Derder, I glimpsed recognition in her eyes. She gazed at him as one might stare at an unfamiliar reflection.

In all our time together, I had never asked what curse strengthened my beautiful girl. After seeing that spark in her eyes, I thought I knew.

Boskin marched on in happy ignorance, blind with joy and madness. In Bharat, I'd promised myself I would know I was dying, when the time came.

I thought of my mortal soul and swore the same.

CHAPTER THIRTY-FOUR

Even without my old akwag surplus, my forces possessed more Aqua Ghyranis than a tyrant might scorn. We drank this freely. I saw no need to hoard our wealth. In the Cardand I would liberate, inanities like currency and ledgers would become extinct. Mortals would protect and provide for each other. We would have no more need of gods and wealth. Parasites like Se Roye would be banished, as would their exploitations.

After we returned, Kaddarar was displeased to learn I had spared Boskin. I let Boskin defend his long truancy himself.

We gathered for his trial. Warriors of many tribes collected beneath the eaves of vagabond temples and the roiling skies. Our banners beat in the wind, casting shade across the forum. Uninhibited, Boskin recounted his titles and deeds. He was an earl, the royal bursar, the lord of coin, the chief quartermaster. He was master of the hunt and a decent cavalryman. He had defended my name in his marches, against tribal Parcher villains who'd had the gall to dwell there before his arrival.

In times of trouble, Boskin swore, he had spent our old akwag treasure judiciously. In better times he had conjured his spoilt blood stores with that foreign Azyrite arcana, taxation. The reason for the depopulation of the marches around Motte Pasheter soon became obvious. None asked whom Boskin had taxed for his casks of enchanted blood.

Yet he enumerated them. He'd taxed robbers and liars, miscreants and rakes. Scoundrels, profligates, dreamers. Fishers and rangers, theologians and misspellers, and those who spelled too correctly. Boskin had taxed men, women, old, young. Their bones rotted in Pasheter's dungeons, their entrails decayed in its moat – and their black ichor enriched its treasuries.

Our sides split with laughter, listening to him. Boskin's obvious insanity dissuaded Kaddarar, who stalked away in the middle of his defence.

'Seeker!' I called over the crowd's roaring laughter. 'You find him innocent?'

Flint in her eyes, Kaddarar bound her black hair up with a string of dried sinew. 'They'll see. Then they'll know, as Boskin knows. Let him live.'

After that day, the little war began anew. Not against the Azyrites, but against the foreigners and barbarians who had burgeoned in Cardand during my absence.

I picked my battles wisely. One by one, my rivals submitted. As time passed, encampments carrying my black banner multiplied across Cardand. Chieftains and warlords bowed before me, accepting my warriors into their ranks, abiding by my decrees. We sealed our pacts with the blood of their desecrated champions. Any who had pledged themselves to the Dark Gods and their many aspects – Five-Tails, Knife-Eyes, Longtongue, or the Prince of Dreams – continued their worship unabated.

Yet within this pantheon, all accepted the supremacy of Kaddarar's Godeater.

I thought it all nonsense, but I was practical. I would not crush morale with proscriptions against faith in the gods. Let my warriors mutter to the winds whatever secret prayers they wished. So long as they fought for me.

My growing army was a portent of my intentions for Candip. Yet try as I might, I could not fill the cracks in my castle. My horde was a league, a confederacy, half-divided. We were nothing like Sigmar's imperial demesnes. I grew cynical. Candip could never be taken like this. Azyrites fought as one; we were a rabble of pagan raiders. Azyrite officers counted their soldiers' weapons at dusk and dawn, reporting these counts to their marshals. My champions simmered in firewine and hubris, duelling each other over matters of ego.

Slovenliness. This would be our downfall.

And then there was the Refuser. Her Stormcast Eternals still prowled Bodshe's reaches and lurked in Candip's depths, waiting.

I knew not how I might dispel these challenges, or if the enemy's hammer would fall first. My horde was an army in name only. Cardand's outlands were ravaged and spent, and those fiefs which remained were too close to Candip to dare. Across our Cardandish territory, tribes and warbands flying my banner battled each other for glory. They were restless, hungry, whittling themselves down. So was I.

One night, I sat in a night market. Those parts of Cardand I ruled enjoyed prosperity and peace, or some shadow of it. Locals laughed with each other, jovial and drunk. Children sword-fought with switches, asking if their savage warrior-mothers had seen this flourish, or that. I paid them all no heed, fixated by the gnats swarming over heaps of smashed sweet-cane and severed capon heads. The flies crawled on the roosters' rolled eyes, drinking the red milk of their slit wattles.

Then, the answer came to me. Command was a skill like any

other. The Refuser had devoted a lifetime to war's craft. But when she had been my mother, what had she known of war? For hells' sake – she'd gone to fight the beasts with a pan! All the abominable Stormcasts must be similar. What had made them peerless warriors?

Practice. Now I must do the same, to become a commander. Not a champion, nor a symbol – but a warlord. The answer was simple.

I breathed gratitude to the flies for their revelation, to Yron for her faith. Perhaps that was all faith was: a cypher for secrets hidden in the creases of the realm, longing to be found by those with eyes to see and ears to listen.

Or perhaps I had drunk too much spoilt blood. Boskin was right. The grim tonic made for a potent elixir.

On the morrow I sent heralds to my warbands, to summons them from their Ashwilds wanderings and their raiding grounds in Cardand. This muster took days. Boskin disappeared, so focused was he on the logistical challenge of feeding our gathered horde on scraps and housing our wild legion in the relic-kingdom's nooks. I required instructors, so Jujjar gathered the Ashstalkers, our core fighters, and prepared them for this special task.

We would train, as all armies train. Jujjar and his veterans would teach my barbarian marauders to fight smarter. Their needless thirst for glory must be dispensed with. We must learn to fight for victory, at any cost. We must be low when the enemy was high, far when they were close, fast when they were slow.

Glory had no part in that, for war was not glorious. Glory must be mastered – or the costs of its achievement would defeat us.

Discipline was the Azyrites' secret. To surpass them and formidable rivals like Malokal, we required discipline. For unlike gods, mortals ruled precious little in the realms. The Dark Gods' boons were real but capricious. Only the weak and the blind might become reliant upon them. I was neither.

Ourselves, the flies whispered. That was what we must control to win.

Because after that, we controlled nothing.

Time's fickle witherings had made many of Cardand's unterways crumble into themselves. Some of the old roads had been massive. The rubble-strewn depressions and pocked ancient squares made for an ideal simulation of Cardand's worst battlefield terrain.

We used this to train, and the derelict temples elevated around the dusty craters and trenches served as command outlooks. The warbands drilled, and we practised communication and coordination. I commanded our battle line, imposing my will upon multiple formations, harmonising their manoeuvres. We rehearsed that most despicable of Azyrite tactics, fighting in straight lines. But this could be sensible, too. Everything depended on circumstance. The more we trained, the more I saw.

Of my captains and champions, some enjoyed training, others less so. But all relished the fury of our mock bouts, and they drilled their units' immediate reactions to various situations to perfection. This, I hoped, would be the crux of any possible triumph in the future. I had fought in a Freeguild and knew I could not out-command trained officers like Boskin, let alone the Stormcast Refuser. But if each of my elements could act as they needed independently on fields of death and chaos, I wouldn't need to out-command anyone. Each of my warbands would be able to function without me. I just needed to instil cohesion between them.

One day, at sky's high flame, a brawl broke out. Heat and sweat-stung eyes had made wraiths of us all. In the training square, Yrdun and Beltollers squared off against a cohort of the *Rottii*, armoured spear-husbands whose ship sails on the Polychromatic Sea had been stitched from lions' hides. The Rottii were a Vitrolian warband that had smelt blood on the Parchward Winds and come to the Pale.

Welwary was trying to fight the Rottii's commander. I pulled her away and put myself between them.

'You're not satisfied with a real enemy, in Candip?' I shouted. 'You'd rather just kill each other and save them the effort?'

My presence calmed them, barely. The Rottii's captain was Laklien. She was easy to recognise with her back-crest of griffon pinions and her wicked blade. Reflective armour-scales of cool metal protected her from the swelter. Her shield, like her warriors', was a round mirror. The Rottii's skin glittered like pyrite. A trick of mutation, or maybe simply heritage.

'Your people are weak,' Laklien snarled. 'You fight like savages. No shields, no pike walls, no archers. How can we win like this?'

I knew Laklien – I'd killed her predecessor myself. She was blunt, but loyal, at least for now. Yet the subject of her complaint had been a point of friction for weeks. So had questions regarding the need for training at all. Few understood why I delayed marching on Candip, or seeking greater victories against rivals like Yron's Malokal.

The warriors craved blood. Somewhere, I knew doubt might settle in the cracks. Doubt in me.

I decided to settle the matter once and for all. I passed Micaw's reins off to a warrior she respected, a warrior she would not savage. I drew my black blades and thrust them into the dry ground. I dusted sand between my fingers, drying the sweat.

Then I slid my blades out from the sand.

'Laklien. You and your Rottii against me and half as many Ashstalkers. Defeat us, and my life is yours. This army, yours. You'll decide my fate, and that of Cardand. If you can.'

Laklien stared, wary. We had forged our pact in the spilt entrails of her former captain. For many free warriors, the line between treachery and honour was a thin one. Not everyone was Yron. Little more than greed and caution guided most of my horde's fighters.

I sighed. 'This isn't a trap. If I wanted to kill you, I would. Deceit takes too much effort.'

Laklien agreed, and we formed our lines. Any warrior not training or toiling gathered around the collapsed unterway to watch. Jujjar took half his Ashstalkers back to the arena's rim. The rest remained with me, forming up against the impressive Rottii, a mirrored block.

My warriors huddled. I issued my orders. We dispersed. I already knew how this would go.

The horn sounded, and the Rottii hardened into a shining square. Laklien barked hoarse commands. The spined, mirrored tortoise advanced, their lockstep gait pounding through Aqshy's crust.

My Ashstalkers dogtrotted out of their way, re-forming into a cloud at their back.

The Rottii reversed march, moving the way kaleidoscopes turn in on themselves. Again, they advanced.

This time, my Ashstalkers scampered from the collapsed unterway into the wide avenues of Cardand. We pushed aside the audience on the arena's rim. Their taunts and jeers faded into bemused silence. We had broken the rules, someone cried. What rules? another answered. This answer was correct: war's rules were what we made them.

Laklien's Rottii plodded after us, relentless. She knew better than to break ranks and give chase. But just the same, I knew better than to come at her. When that time came, I wouldn't need to lift a blade.

The minutes crawled, each moment dilated by the sun's excruciating heat. The fool's chase continued. Yrdun are built for the heat of Bodshe. We spend our lives with fire at our feet and the sun in our eyes. The Rottii were Aqshian, too, but their need for glory had mastered them. They spent all their energy without reserve. We preserved ours, quite relaxed.

After an hour, Laklien finally saw through my ploy. The Rottii returned to the square, and my skirmish cloud sauntered back. The brazen mirror-mercenaries could hardly lift their shields, exhausted.

We gathered around them. The heels of our javelins chanted on the stone, a litany, an omen.

Laklien dropped her spear and raised her hands. 'I yield, God-eater's Son. You prove your point.'

The chant of our javelins ceased. I strode forward and struck Laklien hard across the cheek. She collapsed, too tired and parched to resist.

'*Now* I've proven my point,' I growled, aggravated. The hours of this game had worn my patience to crumbs.

I summoned all the others who had watched. 'Any of you who think you might've done better are wrong. I know how each of you fight. I defeated most of you myself. What I did to beat Laklien and her mirrored killers, I wouldn't do for every opponent. Every foe's different. So must we be.'

'But you're enough, Godeater's Son,' a Sur-Sur-Seri spearwife said.

Others mumbled agreement. 'Why train when we have you and the gods?'

I listened to their objections. I saw in their eyes reverence and realised I'd accomplished what I set out to do, so long ago. I was a symbol. A champion. But these mortals needed a dose of the truth.

'These rumours spun of me…' I began, contemplating each word with care. 'The rumours I fought the Refuser to a standstill, that I wrestled her for eight blazing days, that only her God-King's lightning defeated me… These are lies. Ask those who were there. Hear the truth in their silence. The Azyrites crushed us at Candip. The Refuser would have killed me, if not for our Seeker. You're all proud – and that's good. But do not be proud fools. Azyrites are not weak. They're organised, and this makes them strong. Eight years ago, they had will and patience and I did not. When we fight again, that must change, or we're all ash in their seeing fires. Many of you claim to seek glory. You think I don't want it? My mouth waters for triumph. I want this more than akwag, more than meat, more than air. I crave to win Candip and stamp their guts into the ground and dry my hands of this. But I will set my cravings aside and cool the fires in my heart if that means winning this war. Is there not glory in that? Is there not power?'

Murmurs rippled through the assembled. I'd wanted cheers and cries, but none spoke up, bent with the day's exhaustion. And what I presented now – a radical change to their tribal traditions, and their gods' demands – was perhaps too much.

I cast my gaze across the hundreds of them. I'd driven them all mercilessly. I had offered no revel nor rest to appease their pagan hearts.

'Go, rest,' I said. 'Take this night and reflect on my words. Tomorrow, we do it again.'

Kaddarar awaited me that evening on the outlook. She scanned the horizon, leaning against a pillar, towering. 'You're so clever.'

I grunted, splashed water down my neck. 'My gratitude.'

'It's not a compliment. *Clever* won't get you far in this endeavour. Better if you'd made an example of them.'

I could have laughed, but the day had baked me dry. 'We can't fight like brutes any more. We can't fight like you. To take Candip we must beat the Azyrites at their own game.'

'You cannot beat them at their own game. They'll always do it better. Fight as they fight, you'll die as they die. You must fight as they *don't*.'

'That' – I raised my voice – 'is exactly what I'm teaching. I thought you'd agree.'

'No. You're teaching cowardice. I showed you how to be unpredictable, so that next you meet a demigod, you'd have a chance. You think I taught you this? To prance around the enemy? You're not *seeing*. It's like you don't want to.'

'Patience isn't cowardice. Neither is self-control.'

'Patience and self-control have made nothing of you but a godless brat,' Kaddarar said. 'You need the gods on your side. This is what you keep forgetting – what you cannot grasp. Don't you remember? The mountain, Fall. Asharashra. Khorne.'

I clenched my teeth. 'I remember. I want nothing of it.'

'It's too late for nothing. Far too late. You have the gods' eyes – now accept their blessings. Fight like it means something.'

'What, through sacrifice?' I sneered. 'You're that desperate? What's next, rain dances and berserker tinctures? Reading auguries in pigs' entrails?'

Kaddarar scoffed. 'You cannot read auguries in pigs' entrails. You must set someone on fire and look at their falling limbs.'

I felt the sweat running beneath my mask, the sand which adhered to it. 'Don't you get it?' I spoke softly. 'I'm not who you sought. I'm not the Godeater's Son. I'm Heldanarr Fall, and I want victory, not skulls. I want to make Candip free.'

I thought Kaddarar would lose her temper, but she was as cool as ever. The quartz in her eyes glittered, making my heart skip a beat.

'What a brute you must think me,' she said. 'A fanatic, a fiend. Like broken Khaine and his Daughters of Murder. I tire of killing too, you know. Sometimes it sickens me. Sometimes I drink gore up to my eyeballs and I can't see through the red. I seek victory too, Fall. But final victory – not this halfway drivel.'

'I don't have time for this.' I turned. 'Get out. I've a war to prepare for.'

'But I see no wars. Just burnt-out wastes and the starving serfs who fill them. Just you and what you wish to be. Something must give. Surely you see that. This horde you build cannot be two things at once, and neither can you. I've seen better mortals try. I've made chalices of their skulls.'

Her words chipped at my spirit. I faced her. 'Is that a threat?'

She sighed. 'Just the truth. In the end we're much smaller than you think. But it doesn't have to be that way. Godeater calls. Just answer.'

'You said the thing beyond those gates was not Godeater.'

She straightened. 'I don't know what I saw beyond those gates. But I still believe in Khorne, as I ever have. That is enough for me. What more do you want?'

I wrinkled my brow. 'Freedom.'

She pushed off the pillar and started to leave. 'I'll be with you to the end. Yours, or mine. You know I won't let anyone take a skull I've claimed. You think I twist all I see into shapes I like, shapes I believe in. You think everything I see confirms what I believe because I wish it to.'

'Yes,' I said.

She huffed. 'You're right. But that doesn't mean I'm wrong. When the time comes, if you truly are Godeater's Son, you'll wish you had prepared for what awaits you.'

I couldn't tell if she was toying with me. 'That's what you're for. My guide, until you kill me or I kill you. You always say it.'

She considered her next words carefully. 'Khorne-Godeater loves us no matter who we are. Because in the end, we're all exactly what he wants us to be. Slayers – or the slain. So believe, or don't. You know it's the truth.'

CHAPTER THIRTY-FIVE

I was not too small to see the truth in Kaddarar's words. Yet her warnings were needles in my ribs, obliging me to scream – and I held my lungs for spite. I resented that little compulsion to defy her. I resented my urge to prove her wrong.

But she wasn't wrong. For all my efforts, the months following our flight from Bharat had brought us not an inch closer to the exorcism of Azyrites from the Pale. Yrdun still haunted Cardand's ruins like feral dogs, condemned to squalor in the woeful nooks of the realm. We suffocated beneath the history of lies we'd buried ourselves in. We suffered, and the last eight years had improved nothing. Foreign barbarians wandered the Pale. Our situation had only worsened.

So the filigreed vellum scrolls which arrived bearing the sigil of Arad's Sorcerer-Malus, Malokal, were a small salvation, one of those fortuitous pebbles which may accidentally accumulate into the mighty mountains of fortune. Malokal demanded parley, and I accepted. As soon as my herald departed with my reply to

Malokal's summons, my fighters' spirits lifted. We would march in force, ready for war.

The Sorcerer-Malus had stipulated a meeting between equals at Teller's Ravine, an abandoned syrwanedd sanctuary near the Losh. Equality suited me. And if we remained equals overlong, I would grant him the equality of battle. Whatever wiles the sorcerer and his cabal possessed, I was determined to leverage the discipline and will of the horde I'd built.

I would listen to his words. If he would not submit, I would have his head.

Teller's Ravine was once a mesmerising palace of squared sandstone canals and coursing blue waters. You could still sense its legacy in its smell and bandit flow. Ages had passed, and the Everqueen's syrwanedd children had gone extinct here. Tall skeletons of greying trees rose from rubble hills and rugs of decaying humus. Ancient roots jutted up from blankets of half-rotted leaves, bulging beneath sandstone like leaden bones. Ash spiced the air, part of a haze which often covered the lands in the Season of Smoke. The Losh's maverick waters burbled over river stones as smooth as Draconith eggs.

This place felt older than time, beautiful and barren and purified by extinction. I was unsurprised to find Malokal's battle lines drawn in the ravine. They stretched into the ash haze up either course of the shallow stream. My horde occupied the overgrown heights opposite, ghosts in the cliffs and canopy, their faces buried in war paint. I took Micaw, plodding, down three switchbacks to the ravine's babbling waters. With each step, her barding gave a muffled clank. Her warmth was an assuaging heat.

Easy to know Malokal when I saw him. He wore an ostentatious crown of stag's antlers. His long-clawed hands gripped a crooked staff capped with a lifeless tongue. His mouth was sewn shut.

Yron and her tribe stood at Malokal's back. They were his

honoured Hullet retinue, their eyelids painted, temples shaved, war-braids clean. Malokal's other warbands were a motley mix – yet they were many. Parchers, Palers, marauders, with wicked blades and jackets of matted fur. Some wore armour of twisted bark, stinking of mutation and halitosis. Coming closer, I realised the bark was their skin. Mad light spiralled in their eyes.

For all his corruption and devilry, Malokal retreated in my presence. Maybe the black flames in Micaw's maw spooked him, or the charred grimace of my unclean mask. Or maybe all of us on the heights, staring him down with the hunger of those who had lived on bones and nothing else.

I halted.

Then my warriors chanted, solemn, their basso voices pealing through the dead glades like the pulse of the realm. Weapons hammered shields. Heels pounded stone. The trees shook, once for each breath. We made a drum of the world, and soon the reek of Malokal's witches' fear saturated the air.

I raised my fist, and the chant and rhythm ceased. Crows cawed in the dissonant gloom. Malokal's goat-eyes fluttered.

'All you need do is bow,' I said. 'Bow, and we'll seal a pact that shall make the Azyrites tremble. We'll banish their god from these lands. We'll make a place for all our people. All you need do is bow, and I'll offer you what I give my own kindred. Sanctuary. Hospitality. Revenge.' The words curled my lips. False, Yrdoval was, yet a promise as good as any.

Saliva oozed from Malokal's sealed lips. He gurgled, and I glimpsed drooling blackness in the sutured seam of his mouth. The tongue on his staff spasmed and flapped.

'Bow,' I said. 'Or don't, and let us consecrate this place in our blood.'

One of his champions stepped forward, a muscular daughter of Arad with a metal plate hammered over her eyes and insidious light glowing beneath. 'I speak for the Sorcerer-Malus, Great Malokal, defier of daemon-queens, truest thrall to the magus-king and knower of all plots. We serve holy nine-ways Tzeentch.'

I winced. The ugly syllable of their god's naming screeched up the hollows of me.

'I listen.'

The pale champion raised her glaive. It spoke volumes of the force and swiftness of the Azyrites' rise, that even their enemies spoke the Azyrite tongue in matters which did not concern them. The champion's dialect was ancient.

'Great Malokal asketh,' she began, 'be this not the parley he was prayed? Great Malokal speaketh, if thou comest in earnest, prostrate thyself and be done. Great Malokal sayeth, surrender was promised, and submission. Great Malokal sweareth, he be merciful and compassionate. If thou wouldst resile, Godeatersson, Great Malokal shall spare thy life and receive thy service. Thy warriors shall receive blessing. Thy soul shall be consecrated. Thy mind shall know the nine names of wisdom, in servitude. But first, sayeth Great Malokal – bow thy head, and bend thy knee.'

I recoiled. Her words were more than the sum of a wizard's pluck. Malokal had summoned me. I had not prayed this parley. Which of us was playing the games? Him, or me?

Fool I was, that I didn't see the trap. Not until the first muffled booms of remote artillery resounded in the distance like a snare of thunder on storm-ridden horizons.

Cannonfire screamed overhead, shaving branches from the bowers, splitting tree trunks, cracking like thunder. A blur skipped along the riverbed – a cannonball – shredding an entire rank of Malokal's fighters.

'Treachery!' the champion of Arad screamed.

But the storm was here. Explosions blossomed in the grey. Cannonballs mulched sandstone, and fragments of flying lead shaved old moss from ancient wood. The seconds of that resistless cannonade splintered bones and jellied flesh. The Arad herald-champion was the first to react, leaping and swinging her glaive at my head, but a lead boulder severed her legs at the knees, tossing her mid-air. She pinwheeled and landed headlong, dying in a pile of decrepit flesh.

Micaw had never failed me. But that day, the truth spoke to her – and she broke. My steed reared, whinnying, tossing me into cold waters. She bolted off, trailing black fire, her screams drowning in the din of the barrage.

All of this lasted moments. But when the first cannonade was complete, the damage was done. Nothing more remained but battle.

I roared to disengage, but I was not louder than war. Horns blew, and drums beat. My warbands reacted as I had trained them to react. The old bowers darkened under a cloud of javelin and arrow and stone. Raiders charged, meeting Malokal's lines at the river.

Drenched and shivering, I regained my bearings. Malokal glared me down. The witch-lord thought this my work. He cast off his mantle and revealed what his god's devilry had done to him. The sorcerer was all scrawn and bulging belly and willowy, bent limbs. He dragged a claw across his lips, splitting the stitches in his mouth.

His jaw fell down to his knees. His stomach emptied, and a cloud of bilious flies surged out. They swarmed me, biting with ten thousand razor-sharp teeth, burrowing like lampreys for the ice in my veins.

But just as soon as it started, the pestilence of flies showered the water, dead. I searched for Malokal, but he was a carcass, his throat slit.

Yron stood panting over the Sorcerer-Malus, her iron knife wet with his blood. I was astonished. All that talk of honour and glory, and now loyalty had made a traitor of her. Yron was faithful to me, to the point of perfidy.

'Godeater's Son!' she barked. Her kindred closed around her, resisting Malokal's shambling fighters. 'Go, find the true enemy! The Azyrites! We'll handle this.'

Flinging river silt from my blades, I howled for fighters. They answered. All the little timidities of the boy I'd been disappeared. We cascaded up the far side of the draw.

Of the horrific slaughter at Teller's Ravine, no record remains but the recollections of sinners and the gheists of the dead. Before that day I'd witnessed the flames of pyromancy but nothing like the corruptions which a true devotee of the Dark Gods might unleash. Amidst the carnage, walls of green flame whispered insanity. Worms spilt from the blubbering mouths of the afflicted; their eyes ran like spoilt eggs. Malokal's mutant warriors were terrible, their bark-skin shedding away as malefic doppelgangers of the flayed things they had contained, then assailing us. Only in blade-craft and heart did we match the forces arrayed against us. That had to be enough.

I roared to disengage, but it was too late. Malokal's corrupt fiends thought I'd come to eviscerate them all. They would fight to the death. My army could defeat them – I estimated attrition would favour us. This was like guessing futures from tea leaves or falling limbs at witch pyres. Yet even if we defeated our rivals, the deluge of Azyrites which followed would rinse away the meagre embers of our victory. We were trapped.

To have any hope of true triumph, I must seize control of the chaos. I needed to understand what we were up against. I needed a commanding view.

We scrabbled up overgrown canals on the far side of the draw. For each warrior who fell at my side, another took her place. Across the smoke and bleeding gloom, Kaddarar's bellows echoed, brutal and magnificent, before her voice disappeared into the greater din of war.

She could not fall, I thought. But if she had, this was no time to sing our lamentations. I cast a desperate glance across familiar terrain. I knew this place. Above the draw of Teller's Ravine, dilapidated Yrdun temples weighed down the rise. If fortune favoured us, I could find the Azyrites' positions from there, then devise orders and signals for my warbands. We could force Malokal's broken horde to submit, or work with us. I believed that on faith alone. For I had nothing else.

We pushed, fighting with notched blades and bleeding hands and burning limbs. We broke through Malokal's pathetic rear-guard, then crested the commanding heights beyond. I cast my gaze across the ruinous landscape of Cardand.

A wall of grey tissue filled the sunless sky. A soft halo of rain – only rain – blanketed the lands. Cold pinpricks of water tingled on my skin, stinking of sulphur. At lowest flame, the Season of Smoke was always like this.

But an omen hung over distant Candip which did not belong. A massive fortress, a winged mountain, greater than any metalith I'd ever seen. Domed temples armoured its surface. Its slopes, filled with gun banks, seemed oceanic and infinite. The fortress-metalith loomed in the stormhead horizon like the wall of the world. Artillery rumbled from its battlements. Shells sliced from the gun banks, streaking through the rain like lace. Below, in Teller's Ravine, the answering impacts boomed, and mortals screamed.

The fortress was enough to break my spirit alone. But beneath it, on Candip Plain, an army marched. Each regiment was a patch of bright fabric beneath the shadow of our doom. Worlds-thick chains ran from that host to the storm-veiled monstrosity above.

They had *hauled* it here. Pulled it, with their own screaming limbs.

I could not believe this. The Azyrites had dragged that mountain, on land and by sea, along the Paleward Winds. A host of soldiers and flagellants, zealots and war priests, allies and parasites. Their Hammerhalian banners fluttered and swayed like fields of damp wildflowers. Airships crowded the forlorn skies, embarking troops from the fortress-metalith's ramparts, disembarking them elsewhere. The sight was too much to bear.

Airships were here, too, on the rise. They had been moored to the despoiled temples festooning the rugged hill to deploy troops, their groaning engines faintly audible from where I stood. Those soldiers glimpsed me and mine. They shouted, rushing about in ungovernable urgency.

The frantic fools. They didn't know what I knew. One hundred victories at the Losh could not expel this army from Bodshe. This was not a legion; this was a crusade. They had nothing to fear but victory and victory's shame.

I felt revolution in my veins, then. *Fall*, the changing of all things my father had named us for. And how apt the name. Fall my nation and my people. Fall our kingdoms of yesterday. Fall my story and my family and the fools we had been. Fall the fools we'd become.

We all fell, long ago. Now the Azyrites were just making a point.

'They must be tired.' My words confused my warriors. I pointed to Candip Plain, to the wall of the world and the ten thousand flickering campfires beneath it. 'They've no room to sleep. Too many of them.'

My fighters glanced at each other. Some chuckled nervously; these chuckles swelled to hysterics. Of all times and places, this was the *when* and *where* my warriors kindled despair into hope.

Cheers rose. Spirits lifted. I chuckled, too. We really were barbarians.

All of this was nothing. Sigmar could stride here on his fat feet and it would have changed nothing at all. What did it matter if we died? Had we ever hoped to live?

Nearer, airship engines droned to life. The ironclads moored in the crumbling temple grounds rose. Frigates wheeled around, bringing their broadsides to bear. Domed turret guns clicked and clanged as they oriented on us.

Our window was closing. The disembarked Azyrite soldiers were still in disarray, caught off guard. I sensed their greenness; I smelt it like fields of fresh-mowed grass. Marder Mosh's lone charge against a mercenary Helblaster had won us the day at the Losh. Had he known he had saved us all, before Ildrid stamped out his life's fire? On the whitewood, a lifetime ago, the boy had claimed I inspired him. He had inspired me, too.

Life. Victory. Death. A circle without end, a path. To what? Glory, they'll say, but I still don't know. Perhaps I never will.

I looked upon my enemies and raised my falx. I gave the only order I could.

CHAPTER THIRTY-SIX

We barrelled towards the closest of the moored ironclads. The colossal vessel towered, a groaning bulwark, its engines roaring to life.

My limbs were aflame. Grit scraped beneath my heels. Then I leapt, my legs pumping me from a temple forum into dreary sky. Two dozen warriors jumped with me, into oblivion. We slammed into the airship's hull, scrabbling for purchase. Some slid screaming to their deaths. I craved to join them. Or merely linger, and expend the last moments of my life enjoying the breeze and the view.

Above, duardin arkanauts turned aethermatic guns down the gunwales. Shots cracked off their vessel's iron hull, dropping more of my fighters.

I dangled and bounced on the bolted-plate hull. My nails split, my fingers ached. I hadn't the strength to climb. So I imagined Varry on the airship's deck, beneath the looming metal moons of its ballast tanks. I imagined climbing back in time, to change everything that had happened. I'd change the moment I found that priestess, and the dusk when the beastkin came for us. And if I climbed far enough, I'd stop Sigmar's lightning from stealing my mother. I'd change the doomful coming of his tempest to Aqshy. I'd change all the realms, if only I climbed faster. I would change myself.

Then I was on the ironclad's deck, slashing, thrusting, battling for survival. More warriors clambered over the gunwales. Our war cries filled the air, litanies of fear and its sole cure, valour. Why do we fight, when no hope remains? No answer to this question exists. Instinct and inertia push us on – but why?

The duardin airship groaned with its desperate manoeuvres. The deck tilted. Arkanauts pressed in from the upper berths, the pale glow of their aetheric lanterns illuminating our melee. Each duardin fighter bristled with cutlass and pistol of unfathomable invention. Our brawl vibrated through the metal deck, up my heels.

I killed an arkanaut, then surged towards another. The stink of iron-rich blood assailed my nose. Carnage underlined by the airship's roaring engines besieged my ears.

Then the vastest warrior in the realm erupted before me. Another arkanaut, clad in alien carapace, a worked-metal beard below his bug-eye goggles. His weapon's many barrels spun, priming to fire. Bead-laden braids clattered on his bracers. He was as wide as the world. An airship could have docked on the breadth of his shoulders. Give him a chain, and he might have anchored a metalith. His spine was shorter than mine, but that mattered not. He was as thick as mountain ranges, the mythical womb of his duardin people.

But worse than all this – I knew him. He was Hewer Durandsson, stout in many ways. Most of all, in friendship.

At the Losh, Marder Mosh had been bold at the proper hour. My suicidal rush onto this craft had been little more than fanciful escapism. We handful of boarders were doomed. The arkanauts outgunned us. I had meant to die, I think. Only death could have saved me from the doom over Candip and the extinction it had heralded – the humiliation.

But Hewer was here. I cast down my blades, tore off my mask. 'You ugly thing!' I screamed. 'You stink like the day I met you!'

The lull in the brawl was evanescent. Two savages and a duardin died during that breath.

Then hesitation gripped the edges of the peace, widening it. Violence faded, like a kettle's vapour steaming away. The heat remained. The simmering tension.

Hewer barked at his duardin. My few fighters and I gathered, back to back, surrounded. The arkanauts' leering goggle lenses gleamed with fastidious blackness. The air stank of burning oil.

Then Hewer removed his helm. His braided beard bulged from his armour collar. 'Well I'll be three ways in debt,' he said. 'Heldanarr Fall, you lad. You're one of these scurvy rebels and knaves? What're you doin' here?'

I brushed sweat from my brow, ignoring the poison which had summoned it: embarrassment. I had grown so accustomed to veneration and fear. This look Hewer paid me contained neither. He gazed at me as an older brother might have. He was healthier than ever, his cheeks ruddy and shining, his nose gleaming red.

I was lean, unwashed. My face was a revenant's. Sun-daub tar and the blood of foes encrusted my skin. How far I had fallen. What *was* I doing here?

'I don't know,' I said. I couldn't. Not when my army lay scattered below, hemmed in by foreign foes. Not here, in alien skies, at the mercy of a duardin who had been an uncle, a neighbour, a friend.

What had I meant to do, at the beginning of all this? Where could I go from here?

The sky's fog encompassed the ship. The ironclad's deck

machinery whirred and clunked. Pistons hammered, steam hissed. In this brimming quiet, war seemed a theory of violence. But corpses littered the deck, and spent powder stung my nose. Blood pooled, sticky beneath our feet. The war was real. These duardin were our enemies.

Hewer ratcheted his weapon, a mean look in his grubby eyes. 'Whatever it was, it's over. Down wit' your warriors' arms. Up wit' your hands.'

None of my fighters complied. Neither did I. 'Where were you?' I said.

'Where was I, when?'

Hewer's vain response puddled in my head. Where he had been didn't matter. He wasn't there when the warborn had come. He wasn't there when we'd dragged Elene home. He hadn't waited to meet us, to take the mewling priestess to Candip. If he had, maybe the beasts never would have found us. Maybe this war never would have started. But all those *maybes* and *would haves* were sorcery, formless spells I could never cast.

Hewer stooped, retrieving my mask. His eyes wrenched up. 'All the aether, Held. Is this what I think it is?'

I reddened. In all my life I'd never seen Hewer's shock. All the colours of his greed, the shades of his dismay – but never shock. I nodded.

Enraged, he shook. 'Bloodbound be coming. And so many more. Timestolen, and the Crimson Horde. Khul's Goretide rises this way, lad. Bigots, fiends, gut-chewin' cannibals. Bodshe's *dyin'* – and here I learn little Varry's brother is what caused it all! I thought you dead, lad, but you're him! You're the Godeater's Son!'

Hewer hurled my mask at me. I caught it.

'Never woulda thunk it. But here we are, lad, my muzzle on your mug. Slaves to Darkness never know what they are, it's said. I didn't unnerstand 'til now. But your eyes tell me it's true, you don't know. You hear the rumours on the winds, lad? 'Twixt here and Hammerhal? Barbarians chant your name, by their bonfires, in great feasts. *A slaughter stirs in Bodshe,* they say. Blood portents, and bones raining from the Cursed Skies like hail. It's you, Held. It's all you. For what? Power? Or did you just decide the bright-stone should be yours? What was it?'

I winced at the echo of Ildrid's question. 'I don't even know what brightstone is.'

Hewer scoffed. 'Don't even know what... you think me daft, lad, that it? You and Varry *sold* it to us! And you expect me to believe that?'

Hewer leered. I leered right back.

Then he sighed a great gust. 'Endrineer Orlog. Bring us a burnin' stone from the hold. Show the crow his trinket.'

We waited. The moments of that withering quiet passed as ages do. When the so-called brightstone was finally tossed to the deck, crackling and snapping, I couldn't believe my eyes.

For it was magnure. A glittering, burning ember, same as I'd sought out and wrapped in spellbound cloth scrims. It brought my blood to boil, thawing the ice in my soul. Varry and I had sold magnure for mere droplets. But the lavamander ordure we had spent a lifetime collecting was brightstone, more precious than Aqua Ghyranis – or so Kaddarar had said.

Yet it must have been. Ildrid had asked about it, and now Hewer said it plain. Azyrites had gone to war for this. Nations had gone extinct for it. I felt sick.

That sickness was nothing compared to my rising bile. Varry and I had lived as feral dogs lived. We had eaten the ends of boiled bones for nourishment and gnawed on the roots of weeds. We'd slept under walls of rubbled stone. We'd washed with brimstone waters and drank them too, our clothes stiff with the days and weeks of our sweat.

All my life I'd spent in squalor and filth, right as I plundered my people's lands for the Azyrites, in exchange for droplets.

For ovens, they had said. For stoves.

The truth lay written on my face. Hewer's brow smoothed. 'You really didn't know.'

I collected myself and explained the truth. The lie Varry and I had believed, like many other Palers.

Hewer lowered his eyes. 'Never did understand your rates. Or why you called it magnure.' He shrugged. 'Clever name, though.'

'Aye,' other arkanauts muttered, glancing about, nodding. 'Clever name.'

'You didn't think to say something?' I said.

Hewer scoffed. 'We're not in the business of questionin' good bargains, lad. It weren't personal. Just business. We're all business.'

'Aye,' the others parroted. 'Aye, all business.'

Everything changed, then. The arkanauts relaxed. So did my warriors, baffled as they were. The wrath melted from all of us. I felt it thaw in my heart.

Hewer gritted his bearded jaw, pointing to the fog around us. The fortress-metalith's barrage still echoed. Each volley flashed gold in the silver haze.

'That's a crusade, lad,' Hewer said. 'Real Dawnbringers. They came for two things. First, to squash you. Second, to bring Candip to heel. Eternals are here – Hammers of Sigmar, led by a tall warrioress with a gold face. She wants to stop the war brewing between the Cities of Sigmar. You don't know what ambition does to folk. It makes us what we don't want to be.'

'I want Bodshe to be free,' I said.

'I believe you. Can't believe it, but I do. But, lad – Hammerhal won't back down 'til they get Bodshe's brightstone. Se Roye's been claimin' you've been raidin' and hoardin' it. Not a soul unnerstood why she wouldn't swallow her pride and accept Hammerhal's help.

And three days ago, when the Crusade came, she doubled down. Demanded we smash you, then renegotiate Candip's ancient trade charters.'

I pointed to the brightstone. 'We've none of this. We've only ever fought for freedom.'

'Aye. Se Roye's lyin'. Playin' her own folk, and baldly.' Hewer's thick lips curled. 'And that means we've been played, too.'

'Aye,' his duardin mumbled in agreement. 'Played, baldly.'

'It ain't fair!' another said. 'Our rates are wrong!'

Hewer nodded, sighing. 'I look at you, Held, and I see a lost lad who eats string and doesn't wash. I see a boy who fought for Free-guilds and now chews them up for meat. You got rocks in your head, and stones as big as any. But you ain't rich in brightstone, lad, no.' He paused, grimacing at my fighters. 'And despite your company, maybe you're no Slave to Darkness neither.'

Stone-tongued murmurs rose between the arkanauts. The glowing brightstone disappeared into the hands of the endrineer who'd brought it. The Kharadron kept their weapons trained as Hewer whispered with the senior mates of his crew. The fates of me and my desultory comrades were being written in the hiss of their hushed exchange. I tensed my shaking fingers, calming my breath.

Hewer lowered his gun and faced me. 'It's decided. What we have right here's a violation of contract.'

The other duardin nodded, lowering their weapons.

I blinked. 'What?'

'Our airfleet signed on to help squash you, lad. But you knaves were supposed to be obstacles, not objectives. No one in the realms fights pagans and savages for the fun of it. First clause of our oath-charter dictates certain outcomes. Relevant here, line the third. I quote, "Our endeavour shall be made for securement of supply enumerated below – aqthracite, as previously defined, of which ten per cent shall be paid in compensation to the Geldraad."'

'Should I understand that?' I said.

'If you were signin' the contract, you'd want to. But the long and short of it is, if you and your rabble aren't responsible for the brightstone shortage, our contract's void. We've been ripped off for work that needn't be done.'

The duardin whispered, of *Geldraads* and grudges and broken pacts. I sensed their dissatisfaction, crystalline and hard.

I seized the only chance I'd get. 'Help us.'

Hewer's lips curled. 'No, lad.'

'They lied to you. To all of us.'

'Aye. Clear breach of contract. But I'm not about to betray Hammerhal because of a greedy colony's lies. The Twin-Tailed City is too much good business.'

I hesitated. We'd had these conversations before. I knew how to make Hewer budge. 'What if we made it worth your while?'

'No, no, *no*, lad. I'll lodge a complaint with the Geldraad. But that's just for the sake of precedent. If you're tryin' to bargain, profit won't hardly tempt us. We're not harlots.'

My eyes bulged. I didn't miss the shade of greed in Hewer's voice. I'd heard this before. I knew where it led. He was actually considering this.

He tried to hide it. Kept his face flat, his eyes glittering. 'But' – he raised a stout finger – 'just to be thorough, I'd like to hear what you're offerin'.'

I couldn't believe it. 'Name your price.'

'Full control of Bodshe's skies,' he answered. 'And assurances you won't betray us.'

'I'm no traitor. You know me.'

'If we were sittin' in your hovel, I might take you at your word.' Then he nodded to my fighters. 'But I don't trust them past the lengt' of my beard. You'll be accountable for them.'

His duardin murmured consensus. I shrugged. 'Done.'

'And,' Hewer said, 'I want sworn protection for the mountain kin. You won't touch any slayer lodges or barak holds. They won't give you trouble. They're far from here, beyond the wastes. Swear it.'

I tried to read the other Kharadron. I understood why they always wore their masks, now. 'I so swear.'

'And,' Hewer said, 'you killed sixteen of my crew.' He pointed to the dead arkanauts on the deck. He enumerated their names and debts. 'I'll want indemnities. For myself as their captain, and their families, and their sky-ports.'

That Hewer thought I could provide this suggested I possessed far more bargaining power than I'd thought. I straightened, growing confident. 'Done.'

'And–' he said.

'How many more demands'll you make?'

'*And*,' he said, 'you'll swear on this and sign an oath-charter. Break your word, or if the hordes from the Parch break it, don't think we'll forget. We hold grudges against Grungni, lad. We don't forget.'

'I don't control the Parcher hordes.'

Hewer seemed to doubt that. 'Let's assume they'll be amenable to your suggestion.'

Again, I nodded. 'Done. Now what do I get for all this? I'll want that in your oath-charter, too.'

Arkanauts muttered, shaking their heads. Evidently they'd hoped I wouldn't ask.

Hewer bit his thick lip. 'We'll drop you off safely, below. Then we'll leave.'

'I want more than that. I want assistance.'

'Or how about we turn you over to Candip?' Hewer said. 'Don't push your luck.'

I shook my head. None of this discussion would be possible

if my position weren't more favourable than I'd thought. Hewer knew things I didn't. He sailed the Parchward Winds. Whatever armies marched to war in Bodshe, their weight had stacked this negotiation in my favour. Hewer seemed to think whatever reprieve the Azyrites might win today could only be temporary against what I'd started.

This was only a gut feeling, but the point remained. I held more cards than I'd thought. Maybe all of them.

Against my silence, Hewer finally broke. 'Name your terms.'

I did. The Azyrites had turned Malokal's horde and mine against each other. In the right circumstances, I could do the same to them. With Hewer's assistance, I sensed an opportunity I could not miss.

After I had spoken, Hewer's ruddy cheeks blanched. 'Hammerhal might be rivals wit' Candip, but they'll take that as personal. And you still ain't sworn a thing.'

'Think of what you get in return,' I said, assuming Cardand's skies were worth as much to his people as its lands were to mine. 'Look at us, Hewer. You really think we can hurt you? Eating strings, rocks in our head. We need your help.'

Hewer gave a hollow laugh. 'Lad, if you think Sigmar's enemies need help, you really ought to get out of Bodshe.'

That was a thought.

Hewer exhaled. I wasn't sure if it was a show, as if his accession to my terms was unwilling, and therefore precious. Still, I knew this game. I had clearly not played it well before, given magnure's true nature. But I went along as if we were only at night market, talking over the prices of food and firewine.

'I accept your terms,' Hewer said. 'But I still want it oath-signed.'

I sashed my blades. 'I swear to abide by these terms.'

Hewer stamped his foot. 'No, you damn lad!' Another arkanaut produced a wax tablet to record our agreement. 'Do better. Swear on somethin' precious. Swear on your sister.'

I cooled. 'Varry's dead.'

'Oh.' Hewer moistened his lips. 'Consolations. Anythin' you believe in will do. But only somethin' real, and don't lie. The ink always knows.'

I glared at him. I had seen the truth in Bharat, in Khorne's hell beneath the world. I felt it again in the perfidy of Hewer's apathy. How many times had we broken bread and shared cups? Varry had honoured Hewer with the Yrdoval! Hospitality, as he kept his thick lips sealed and ripped us off. Now the fact of her fall slid across his face like oil on a skillet, gripping nothing, blistering my hands.

Hewer wasn't friend or neighbour. He didn't care. Like Azyrites, he measured the realm in profits, counting its miserable people off like drops of Aqua Ghyranis.

For all I'd come from and everything I had seen, I could not be hurt by this.

'Something I believe in...' I thought long and hard. Tominer had been right, in Bharat. All flames guttered out. And when time's hand finally ceased its turnings and the realms burned to ash, only our names would remain. Our deeds.

If my story was all that would survive the realms' ruin, let it be worth praying to. Let it be worth believing in.

I lifted my chin and spoke from my chest. 'I swear on my name,' I said. 'Heldanarr Fall, the Godeater's Son. I swear on me.'

CHAPTER THIRTY-SEVEN

Walking off the ramp of Hewer's ironclad was a long moment of latent peril. I expected the arkanauts' aethermatic munitions to thud into our backs, a dirge of screams rising as my fighters toppled around me. I thought they'd leave us half dead, bereft of cairn and eulogy, life rattling from our lungs like the mortals in Lurth. Those had suffocated to death where the beasts piled their kin's corpses atop them, drowning in blood and filth. So would we.

But as Hewer's airship groaned into the smoky skies, I exhaled. He would abide by the glowing ink of our oath-charter. Whether he would do *exactly* as promised was another matter – but that I could not control. Hewer had sailed from my life a long time ago. I did not count on his assistance any more. What would be, would be.

Hours passed before we found Sertorix and his *Dospekhs*. Sertorix was the rare warlord who had pledged fealty to me without shedding a single drop of blood. He was a true believer, like Kaddarar, who had always seen in me the will of his gods and twice as blindly bought into it.

In a steaming forest near the site of our battle, I surveyed their pathetic encampment. The Dospekhs had marched to Teller's Ravine, but to judge by what I saw now, few had survived. As I passed through the camp, Dospekhs' heads caged in ferromantic helms craned towards me. The iron lungs of their battle armour wheezed as they rose and pushed aside vines to watch. Greener fighters filled out their camp, but none of them were Sertorix's. Their warbands must have been routed. Our casualties in the draw had to have been high. The Losh ran red again, this time with the blood of *my* warriors.

My mask hung from my belt, and few recognised me. Those who did quit their rest, sauntering over like ghosts, following me and those warriors who had stood beside me on Hewer's ironclad.

On a sandbar surrounded by trickling silt-red waters, I found Sertorix speaking to a handful of Ashstalkers. Mist obscured the trees and hanging vines around them. Jujjar and his veterans were here. At Teller's Ravine they had been our reserves.

I tramped closer. 'So you lived.'

Sertorix's jaw slackened, rotting teeth jutting from his greasy lips like mossy stones. 'Godeater's Son! I thought you fell.'

Disbelief wrinkled Jujjar's nail-studded face. Old tension resurfaced as my Ashstalkers – his? – parted for me.

'I did not fall,' I said. 'I rose. Are we all that remain?'

Sertorix grunted. 'No. Malokal's host is broken. And ours, many fell, but many still remain. Jujjar-Yrdovaler and your kin-swords rally them.'

I stared at Jujjar. I knew he wasn't doing this for me. This was what he wanted, same as when Ildrid broke my warband in Candip. Jujjar longed to take my place, to do differently than I had.

The studs in his brow were like gems in furrowed stone. He looked cold, as I did.

'I did what you would have wanted.'

I nodded and gripped his shoulder. 'I'm glad you live, too.' Then I hardened, gazing at Sertorix. 'I bear tidings. It's time to finish this war. Gather your fighters.'

Warriors collected around us, some wounded, many weak, a pack of dogs that had sniffed out some carrion hope. I gave Sertorix orders to organise our warriors and dispatch trusted messengers across Cardand. The horde had been scattered, but more remnants must have survived. To have any hope at accomplishing my designs, I needed every fighter we could muster.

Sertorix complied. Dark hope glimmered in his eyes, like flames limning smoke. He barked gravel-tongued orders to the Dospekhs, who rallied the rawer warriors and set about enacting my commands.

As they attended to this, Jujjar and the Ashstalkers closed in around me. The sour smell of their breath filled the air, tinctured with heat I couldn't recognise.

'What did you intend to do?' I asked, in Azyrite.

Jujjar hesitated. For my face, I realised. He hadn't seen me in so long. He had only seen what everyone saw. My father's mask, the face of the Godeater's Son.

Not Held Fall. Not his friend.

'I thought you were dead,' he spoke, in Yrdo.

I glanced around. I still remembered the names of the Ashstalkers present.

'You don't look pleased I'm not,' I said.

'I am.'

I licked my lips. 'Where were you in the draw? I fought clear with outlanders and Beltollers, but not a single kin-blade. Not a single one of you.'

Jujjar clenched his teeth. His bushy beard concealed the emotions written on his face. 'We held in reserve. Just as you ordered. And when you ordered retreat, we handled that. Brother.'

A slipping feeling lubricated my innards – the touch of a lost grip, the slide of inevitable betrayal. Sertorix was too naive to see it, too faithful. Only a mortal once sibling to these Yrdun could sense the gaping void of their fraternity.

I met each of their eyes. 'So.'

None moved. Their hands gripped their hilts, as a good warrior's fingers must. But this was more than martial instinct.

Jujjar hardened himself for what came next. 'If it came to it, would you kill yourself for the Yrdun? Would you die for our people?'

I knew these Ashstalkers by name. I still remembered their stories from that night on the whitewood and all our common travails.

'Not for the Yrdun,' I said, glaring. 'I would die for you, Jujjar. I would die for all of you.'

Jujjar's countenance softened. Doubt chipped at whatever had poisoned him and the Ashstalkers against me. My answer had surprised them. Perhaps they didn't know what to think.

I did. All the stars in the sky, all the kingdoms in all the realms; all the truths, all the lies; all the great gods and little men, the dead sisters and abandoned sons; all the blood rains and bloodied blades; all the Azyrites' faith, and their treachery… All this could not stand between us. All this could not change who we were. Yrdun, yes, but also comrades. We fought for each other and nothing else.

Jujjar was a man at war with himself. Finally, he nodded.

'What does Heldanarr Fall command?'

Jujjar took our Ashstalkers to scout the unterways running into Candip. The rift city was the nexus of Cardand's unterways and high roads. The passing of ages and the machinations of despots had sundered many of these paths, but many more remained open.

How else could Se Roye's army have marched to the Losh in the growing scorch of the Season of Flame? Even if they did not know the lands as we did, they commanded its passages.

If I could secure the unterways leading to Candip, my horde could enter the city's crevasse. I could find the Refuser, tell her the truth of what Se Roye had done. Ildrid had said she despised Se Roye's methods, and she had wanted to solve the riddle of Bodshe's brightstone. If I revealed the full extent of the Lady Lellen's intrigues, I was certain I could turn my Stormsworn mother against her.

The cynic in me whispered this plan was folly, but my nascent hope told me it could work. If the Refuser truly believed I was worthy of redemption, then once I laid bare Lellen Se Roye's exploitations, perhaps the viceroy-regent would be deposed. Perhaps she'd be pilloried in one of Candip's market squares like common scum. And with my forces in Candip, perhaps I could force treaty with Hammerhal from a position of strength.

Perhaps, we could have peace.

Perhaps – a scant word filled with all the possibility in the realms. Candip could never be returned to us, that I knew. But what if the Azyrites permitted us to build a new home in the bones of Cardand? A kingdom for all who had known the sting of loss. Let the Azyrites ordain the city they had stolen from us. Let it be another jewel in their God-King's crown.

All I wanted was the future taken from me and Varry. All I wanted was to live.

I was under no illusion about how difficult this endeavour would be. If I came to Ildrid Stormsworn alone, my life would be forfeit. We needed to fight our way in. The Dawnbringers had come for Candip as much as they had come for us, so with Hammerhal's crusade on Candip Plain, the city's garrison would be on alert. Then, even if we secured passage through Cardand's unterways, we would need to penetrate Candip's internal defences to find the Refuser. The odds of success were longer than a rich woman's life.

Yet... it could work. My forces were far too few to defeat the Azyrites' combined armies on the field, but we were skilled. My smaller force, now battle-hardened at Teller's Ravine, might even be more effective than the unwieldy horde I had commanded before.

For all this to succeed, Hewer's assistance was critical. He had refused to go so far as attacking Candip – no Kharadron would so eviscerate their sky-port's reputation among their best clients – but he had been eager to spread the truth of Se Roye's deception among the Kharadron airfleet. Kharadron despised deceptions when they were the ones deceived. For this they even held grudges against their god.

On the second sunrise after our meeting, Hewer would distract Candip's defenders with an unexpected show of force, a manoeuvre which his arkanauts termed a *flyby*. Since Candip's defenders feared attack from the Hammerhalians, the Kharadron flyby would shift Candip's attentions outwards, to the Dawnbringer Crusade on Candip Plain, away from the unterways leading into Candip.

They would not be expecting us. So I hoped.

The success of Hewer's feint depended on confusion and the fog of war. If it worked, the opening would not last long. Azyrites made peace far more easily than the barbarian tribes I'd hammered together into a horde. I envied this quality about them, even as I hated them for it. But I could no longer pretend everything they did was wrong.

Hewer had been scrupulous with the terms of our oath-charter. This boded well. But if the arkanauts didn't come through, I would make do. As Hewer himself had put it, I didn't trust him past the length of his beard.

Then again, I had never seen the length of his beard.

With that second sunrise looming, I hardly had time to reorganise my army. Sertorix's Dospekhs gathered who they could. The Rottii were intact, but the same could not be said of many of my more impressive warbands. I was forced to rely on tribes I did not wholly trust. Ushara warborn, who had pledged their sand-iron to my cause in exchange for promises of independence. Holmon delvers, duardin better known for their enmities than their grit in battle. The Doomsteed Riders, the Smiling Sword clans. So many more.

But we numbered mere thousands. Many had fallen at Teller's Ravine or succumbed to the wounds and spiritual rot inflicted by Malokal's sorceries.

As new blood filtered to our camp, I felt it again: my slipping feet, my lost grip. The warriors sat, sharpening their blades. They made nervous jest in tribal tongues, or supped on meagre meals in morose silence. *They are not enough,* fear whispered within me. I forced myself to believe they were – that if we could draw Ildrid Stormsworn out, we at least had a chance.

At dusk, in the shadow-wreathed foundations of a crumbling ziggurat, my warriors gathered in long queues to be inspected by my veterans and champions. I worked among them, checking the edges of each of our fighter's blades, examining their gums for disease and their bodies for corruption, pawing at their equipment to ensure they were ready. I checked to see if mutation had twisted them. I asked them what was to be done in this event or that, to see if their captains – or whoever had risen to lead them – had prepared them properly. Then I dispensed cuts of fat and thick bread, so they could eat well one last time.

My mask still hung from my sash. The thinnest touch of sun-daub provided me a semblance of anonymity. The horde knew the God-eater's Son lived, but this final day I had wanted to mingle with my mortals, to see them with my eyes and hear them with my ears. Being nobody was liberating. We laughed together. I taunted the rawest fighters, assuaging their trepidations with brotherly ridicule. Only warriors might understand this. And warriors we were.

A boy in dyed Beltoller shawls told me he feared widowing his wife in the Ashwilds. I told him battle is nothing to a wife's anger – that's how I knew he would live. He blushed and went on but seemed braver than before. I gave similar words to others. I felt good.

After the horizon had broken up Hysh's last light, someone tapped my shoulder. Yron stood behind me, still battered from Teller's Ravine, her temples thick with a day's growth of hair. Malokal's gore had stained her face black.

A seasoned fighter replaced me on the queues. I brought Yron to a tabernacle in the ziggurat. Candles of mortal tallow with hair wicks and guttering flames weighed down a timeworn altar. Totems overflowed from it, offerings of bird skulls and flower petals. The chamber smelt sickly and strange.

'I didn't think I'd see you again,' I said. 'Will you stay?'

Yron offered a fragile smile. 'I'll go, if it pleases you. I'm done.'

I had been grinning, but my grin melted away. Some spiteful boy in me screamed for her to stay. I could have commanded it. I could have held her hostage and forced her kin to fight with us. We needed every blade we could get. Everything had led to this moment – and now Yron wanted to leave.

But I was tired, half broken. I sighed. 'Why do it? Why betray Malokal and help me, only to leave?'

Her face flickered. 'Would you believe me if I said glory?'

I tilted my head. 'Would you?' When she didn't answer, I took her hands. 'The glory awaiting us tomorrow will be greater than any we have ever shared. This is the end of the war, Yron. I feel it.'

Her smile must have ached on her lips. 'Glory walks with you, Yrdun-son. But not with me. Not glory I can bear any longer.'

'Your tribe,' I said.

'I'm beginning to think there are safer ways to protect my kin-folk. But not here. Not in the Pale.'

I gritted my teeth. 'Why not?'

'Maybe I've seen too much. Or lost too many.' She shook her head, her braid swaying behind her stiff neck. 'I see where this path leads, better than I did before. I can't go there. I won't be like the Seeker.'

'Like me.' The despair in her eyes was infectious. 'You lack that much faith in me?'

'No. The gods walk with you. They watch you. But not me. I've seen the price of their favour too many times and lied to myself, pretending it's just. But Tul… or Kaddarar, who slaughtered my kin-fighters for being in the wrong place at the wrong time… We're supposed to be on the same side. I don't think we are. At least, not all of us.' She raised her chin. 'If you asked it of me, I'd hold my blade for you. I'd fight with everything I have left. But in the end, it would only earn me death. I've no more faith left to give.'

I bristled, not only at Yron's desire to leave. Kaddarar still hadn't been found. At Teller's Ravine, warriors claimed they had seen her carve her way into a press of Malokal's crow-eyed barbarians. Rumours passed she had fallen there, and the Losh's mourning waters had carried her clear of the draw.

Half of me hoped it was true. The other half hoped she was still out there, fighting, killing. Becoming whatever her god demanded she be. That had been what she wanted.

It all felt so weightless and futile. Kaddarar had wanted to teach me something, but I still wasn't sure what, and now she was gone. Yron had wanted to, too, but now she prayed to leave when I needed her most. I had crossed a vast distance since Varry's death. What were all these ordeals supposed to mean?

'I could really use you tomorrow.' I feigned cool indifference.

Yron's eyes moistened. 'I believe in your Path to Glory, Yrdunson. Not in the others who walk this road – but *your* path, *your* glory. But I can't go as far as you have. The way is supposed to be a means. For me, it can only ever be an end.'

I could respect that. I searched for words and found nothing. Yron had always been so certain. Here I learned all that certainty had stood on a bed of ice. Now it had melted away.

Her shoulders tensed, and she looked at me. For the first time since we had spoken on the trek to Whittale's End, I glimpsed the human behind the grey war paint.

'Come with me,' she said.

I blinked. Desire sliced away at me, and ancient loathing filled the cracks. 'These lands hold my heart. My people, my *fighters*–'

'There are other things worth living for.'

I fell silent, for three breaths. The span of a life's beginning and its end. The time it took kingdoms to rise and fall.

'Not for me.' I exhaled. 'Go, Yron. Live in peace.'

Before she left, Yron begged for two casks of Aqua Ghyranis. With that much akwag a human could spend three lifetimes in luxury. A small tribe could build a village, or simply buy it. They could use the waters to grow red lands into sylvan glades. They could farm fields of smoking rye and nourish sleeping giants. They could feed on things they hadn't killed. They could start again.

I gave Yron my mask to show Boskin she had my blessing. Then she embraced me and departed.

For a long time, I waded in reflection beside the altar, wondering at the life I had lived, the people I would never see again. Then I returned to the queues.

Hundreds of warriors remained lined up on one side of the temple nave. The others had departed for other matters, to their naked revels and tribal feasts and ritual fires entreating the gods for their blessings of victory. Some had gone to spend this last eventide in solitude, as I intended. First, work. But before I could find my place at the queues, Boskin trundled towards me, lop-sided and heavy, pistols rattling in the holsters on his baldric.

He shoved the beaten metal mask I had given to Yron back into my hands.

'You're serious? The king just passes off his crown as a writ for rations?'

'I'm not a king. That's not a crown. You're not a lord.' I frowned. 'Please don't say you shot her.'

'Yron? No, she's fully bulletless, your majesty. I gave her what she wanted. Plus the good stuff.' He winked. Then he tapped my father's death mask. 'You can't just give this away. I'm serious. It's important. Really important.'

I held my father's face in my hands, burnishing char away with my finger. Beneath the bullet dents and blade scars, the scorched metal and ugly grimace, the mask didn't even resemble my father any more. It was the face of the Godeater's Son. It was mine.

Then Boskin's eyes lit up. He reached beneath his breastplate, retrieving a wrapped bundle. 'Almost forgot. Cillus said this belongs to you.'

'Cillus?' I scowled, unwrapping the cloth bundle. It contained Cillus' metal gift from beneath the whitewood, a lifetime ago. Time had replaced the metal's black with the hopeless hue of Yrdun flesh. A heatless smoulder still shone in the metal's cracks, but the shape of the ingot had changed.

It resembled a face, or a death mask. But no rictus twisted its lips, nor anything to scare away the daemons and the Nighthaunt ghosts.

I tucked it into my sash for luck. 'You really are mad,' I told

Boskin. 'Cillus is eight years dead. Worms in his eyes, dancing in Shol. Dead.'

Boskin smiled, shaking his head. 'Nah. He's one of my vassals. And my friend.'

Who was I to blame Boskin for the lies which sustained him? I had seen Cillus, too, delirious in the Ashwilds, broken by the Refuser's hands. I merely nodded.

'What of Micaw?'

'I'm fine, your majesty, thanks for asking.'

I shoved him. 'The horse. Have you found her?'

He cackled, nudging back. 'I know, I know. Just jesting with his majesty. No such luck. She's gone as Grimnir, as the stunties like to say. But I'll let her keep my name. And now, my liege, you *must* don your crown. The people need a king to lead them, not common filth.'

I hesitated. Then I fastened my father's death mask to my face. I felt right. Better than I had without it.

Boskin gave a pleased nod. Watching him go, I couldn't help but wonder what fluke of fate had brought us together, or for what flaws of character we had stayed together. People like us weren't forged or tempered – we were warped. Yet here we remained, the boards of our lives still seamlessly joined.

'*Boskin!*' I shouted.

Heads turned, and not only his. My warriors knew my voice by heart, its commanding tone branded into their bones after hard hours of training and the ruthless battle at the draw. When they heard me call Boskin, the ziggurat's hollow fell silent. Greener warriors murmured to older veterans; the veterans murmured back. I had been cruel before, many times. Maybe they expected cruelty now. Maybe they thought I'd finally kill the Derder traitor, for his Golvarian blood or his madness. I had always been a frail man. Hating in others what I saw of myself.

Boskin peered across the javelin's throw of sand which separated us. 'Your majesty?'

I spoke loud enough for all to hear. 'Can I rely on you and your vassals in the battle ahead, Lord Earl Boskin?'

His eyes clarified. He crossed his breast in salute and bowed. 'We'll stand by you, we'll fall by you, we'll rise by you. No place else but by your side, King Fall.'

Laughter rippled from the crowd of fighters in the ziggurat. Some jeered, or hollered tribal honours to the so-called earl. The Mad Derder bowed deeply again, the yellow of his teeth flashing in his silly smile. I bowed back.

I returned to the queues and my inspections, speaking to my warriors, accepting their reverence, ignoring their fear. Spirits were high. That was all I could ask for. We needed courage for the fight ahead – for we had nothing else.

CHAPTER THIRTY-EIGHT

Three unterways led into Candip's heart. Boulders and hushed darkness choked the monumental passages. The half-stirred dust of ages blanketed the stone. Earthfire rills trickled from underground channels, casting a dim glow. From those old defensive canals, much magma had been harvested and sold off, to warm the bathhouses of fair ladies or boil water into steam in Ironweld engines.

For all I knew, earthfire was brightstone, too. For all I knew, all the Pale was precious. Only its people had ever been worthless to the Azyrites. We were the maggots in their plates, to be picked free and mashed.

Today, that insignificance reassured me. All my life had been the defiance of powers greater than me. I had made war on the Azyrites and their lies. Then I had seen the truth beneath the realm and made war on it, too.

Today, everything changed. Tomorrow, the world would be better.

Dismounted Derders patrolled the unterways. We slit their throats, or slipped daggers between their vertebrae and laid them down for final rest. Jujjar had assured me only Derders guarded the unterways leading into Candip. He stalked beside me now, at the head of our massive column, on the lookout for the Ashstalkers he'd left behind to monitor the passages.

'They're concealed,' he said. 'At the entrance to the main plaza. They'll lead us into Candip.'

The hushed breaths of our heathen thousands shifted the air in the tunnel's suffocating darkness. Ahead, the orphan glow of Candip's orreries and pyromancy gave us a light to move towards. I counted the beats of my restless heart, licking away sweat on my lips. I heeded the hissed prayers of my pagan horde and for once did not scorn them. I understood why they prayed, now. How I understood.

Hewer had promised we would hear a signal when his feint was complete. But the longer we stalked through the still shadows, the more the quiet ate at my calm. Hewer's feint might never come. He might even give us away. Perhaps his scrupulous negotiations had all been a show to lure us here. Perhaps our oath-charter was as meaningless as his empty affections had been.

I steeled myself. I was a blood-hungry beast, not a sun-scared rodent. In a hundred heartbeats I would lead this attack with or without Hewer's distraction. New plans could be devised on the prowl.

But then I heard the distant buzz of a Kharadron fleet. Closer it came, first like flies in my ears, then the snores of sleeping gargants. They were flying above Candip's upworks, on the surface. A brief cannonade resounded, the signal I had been promised. This was to be expected. Visiting airships discharged their cannonry before entering Candip's crevasse. The real confusion, Hewer had said, would begin once his formation bypassed Candip's port tunnels and rose again to the Parchward Winds, to return to Hammerhal Aqsha and reveal the egregious error in their contract.

Despite my nerves, I smiled. Hewer had been good to his word. Greed was useful for something after all.

Forward we stalked, low and tight, our eyes staked to the dim glow at the tunnel's end. I listened to Candip beyond, to the choral babel of a city that suspected nothing.

Boom. Boom.

The tunnels shook. Grit drizzled from the ceiling. I paused, blinking. That had not sounded like a feint.

Boom. Boom, boom. BOOM.

Epiphany ran through my blood, weightless when it hit my belly. Candip had fired upon the Kharadron. Had the cogforts done it? Or the surface defences? I didn't know – but our window had just grown larger.

Grinning beneath my mask, I peered at Jujjar, who seemed fretful. We moved faster, the sandstone trembling from our horde's migration. I only needed to find Ildrid. We would show our strength to the Azyrites, and Ildrid would not be able to stomp out all the fires we would start. She would have to bargain with us. Once I told her the truth about Lellen's intrigues, she would *demand* it.

The unterway's entrance yawned overhead. The light of Candip's crevasse beamed down. In Candip's plaza, a rib-vaulted ceiling covered a sweeping sandstone square. This covered square led through a pair of arches to a second, wider square.

Through those arches, a raised ledge surrounded the plaza. Buildings were perched on that shelf; Candip's great cut soared beyond it. Closer, I vaguely made out the shaded entrances of other unterways. Dirty fighters from my other columns teemed from their mouths into the first square of the plaza. Good – they had arrived just as we had.

Then my heart dropped. Below the arches which led into the second square, thick ranks of shouting soldiers mustered to defend the passage. They were Cossery guard, House Se Roye's lauded retinue. Their spiked helms and star-stitched lamellar were unmistakeable. Their flamboyant great swords, too, each a Draconith tooth of undulating steel.

The Cosseries' banners and their Capilarian pennants sagged from the weight of their victory streamers. Their gazes reached out across the plaza and touched us, stark with astonishment but focused and lethal.

I stared at Jujjar. 'You said only Derders.'

Boom. BOOM, BOOM, BOOM.

Jujjar donned his own mask, the parody of mine. 'And you said only a feint.'

I scowled and pushed my way to the front. Across from us, the Cosseries tightened until they filled the space between the arches. Their lines bristled with great swords like a spiny wall. Their captain shouted orders, and her orders echoed up the battle line in the gruffer voices of sergeants.

I glanced up and down the Cosseries' ranks, my breath quickening, my heart hammering at my ears. I had been so certain my gamble would succeed, but all gambles seem certain in our heads. Faced with resistance I hadn't expected, my certainty rusted to dread. The Azyrites had outwitted me.

Kaddarar's counsel struck me with the clarity of lightning. She had been right. Try as I might to fight like the Azyrites, they would always do it better.

But… we needed not fight like them. My horde's warriors seethed and tussled behind me like the wrathful waters of a stormy sea. All they needed was the word, and the tide would be unleashed. Ahead, the Cosseries called for gunners, gunners, more gunners. They shouted themselves hoarse, and the despair in their voices revealed the truth. My fighters and I possessed the only advantages that mattered. The weight of our numbers, the force of our fury. The Azyrites' forces were spread throughout Candip Plain and the Pale. Stuffed into this single choke point, we could overwhelm them.

I felt the Dark Gods' eyes, then. I relished the touch of their gaze. Their favour burned in my warriors' hearts, and mine. The Azyrites had nothing but a jealous thundersmith. We had a pantheon born from the primordial fires of annihilation.

And righteousness. We had come to take back what was ours. That had to be worth something.

I turned and raised my falx, and an eerie quiet fell over my horde. No battle cries followed. No speeches, no chants. No invocations to the gods nor oaths for the enemies we'd slay.

Only wrath.

I swung my falx down. Three volleys of javelin and arrow whistled out from my warriors' ranks, softening the Cosseries' formation. Wounded swordsmen screamed and toppled from their forward ranks, skewered through their bellies and legs.

Without paying Jujjar a second glance, I roared my command. As one, our horde stampeded into the Cosseries' lines.

CHAPTER THIRTY-NINE

You have seen lines crash in battles on fields more gruesome than mine. I won't tire you with the trite horrors of bloodshed. Yet often I've pondered how bards blind to the visions of war dare claim their sagas reveal its truths.

The angst. The slaughter. The heinous breed of glory.

Often melee comes in pulses and waves. Ranks dance off ranks, retreat, then charge forth again. Sometimes battle is a menagerie of single combats. Sometimes, wet drudgery, like two fruits smashed against each other and the juiceless pulp which remains.

I don't know what it was this time – for I was in the middle of it. Blood and spittle from strangers' screams moistened my lungs and misted my hands, a rain we all danced for. The reek of mortal entrails – and ordure as they were crushed under heel – was intoxicating. We trampled the dead and dying, all of us grapes for slaughter's wine. I unsheathed the wet metal of my dirk from a Capilarian Cossery's skull. The blade glistened crimson in the plaza's maverick light, an ugly eye impaled upon it. The eye's roots waggled in the air until I flung the bulb clear. I retched and fought on.

My lungs were on fire. My wrists and arms were sore from our grim toil. The Cosseries had to feel the same. I hewed an enemy's arm off, then ran him through when he fell. I slashed my dirk across the throat of another Cossery whose back faced me. The battle was like a thousand little wars between strangers and friends harvesting each other like grain. It was not sacred, not glorious, not as the ballads are sung. Just a little war followed by a little massacre, then another all over again.

The Cosseries fought well, as one entity, in such ways a novice commander like me never could have hoped to train his marauders to emulate. But the force of our numbers worked against them. The walls of our dead grew tall. Screaming, we toppled this corpse mountain onto the Cosseries' thinning ranks. Some were crushed, but others receded, giving ground in measured steps, arching their line back into the second square. Bobbing tongues of pyromantic flame illuminated those grounds for gunners and crossbow militia on the ledge surrounding the plaza.

I halted and scanned that second square. Stairs of carved stone climbed up the surrounding ledges, reminding me of Whittale's End. Flat-topped buildings rose above them, their roofs heavy with the enemy. Derders raised their pistols. Mercenary gunners rested their fusils on the stone, taking aim. I recognised their battalions.

I recognised the Ashstalkers, too. *My* Ashstalkers, standing beside the enemy.

A trumpet sounded twice. As one, the Cosseries peeled back. Our vanguard staggered forward as the enemy's resistance evaporated. We hesitated in wide-eyed astonishment.

Ashstalkers, on the heights. This was wrong. Everything was wrong.

I craned my head around. *'Jujjar!'* I roared.

The gun line barked with the volume of four hundred hounds. Bullets thudded into flesh, or snapped off stone. Pain pierced my side; wet warmth drenched my ribs.

Blood. But we were so densely packed I couldn't even see my wound.

My boldest barbarians surged forward, to loose what final darts they could. Javelins lanced out. More gunfire barked back and they toppled like felled trees. I collapsed, shielding myself, waiting for the storm to end. Around me, warriors died. Others pulled back to the unterways, trampling our own wounded to death.

Then I lifted my head. We littered the killing grounds, and they. From the dying, hands reached out for help that wouldn't come. Tremulous cries rose for mothers and sons who couldn't save them. A haze of smoke rolled over us, accompanied by the acrid cut of spent powder.

Then someone gripped my arm. 'Held,' Jujjar wheezed. He cradled his maimed hand in the crook of his arm. His belly was savaged, his death mask hanging at his neck. 'Held.'

The Cosseries re-formed at the bases of the stairs leading up from the square to the ledge. Above, beyond the city's ceiling, artillery rumbled on Candip Plain. Battle had been joined above, between Hammerhal's crusade and Se Roye's paid mercenaries.

The Azyrites' temporary discord couldn't save us. Only Ildrid could. I had to find her, to speak with her. I had to tell her the truth of Bodshe's brightstone. Yet Jujjar was dying before my eyes. For the first time, my whole war seemed like folly and despair. Even if we won, what would remain afterwards? Grief, and victory's shame.

I shifted both blades to one hand. I clasped Jujjar's arm, eyeing the enemy on the heights, their weapons staring us down. Azyrites, and Ashstalkers. So many questions I had, but nary a when to ask them all.

'I'll stay,' I told Jujjar. 'I'll stay, brother.'

He coughed blood. His absent eyes wandered the butcher's square. Treacherous Ashstalkers rained javelins on us. Quarrels hissed from Freeguilders' arbalests, the opening drizzle of a merciless storm. In the chasm beyond, a Stardrake's roar echoed, terrible and prophetic like all the portents of Azyr.

We had come so close. Yet here we were.

'I was going to join them,' Jujjar said. 'And they shot me. They shot us like dogs.'

I flinched. 'What?'

He croaked wetly. 'I found Se Roye's captains while scouting the unterways. Told them your plan. We betrayed you, brother. I betrayed you. I did it eight years ago, too. I let word of our raid slip.'

Jujjar's eyes did not lie, nor the bloodless white of his brow. 'Why?'

He shuddered. 'I wanted you to fail. I thought you betrayed us first. You traded Yrdoval away. For what? Outlanders, Parcher allies. I wanted… to take your place. I thought I deserved to lead the Yrdun more than you did. I thought I could fix things. For the Azyrites' favour, I offered up your life and your horde. They promised to return glory to our people. But the bastards shot me.' He chuckled grimly. I heard pebbles in his lungs. 'They couldn't even tell us apart.'

My side burnt with pain, but my gunshot wound was nothing compared to Jujjar's betrayal. He had been jealous. He had never loved what I had built. He had always despised Beltollers and outland Parchers like Kaddarar. He'd sought a different way. But I couldn't fathom what he'd hoped to accomplish. He and a handful of our old comrades could not change a history millennia in the making. The Azyrites would never settle for less than everything.

Then I winced. Hadn't I wanted everything, too? Hadn't I chased my own vain dreams in this war?

I should have killed Jujjar. Instead I clenched my teeth and gripped his arm.

'I'll stay, brother.'

Jujjar prised my fingers from his arm and pushed me away. 'Don't. You're not one of us, Held. Only now do I see. You're something more... something less. But still my friend.' He swallowed the blood pooling in his throat. 'You said you'd die for me. So let me die for you. Let me fix this.'

'This cannot be fixed,' I sobbed. 'We cannot change the past.'

'Scorch the past.' Jujjar's eyes were burning iron. He slid his mask back upon his face. 'Change the future, Held. Rally your horde. I'll fix this. I *will*.'

I understood. I flew back to the unterways, pain twinging through my ribs. I roared myself hoarse with commands for my chieftains and champions. If glory truly existed, it was only in moments like these, staring down the miscarriage of our lives, standing tall in defiance.

Jujjar clambered to his feet in the second square. He stumbled forward. A farewell quiet fell over the killing grounds. Only the moan of dying mortals resisted that silence. Only the rumbling barrages above.

A legend exists, first spawned by my defeat at Ildrid's hands, cemented that day by Jujjar's redemption. Sigmar's slaves believe the Godeater's Son cannot be killed. They believe he is invincible. Slay him, and the Dark Gods will raise him up, as Sigmar raises his Stormcasts.

This was not yet true, then. Only Jujjar sold the lie.

'You wanted me!' he shouted, in the many tongues he knew. He pointed to his mask. 'Here I am! Heldanarr Fall! The Godeater's Son! Come, you bad-breathed swine! Come die with me! Ride your god's lightning to his stinking pens! And tell him he's next!'

Jujjar's voice frayed from his screams. But the Cosseries came, the arrogant fools. They came, exactly as Jujjar demanded. First in ones and twos, fissuring their formations. Then in the dozens, unchained, like rabid dogs. Their captain could not stop them. Not when each would kill the Godeater's Son and become a hero, or fall by his blade and be made Stormcast Eternal. They were no better than my own horde's heathens. Crowing for glory – for immortality. Oblivious to its price.

I imposed my will on my army. In the second plaza, so many Cosseries fell upon Jujjar I could not see them tear him apart. His roar melted away into a howl. Pieces of him flew in the air, like discarded offal in Bharat's abattoirs. My treacherous Ashstalkers must have known it was Jujjar, but they were too few to stop the others. The trap was set – this time, ours. Jujjar had broken faith, and I cursed him for it. But I would not waste this moment of his sacrifice.

I gave my order. As one, my horde washed across the plaza like a tide. The Cosseries – assuming they had slain me and routed my horde – had abandoned their defensive formations. We swept through them as a fire blazes through dry forest, then attacked the gunners on the ledges. In the butchery which followed, we made sons fatherless, and mothers daughterless. We ended bloodlines which might have traced their roots to Sigmar's tempest. Let the halls of the Azyrites' tyrant-cities wail with mourning for the price we extracted that day. Let the bells of his haughty churches toll for their countless dead. We slew them all.

We seized the heights overlooking the second square. At last, I thought the battle was over. I could not rein in my horde's warriors, so I let them pass into Candip, to take their pound of flesh and fill their flasks with the enemy's blood. The Azyrites' resistance had been broken. Only Ildrid remained. I would find her and reveal the truth of Se Roye's deceitful intrigues – the truth of Bodshe's brightstone. Then I would negotiate peace from a position of strength.

This war would end. The Pale would be ours.

But our fortune had exhausted itself. The Stormcasts were already here – and not to bargain.

CHAPTER FORTY

First, the stink of ozone. Then, a shadow over us all. The skull-scrubbing scream of an Azyrite monster filled my head.

The Stardrake. I had forgotten about the Stardrake.

The abomination crashed into the plaza. A shockwave of white flame scalded my skin and burnt ghosts into my eyes. The Stardrake blared, my toes curling from its noise. Heat blurred the air around the furnace in its throat. The beast shovelled its twisted crown through the square, dragging panicking fighters across the plaza. Its horns and claws gutted the living and the dead, ripping warriors' limbs free like snapped lengths of dry-rotted rope.

My horde continued pouring from the unterways into the plaza, then up the stairs leading into Candip. Nothing could staunch their flow. I don't know if wild courage spurred them, or the madness of the mob, or panic.

The drake crushed those it could. Lightning blasted from the lance of the templar on its back, carving through the square. The monster turned the blazing stars of its gaze on me, and my temperature rose. The beast's breathing grumbled through me like earthquakes.

But so did something else.

The ground shook, until a gargant barged from one of the unterways, tearing stone free, tossing everything in its path.

Stinking Gomurtha swelled forward and gripped the drake's horns, then tossed the beast down. She was the mountain which had slept by windmills in fields of smoking grain. A fell rune smouldered in her belly; a pair of empty casks clanged at her girdle. For the gargant, they must have been nothing more than cups.

I laughed like a fool. Nothing had been able to stir Gomurtha. Only the promise of a filled belly, and the invocations of Yron's people. With my parting gift of akwag, Yron had awakened the Hullet's sleeping gargant, purchasing its aid. What else had she promised? Meat, from our allies and enemy dead. So be it. I hadn't wanted this, but I hadn't wanted many of the things which were mine. I had a battle to win. Thank the gods Gomurtha was here to help me.

The drake's claws scythed at the gargant's flesh. Gomurtha's blood bubbled from the wounds, sheeting to the plaza in a mudslide. She planted her continental grip on the drake's wing, then snapped it with the sound of a falling tree.

The drake screeched, arching back. Gomurtha stomped its leg into the stone. Somewhere in that desperate clinch, lightning erupted – the Stormcast Templar had been crushed beneath his mount. The drake rolled over, dragging Gomurtha with it. They avalanched over the second square, crushing buildings as they slid down into Candip's canyon and disappeared.

I had no time to relish this minor triumph. Stormsworn was here. Her retinue carved through the warriors around me, silent as they ever were. More Stormcasts emerged on the heights, cutting my warriors apart, caging us back into the plaza. I glimpsed fewer Stormcast Eternals than the last time I was in Candip. The others must be chasing my warriors who had spilt into the city. Or perhaps they were above, on Candip Plain, seeking an end to the infighting Hewer's flight had accidentally unleashed.

Ildrid came at me like a landslide. I stumbled as her arm lanced out for my neck. If her armour encumbered her, I couldn't tell. Her two praetor bodyguards lumbered closer, hemming me in. Their halberds were lowered, their capes hanging like flags from castle walls.

Then a pair of pistols barked. Sparks spat off the praetors' pauldrons. The Stormcasts swivelled on their assailant, my saviour.

Boskin stood there wide-eyed, slack-jawed, chewing his lop-sided moustache. He dropped his pistols and raced off with high knees, tittering in joyous madness.

'Long live the *king*!'

Where Boskin had stood, more of my warriors gathered. The mirrored shields of the Rottii formed into a wall alongside marauders from the Arad. Sertorix and his cage-helmed, iron-lunged Dospekhs punctuated the Rottii's line, each an engine of war. From behind them, Welwary's periwinkle-skinned rangers peppered the Stormcast titans with arrows, baiting them forward.

'For the Godeater's Son!' Laklien howled, slamming her visor down, her helmet crest shaking. 'Death to gods! Glory! *Death!*'

'Deal with them,' Ildrid said. Her praetors and other Stormcasts thundered towards my warriors.

Against all expectations, Laklien ordered a withdrawal. The Rottii and others melted back, rank by rank, luring the Storm-casts into the first square. They were adapting as I had taught them to, retreating so our forces could more easily envelop the enemy from the plaza's adjoining unterways.

I had no more time to admire them. Ildrid cracked forward, hammer raised, the void in her eyes.

I raised my hands. '*Stop!*' I shouted. 'I would have words!'

She swatted her massive hammer down as one might kill flies. I dived. Stone crumbled behind me.

'No,' she said. 'You would not.'

Her backswing sent me flying. I thumped down and slid breathlessly over hot grit and bloodied stone. Coughing, I rose. 'Refuser–!'

She swung again; again I dived. Where I'd stood, a crater yawned. She wouldn't even answer me.

I roared. 'That's it? No more prattle of redemption?'

'What are words before action?' Ildrid lurched closer. The crushed meat of an Ushara warborn dangled from her weapon's head, wet and stringy. 'Accept the redemption of my hammer.'

This time, I dared parry. Pure force rattled through my bones. My falx wheeled from my grip. I staggered back, cradling my fractured arm. Ildrid loomed ever closer.

I should have told her of Se Roye's machinations, of the brightstone she surely hoarded. But I couldn't rein in my spite, nor master my anger. All I wanted was to hurt the person who'd hurt me. All I wanted was to make her understand.

I groaned, shaking the agony from my arm, pounding my chest. 'A liar! That's all you ever were!'

'I have only ever told you the truth,' Ildrid said.

I held her midnight gaze. 'What mother gives up her children to serve her god?'

Ildrid hesitated. The barest flicker of emotion enchanted her near-expressionless face. Then she resumed her march, thundering closer.

'A mother who knew love would not protect you.'

I cackled. 'You're going to kill me.'

'No. I am going to save your soul.' She raised her hammer. 'Then I will repair this mess. But for you, boy, death will be better than the torment which awaits you. Even if you have earned both.'

All my best-laid designs were ash in the wind. I had been here, eight years ago. But this time, Kaddarar would not save me.

The Seeker's words from Bharat reverberated in my skull.

Do what they do not expect. Do what you do not expect.

I lashed my dirk at the galling mass of Ildrid's armour. The blade sank into a gully of plate at her waist. Howling, I shoved it hilt-deep.

Instead of blood, lightning blasted my fingers. I stumbled back, hand buzzing, nursing the blackened stumps of my knuckles. My fingers were gone.

Ildrid gazed down, eyes trenchant. She reeked of the void. Then she jerked my blade free, electricity sputtering from her wound. She wrapped her other hand tenderly around my back and jerked me forward, spitting me on the dirk Jujjar had gifted me so long ago.

I gasped. Life and fire bled from me. Deeper within, a hole gaped where my soul had been. The slavering maws of laughing things snapped at the nothing which had replaced it.

'Mother,' I wheezed.

'I am not your mother,' Ildrid spat. 'I refuse you.'

CHAPTER FORTY-ONE

I was the bloodied sword and the thrust dagger. I was the broken shield and the maul and mace. I was my people's death, and Bodshe's damnation.

I was mortal, and nothing else. Blades kissed me, and my flesh parted like any other's. I had run the gauntlet of life and fallen. In the end, in the beginning, I was the same as anyone. I was the same as you.

With Jujjar's gifted blade erupting from my back, my spine had shifted and broken. I collapsed atop the futile heap of my legs. Ildrid spared a final look, decadent with pity. I thought I'd see regret in her eyes – I even dared hope.

But I saw only grim relief and blank-eyed disappointment. She turned her back on me, and I finally understood who she was. Immortal, certainly – yet as human and imperfect as any of us. A woman who could not atone for her failures, worshipping a God-King who would not justify his. Between them both, redemption: their miserable consolation to the worlds they had left behind.

Everything faded. The ghastly spectre of war, and agony's secular blaze. Greater oblivion consumed the numbness in my legs. A dead man's ruminations haunted the hollow I became. That was the delicious irony of my vain quest for control. In the end, all lives lead places we do not choose.

Kaddarar was right. So was the Refuser. All I had ever wanted was freedom. But I could not choose my fate, nor change my sister's. For all the power I'd held and the glories I'd earned, every triumph had brought me nothing closer to what I longed for.

Control. The will and power to master myself and the life inflicted upon me.

I had never controlled a thing. I had always been a slave in the Mortal Realms, as were we all. The Azyrites had not ruined me. Nor the Smoulderhooves, nor Se Roye's greed, nor Ildrid's obsession. Life had done it. *I* had done it.

I had refused the truth in Asharashra. Now that truth pounded beneath my soul, peeling up the corners of me.

Annihilation. I controlled nothing, nothing at all.

Khorne's shadow fell over me, in darkening plains of blood. I glimpsed a distant throne which dwarfed castles. Sitting atop it, vague like a far-off mountain, the red god leered. *All must slaughter,* its sickness within me hissed. *All must be slaughtered.* I was dead, damned to the realm of Chaos. Skulls fell in cataracts from the crimson skies, piling into mountains around me. Distantly, a kingdom-come crown of brass and iron sat on the Blood God's endless brow, shining with grievous glory. Khorne's legs were the pillars of creation. Its oceanic eyes were blood and swirling flame.

Oh, for the hell in those eyes, glaring through me. I was the ant in the machine. I'd thought I'd known dread. But one has not felt dread until the end of worlds stares through them and beckons.

Khorne watched me – and *beckoned*. My end had not yet come.

Not in death, not in damnation. Too much remained unfinished. I had parts to play yet.

Beyond the Blood God's lascivious gaze – beyond the fields of fire and the butcher's skies – I saw them again. Tall towers, twinkling with dark light, winking through time. In their infinity, I heard my name. The towers summoned me forth.

The call, the call. Godeater's call. You were always there, speaking to me, but I hadn't listened. Kaddarar had told me – *and I had not listened!* You were never Khorne at all, were you? You were far, far worse.

Chaos. The word drew chuckles from my desiccated lungs and blood-basted throat. Words were minor magic, conveying so much meaning in the spells of their sounds. But no word could ever encompass the endless truth of Chaos.

The same was true of you, Godeater. You had always wanted me. The beastkin, Sigmar, his slaves – they were nothing but links in the long chain of your terrible summons. That is all suffering is: a long, long chain. Not incanted from nothing, not conjured like a spell. Suffering is physical law, a transitive property, migrating like heat through metal. The hurt done to me, I inflict upon another. *They puts it down; I picks it back up.*

At the root of this endless evil, you brooded. An eternity ago you had started this chain and marked me. One sin had avalanched into the next, accumulating through ages, enduring the extinction of worlds – all to bring me forth.

From the moment Varry fell, I had been doomed. From the day the Smoulderhooves came, from the day I was born. From the moment my father and mother met in Cardand's crowded night market. From the years of Bodshe's despoilment, back to the age of its mythic rise. From Bharat's tribulations and the dawn of Chaos and the forging of the universe. From my many humiliations and unending, meaningless hurt.

For all this time, your greedy eyes watched me. You waited as I was torn from my mother's womb. Waited until my suckling had ended and my hunger began. You waited for Ildrid to leave, that I could rise. You waited as the Dark Gods' eyes gathered over me like storm clouds.

What had I ever controlled? What could I have ever changed? For all eternity, all of this had been in motion – and it had all led here. All the suffering and sacrifice. All the bodies and blood, the death and dearth. A soul was old in me before my body was young. My fall had been preordained.

Faced with my utter helplessness, I did the only thing I could. I gave it all away.

My pain, and my past. My story and my name. I gave away everything, to the powers which had damned me. I gave them my faith freely, for I controlled nothing else. I *believed* in the gods. What other choice did I have? This had not been my life. Nothing had ever been truly mine.

So I let it all go. And for the first time – I was *free*.

Power possessed me. The Blood God's gut-churning laughter became ear-blistering roars. Khorne shoved baleful blessings into my hands, demanding my affections. Boundless force raged through me in wild torrents.

This. This was control. Faith, in the cackling god pawing at the scraps of me. Khorne cared nothing for me – Khorne only craved my soul. Against Khorne's hunger, faith was my only currency. Faith protected me, because only I could dispense it. And what was freely given, even from an ant like me, could be freely taken away.

I would have laughed, had I lips to smile, lungs to breathe. The Path to Glory was faith. The path to freedom was slavery. What hellish paradox filled the realms. But the truth was hell.

From the realm of Chaos beyond place and time, my consciousness flooded back into the enchanted husk of my body. To return and find my soul gone was like clambering from a raging river and finding nothing beneath my feet. I didn't know when it had disappeared, or how. All at once, shattered by some heinous atrocity? Or bled away in the little moments and sins until only this black hole remained?

It didn't matter. Whatever else life had inflicted upon Heldanarr Fall, I – the Godeater's Son – had annihilated him. Everything else was smoke on the wind. I only knew what I knew. What I had seen with my eyes, and what I had heard with my ears.

So what came next, I could not have expected.

CHAPTER FORTY-TWO

My mind ripped its way back to my body in Candip. Everything was red. The city, the corpses blanketing the plaza. Even the Azyrite orreries shone like blistering scarlet suns.

Stormsworn strode away, calling for her Sequitor-Prime to come capture my soul.

I found my feet. From the puncture in my belly, blood drooled. The wound gnashed itself open. Enamel spurs protruded from the ragged gash, then hardened into yellowed fangs, wolfing down the old flesh.

A maw, in my midriff. My blessing and my curse.

I looked upon myself and shuddered. New muscle bulged through my riven flesh. Over this indecent frame, skin tore into webs, then reknitted. What a horror to behold, but I felt no pain. I had given that away with everything else. New flesh, wan and fell, sealed around my bones. I craved violence and the wet iron warmth, blood. Yet to this craving, I did not yield. My frigid will mastered my blazing war-lust. I refused to surrender completely.

I believed, where once I hadn't – but if my faith was my final currency, then I was a miserly steward with it.

Tominer might have called me hard-headed. I called it something to prove.

Overlaying the slaughter around me, ghosts crossed my eyes. The twinned image of numberless swine plunging from overturned mountains, sickening and corrupt. I blinked away these phantoms, focusing the bleeding lines of my vision until they became Ildrid's broad back.

'Refuser,' I growled.

Stormsworn froze. She turned, her armour creaking. 'No. No… *No.*'

Stormcast Eternals solidified around the Refuser into a burnished metal battle line. They shouted now, in great baritone voices, just as the Cosseries had. Orders, commands. Calls for vigilance and courage. For the first time, I made them wary.

Ildrid anchored this impossible wall of shields and hammers and spears. She raised her chin. 'So I was wrong. Look at you. Just like them – a Slave to Darkness.'

Around us, the corpses in the plaza sank into crumbling stone. Brutal passages formed in the ancient square, maws like the mouth in my belly. They were Bharat's unterways, the same as I had seen with Kaddarar so long ago. Ribbed like oesophagi, flaring with nether heat.

Tominer emerged with the first of Bharat's warriors. She wore her shale armour, thudding a maul-axe of black iron embedded with fangs into her palm. Her warriors reeked of soot and smelted brass, and the spines in their helms rattled. The heat in their blood could have fractured crucibles.

Tominer canted her head at me, staring through the prism. I caught a glimpse of her black teeth as she spoke. 'It seems you were indeed our awaited one, Godeater's Son.'

For me, weeks had passed since Bharat. For Tominer, it might have been minutes. I gestured to the Stormcasts, to Candip's canyon beyond.

'Spread your good word, Maal.'

Tominer craned her head at the Stormcast Eternals. 'The final war. As was foreseen.'

Two armies rallied behind me. The horde I had built, possessed with new courage, and the warriors and Chosen of Bharat. Ashar-ashra's malevolent Champions stalked forward, sacred animus glowing in the seams of their cursed armour. Hellish knights trundled from Bharat's portals, their juggernaut mounts like infernal mechanical bulls. The beasts chugged and clanged, each a walking furnace.

Then the spilt blood in the square coalesced around my boots, trickling up my legs, each droplet a seething maggot. The worms returned my falx to my hands, then accumulated on its edge, scabbing into rough metal. Soon the scythe-like blade glittered red, long enough to match my new dimensions, or my mother's, or any of the Stormcasts.

Our cramped lines stared each other down. The Chosen of Chaos, and the Chosen of Sigmar. Patient pressure burdened that fragile quiet. I would give the order to attack. First I wanted them to see.

The voice of an Azyrite herald broke the silence.

'A horde!' she screamed. 'Another horde on Candip Plain, from beneath the ground, attacking the Dawnbringers!'

Ildrid Stormsworn bared her teeth and roared: *'First to be forged!'*

'Never to fall!' her Stormcast Eternals thundered back.

I only chuckled. 'Bold claim,' I told my warriors. 'Let's put it to the test.'

CHAPTER FORTY-THREE

War is Chaos. One kills another, then another kills them. Another, and another. A relay without end.

The plaza slaughter became ungovernable. The conflagration of battle engulfed Candip's crevasse. Church bells pealed across the city's canyon, to instil in its defenders hope. My heathens ransacked one church after the other, cutting down the bells. Their last tolling was the sound of them breaking on stone.

Through this storm, I battled Ildrid. She had held back before, I realised. Now she didn't. Each swing of my cursed falx left scars in her sun-bright warplate. Her hammer strikes rang through me, each blow more painful than the last. She was fast, and strong. So was I. We were evenly matched. But she had lost control. I had not. Righteous anger filled her, distracting her. I was nothing more than a vessel for violence.

Stormsworn shoved me off, shaking the stone as she staggered back and refreshed her hammer grip. I launched into another attack. My blade chomped into her side. Lightning spurted from the wound like an oil fire. So she did bleed.

Groaning, she rammed her hammer's head into my chest, then pushed forward in a trampling rage. This time, I regrouped.

We came at each other, and again. Elsewhere, barbarians swamped the Stormcasts. The immortals were powerful, but their plight was beyond hope. Their allies scattered across Candip were beleaguered at every turn, unable to assist them. The charnel stink of death com-mingled with the acrid reek of burnt timber, scorched hair and oxygen flames.

'You are worthless,' Ildrid spat. 'All of you. And to think I bothered trying to save you.'

She had so much time for words, I almost couldn't believe this was the same woman I'd fought before. I hacked down. My blade chewed through her gauntlet. More blood and electricity spilt out. She slammed the butt of her hammer into my knee.

Something cracked. I couldn't walk straight but kept my feet. I chuckled, relishing the pain.

'We were *all* worthless,' she continued. 'You. Your brothers and sisters. Me. We are powerless without Sigmar, Heldanarr. When I went to fight those beasts, I knew I would die. But not for you, nor any of your family. It was for *him*. For the God-King. It had to be. That was my only choice. I would make it again.'

I said nothing. I believed her.

She swung for my head, then swept below my feet. I went down hard, cracking stone. She raised her hammer. Its head snapped and spat with power. 'This is for him, too!'

I grunted and braced my blade. Her hammer crashed into it. My falx seared at the contact, then snapped. The hammer crushed my midriff. Ildrid's force ached through my core.

Then the jaws in my belly rattled open and champed down. Pain twinged up those curse-jaws, as if I'd bitten the hammer's metal with my own teeth. Azure flame spat from the contact. Black bile trickled from my belly.

Then rivulets of blood snaked up my falx's hilt, hardening on the blade, remaking it whole. Howling, I rolled and twisted my weapon up. The scythe-edged blade plunged through Ildrid's breast.

She gasped, staggering. Her hammer clanged down.

My curse-maw closed, and I regained my feet. Arrows snapped and skittered along the damp stone, or thudded into the carpet of the dead. I slid my blade from my mother's breast. More blood and lightning spattered my mask. The contact stung, then seared.

Stormsworn crumbled to her knees. I shielded my gaze. Wounded though she was, I could not look upon her for long.

She cast her vacant eyes upon the fallen city. Candip was in flames. Our city, the city they had stolen. The battle raging in its canyon carcass was only a beast's death throes. Blood seeped from the ceiling of the covered chasm, from the defensive plains above. The blood rains had returned, same as that day beneath the Orb Infernia when Varry was taken from me.

I followed the sweep of Ildrid's eyes. Distantly, gluttonous Gomurtha lounged beside a cliffside chapel. The gargant ignored the arrows bristling from her callused flesh. She reached into the chapel's nave, its threshold crumbling around her titanic arms. She pulled weeping refugees from their sanctuary, then crushed them between her teeth like wild grapes.

Elsewhere, in the coiled snakes of Candip's streets, pockets of Azyrite resistance fought their gallant last stands, shouting their final cries. For each fallen Stormcast Eternal, a crack of thunder and a flash of lightning erupted in salute.

The city was being devoured alive. My marauders pillaged domiciles stolen from their ancestors, and Bharat's warriors butchered all who fled. I had come to liberate Candip. Instead I had inflicted my own hellish past upon it.

Ildrid took all this in, then calmed. Her shoulders relaxed. She panted, merely a dying woman, her breast heaving for the pierced bellows of her lungs.

'Oh, little Held,' she said, gurgling blood. 'I would have done it all again. I did the right thing. By Sigmar, I did the right thing.'

I sauntered forward, my wounds knitting themselves closed. A sneer curled my lips, but it was a forceless thing. I had no more spite; I had given that away, too. Yet as whole as my victory had become, I wished to break my mother's spirit as I had broken her body. I knew what to say to do it. I would tell her of Se Roye's manipulations and lies. I would reveal the truth of Bodshe's brightstone and show the Refuser in utter clarity how her people's greed had brought me upon them, just as Godeater had intended.

With this parting gesture, I could poison her faith. I would revel in the fullness of her defeat.

But before I could speak, Ildrid's eyes lanced through me, holding me at arm's length.

'I named you for the glory of Sigmar,' she said. 'Look at you. Look at what you became. Look at what you've done. Imagine what you could have been, had you been with us.'

Khorne's curse filled my veins and fuelled my rage. But I was still human beneath the hell. I sensed the regret tainting my mother's tone. The guilt. All this time, she had sought to convince herself she'd done the right thing, leaving us. She did it now, too, in the throes of death, on the precipice of wherever that would bring her.

I hated Stormsworn. But I loved her, too. The only way a man could, deprived of his mother for so long. The leaden nail of that love ached through me. I could not blame her for what life had made her. She had become what she must, as I had.

I raised my blade and said what she wanted to hear. Let Ildrid think this was unavoidable. Let her think she had made the right choices.

Because I forgave her.

'Blood for the Blood God,' I said. 'Skulls, for the Skull Throne.'

She closed her eyes. I took her head. She exploded into the storm she'd sworn herself to, then cascaded into the stone skies. Through the pyromancy and blood rains, into the void and aether beyond.

CHAPTER FORTY-FOUR

Weeks were required to consolidate our triumph in the Burning Valley. In that time, I came to learn exactly what had occurred during the Fall of Candip.

Se Roye had ordered her city's upworks and cogforts not to fire upon the Kharadron. In spite of her desperation in those days, Jujjar's betrayal of my plans had afforded the Lady Lellen a cool head. She knew my intentions down to the last detail.

The same could not be said of Candip's artillerists. The duardin ironclads' flyby had spooked the city's defenders. After three duardin airships crashed into Candip Plain, the Hammerhalian host thought they had been betrayed. Dawnbringer marshals gave the order to smash Candip's cogforts to smoking ruins, and a siege assault began. By the time Ildrid's Stormcasts intervened to stop the fighting, the damage had been done. Order had broken down, and confusion reigned. Many had died.

Then, Bharat's legions had arrived.

I thought this the irony of fate. But it was preordained, wasn't it?

I remembered my flight from Bharat, plunging from the upturned mountain and the brass gates to Khorne's hell. Kaddarar and I had awoken the city's Chosen before we escaped, and they had followed us. Khorne even bestowed on me a vision of them: the twinned image of possessed swine, tumbling into abyssal skies.

My war did not end with Candip's sack. Azyrite fiefs remained in Cardand – too many to count. Not outland manors, but mighty keeps and bailey-towns which buttoned down the Burning Valley like a noble's frilled coat.

Then there were the Stormcasts. We had not killed them all in Candip. Those on the plain rallied the Dawnbringers and Candip's scattered defenders. Upon their fortress-metalith, they fled. Merchant airships and endless columns of tethered fanatics towed them away, into the wastes. Se Roye escaped, along with many of my treacherous Ashstalkers.

I assumed Hewer survived, too. Picking through the burnt-out frames of the duardin ironclads, we never recovered his corpse. How he might explain what had happened to his people, I did not care. But for the time being, I stayed true to my word. Let his people think they were safe, in their earthfire lodges and subterranean kingdoms. The truth would come for them, in time. Annihilation always comes for us all.

The forces of Order were not my greatest concern after Candip. The real threat came from others like us. Parcher warbands, pouring into Bodshe by air and sea. Or the scattered fragments of my horde and Malokal's mutant usurpers.

I showed them all their place, in time. This little war dragged on for a little age. To wage it, I remained in Candip's blood-drenched halls directing my legions, administering my domains. I fed my subjects and soldiers the cooked meat of our enemy dead. For all meat is meat, just as all blessings are blessings.

The day came when my domination was complete. Ranks

of Bharat's Chosen and Cardand's tribal champions lined the nave of Candip's despoiled cathedral. Mortals from near and far pledged their blades to me, or begged my protection. I met the Doombringer of the Ushara warborn, the *Raz-Mechati* of the Sleeps-First clans. The Smoulderhooves' heavy-horned alphas and crook-backed shamans lowered their heads, or exposed their throats. The phantom of who I had been wondered what might be proven if I slaughtered them and all who had ever defied me. But the past was too far to hurt me now, and the gods had taken away my spite.

The truth: annihilation. We would all die. Enemies and friends, lovers and children, now or in ten thousand years. Like the Azyrites, or Heldanarr Fall. From annihilation, none of us were exempt.

I would never again see the people I wished to most. Varry was gone, wherever death had taken her. Jujjar had sold his honour, then his life. Often I saw Yron in my dreams, laughing with kin in distant deserts, an infant mewling at her breast. I dreamt she died of old age, in her sleep. Unremembered – but unhaunted. And when the Ushara warborn brought tidings they had hunted down the Hullet and murdered them to the last, I pretended that, too, was only a dream.

And Kaddarar. She had taught me what she came to teach me. But that did not heal her absence.

But what of the Reclaimed smallfolk, who had believed in Sigmar? The little people who had suffered as I suffered, thirsted as I thirsted, hungered as I hungered? I had started all this for them, in part, just as I had finished it for myself. We had been the same.

I answer this question with my own. Where were they when I needed them? Where were they when I saw our enemy and learned the truth? Why hadn't they fought beside me as others had? Some were the family and kin of our fighters, and when those tribes bowed their heads and bent their knees, I gave them a measure of peace.

But those who had tried to stand on the sidelines and survive? Those who had done nothing at all? They should have picked a side. We all must choose, and they had made no choice. So that alone I gave them. Not mercy, nor protection. Only the power of choice, the only freedom a mortal could ever have.

'Bring those who continue to resist us,' I ordered my champions. Kalkien, Sertorix, Welwary. Many, many more. 'They shall have the choice to join us or die.'

'And the others?' Sertorix asked.

My burning gaze gave him his answer. There would be no others. Only skulls, and flames, and the chains of ceaseless suffering they forged.

I searched Candip's depths for a long time. I walked its ancient delvings alone, running my scarred hands over rough stone carved by Holmon duardin in the days of the great houses. I had not known how deep Candip's ways went until I found Se Roye's vaults. But I knew what they contained before I opened them. The heat blazed in me, thawing my gelid heart.

Magnure. Heaps of it, smouldering and crackling in nullstone crucibles, burning with never-ending flame. Brightstone, the source of Se Roye's wealth, the object of Hammerhal's desire.

I would learn to employ this treasure, in time. For now, the woman who had hoarded it occupied my mind most of all.

Hammerhal's crusade had slipped from my fingers at the Fall of Candip. The Stormcasts and crusaders had spirited Se Roye and her household troops away. This was a great wrong. After I rechristened Candip in the ancient tongue of my people, as Carnd-Ep, I hunted down the Azyrites who had fled into the burning wastes.

We found the fortress-metalith wandering the flaming barrens, its tectonic motion powered only by the blistered feet of trudging zealots and guttering Ironweld engines which dragged the great chains that were their sigil. My forces encircled them. The eight-day siege that followed is worthy of its own legend, but I took no part in it. I had no interest in offering my neck to the Refuser's Stormcast remnants or Hammerhal's Freeguild survivors. Let my horde's fervour and sheer numbers drown them. Let the Azyrites and Dawnbringers be crushed beneath the weight of the foe they had forged.

From a distant ridgeline, I observed the siege. Far-off lightning cracked and lanced into the Cursed Skies, piercing that roiling veil, or being devoured by it. The fortress-metalith's desperate defenders held out against the inevitable fall of their floating fastness.

I did not miss the sand barque and skiffs which sailed from bays in the metalith's craggy mass. The squadron impacted the sand, then raced for the hard hills on the horizon. The Mad Earl led a raid of juggernaut cataphracts and lighter javelin cavalry to intercept them. By the time I arrived the fugitives had crashed into the cover of a ridgeline, their vessels as broken as the hill I once called home. In the stagnant air, beneath the complacent light of Sigmar's stars, I felt self-effacing peace. All the sin in the realms could not haunt me. I had given away my conscience, too.

I trudged through the sand flats, between pools of bubbling magma, to my lingering raid force. Cursed cavalry circled. Under the heat of the juggernauts' glowing metal hooves, sand steamed into glass.

'What are you waiting for?' I said. 'Sigmar? He won't come.' He never does.

My raiders shuddered at the God-King's mention. Boskin, a mad glint in his pupilless eyes, merely pointed.

Ahead, two skiffs lay overturned beside veins of exposed

earthfire. Flames licked up their splintered hulls, curling their sails to ash. A tor had broken the keel of the greatest vessel, the sand barque. Beside it, an unholy steed snorted and pawed at the ash-covered sand, gnawing on the gristle of a dead mortal.

Micaw.

We approached. Boskin's pistols were drawn, his pupilless eyes fluttering. Bharat's curse-warriors kept their heads on a swivel. They were eager for violence.

I stroked Micaw's neck, kissed her brow. 'Good girl,' I whispered. 'Good slave. Like me.'

She whinnied and returned to her grisly feast, anchoring the carcass with hooves that had begun to twist into claws. The movement of lavamanders passing under our feet shivered through the earth. With the Azyrites gone, many had returned to Bodshe. Things were as they had been.

Boskin clambered up the barque's side, clearing the deck. I followed. Sand trickled onto the battered wooden planks. Stone had smashed the aft cabin, but that was not what had killed its crew. Dead mercenaries – Se Roye's soldiers – littered the glistening, wet planks. Blood puddled beneath the corpses, soon trickling towards the gravity of my presence. Some fell force had eviscerated them all. Of the one who had killed them, there was no sign, but I recognised a scent of pumice and foreign flowers.

On the deck, Lellen Se Roye lay in a foetal curl. Tears streaked from her weary eyes, gleaming on her bruised ebony cheeks. Her suit was sullied and tattered from her desperate flight. Her breathing shook as she reeled from whatever had destroyed her soldiers.

I towered before her, smoke licking up from the planks beneath my tread. The echoes of the fortress-metalith's distant siege carried from the wastes.

When her eyes lifted to mine, her whimpers became wails. Then she vomited on herself.

'Please,' she said, wiping her lips on her ascot. 'I've a great wealth. Aqua Ghyranis, oceans of it, like you wouldn't believe. And brightstone. Oh, brightstone! Hidden beneath Candip, in vaults guarded by ancient duardin runes. I'll tell you where. Only let me *live.*'

I stared. Lellen was a child, like her sister had been when the warborn had chased her.

Recognition stirred in her sick eyes. 'Oh, no. Heldanarr Fall, no, no, no. Great Drake have mercy. Not this. Not like this.'

'I killed your sister in Lurth,' I grunted. 'Do you want to know why?'

'Please, no. I have Parch holdings. Spare me and my wealth's yours. I'll send word, to have it brought here. Riches, riches beyond a greedy duardin's dreams. And together... I'll swear myself to you. I'll *fight* for you. We'll turn on Hammerhal. The bastards, Fall, don't you see? It was always us against them. They wanted to *control* us. Our enemies... we're the same. We fought them, back in Candip. Together! I didn't see then. But I see now! We'll take what we desire, Fall. We'll have everything we want!'

Like the motion of worlds in Candip's cast-down orreries, the high gravity in my gaze crushed Lellen's words into silence. I knew what I should say to her. That I had never had anything I wanted, and that now I never would.

But she must have seen it. She ran when she had the chance. None of us followed.

'Leave her for the beasts when they come,' I said. 'Or the warborn.'

Then, Kaddarar came.

I felt her before I heard her, heard her before I saw her. The Seeker charged from the shadows of the splintered aft cabin. She pounded along the deck, shaking the barque. Planks splintered beneath her ironshod boots, and her bladed mauls threshed through the air.

'GODEATER'S SON!'

I threw Boskin from the ship, over the gunwales. He tumbled into a dune.

Then I dived, just in time. Wood snapped beneath Kaddarar's first strike. She recovered, regarding me, a universe of hate blazing in her eyes.

Her chest heaved with each hurricane breath. 'Everything dies,' she said. 'You just have to kill it.'

And here it had come. Her final trial.

Kaddarar swung again, and again. I dodged, until she whipped her flails forward. The mauls cracked against each other, and the shockwave sent me spinning.

She drank me up with her eyes, mirthless, then came again, and again. But I knew how Kaddarar fought, and I filled the spaces between her blows. Three chances I had to kill her. Each I left unexploited.

Then I reversed my blade-grip and tumbled against her. I rammed her to the deck. We wrestled, consecrating ourselves in her victims' blood, our weapons gouging tracks into the fire-hardened planks.

I pinned her black hands down, her disgusting fingers skittering along the wood. I drove my knee into her belly and pushed until she wheezed. The maw in my midriff slavered, hungering for her blessed meat.

Kaddarar grimaced with pleasure, spittle roping down her chin. 'Skull, or skull-taker,' she growled. 'Which are you?'

She lunged, champing at my face, so I butted my head into hers. In that dazed moment, blood sluicing down her nose, our eyes met.

Then I did what she had taught me to do. The thing we did not expect.

I kissed her. Through the living metal of my mask, I tasted her lips.

She spat me out. She could have chomped off my tongue, or ripped my lips from my skull, but she hadn't. Kaddarar, wherever her soul had gone, was still human. The wrath and fire guttered from her eyes. Red quartz glittered in their coals. She threw me back, scrambling away, her jet hair uncoiling behind her.

Then she calmed, spitting again, rubbing her lips raw. She watched me. We were silent for a long time, the barque smouldering around us.

'You,' she said, 'are the strangest man I never killed.'

I laughed. I, the Godeater's Fall – father to bloodshed, son to slaughter, warlord of a thousand tribes. Here had come the moment of the Seeker's final tribulation, and I had bested her with a kiss.

We departed and returned to the distant siege, which had not abated. We watched from high bluffs.

'How did you know it was me?' Kaddarar asked.

I patted my cursed steed's neck. 'Micaw. You both disappeared at Teller's Ravine. Call it faith, or a fortunate guess.'

She was silent for a moment. 'You should have killed me,' she said. 'Now I'm stuck with you.'

'We're all stuck,' I said.

Beneath the distant fortress-metalith, bound djinn summoned serpentine lengths of rope from covered baskets. The gleaming Rottii climbed the ropes, their shields and spears strapped to their backs, then scaled the metalith's crags. The Azyrites would never see them coming.

'I can't understand,' Kaddarar said. 'You pledged yourself to Godeater, yet I don't see the eight-way mark. And you didn't kill me, either. You didn't take my skull.'

'You were right in many things, Seeker. But Godeater is not who you thought. He is not Khorne.'

She stared at me, a million questions in her eyes. Kaddarar was a woman of faith, as my mother had been. 'So who is he?'

'You'll see,' I said. 'Then you'll know.'

Some part of her accepted this. Her garrulity died. Wind blew jet hair into her brow, and she brushed it aside. When she spoke again, humility laced her expression, and reverence undergirded her tone.

'Tell me who he is, Fall. I am listening.

CHAPTER FORTY-FIVE

When Cillus' gift assumed its final form, it was indeed a mask, but not the one I had expected. It was my face. Or, *his* face. Heldanarr Fall, as his sister might have remembered him. All the things time had erased from him were forged in that metal countenance. The terrain of his cheeks, the shade of his skin, the downward cast of his eyes.

I thought to try it on, once. But when I reached up to remove my father's death mask, I found it sealed to my skull. A lifetime ago, beneath the whitewood, I had asked Cillus what Godeater wanted. His gift had been his answer, though I hadn't realised it. Godeater wanted me.

So let these words end my first and final prayer, for all the things I have not attained. I will find you, Godeater. This war is not over. Fires die and embers cool, but beneath every ending is buried a new beginning. In the ashes of war, conflict kindles anew. Forgiveness is breeding ground for spite.

I forgive the Azyrites. I forgive Se Roye and my Storm-cursed mother. I even forgive myself. But I will never forgive you. You, who proved fate is unwritten, yet whose vast hands encompass mine. You, who defied gods, and who will one day master them.

I'll master them too. I know how that sounds, to make such a claim after surrendering so completely. But I needn't explain this paradox to you. The Dark Gods are your masters – just as they are your slaves.

You still call me in my dreams. To come to your tall towers of dark light and pass your trials, to bend my knee. You set all this in motion. Always you and your empty throne and the life you forged for me – the life that will not let me go.

You thought I didn't see you. I do. You thought I'd accept Chaos and give in to the mindless fall that follows. I won't. Even stripped of my soul, I am whole of body and mind. I have learned the lessons you sent the Seeker to teach me. I will walk this Path to Glory and see how far it goes.

But when our time comes, know this: I will not serve you.

Let us meet, Godeater. Let us see who is stronger – which of us the skull, and which the skull-taker. Do not underestimate me. In the years that have passed, I found your name in the libraries of Candip and the abattoirs of Bharat. In the ruined temples of Cardand, within dusty tomes and daemon-bound grimoires. Your myth, older than the Mortal Realms, whispered into my ears by flies.

Everchosen. Three-Eyed King. Archaon.

So answer my final prayer, Godeater, and I shall answer your final call: where in the Mortal Realms does the Lord of the End Times hide?

ABOUT THE AUTHOR

Noah Van Nguyen is a freelance writer who lives in the U.S. with his wife. His tales set in the Mortal Realms include the novels *Godeater's Son* and *Yndrasta: The Celestial Spear* and the novella *Nadir* from the Warhammer Underworlds anthology *Harrowdeep*. He has also written several stories set in the grim darkness of the 41st millennium, including 'The Last Crucible', and the Warhammer Crime stories 'No Third Chance' and 'Carrion Call'. When he's not writing, Noah enjoys studying foreign languages and exploring far-off lands.

An extract from
Bad Loon Rising
by Andy Clark

Zograt would forever savour the expression on Skram's face in the instant before the Loonboss turned and fled. He knew he would recall again and again that look of dawning comprehension, of ignorant belligerence melting away to expose the panic of a hunted animal. He suspected it would bring him the same surge of pleasure every time. It felt almost as good as the magic that flowed through his body, churning his guts and tingling his fingers and scrabbling like spiders' legs behind his eyes.

As Skram vanished through a rent in the side of the hut, Zograt fixed Stragwit with a beady eye.

'Yoo scared o' me, Brewgit?'

Stragwit nodded vigorously.

'Rememb'rin' all dem times yoo made me carry scaldin' 'ot potions and gave me beatings when I dropped 'em?' Zograt asked, enjoying the new rumble that lent menace to his reedy voice. 'Finkin' about dem names wot yoo called me, dem nasty brews wot yoo tested on me?'

Zograt twiddled his fingers, experimentally flexing his new-found powers. The insects surrounding Stragwit shrilled and seethed in response. The Brewgit screeched. He tried to pull his extremities in further as the many-legged tide flowed upward, but only succeeded in overbalancing.

The Brewgit toppled with a forlorn wail and was immediately buried in insects. Zograt giggled at the sight of Stragwit's flailing, the sound of his shrieks turning to choking as insects wriggled into his mouth.

Then the question struck Zograt of where the tribe would get their potions, if not from Stragwit. He heaved a put-upon sigh and looked up at the Dankhold troggoth towering over him. The creature was tall enough that his head scraped Da Big Cave's ceiling. His warty hide was mottled pale purple, encrusted with fungi and waxy-looking mineral accretions. Near as many insects scurried and squirmed across him as nestled in Zograt's robes. The troggoth's boulder-like knuckles dragged along the ground.

'Wot ya reckon, Skrog? Dunno 'ow to brew potions meself.'

Skrog returned Zograt's stare with all the comprehension of a granite slab. A scutterbug clambered from the troggoth's ear, waved its antennae fussily, and set off down his neck for points south.

Zograt nodded. 'Yer right, lad. We need 'im.'

Zograt wiggled his fingers again and the insects scuttled back to leave Stragwit in a ring of clear space. The Brewgit struggled to his feet, retching up a throatful of squirming things. He wiped a bug-bitten hand across his mouth.

'Don't kill me,' Stragwit croaked.

'Not gunna,' Zograt replied, exhilarated at the sense of holding another creature's life in his claws. His tribe had only ever looked at him with contempt. The terror and hope now warring on Stragwit's face gave him a sense of power like nothing he'd ever known.

'Not gunna?' echoed Stragwit.

'Not if yoo does wot I tells ya,' replied Zograt.

'Wot, like yoo'z da boss?' Stragwit cringed at his own incredulous tone, his eyes flicking to the circle of insects surrounding him.

'Stragwit, ya daft zogger, I *is* da boss now,' said Zograt.

'Yoo'z da boss?' That tone again. Zograt twitched one finger. Several hundred insects took a collective step closer to Stragwit.

'Yoo'z da boss! Yoo'z da boss!' screeched Stragwit.

'I'm da boss,' said Zograt. The realisation left him light-headed. He steadied himself against one of Skrog's pillar-like legs.

Zograt.

Not the runt.

Not the tribe's punching bag.

Not face down in a mountain of squig dung.

The boss, by the say-so of the Bad Moon itself!

Zograt couldn't hold back a mad cackle that bubbled up and echoed around Da Big Cave. Something in his new-found magics amplified the sound so that it boomed fit to shake the cavern. Stragwit cringed, hands over his ears.

As the echoes of Zograt's laughter died away, the chitter of insects and the distant cries of terrified grots could be heard again. Stragwit ventured to speak.

'Boss, if yoo'z da boss now, wot about… da boss? You gunna let 'im leg it?'

'Course I ain't,' replied Zograt.

'But ain't 'e gettin' away?'

'Nice fing about Da Big Cave, Stragwit, is it's big,' said Zograt. 'Takes a while t'get across it through all dese bugs.'

Zograt limped past Stragwit, insects flowing in his wake as though caught in a tidal pull, forcing the Brewgit to scurry alongside him or be buried again. They both looked out through the tumbled hut wall. In the wavering 'shroomlight, Skram could be seen wading through biting insects, shooting fearful glances over his shoulder, making for the tunnel that promised escape. Zograt saw Nuffgunk leading the fleeing remnants of the raiding party in flight. He realised he had taken too long tormenting Stragwit, that Nuffgunk was within a few yards of reaching the tunnel.

'Can't be 'avin' dat,' Zograt said. He reached for the power within. It responded eagerly, flowing at his command. A detached part of Zograt marvelled at that. Old Spurk, the tribe's decrepit shaman, always made a literal song and dance over conjuring his powers. Even then, half the time they just gave him a nosebleed or made somegrot's head go bang. Yet Zograt's power felt as though it were part of him, a reservoir he could tap into as instinctively as breathing. If that wasn't proof of the Bad Moon's favour, he didn't know what was.

Now he drew deep upon that power and sent it coursing into the bedrock of Da Big Cave. It raced beneath the feet of the fleeing grots to the tunnel beyond. He heard Stragwit gasp as a mass of insects spilled from the tunnel mouth, causing Nuffgunk and the others to falter. Bulky shapes swelled in the darkness, then a mass of multicoloured fungi ballooned outward to block it. Zograt watched Nuffgunk turn and flee back into Da Big Cave. A couple of his ladz weren't so quick-thinking. One got a leg trapped under a grotesquely swelling mass of stinkcranny fungus, which rolled over him and crushed him flat. Another grot was pierced by swaying tendrils and lifted off the ground, limbs thrashing as his body bulged and tore through his robes. Taut skin split, blood drizzling onto the bugs below as a forest of glowing 'shrooms erupted from the luckless grot.

'Oh, zog me,' whimpered Stragwit. Zograt watched with satisfaction as his victims performed a scrabbling about-turn and fled deeper into the cavern. Skram pulled up short, looked frantically around for an escape route, then dashed off after his fleeing ladz.

'Dat's better, off to Da Soggy Cave dey goes,' he said.

'But boss... dere's uvver tunnels down dere, uvver ways out,' said Stragwit.

'Wot makes you fink I didn't 'shroom dem up too?' Zograt shot a toothy grin at Stragwit before limping off in pursuit of Skram. 'Come on, Skrog,' he called. Behind him, Zograt heard the troggoth grunt, followed by a series of rending, crashing sounds as he ploughed through the remains of Skram's hut.

As Zograt limped down the wide, slanting tunnel that led to Da Soggy Cave, Stragwit caught up to him.

'Boss?'

'Wot?'

Stragwit's jaw worked as though he were fishing for the right words. They picked their way down the tunnel between stalactites, and across overlapping slabs of stone between which foetid streamlets gurgled.

'Boss, 'ow come ya got da Clammy Hand? Wotchoo do?'

Zograt had known the question was coming, but wasn't sure how to answer because really, what *had* he done? His memory of the events leading up to his sudden apotheosis were hazy...

Zograt recalled being thrust face down into the dungheap until he must have lost consciousness, because the next thing he recalled was Driggz hauling him out of the filth. He had been surprised that the other grot had dragged him to safety instead of rifling his pockets, until it occurred to him that he had nothing worth Driggz's while to steal. Zograt suspected Driggz maintained their shaky alliance mostly because, with Zograt around to pick on, he himself was spared the worst of the bigger grots' attentions. Ergo, Zograt was worth more to him alive than drowned in squig turds.

It was about here that Zograt's memory grew hazy, yellowing in his mind's eye as though his thoughts had become mildewed. He remembered shrugging Driggz off, limping through the caves to his hidey-hole, the cramped grotto where he went to skulk and lick his wounds after each beating. His mind had been boiling with thoughts of vengeance, the desire to drive a shiv into Skram's back even if it killed him. The crawl to get to his grotto through a narrow fissure was hard on Zograt's bad leg and bruised ribs, but it was worth it. He was the only one of his tribe small enough to reach the hidey-hole. It was the one place where he could feel safe for a few precious hours.

Only, had there been something different about his grotto this time? Was that what curdled his thoughts? Zograt wondered. Was that what sent glowing mycelia burrowing through his recollections and rummaging through his brain until they burst from his scalp as malformed fungal braids? Zograt dimly remembered a leprous light washing over him. A bitter taste danced on his tongue, his saliva burning as he felt again a sponginess yielding between his teeth.

A sense of delirium followed. Zograt recalled nonsensical images tumbling over one another like a river of insects. He shuddered as his memory brushed against something vast and foul that stirred amidst darkness and stared with yellow eyes as wide as craters.

Zograt's next clear memory involved limping along one of the lurklair's outermost tunnels and feeling powerful in a way he never had before. He had registered the scrabble of insects infesting his robes and welcomed it, known it for the blessing it surely was. He had felt the potential squirming through him and watched in amazement as fungi bloomed from the tunnel walls in answer to a wiggle of his fingertips. A glance over his shoulder had caused Zograt to halt in surprise as he saw the hulking troggoth that followed him. Zograt had looked the huge beast up and down, felt it sizing him up in return. He had observed the infestation of insects scampering over its body just as they did his own. Zograt had known in that moment that he should have been fleeing for his life, for he had never seen this troggoth before and as far as he knew the huge creature fancied him for a snack. Instead, he had felt a sense of rightness in that moment. There had come a sensation that it took Zograt long moments to identify, so alien was it to him. This beast made him feel as though his hiding grotto had somehow come alive in troggoth form.

To his frank amazement, he felt safe.

'You wiv me?' he had asked. The troggoth had appeared to consider this question for so long that Zograt wondered if it understood. It had held one huge hand outstretched, patiently waiting for a fat-bodied spider to descend on a strand of silk then scuttle away across the tunnel floor. At last, the troggoth had jerked its head and given a grunt that sounded to Zograt like 'Skrog'.

'Skrog, is it? I ain't got a zoggin' clue wot's 'appened to me, and I dunno where yoo came from, but zog it, I can feel da Clammy Hand on me!'

The troggoth had stared down at him. Moisture beaded on the end of its nose like water on a stalactite and dripped to the floor.

'Glad yoo agree,' he had said at last, realising that he had more pressing matters than holding a one-sided conversation with a troggoth. It had dawned on Zograt that he needed to find his way back to Da Big Cave. He had been blessed with strange new powers, and he couldn't think of a more deserving bunch of gitz to practise them on.

'Skram Badstabba, yoo'z about to 'ave a zoggin' 'orrible day...' he had chuckled to himself as he set off...

'Boss?'

Zograt came back to himself. Stragwit was staring at him in confusion while he stood muttering under his breath. Zograt glanced

up at Skrog, who had halted a few steps behind and was ponder-
ously licking moisture from the wall. The troggoth seemed to feel
his gaze and turned to regard him with glacial patience. Zograt
felt again that inexplicable sense of safety in the beast's presence.

'I got da Clammy Hand cos I deserves it more dan da rest
o' yooz,' said Zograt. 'I'm smarter an' meaner, an da Bad Moon
knows just 'ow bad I want to stick some shivs in some backs. Don't
worry 'bout what I did, Stragwit. Worry 'bout wot I'm *gunna* do.'

He set off down the tunnel again, Brewgit, troggoth and a chit-
tering sea of insects following in his wake.